The Tender Vine

Rocky Mountain Legacy
◆◆◆◆◆◆◆◆◆◆◆◆◆

Honor's Pledge
Honor's Price
Honor's Quest
Honor's Disguise
Honor's Reward

Diamond of the Rockies
◆◆◆◆◆◆◆◆◆◆◆◆◆◆

The Rose Legacy
Sweet Boundless
The Tender Vine

◆◆◆◆◆◆◆◆◆◆◆◆◆◆

Twilight

KRISTEN HEITZMANN

The Tender Vine

BETHANYHOUSE
PUBLISHERS

MINNEAPOLIS, MINNESOTA

The Tender Vine
Copyright © 2002
Kristen Heitzmann

Cover illustration and design by Dan Thornberg

Published by Bethany House Publishers
A Ministry of Bethany Fellowship International
11400 Hampshire Avenue South
Bloomington, Minnesota 55438
www.bethanyhouse.com

Printed in the United States of America by
Bethany Press International, Bloomington, Minnesota 55438

Library of Congress Cataloging-in-Publication Data

Heitzmann, Kristen.
    The tender vine / by Kristen Heitzmann.
       p. cm. —(Diamond of the Rockies ; 3)
    ISBN 0-7642-2417-4 (pbk.)
     1. Triangles (Interpersonal relations)—Fiction. 2. Italian American families—Fiction. 3. Rocky Mountains—Fiction. I. Title.
    PS3558.E468 T46   2002
    813'.54—dc21   2001005675

To Lisa with love

Near indeed is his salvation to those who fear him,
glory dwelling in our land. Kindness and truth shall meet;
justice and peace shall kiss. Truth shall spring out of the earth,
and justice shall look down from heaven.

PSALM 85:10–12 NASB

One

I look on her whom life has bruised in heart and mind and soul.
Though other hands have broken her, now mine must make her whole.

— Quillan

SOFTLY SCENTED PINE. The downy embrace of a feather mattress. A slow paling of sleep.

Then the dull throbbing of every bruise drew Carina from her stupor. Someone stoked the fire in her stove. Raising heavy-lashed eyelids, she expected to see Mae's soft, undulating form, but it was Quillan's muscular back that bent to the task.

Panic brought her fully awake. Too many times she'd seen Quillan's back, his stubborn gait carrying him away. His mane of light brown hair hung loosely over his shoulders, and she wanted to sink her fingers in—and grab hold. Oh, she knew his back. It was his face she longed to learn. He must have sensed her watching; he turned.

Would he cut her with cruel words after the closeness they'd shared last night? Not the intimacy of husband and wife; her injuries precluded that. But they had woven their hearts, and she feared now that he would pull away as he had every time he got too close.

She searched his face, hoping the things he'd seen and learned had changed him—Wolf's cave, his mother's diary. Had he made peace with his past, his parentage, as it seemed last night? And was it enough to hold him? The fire gave his gray eyes the luminescence of a storm cloud sunlit from behind. His brow pulled together, but his voice was soft. "What's the matter? Are you in pain?"

She was stiff and sore from the thugs' beating, but she shook her head. "No, I . . . I thought for a moment you'd be gone." Like their unborn child. A stabbing grief found a hollow place inside and lodged there. They'd hardly spoken of the baby last night. No more than to acknowledge the loss. Who would their child have been, had the beating not destroyed the baby inside her? She wanted to lash out, but Quillan's repentance, his anguish that he hadn't been there to protect her, was real.

He left the stove and crouched beside the bed, resting his forearm on the coverlet, the roping muscles visible beneath his cotton undershirt. "I told you I'm not leaving."

He must see her doubt. And why not? In six months of marriage they were still strangers with a powerful bond neither could ignore, but in which she had yet to trust. She was the one pulling away this time. His tenderness left her more vulnerable than his gruffness ever had. He was the most unpredictable, annoyingly irresistible man she'd ever known. And when she considered her papa, her five brothers, and all her male cousins connected by blood, marriage, or otherwise, that was quite a laurel for Quillan.

He spread his pirate's smile. "You should have chucked me, not the rocker."

Carina glanced swiftly at the empty corner of the room. So he had noticed. How could he not? Perhaps he had even seen her deliver the rocking chair to Èmie, though he'd said no word about it when he carried her back to bed like an invalid child for all the world to see.

"Oh, Quillan." She reached for his arm. "I wish I hadn't."

"Think of the pleasure the Simms will have of it."

So he did know. He was baiting her, mocking her rash, vengeful act.

He shrugged one shoulder. "Besides, I deserved it. A more eloquent thrashing I've never had."

"I was angry! And hurt!"

"I know." He ran his fingers over her sleeve, down her hand, and along each of her fingers.

Her stomach shrank tight, and she reached up to his beard-darkened cheek.

He drew back. "I haven't shaved yet. Just barely let the dog out and stoked the fire."

She smiled. "You should grow real whiskers, not this roguish stubble you're so fond of." She'd seen him both overly mustached and clean shaven, but mostly as he was now. Just enough whiskers to look dangerous and disreputable.

He rubbed his scratchy jaw. "Roguish." He looked down at her lips and she felt them warm, anticipating his kiss, but he didn't come any closer. Nor had he kissed her last night, though he'd held her in his arms. Must she show she was willing? She started to raise her chin, but the whining and scratching at the door took his attention. Quillan stood and admitted Second Samuel, who bounded in, shaking frosty fur powdered by the morning's snowfall. He crowded in to lick Carina's hand.

She looked from the dog to the amused face of her husband. "What?"

"Nothing."

"You're thinking something." She waved her hand in small circles. "I see it in your face."

"What do you see?"

She stroked the velvety softness of Sam's ear as he continued to lap her arm with his tongue. "I probably don't want to know."

He grinned. "But it'll drive you mad until you do."

"Oh!" She pushed the dog away and flounced into the pillow.

He laughed. "Go ahead. Finish it."

"Finish what!"

"*O-maccio*. Isn't that what you meant?" He moved Sam aside and towered over her. "Omaccio, cad, ill-bred man. It goes with the whiskers."

"Are you enjoying this?"

He leaned down, one hand gripping the maple headboard. "What did you expect?"

Carina looked from his face to the mottled brown-and-white mug of the dog, still hopeful for attention. She threw up her hands. "I don't know what to expect. How could I know?"

Quillan tucked one arm behind her and raised her gently as he shoved extra pillows behind her back. Then he sat on the edge of the bed. "I'll tell you. First, Sam and I are going to see you're comfortably set. Then I'm going to learn what needs to be done for your restaurant."

She opened her mouth, but he covered it firmly with his hand. "After that, I'll meet with Alex Makepeace."

Did she imagine the flicker in his eyes? Meet with Alex for what? Don't be silly. It was natural he would meet with his mining engineer. Did he see her discomfort? He must, because he turned away and contained himself. His hand came away from her mouth.

"And what am I to do?" she said.

Quillan stood, crossed the small room to the far wall, selected a book from the shelf, then returned, laying Emily Brontë in her lap. "Maybe Heathcliff will put you in mind there are worse rogues in the world."

She wasn't surprised he'd read the story. But as for rogues . . . "Well, I don't have to live with them." She waved her hand. "You think you can take over my business? Handle it without me?"

"Not a chance. But Mae and Èmie and all those little girls you've taken on . . . I'll just see they do what needs doing."

"Un gross'uomo." A big man.

Again he laughed. "I'm sure you have a wagonload of things you'd like to call me. You can thrash me with them all the way to Sonoma if you like. But just now you're following doctor's orders and staying abed until you're out of danger."

"Oofa! If I need a papa, I'll tell you."

His lips hardly smiled as he appraised her, but his eyes were filled with wicked mirth. He was enjoying himself. If she had something to throw, she would have thrown it. But she wouldn't damage *Wuthering Heights* on his bony skull.

"Now sit up like a good girl, and Mae will bring you some breakfast."

"Bene!" She jutted her chin at him. "Have your fun."

He left the room for Mae's with a chuckle that made her reconsider whether she could replace *Wuthering Heights* after all.

Quillan strode into Mae's kitchen feeling jaunty. Mae sat at the table holding a steaming cup of coffee, which was turning her florid cheeks redder than usual. She looked up with a blend of surprise and amusement. "Won the war already?"

"Not completely." Quillan sprawled onto the bench across from her. "But I will."

"Famous last words." Mae's chest rumbled.

"How long before breakfast?"

She tipped her face down without changing her gaze. "I'm only just opening my eyes."

Quillan glanced out the window, the sky still dark with winter dawn. It was early yet. He might have stayed abed longer, but having Carina beside him made it impossible. And he was by nature an early riser. Lying inert chafed him unless he was working his mind over a book as diligently as he worked his muscles hauling freight.

He considered his selection for Carina. Heathcliff was one of the better rogues he'd encountered. Quite similar in many ways to himself: socially unfit, disgraced, yet determined to win the woman he loved—Alexander Makepeace notwithstanding.

A potent surge of jealousy struck Quillan, a feeling unknown to him before. He wasn't sure what to do with it.

"I'll fetch you some more wood." He stood, hoping to prod Mae into action, but she watched his exit with vague interest. Her woodbox beside the stove was full, and there was a stack of split wood along the back wall outside. But thoughts of Alex Makepeace had put Quillan in the mood to do violence, and he did it on a half dozen thick logs that awaited splitting.

He'd seen Carina's discomfort when he mentioned Alex Makepeace. Quillan brought the ax down with splintering force and cleaved the log deeply. She had feelings for the man, but he'd be switched if he'd share Carina with Alex Makepeace or anyone else short of God. He lifted the ax with the log still clinging and slammed it onto the chopping stump. The halves flew as the edge of the blade bit the stump with a thud.

Carina had said nothing, but he wasn't blind. And it was Alex's name she had murmured that night in the delirium of pain and laudanum. Quillan figured it was just as well Carina wanted to go home, to leave Crystal. A clean break was what they needed. And as soon as he could wrap up their business, they'd go.

Quillan retrieved one of the split halves and balanced it on the stump. He raised the ax and sundered it with one stroke. Twenty-eight years of imprisoned emotions rendered him helpless against these new feelings. No, not helpless. He would govern it. He just needed to reduce every one of the logs to kindling.

Be careful, something inside him murmured. Maybe his conscience, maybe something more. Careful of what? Chopping wood? But the thought was gone, leaving only a nagging echo. Quillan brought the ax down again and again. Exhausted at last, he finished stacking the wood and carried an armload back into the kitchen. He dumped the wood into the overflowing box and turned.

Still seated at the table, Mae fixed him with a knowing stare. "Sit down, and I'll rustle you up some smoked venison and hot-cakes."

He nodded. "I'll just bring Carina some coffee."

"You fetch me some fresh water. *I'll* bring Carina some coffee."

He met Mae's frank expression and decided not to argue. If Mae wanted to see for herself that he had things in hand, let her. He did. At least he planned to. As Mae left, he glanced toward the ceiling with the uncomfortable feeling that everything he thought, everything he did was known. Surrendering to God in Wolf's cave, as difficult as that had been, seemed less consuming than this day-to-day accountability.

Carina looked up from Emily Brontë's prose when Mae entered with a cup releasing rich coffee aroma into the room. "Good morning, Mae. You've seen my husband?"

"I've seen him."

"He thinks he will run my business."

Mae smiled. "Well, honey, you and I know that's impossible."

"Oh, he won't cook and serve and wash the dishes. He'll just crack his freighter's whip, and you and Èmie and the girls..." Carina waved a hand. "He has it all planned."

Mae handed over the cup. "It did run rather well last night. The men were sure pleased to have the doors opened again. Though to a one they asked after you and sent their condolences." Mae straightened. "But Quillan did keep things in order."

Carina huffed. "I thought *Italian* men were difficult."

"All men. Except maybe my Mr. Dixon." Mae's eyes turned dewy. "He had the sweetest nature ever a man possessed. There was no contention in him."

"Quillan makes up for it."

Mae laughed. "Seems you're chewing both sides of that bone. Either you want him home or you don't."

Carina took a quick sip and set the cup down stormily.

"Home, fine! But insolent and difficult? *Beh!*"

"Watch that china. I've an order for more, but until it comes, I'm running short."

Carina loosened her hand on the cup. "He makes me so mad I could—"

"Now, Carina. He's doing his best by you."

Carina rolled her eyes. What should she expect? Mae had been defending Quillan from their first conversation. He carried the sun and moon on his back in Mae's eyes. Never mind that he'd married Carina, then run off at every opportunity, leaving her to face . . .

Tears welled up in her eyes for the child she'd lost. How she had dreamed of that child bringing her husband home. But hadn't the loss done as much? He was home. Though now Carina was not so certain how to handle that.

Signore, I should be happy, but I'm all torn up inside. I don't know what to think of this man you've given me. She thought for a moment of Flavio, whom she had known since childhood and loved. He would not have been a stranger. Would it have been better so?

Never! Flavio was *infedele*, unfaithful. Flavio and Divina, her sister. But why did she think of that now? Because she'd dreamed last night of going home? Quillan had said he would take her. But that in itself set a new problem in her mind. She had yet to tell Mamma and Papa of her marriage.

She'd married outside the family, outside her people, without Papa's consent, Mamma's blessing, without all her *zios* and *zias* cousins and brothers and sister. She had stood before Father Antoine Charboneau in Mae's parlor and pledged herself to Quillan. And then there was Quillan himself. What would Mamma think? And Papa?

. . . .

At sight of him my heart pumps fire whose coals I bank in silence.

While in my mind the thoughts conspire to force my soul to penance.

— *Quillan*

HAVING DRIVEN HIS MUSCLES to the point of pain while chopping wood, Quillan approached Makepeace's office relatively confident he'd do nothing he'd regret. The man was, after all, in his employ, and there were questions Makepeace was most qualified to answer. It was ridiculous to avoid the man because a friendship had developed with his wife.

Friendship? Quillan fought the dangerous thought that followed. Of course friendship. Anything more would be unworthy of Carina. *His* wife. To consider her affection for Alex Makepeace anything beyond proper would dishonor the woman he loved. Loved with an almost crippling ferocity. If he'd known how it would be . . .

Would he have it any other way? But it was all so new. Love. Faith. What did he know about either? He needed his old friend Cain. But Cain was gone. Quillan would have to learn on his own. He knocked on the wooden door of the shed near the mine workings.

"It's open," Makepeace called from inside.

Quillan turned the knob and walked in.

Alex Makepeace removed his small oval spectacles and laid them atop the papers on the desk. His thumb was stained with ink from the well and pen just to the right of his felt writing board. He hesitated only a moment. "Good morning."

For the first time Quillan considered the man as Carina might. Pleasant enough in looks, trim, well-kept beard, no rogue's growth, hair a darker shade of brown than Quillan's. Regular features and modest physique. Some might say handsome. But there were signs of strain. Was it Quillan, Carina, or the business that caused it? "You're busy?"

Makepeace shrugged, waved his hand over the desk. "My report to the powers that be."

Quillan looked around the small room. Neat maps, topographical and survey, hung on the walls. A plane table stood on its tripod in one corner, a stove in the opposite. Beside the stove, a cot. He returned his gaze to Makepeace. "I have some questions." The man's lips narrowed, and a tightening around the eyes showed his unease.

Quillan was tempted to make him squirm but said, "I want to know who attacked my wife and why."

Makepeace interlaced his fingers. "What do you know about the mining business, Quillan?" He motioned, and Quillan took the chair in front of the desk.

"All I want is names."

"So vigilantes can string them up like the last bunch?"

Quillan flinched. He didn't like to think of that ugly affair, though he wasn't surprised Makepeace had heard of it. Even the Tabors in Leadville had heard of it. He'd tried to avoid that action, but would Makepeace understand that? The names Quillan and Carina provided from Beck's ledger had been the fuel. Cain's murder had been the match.

"The fact is, most of those high-minded vigilante citizens were probably in on the threats made to your wife."

"Threats? I don't consider what happened a threat. I call it an attack."

Alex Makepeace dropped his gaze to his hands. "The attack she brought on herself, Quillan. And don't think I say that lightly. I wish ..."

"You wish what?"

Makepeace aligned his index fingers, unconsciously pointing them at Quillan's chest though his hands remained resting on the desk. "I wish I'd seen the danger."

Quillan wanted to contest that, to say it wasn't Alex Make-

16

peace's place to protect Carina. But that would only illuminate his own failure to do so.

Makepeace met his gaze. "The men who attacked Carina were spirited away before the echo of my shots died out."

Quillan winced at the man's use of Carina's name. Such familiarity was not easily won with his wife and proved his suspicions. There was also the subtle reminder that it was Alex Makepeace's gun that had sent the attackers running.

Makepeace said, "You won't find them. I've given the names of those behind the threat to the authorities. Their statements have been taken. I'd wager nothing further will be done. Such action against the most powerful citizens in Crystal would bring chaos. Your fledgling law officials can't risk that. Besides, what happened was, at least in part, my responsibility and your wife's." He stood, walked to the wall, and studied the framed map that hung behind his desk.

Quillan frowned. Maybe Carina and Alex Makepeace had crossed a line that caused trouble between the miners and the management. But he couldn't ignore what had been done to his wife. That the powerful mine owners of Crystal would resort to hiring thugs to frighten and, yes, even beat a woman ... He had to understand why.

"How would helping the families of dead miners bring that kind of repercussion?"

Makepeace turned. "Because it isn't done. Can't be done without turning the industry upside down. The mining company cannot be responsible for accidents or carelessness. By paying the families, it appeared the mine was accepting blame. I should never have compromised the New Boundless that way. Should never have acted against my better judgment. I don't know why ..." He sighed.

Quillan sent him a cold stare. He knew why. Carina Maria DiGratia Shepard. Was there a man alive who wouldn't buckle under her spell? Especially when her heart was in it? Especially if his was captured already.

"It was an inexcusable lapse." Makepeace tapped a letter on the edge of the desk. "Hence, my resignation."

Quillan eyed the letter. "Why?"

"I compromised the standing and safety of the organization."

"You showed compassion in the face of tragedy. I might have

ordered it myself." If he'd been there when the mining accident, which took thirteen lives, occurred. He felt a fresh guilt for the months he'd left Carina in Crystal alone, though not alone after all. . . .

"And I would have refused. With all respect." Alex bowed his head slightly.

"But you didn't refuse Carina."

Alex Makepeace leaned against the wall. "No," he said, leaving Quillan to make what he would of that.

Quillan frowned. "I'd like to see the mine records."

Makepeace raised his brows. "The financial records?"

"All of it, everything."

"Are you suggesting I've acted with less than integrity where your interests—"

Quillan shook his head. "I'm not suggesting anything. I just want to see them, to see how it all works."

"Your instructions were to deposit your profits directly into the bank. That's been done except . . . the one time Mrs. Shepard had them diverted."

So it was back to *Mrs. Shepard*. "I'm not questioning your good faith. I'm trying to establish what my portion of the mine is worth."

Makepeace stood in silence a long moment. "For what purpose?"

"For the purpose of sale." He watched that sink in. "Carina wants to go home. I can hardly look after my interests here or those of D.C., my partner, from Sonoma, California."

A look of fatalistic resignation passed over Makepeace's features. And it wasn't Quillan's ownership he would miss.

Quillan said, "As much as the mine meant to his daddy, I think D.C.'ll be willing to sell out if I do. I'd appreciate it if you didn't send that letter just yet."

"Why not?" Alex Makepeace glanced at his resignation as though it might hold some explanation.

"I'd prefer to keep things stable until this is concluded. You think you acted irresponsibly, but I don't see it that way."

"You don't know—"

"The industry. You're right. I'm reminded of that at every turn. But I stand by what Carina did. What you did. And I want to make that clear to every man who acted against my wife. That's why I'm making this offer. I want you to own the New Boundless—my stock and D.C.'s, if he sells."

Alex Makepeace stared at him, looking as shocked by the offer as Quillan was himself. Where had that come from? He'd had no intention of making such an offer to Alexander Makepeace. This man who'd cozied up to Carina, shared in the secret of Wolf's cave, half caused the trouble that might have killed her, that had miscarried their baby...

Makepeace spoke low and a little coldly. "I couldn't begin to afford it. Without looking I could tell you your holdings together are worth a hundred thousand at least. The investors—"

"I don't care about the investors, or anyone else in town who might want a piece of the Boundless. I'm offering it to you."

Alex Makepeace sat down in the chair, resting his palms on the edge of the desk. "Why?"

"Because you saved my wife's life." There was the truth.

"And I was at least half responsible for it being threatened."

Quillan ignored that. Maybe it was God who had brought things in this direction. Maybe if he focused on the fact that Makepeace had driven away the thugs, if he found a means to compensate that debt ... maybe then he could keep the crushing jealousy in check. "I have a friend in Leadville who might front you the money. You can make arrangements for repayment with him. If you're interested."

Alex Makepeace looked dazed. "A friend?"

"Horace Tabor. You've heard of him?" Quillan quirked an eyebrow.

"The silver king?" If it was possible, Makepeace looked more dumbfounded yet.

Quillan hiked one side of his mouth. "I'm off to see him later this morning if the weather holds. Should be a two-day turnaround. Get the records together for me and consider coming along."

Alex Makepeace dropped his forehead to his fingertips, as though the thoughts that coursed through his brain made it heavy to hold up.

Quillan said, "Think about it. It'll be an hour or two before I'm ready to leave." He stood, met Alex Makepeace's eyes briefly, then turned and left.

Carina laid the book down across her lap when Quillan pushed open the door with a burst of wintry air. Sam scooted in around him, greeted her, then returned to Quillan's side, tail wagging, as though he shouldn't let him far from his sight. Carina felt a tingle of foreboding. Something in Quillan's expression . . .

He stopped at the foot of her bed, parted his buckskin coat, and tucked his hands into his canvas pants pockets. "Carina—"

"Don't say it."

He cocked his head. "Say what?"

"You're leaving."

His nose was chapped with cold, his lips grayish against his still unshaven face. "I'm only going—"

She clapped her hands to her ears. "I knew it! One night you spend with me, and off you go. Why did I think anything would change? Why did I—"

In three strides he had circled the bed. He grabbed her hands from her ears. "Will you listen to me? I'm only going to Leadville. I'll be back tomorrow, weather permitting."

"Why? I thought you would stop freighting. Isn't that what you said? You would do whatever it took to stay here with me?" She started to shake. It sharpened the pain in her back where the worst of the blows had threatened her kidneys.

"It's important. I'm taking Alex Makepeace with me."

That caught her short. What could he possibly be doing with Alex? He eyed her grimly. How long would Alex's name bring a shadow between them? She sagged onto the pillows behind her.

Quillan held her hands between his. His eyes took on the stormy intensity she knew so well, like the tingle in the air before lightning slices the sky. "I'll be back tomorrow."

She turned away. All she knew was his leaving kindled the pain of his desertion and the loss of their baby. "So go." What should she care?

"Carina"—he pressed her hands—"I have things to do."

"So have I." She felt him stiffen.

He reached over and turned her face to his. "No, you don't. You be still and heal."

She didn't answer. She felt too weary to do anything else, but she wouldn't ease his worry by telling him so.

"Give me your word, Carina."

She said nothing.

He scowled. "You have plenty of Italian names for me. I wish I knew the female equivalent of some of them."

She almost smiled, he caught her so off guard. Then the hurt of his leaving chased away her mirth. "Why are you taking Alex?"

"Business." His voice chilled.

"With the mine?"

"Yes."

She raised up slightly. "Has something happened?"

He pressed her back down. "Nothing to concern you."

"Oh!" She pushed his hand away. "As though I haven't fed and encouraged and—"

"I'm well aware of your efforts, Carina. But nothing is wrong with the mine." His voice was level, reassuring.

She was being childish and petulant. She knew it. But this man brought out the worst in her. The worst and the best. She softened. He was trying, was he not? "Can you travel on the snow?"

"The pack should be hard enough. You've seen me use the chains, and I've spiked the wheelers' hooves."

"You have to go?"

He didn't answer, though his eyes said he wouldn't otherwise.

She sighed. "Then I suppose . . ." She looked up at the knock on the door.

Quillan crossed and opened the door to Alex Makepeace. Carina's heart jumped. She hadn't seen him since the night of the attack, and even then she'd been all but unconscious. Mae had mentioned that he asked after her, but he hadn't once come to see for himself. Because Quillan had come home.

Now with the two of them together, the air crackled. Blood burned her cheeks as she met Alex's eyes and realized how far she'd let things go. Quillan must see it, too. She was suddenly aware that she was in her bed, covered with blankets and a woolen shawl over her shoulders, her hair loose over her shoulders. She could imagine the picture she presented.

Alex took off his hat and held it to his chest. "How are you, Carina?"

Her throat tightened sharply. "Better than I might be without your help." How stiff she sounded. "I never thanked you."

"Your husband has."

Implicit in that was the conclusion to their friendship. They could not return to a superficial acquaintance.

Quillan said, "You're ready?" His voice sounded as tight as Carina felt.

Alex nodded.

Quillan moved between them. "I have the wagon provisioned. You have the documents?"

Documents? What were they doing? Business, Quillan said, business with the mine that didn't concern her. Alex nodded, careful not to look her way again. She wished he would, but then she didn't. It was Quillan's glance she craved.

Quillan said, "I'll meet you at the livery as soon as I take leave of my wife."

Now Alex did look. "Good-bye, Carina. I hope your recovery is swift."

She forced a smile, but no words came. It hurt to see him so withdrawn, he who had upheld her hopes and spirits, given her kindness and compassion and good humor. Though chaste, they had crossed emotional boundaries. And he was hurt by it. She must never let that happen again.

Quillan closed the door behind Alex and returned to the bedside. "I won't be later than tomorrow unless—"

"Your safety is first." She reached a hand to his sleeve. "Don't take risks you shouldn't."

He frowned. "Are you afraid for me or for him?" His anger flashed, then receded. He dropped to a squat and clasped her hand. "I'm sorry. I had no right to say that." But she knew he'd seen her affection for Alex, and it burned him. What in another man might be jealousy, in this one was poison.

She started to speak, but he covered her lips with his hand. "You don't owe me an explanation, and frankly, nothing you say would speak more truly than your face already did. But I'll tell you one thing, Carina. No one will have the chance to take my place again. No one."

A soft whimper escaped her throat as he caught her face between his hands and stared at her hard until she thought she could bear it no longer. "Nothing short of a blizzard will keep me away tomorrow." He stood, but his gaze lingered on hers. "I'll even bring Alex Makepeace back with me." He gave her his rogue's smile.

It tugged at her heart, made it leap inside her breast. Certainly he would kiss her; she wanted him to. But he backed two steps away from the bed, turned slowly on his heel, and crossed to the door. Sam sprang up, but he ordered the dog to stay, then left them.

Sam whined at the wood separating him from his master. His whole body swung with the wag of his tail, hoping the door would open and the hand he craved wave him on. As the moment passed and Sam's sharp ears told him Quillan was gone, he dropped his head and padded to her bedside, his brown eyes forlorn.

"I know how you feel." Carina stroked his head. "But he'll be back." She wished she felt more certain of that.

Three

To claim I am a man betrayed and rant against my plight,
I must admit I should have stayed and kept her in my sight.
What fool to flee her sweet embrace, to tear her love apart,
and let another take my place within her weeping heart.

— *Quillan*

QUILLAN AND ALEX MAKEPEACE rode the steep, snow-packed road between Crystal and Leadville. It might have been easier to travel horseback, but with the wagon, Quillan could make the trip count twice. He'd bring back a light load, things he could sell at a profit in Crystal, which was less accessible than Leadville. He'd already resupplied Carina's larder, but there were plenty of others, Mrs. Barton in particular, who would pay well for anything he brought her.

And if they were stopped by a storm, the wagon would provide shelter. He'd spent one night beneath it with Carina while a blizzard raged around them. He didn't warm to the thought of doing the same with Alex Makepeace, but weather was chancy in the mountains. Better to be prepared.

At least Makepeace didn't expect conversation. At most they discussed the mine and a little of the industry. Makepeace was sharp enough and educated. If Quillan cared to, he might learn a lot about mining from the man. But just now his intentions were to rid himself of the New Boundless and cut loose of Crystal. As soon as Carina could travel. As soon as she was well. Dr. Felden believed she would recover if she gave herself time to heal.

Makepeace cleared his throat. Quillan waited for him to talk, but the man settled back into his thoughts. Quillan returned to his own. This trip hadn't exactly been what he intended. Quillan had intended to seek Tabor's advice, but he hadn't premeditated his offer to Makepeace. If that was how God worked, Quillan had better keep his wits sharp.

But it was a sound plan. Owning the New Boundless would keep Makepeace in Crystal, a detail that had occurred to Quillan after he left Carina. A thousand miles between Crystal and Sonoma should be just about right.

Maybe Horace Tabor was not interested in another mine, but he'd know who was. And the New Boundless was successful. Tabor would wonder at Quillan's decision. But then Horace Tabor had yet to get a handle on him. Quillan half smiled. He sort of liked it that way.

They reached Leadville by late afternoon, just as the sun left the sky. Quillan left the wagon in the livery. He paid the ostler for feed, then turned to Makepeace. "First, I have some freight to collect. Then we'll see Hod Tabor. You'll need a hotel." The Tabors would likely offer a room in their home, but he didn't fancy sharing it with Alex Makepeace. The hours in the wagon had allowed plenty of time to stew on Makepeace's relationship with Carina, and the dragon was twisting again.

"Meet me here in an hour."

Makepeace nodded and headed for the hotel on the corner. Quillan worked quickly to collect goods for the trip back. In just short of an hour he returned to the livery and found Makepeace waiting. He took the New Boundless documents, and they boarded the horse car, which carried them to Tabor's street.

They discovered the Tabors were at dinner, and as Quillan and Makepeace were shown to the dining room, Tabor stood. "Quillan!" He gripped his hand. "You show up at the queerest times. Augusta and I were just discussing you."

"All good, I hope." Quillan reached down to where Augusta sat, took her hand, and covered it with his other palm.

"Hello, Quillan. You're quite robust, I see. Altogether recovered since the last time we met."

Quillan softened his gaze. "Thanks to your kindness, Augusta."

"Hmm." She sniffed. "And who is this you've brought?"

Quillan turned. "Alex Makepeace, may I present Horace and Augusta Tabor."

With a look close to awe, Makepeace shook hands with each.

Quillan turned to Tabor. "Have time to talk business?"

Augusta stood abruptly. "Certainly not on an empty stomach. If I know you, Quillan, you've dragged this poor fellow through the snow without a morsel to warm or sustain him. Am I right?" She addressed Alex Makepeace.

"Unless you consider hardtack a meal."

"Humph." She walked to the wall and pushed the third button in the row. A dull ring vibrated through the wall. When the maid appeared, Augusta ordered soup and bread, then turned. "With the sun setting so early we dine at an uncivilized hour." She waved a hand toward the table. "Please. I daresay Horace won't refuse a second slice of pie?"

Tabor settled back into his place at the head of the table. "If I must, my dear." He patted his thickening waist. Still, for a man in his middle years, he was fit and elegant. And he now took charge of the conversation as Quillan and Makepeace ate. Quillan's thoughts wandered when talk turned to mining, as inevitably it would, but Tabor and Makepeace held forth at length and with much gusto.

After a flavorful venison soup and crusty bread, Quillan eyed the piece of mincemeat pie placed before him, then sent a grateful nod to Augusta. Her gaze was on him already.

"And how is your wife, Quillan?" Augusta asked it softly, but Tabor seized on it and pounced.

"Ah, yes, your wife." He turned to Makepeace with a rascally smile. "I only half believe he has one."

Makepeace set his fork on the edge of the desert plate. "He has." He flicked his glance Quillan's way.

"And she's ugly as an Angus heifer?"

"Hod." Augusta frowned.

Makepeace hid his discomfort almost well enough. He shook his head. "She's not ugly. Far from it."

"Now are you satisfied, Hod?" Augusta pushed against his arm. "I hope that's the last we'll hear in that vein. Besides, beauty isn't everything."

From a plain woman, that was especially poignant, and Quillan hoped Tabor would drop it. The last thing he needed was a discussion of Carina's attributes with Alexander Makepeace holding forth.

Tabor swabbed his mouth with the napkin. "You had business to discuss?"

Makepeace seemed surprised that Augusta stayed at the table. But Quillan knew better. She was a businesswoman from the first step she'd landed in Leadville. He met Tabor's querying gaze. "Yes. I'd like to sell my mine." Quillan took out the papers and laid them before Tabor. "I've made an offer to Makepeace here, but he can't do it alone."

Horace Tabor took up the papers and fitted a pair of pince-nez to his nose.

As he scrutinized the numbers, Quillan pointed to a column beside the first. "This much is my partner's. I wired him about selling. I haven't heard back, but I'm guessing he will if I do. He's in seminary."

Tabor chuckled. "Plenty of clergy striking it rich all through these mountains. Isn't there a priest ... Father Charboneau?"

"Performed my marriage ceremony," Quillan said. "But as to striking it rich ..."

Tabor's smile took a reflective curve. "Well, that was years ago. He's likely given it all away."

Quillan's curiosity was piqued, as Tabor knew it would be. "As far as I know, he travels like an apostle with nothing but cloak and sandals," Quillan stated.

"As I said, it was years ago. But he yelled eureka with the rest of us. Panned enough to weight his pockets and then some. Went through his fingers like water to anyone in need, though."

Quillan wondered. Had his parents been among those who received the priest's gold? Surely Father Charboneau would have helped his niece if he still had a stash. He wouldn't hoard it while she and her uncle Henri were barely getting by. Of course Èmie was now married to Dr. Simms, and Henri Charboneau ... Fresh rage seized him.

Henri Charboneau had allowed Wolf to take the blame for a heinous murder, and even Quillan had believed his father, the man they called Wolf, a monster. But Henri was dead by his own hand, and his confession had cleared Wolf. Old legends died hard, though. In the minds of most in Crystal, Wolf still howled in the hills, and many a grizzly retelling of his tale would continue.

"So you're selling out." Tabor laid the papers down. "By the looks of it, the mine's doing well. Why sell?"

"Carina wants to go home." That was most of it. He'd never wanted the mine, and though it had made him a rich man, he felt no sorrow leaving it, except if he thought of Cain and all the mine had meant to him. But Quillan still smarted with thoughts of his old friend Cain. That loss was fresh and raw even though he no longer blamed himself. God had freed him of that. It was also the part the mine played in Carina's attack.

Tabor studied him a moment, then turned to his wife. "Augusta, tell him how many times you've wanted to go home."

"I don't really think that's the point."

Quillan folded his napkin and laid it across his plate. The maid took it away, and Quillan threaded his fingers in its place. "Carina has good reason. I'm taking her to her family in California."

"And then?" Tabor's question was sincere.

"I don't know. Learn the lay of the land, I guess. Never been to California. Heard about it some."

Tabor slapped his thigh. "I tell you, Quillan, you're more like me all the time."

"God help Carina." Augusta's tone was dry, but there was affection in her eyes, affection borne of her own inner strength and Horace Tabor's engaging temperament. She loved him, that was clear; it was a comfortable, staid kind of love. Quillan wondered if his fiery relationship with Carina would ever calm to that.

"As for this," Tabor flicked the papers and included Makepeace in the discussion, "let's play with some figures."

The terms were much to Makepeace and Tabor's favor. Horace Tabor was shrewd and Quillan close to indifferent. He'd never considered the mine his, but he had D.C., Cain's son, to think of, as well. Whatever fight he put up was more for D.C.'s sake than his own. All his belief that money would make him somebody had been washed away by the flood, and he was almost thankful, now, that it had happened.

Still, Tabor was fair, and Quillan stood to walk away from these dealings a very rich man. He could give Carina most anything—*if* she stopped chucking his gifts off to Èmie Charboneau Simms. He thought of the package nestled away among the other goods he'd purchased in Leadville, then brought his attention back to Tabor's outstretched hand. He gripped it firmly.

"You know you could get more from the consolidated operators right there in Crystal." Tabor's bulging mustache bounced with each word.

"I know."

"You have personal reasons for doing it this way?"

Quillan glanced at Makepeace, who'd been almost a silent contender through it all. "I have."

"Well, Quillan, you're an odd bird, but I like you. I've liked you from the start, and it's a pleasure to do business with you. And Mr. Makepeace."

"You'll stay here tonight, won't you?" Augusta included both of them in her gaze.

Alex Makepeace spoke first. "I've already acquired a room, ma'am. But I thank you for your offer." He stood. "I'll take leave now, with your permission."

Quillan stood with Tabor and Augusta. He was not sorry to see Makepeace go, though things had progressed amicably. Once the man had gone, Quillan turned to Augusta. "I'd be pleased to accept your offer."

"And have a glass of port with me." Tabor walked to the glass cabinet, which held his decanters.

"Thank you, no." Quillan smiled. "But I will have coffee if it's available."

"Teetotaler, are you?" Tabor paused at the cabinet.

Quillan shrugged. "I have a difficult drive tomorrow."

"Well, bring him some coffee, Augusta. I'm going to pick his brain while I've got him cornered."

Quillan grinned. He liked Hod Tabor. But then, most people did. The man had a magnetism and generosity and good humor that were hard to resist. But he had another reason for speaking with Tabor alone. "I'd like that letter of introduction we spoke of in Denver."

"DeMornays?" Tabor had a good memory.

Quillan nodded. "If it's possible they're my mother's people, I'd like to make their acquaintance before I leave the area for good."

"Understandable." Tabor held his port a moment, then sipped. "All right, then." He took a sheet of stationery from the escritoire.

Quillan had turned down the introduction the last time they

talked. But things had changed; he'd changed.

Tabor scrawled something, then folded the letter. "Might find him a bit of a stuffed shirt. Railroad baron, you know."

Quillan quirked a brow.

"Then again, that's my impression."

"Well, Hod—"

"Actually, I misspoke." Tabor handed him the letter. "Make your own judgment."

Quillan took the letter and slipped it into his pocket. "Thanks."

Tabor nodded. "You have to leave in the morning?"

Quillan smiled. "My wife expects me."

———

Carina glared at Dr. Felden. "What do you mean, weeks? The pain is bearable, the bruising inconsequential."

Dr. Felden leaned forward and spoke with antiseptic breath, his clipped gray mustache like boar bristles across his upper lip. "Not inconsequential inside, where you can't see it. The kidneys are attached quite tenuously, and you've sustained damage. You must remain still and restful for healing to occur."

"I have been still."

"Not by Mae's account. You were in the kitchen instructing Èmie just this morning."

"Twelve steps from my bed to the stove." She waved her arm.

"More like twenty, but it's irrelevant. Any jostling, any jarring, can mean the difference between functioning kidneys and death."

Carina paused at his blunt words. *Death? Dio, was it so serious?* Yes, she felt weak, depleted, sore, and broken, but death? Like her baby?

"Believe me, Mrs. Shepard, you cannot gauge your condition by what you feel. I understand your frustration, but you must accept my restrictions."

Carina felt like a scolded child, and in truth, she'd acted like one. Èmie could handle the kitchen without her. So what if the tagliatelle wasn't just like Mamma's. Quillan had ordered her to stay abed, though perhaps that had contributed to her rebellion. She sagged into the pillows behind her. "Bene. I'll be still."

Dr. Felden closed his bag with a snap. "And when is Quillan due back?"

Again Carina swung her arm, this time sulkily. "He comes when he comes." She looked at the snow through the window. It had been falling since morning, and of course Quillan's only stipulation for not returning was a blizzard.

"Well, mind my instructions, Mrs. Shepard."

She sighed as Dr. Felden let himself out into the storm. The wind did not blow in. The snow fell in silent descent, hardly causing a stir, but surely making the roads impassable. And she knew how quickly such a storm could become life threatening.

She had told Quillan to take no chances, but her heart ached. She didn't want to spend another night alone, crying, fighting the furious, vengeful thoughts toward the men who had killed her unborn child. This new anger was worse than the original shock. *Signore, help me to bear it. And show me why.* She needed to know. How else could she stand the grief that welled up uncontrollably?

Previously her physical pain had overwhelmed the grief and rage. Now thoughts of the baby washed away all else. *My baby!* She reached for Rose's journal. If anyone could understand, it was Quillan's mother, whose first baby had died and whose second, Quillan, she had been forced to give away.

Carina shuddered. Would she, too, imagine her child until she no longer knew what was real? She stroked her hand over the red leather book cover. How dear Rose's words were to her, but she couldn't face them now. Fear of where the grief could lead made her place the book on her bedside crate. If only . . .

She looked at the darkening window, and tears made warm tracks down her cheeks. Carina wanted to believe Quillan would return, if not today, then as soon as he could manage it. He'd never told her a time before, never even promised to return. Surely—

Motion outside the window startled her. She jerked her face that way with a new but familiar terror. Someone was out there. She stiffened. If she screamed, Mae might hear, but . . . The door flew open, and two snowy forms bustled in and banged the door shut behind them.

"Your husband is mad, Carina. Utterly mad." Alex brushed the snow from his coat.

Quillan caught her gaze and held it. "I told you I'd be back tonight."

She looked at him, hair woolly with flakes, whiskers iced and cheeks raw. She swiped at her tears, ashamed she had doubted him.

He stepped forward and handed her a small red-papered box. "For medicinal use." A glimmer shone in his eye.

She took the box, and before she opened it the aroma told her all. She swept the lid from the box. "Chocolate! Quillan!"

His beard was heavy around his buccaneer smile. He was obviously pleased with himself. "Of course, if you'd prefer Èmie had it . . ."

Carina clutched the box to her breast. "I haven't tasted chocolate since San Francisco."

Alex cleared his throat. "Well, I'll be going on to my room. But you should know I feared for our lives more than once on the road home."

Carina tore her eyes from Quillan's face and smiled at Alex. "I'm thankful you're safe. Make Mae give you your table, and if she's given it away already, have Èmie feed you in the kitchen. It's Mamma's *tagliatelle alle acciughe*, pasta with anchovy sauce."

Alex beamed. "Carina, I'd have braved any road to hear you say that. May I?" He motioned toward her side door, which would save him going back out into the storm.

"Of course."

He crossed the room and went out. She turned back to Quillan's scowl. What now? Would he stalk away to sleep in the livery?

He stood a long moment, then seemed to draw himself in. His eyes softened, and the hard line of his mouth eased. "I hate that." He tugged his gloves off and stuffed them fiercely into his coat pocket.

"What?" she almost whispered, fearful to know the answer.

Quillan stooped beside the bed and took her hand. "You don't just cook, Carina. You create, you put yourself into it. I've watched you, seen the magic your hands work on ordinary ingredients." He turned her palm over and ran his finger across it.

A powerful sensation passed through her.

His brows drew together. "I don't want other men to know you that way."

She stared into his face. It was the restaurant he hated? That she fed hungry men something special? "But . . . you have Mae and Èmie running it."

"That's not what I just saw. If Makepeace wasn't already in love with you, he is now."

"He's not—" But now that it was said, what use was there denying it? She dropped her gaze to her palm lying in Quillan's. "Èmie cooked it. I only told her how."

His hand was cold from hours in the elements, but there was nothing cold in his expression. It burned. What were these feelings that cracked Quillan Shepard's hard veneer?

She didn't know what else to say. The restaurant was more than an enterprise to win men's acclaim. It was . . . a mission. She had done so much good with the monies earned through her cooking—which, yes, was more than just making a meal. Why should that offend her husband?

Quillan cupped her hand with his other chilled palm and forced a smile. "Don't you want to know what I did in Leadville?"

"Of course. You told me nothing." She tipped her chin toward him. "And if I asked, you would tell me less."

"I sold the New Boundless."

Her gaze jumped to his face. "You—"

"Horace Tabor fronted Makepeace a loan."

"You sold it to Alex?"

He pressed her hand to his throat. "You wanted to go home, didn't you?"

She felt his rough whiskers against her fingers. "I do. But Dr. Felden—"

"I know you can't travel yet. But we need to get things in order. I think you should sell your restaurant. Or give it away, turn it over to Èmie or Mae."

So there it was. Until that moment she hadn't thought through the details of leaving. She had only longed to see Mamma and Papa and everyone in Sonoma. She had wanted to flee the place where her baby had been beaten from her body. Tears sprang again from her eyes. Was there no end to them?

Quillan brushed them away with his thumb. "I thought it was what you wanted."

"It is, but how can I leave Mae? And Èmie and . . ."

"Alex?" His tone was caustic.

She glared. She had not intended that. "Alex Makepeace is a friend to me. If you were so concerned—"

"Don't you think I know that?" He dropped her hand, stood,

and paced to the wall. "But it's like a sword inside me every time he looks at you. Knowing he sent your attackers running—"

"You should be thankful."

His fists clenched at his sides. "I am. But it doesn't make it any easier."

Carina tossed her head back and flung her palm upward. "First you don't want me—"

"That's not true!"

"You told me every time you came, 'Go away, end this marriage.' "

Quillan pressed his fingers to the sides of his head. "Not because I didn't want you."

"No?"

"No." His voice was firm, insistent.

She sighed, letting her hand fall. "I don't know where to start."

He came and dropped to one knee beside the bed. Carefully he unfolded the paper from one of the chocolates in the box. He held it up and met her eyes. "Start here." He brought the candy to her lips, and she bit the edge, tasting the rich, velvety confection.

It melted away in her mouth, and she licked her lower lip. "Start with chocolate?"

His mouth quirked. "Why not?"

A pang of fear and loss seized her; fear that Quillan's cold, hurtful side would return. And loss—well, all the loss. Why couldn't it have been this way from the start? *Why, Signore?* Quillan slid the rest of the chocolate piece into her mouth. Receiving it from his fingers was so intimate, so tender, her heart quaked.

He cupped her cheek with his palm. "I want to show you I care. To court you as I should have."

She searched his face. What was he saying? He was her husband, the man she loved.

"I read something last night." He closed his eyes, then looked again. " 'Now I rejoice, not that ye were made sorry, but that ye sorrowed to repentance.' " His throat worked. "I'm sorry to repentance, Carina. You said you forgive me, and God also, but I want to make it right."

She felt the intensity of that desire. She knew it herself, that driving need to right a wrong. She said, "You have. You're here."

He gripped her hand almost painfully. "Don't make it so easy."

"It's all I want."

"You deserve more."

Was he saying he loved her? He'd never said the words. He'd spoken poetry, and twice they'd come together, once shyly, deeply, on their wedding night, the other time in anger. But never had he said he loved her. *Dio, he must.* He couldn't look at her that way unless he did.

She dropped her gaze to his lips and willed him to say it. Her pulse raced, waiting. Surely he would kiss her. She looked up as his face drew close, drawn there, she knew, by her own desire.

Then he brought her fingers up between them, pressed them to his lips. His breath was hot. "I married you to prove that I could best Berkley Beck."

"I put you in that position."

"You came to me for help."

"You helped." But after their wedding, she had faced his desertion, the vigilante hangings, her danger and rescue, then Quillan's repeated offers of divorce.

He pressed her fingers to his lips again. "You've been under my skin from the start."

Under his skin? Was that the same as love?

He opened her hand and kissed her palm. "From the day I saw you on the slope scavenging the bits and pieces left from your wagon."

"Thanks to you," she scoffed.

"If I'd known I'd be paying for that the rest of my life, I'd have dismantled your wagon and killed my team hauling every ounce of it."

Carina stared at his intensity.

His voice thickened. "All I want is the chance to make it right." He laid her hand down and drew back.

She sensed the moment lost. He would not kiss her, not say he loved her. She sank into the pillows. What did he want from her? Would she ever understand this son of Wolf and Rose? *Signore, would you be so kind as to give me a clue?* She could almost hear God laughing. She failed to see the humor.

Four

If travail has a purpose, let me find it now.

If honor needs a taker, O Lord, me endow.

If wisdom is a garment, let me wear it well.

If goodness needs a champion, help me dark dispel.

— Quillan

QUILLAN ROSE EARLY. The need to make things right gave him little rest. It drove his desire to conclude the sale of the mine and make preparation for departure. As Quillan crossed Central at Pine under the clear morning sky, he was hailed by Ben Masterson. Quillan turned and extended his hand with a smile. "Mr. Mayor."

Masterson clasped his hand. "I hear you're selling out."

"From whom?"

"Round about."

Quillan shrugged, trying to look noncommittal. He'd told no one but Carina, though Makepeace might have talked. "I was hoping to keep it tight until I heard back from Daniel Cain."

"Selling out both your interests?"

"I don't know yet. D.C. hasn't answered."

"He won't, either. Not for a while." Masterson sent his gaze upward toward the pass. "Snow brought down the lines two nights ago."

The night Quillan and Makepeace had fought through the storm back to Crystal. It must have been especially heavy over Mosquito Pass, where the telegraph line ran. Quillan frowned. He had time before Carina could travel, but he'd wanted to wrap up this sale as soon as possible. The consolidateds would try to get their hands on the New Boundless, and he was determined to resist their efforts after what had happened to his wife.

He'd offered the mine to Makepeace for less than its worth, assuming D.C. would also sell, and Tabor had set liberal terms. If details got out, he'd have a dogfight with men he'd rather strangle than haggle with. It was critical he communicate with D.C., but the lines could be down for weeks.

"I'm sorry about your wife, Quillan." Masterson looked sincere, but Quillan knew he was only sorry as far as it didn't threaten commerce and peace. He'd been willing to lynch her once.

Quillan nodded.

"Guess it's understandable, your clearing out. Will she be able to travel soon?"

"Doc Felden thinks a couple more weeks abed, then we'll see."

"I'm truly sorry. It's an ugly business when our women aren't safe. I'm just glad those reprobates cleared out after."

Again Quillan nodded. It would do no good taking Masterson to task. He had a political mind, and to him the welfare of Crystal far exceeded Carina's justice. Quillan tipped his hat and continued across Central. Turning left, he headed for the livery.

"Good mornin', boyo." Alan Tavish huddled in a rocker next to the stove, fragrant pipe smoke circling his head.

"Good morning, Alan." Quillan took in his bent, arthritic form. Alan seemed more contorted than ever, and Quillan's heart seized at the thought of leaving him. With Cain gone, he'd drawn close to Alan, and he worried about the old man. Who would check in on him beyond their livery needs, stay to chat, see that he took care of himself?

Quillan dropped to a barrel beside the rocker.

"How's the lass?"

Quillan smiled. Carina would always be "the lass" to Alan. "Better since she's following doctor's orders."

Alan grinned. "Bit of vinegar there."

"A bit." Quillan raised his brows.

Alan pointed with the stem of his pipe. "And you?"

Quillan knew which part of his well-being Alan addressed. "I'm trying, Alan. Courting her as you said I should."

Alan patted Quillan's thigh, his crumpled knuckles upraised like spider legs. "It'll do ye good, boyo."

Quillan leaned his head back to the wall. What he wanted most was to grab Carina into his arms and kiss her breath away, then know her as he had on their wedding night. But he had hurt her once, taken her in anger, and he was determined not to even kiss her again until he'd mended that. Carina had to want his touch, his kiss. Sometimes it seemed she did already, but it was more likely his own desire speaking.

"I need to reach D.C., Alan."

His change of subject had little effect on the old ostler. Alan was used to his close keeping of personal thoughts.

"Ye know where he is."

"I wired him in Northfield, but the lines are down."

Alan shrugged. "Send a wire from Fairplay."

"I'd have to get there."

"Aye."

Quillan shook his head. "I just left Carina. How would it look to go again?"

Alan's silence said too much. *Never worried about that before. Ye must be smitten sure, lad. And it's about time.* Quillan could hear it well enough without Alan speaking aloud.

"Then I'd have to wait in Fairplay for a reply." Quillan raised his hands, frustrated.

"Aye."

Quillan dropped his hands to his lap. "She won't understand. You should have seen her." He recalled her face as he'd told her he was going to Leadville with Makepeace. The twisting started inside him. Ah, that was the root of it now. Leaving Carina alone with Alex Makepeace. He could hardly take the man along this time.

"She'll bide."

Oh, she'd bide all right. With Makepeace to make the biding easier. Never had Quillan felt such possessive malice. But then, he'd never loved before, never allowed himself to love. "I can't do it, Alan. If Makepeace—"

"Ah, boyo. 'Tis a jaundiced eye ye have."

"You said yourself she could love him and would if—"

"That was before ye put your trust in the Almighty."

Quillan sat silently. How did Alan know? Did it show on the

outside, the surrender? And what exactly was Alan saying? That God would keep Makepeace away from Carina? *Lord?* Quillan searched his heart. How did faith work? All the sermons his foster father had spoken, all the truths Cain had touted; had they told Quillan how to live? How to handle this jealousy, this doubt, this aching fear that he'd lose Carina and it would be his own fault?

"I don't know what to do, Alan."

Alan drew long on his pipe, puffed out the smoke. "Pray, Quillan. Ask God. Then trust He'll see to your business better than you."

The thought of turning Carina's safety, Carina's fidelity, over to God, even the God to whom he'd surrendered in his father's cave . . . It was easier to surrender himself than Carina. He shook his head. "I've made a mess of it."

" 'Tis bought and paid for ye are, Quillan. Whatever ye've done or failed to do, sure Christ the Savior has taken it on himself."

Why didn't it feel that way? If God forgave him, if Carina forgave, why couldn't he forgive himself? Just the thought of telling Carina he had to leave town again brought a burning shame. She'd known before he spoke the last time; she had expected it, seen it coming—and why not? It's all he'd given her. His back.

But without D.C.'s okay, he couldn't go forward with the sale. And with the lines down . . . He sighed. Mae had told him to learn to be still. Alan said pray. Maybe today he could do that much. He leaned forward and patted Alan's shoulder. "Thank you, old man."

Alan covered his hand with his dry, callused palm. "Seek Him first, and the rest will come."

Quillan nodded. The feelings he had for Alex Makepeace were certainly not rooted in God. And he couldn't let those feelings rule his decisions. Maybe he would do better to learn God's mind in it. He left the livery and returned to Carina's room, hushing Sam's eager greeting. Carina was still sleeping, and he stood for a moment looking down on her and wondering how he could have been such a fool.

Then, taking Cain's worn Bible from his pack, he sat on one of the two chairs beside the small table as Sam settled at his feet. He laid the book down and opened to the gospel of Saint Matthew. It was the first of the gospels and seemed as good a place to start as any. He was certainly familiar with the scriptures. He'd committed whole books to memory at the instigation of Reverend and Mrs. Shepard, his foster parents. But though he'd memorized the words, he'd never taken them to heart.

Now he looked at the book, wondering if he could learn it differently. He'd read it two nights ago, and that phrase he'd quoted to Carina had jumped out at him from the page as though he'd never seen it before. He closed his eyes. *Jesus, show me what you want me to know. Change my heart, my mind, my being. Make me new.* Where had that prayer come from? It was as though some power had prayed through him, prayed what he needed even though he hadn't known what he needed.

Quillan reached into his pack and pulled out the journal in which he'd begun to jot thoughts and writings, mainly in the form of poetry. He found a fresh page and, at the top, wrote the prayer he'd just prayed. Then looking at the words, he read them back, owning them. The constriction in his heart eased, and he read through the gospel of Matthew.

When he finished, he felt as though he had only just begun to know Jesus and his followers, and he wanted to know more, needed to. He wrote: *Lord I want to know you, your heart, your mind, your being.* Glancing up, he saw Carina watching him. How long had she been awake? He met her eyes and felt the jolting charge of connecting with her. Without touching, they held each other; without words, they spoke. But did she understand? Did she know what she meant to him?

"What is that?" She motioned to the journal.

"My diary. Or something like that." He flipped back to a page nearer the front, stood, and carried it to her.

She took the open journal and read aloud.

"The Road

A winding gash across and up a mighty craggy crown,
Blasted, hewn, and flattened down to form a ribbon where,
The wheels of commerce rolling forward,
    forward up and down,
To and fro and back and forth with ne'er a moment spare.
Carcass bleaching in the sun, horse flesh pushed to death,
Stage behind and bed before, and fate trapped in between,
Wears a face both fair and keen that takes away my breath,
If I had known, if I had done, if I had only seen."

Tears brightened her eyes to dark sparkling pools. They clutched his heart when she looked up, and he stooped beside her, clasped her hand.

She cleared the morning and tears from her throat. "Am I fate, Quillan?"

"Fate, destiny, gift." Meeting Carina Maria DiGratia in the road had changed his life.

She searched his face. "Whose gift?"

"God's." He stroked the top of her hand, so softly the mere touch of it brought him alive.

"Do you believe God put me in your road because he meant us to be together?"

Quillan pondered that. Had he not met Carina stranded on the road, would he have noticed her in town? Would he have looked up long enough to note her face and allowed himself to think about her twice? Had God broken her wheel at just that place to make him stop and pay attention? It was impossible to think he could have cohabited Crystal with Carina and not been swept away by the same force that had him now. But he was not the man now that he'd been then.

"Yes, Carina. I was too boneheaded otherwise."

She smiled, and he wanted so much to kiss her he almost threw away all of Alan's advice and just did it. But he stood up instead, taking the journal with him.

"Can't I see the rest?"

"Sometime, maybe. Some of it." He smiled crookedly. "The parts about you."

"I want to see it all. I want to know you." Her words echoed his own search that morning. *Knowing*—how deep that word.

"I want to know you, too, Carina."

She threw up her hand. "You do know me! You've known me from the start. I don't hide who I am."

His grin deepened. No, she didn't hide anything. Couldn't if she tried.

She raised her chin. "But you? You shoot the head from a rattlesnake, drag me from a mineshaft, save me from lynching, and now you're a poet?"

He spread his hand, helpless to explain.

"You know what I thought the first time I saw you, after you'd thrown my wagon down the mountain? I thought you a pirate.

Standing in the hotel with Mrs. Barton fawning, you looked the worst blackguard buccaneer imaginable."

Quillan laughed. "I wondered what you were thinking. But you were dining with Berkley Beck, as I recall."

"Not dining. Meeting. Trying to save what I could of my hopes and thinking all the while how I would get back at you for what you'd done."

Quillan dropped his gaze. She'd succeeded admirably. There was certainly hurt between them.

"Now you show me these words, and they melt my heart."

His own turned to syrup as he raised his eyes to hers. "I want them to."

Again her tears came, and he felt stung. Was it so awful for her to think he loved her? He turned away. "I have to go to Fairplay, Carina." She didn't answer, and he knew the look he'd find on her face if he looked. "The telegraph wires are down over Mosquito Pass. I have to contact D.C. and know what he wants to do about the mine."

"Won't they fix them?" Her voice trembled, but with sorrow or suppressed rage he couldn't tell without looking.

"It'll take too long." He glanced at Sam lying by the door, head raised. Did even the dog blame him for once again walking out? "We need to act quickly to avoid trouble, trouble for Alex Makepeace." Now he did look at her.

Her face was angry—angry and hurt and confused.

"That's why I went to see Horace Tabor first thing. If the consolidateds know Tabor's involved in the venture, maybe they won't try to force my hand. But if there's a hang-up . . . The New Boundless is too valuable, Carina. Alex Makepeace won't stand a chance if the big boys enter the fray."

"So sell him your part, and let D.C. worry about his own." Her voice was bitter.

Quillan answered softly. "You know I can't."

She started to cry, then gripped her chest and turned her head away from him. But he knew it wasn't physical pain. He dropped down beside the bed. "I won't go. I don't care about the mine. I don't care who gets it. I won't leave you."

She held herself, weeping. "It hurts so much!"

He pulled her to his chest. "I'm sorry."

She tried to push away, but he held her tightly until she

softened and sank into his embrace, now crying silently.

He'd held her unconscious the night he learned of her attack, cradled her and cried out to God for help. He wouldn't hurt her further. "I won't go."

"You have to."

For a moment he wasn't sure she'd actually said that. "I don't have to and I won't."

She pushed back from his chest, deep brown eyes full with tears. "You must do it. For Alex. It's the right thing."

The stab of her words went right through his solar plexus and rendered him unable to answer until the feeling passed. *For Alex.* For Alex she could suffer Quillan's departure. *Stop it!* The thoughts would drive him crazy! "Just tell me what you want, Carina." He sure wouldn't figure it out for himself.

"I don't know." She sobbed. "Signore, help me, I don't know."

"You're overexcited." He laid her gently back. "Rest now, or Doc Felden will have my neck."

"You're leaving now?"

"No."

"But you should?" Her eyes were obsidian pools.

"No. I can stay as long as you need me to." And hang the New Boundless, Alex Makepeace, and all the consolidated miners who would love to add his property to theirs.

She sighed, pressing her fingers to her eyes and dropping her head deeper into the pillows. He stood over her, hating himself for wounding her yet again. Her hands dropped to her breast and folded there, but she didn't open her eyes or speak. He went and sat at the table.

He was a third of the way through St. Mark when she spoke. "In the morning, you can go."

He turned. Once again their eyes met, though this time the storm kept them apart. Quillan was fairly certain he would never undo the damage he'd done her, and even though she seemed to have spent her tears, she was far from pleased. Still, if she were willing . . .

God, what do I do? A peaceful assurance filled him. The Lord would look after Carina just as Alan had said. He nodded without answering, and when her eyes closed again and she fell asleep, he returned to Mark's gospel, devouring it before he went to Mae's for lunch.

He spent the afternoon committing portions of Luke's gospel to memory while Carina alternately rested and read. It seemed strange to be with her inside the same four walls, each holding his own silence. Part of him appreciated the chance to be quiet together. Mostly he worried that he was doing something wrong. Maybe he should talk to her, but what was there to say?

Several times Èmie came to consult about the menu for the restaurant that evening, but Carina seemed listless and disheartened. Perhaps she was reluctant to show her enthusiasm when he was there. If it weren't for Mae's and Alan's instructions to sit still, bide, and pray, he'd ... what? He was hard pressed to think of something better he could do.

Mae brought dinner on a tray for Carina and served Quillan's on the small table where he studied. With a look half amused, half approving, she sashayed from the room, her swinging girth somehow accentuating both messages. Quillan noticed Carina cross herself and fold her hands over her food. He offered a silent grace of his own. He'd been tempted for a moment to speak a blessing as Reverend Shepard had when Quillan was a boy, but he was afraid to break the silence between them.

Though Carina had given permission for him to go, she was not peaceful with it. And he was afraid one word from him would set her off again, her Italian blood something to contend with. The food was flavorful and hearty, Carina's recipe for certain. But it lacked ... what? The touch of her hands preparing it? The graceful communication of her hopes into the dough she pressed and twisted?

He felt an unholy pleasure that the food was not the same without Carina. Not one man in Crystal would experience her cooking again if he could help it. Just the thought of those dirty miners, and even men like Alex Makepeace and the mayor himself—

For out of the heart proceed evil thoughts, murders, adulteries, fornications, thefts, false witness, blasphemies: These are the things which defile a man: but to eat with unwashen hands defileth not a man. The Scripture sprang to his mind from days of memorizing his wickedness at the instigation of his stepmother, who saw nothing good in him. But the words kindled inside his mind as though burned there by a divine finger. Bitter, unkind thoughts would do him more harm than good.

Quillan looked down at his plate, certain the food would now taste like sawdust, just recompense for his thoughts. But it didn't. It still tasted good if not remarkable. He wondered what Carina was thinking, but glancing up, found her nibbling at her portion with little interest. "You need to eat, Carina."

She shrugged. "You sound like Mae."

"Mae's a wise woman."

Carina sighed, pushed the tray away. "I'm not hungry."

He knew better than to force it. He stood and took the tray from the bed and set it on the table. Maybe in a while she would want it. But when he'd finished his and looked up again, she was asleep. It seemed she was getting an inordinate amount of sleep, but then, her body had a lot of healing to do. Gently he removed the extra pillows from behind her head until she was lying down. He pulled the covers over her shoulders, then extinguished the light and got into bed, careful not to jostle or touch her.

He'd spent the day in prayer, hoping the Lord would make things clear. He'd asked to know God, to understand His purpose. And he did seem to grasp something more. The words of the gospels were planted deeply in his mind, held there by the special gift of memory he'd possessed from his youth. He settled into sleep, trusting the rest would come with time.

Five

Duty is a cowardice by which a man eludes,
the deeper call of heart and soul a woman's love exudes.
From her deep unfathomed well, he marches straight and tall.
Certain in resolve and zeal, "darling, I must" the clarion call.

— *Quillan*

WAKING AT THE SOUND of the door opening, Carina watched Quillan go out with Cain's dog—now Quillan's—to prepare for his trip. In her silent thoughts, she had begged God to side with her, to force Quillan to stay, but all God had said was, *I am sufficient.* Bene. Once again she was alone. She sulked. "Is this all I will have, Signore? Am I to be alone? Will you never be finished punishing me? Oh, why did I ever leave Sonoma?" A pang so sharp it vied with her physical injuries stabbed her heart. "I want to go home, Signore."

But wasn't that what Quillan was trying to accomplish? Why did she take his efforts as a personal affront? Because she didn't trust him. How could she? He had deserted her, left her alone to face— She recalled the attack, which had damaged equally her heart and spirit. And her baby.

She clutched her belly. How could she ache so for a child she'd never seen? A child conceived in error, spite, and anger. How could she long for its tiny flutters inside her? How could she not? Even so early, she had treasured the presence inside her. She covered her face and wept.

If God was sufficient, why did she hurt so? She thought of

47

Quillan lying beside her in the bed last night, his back against her like a wall. He had not reached for her, not held her. He felt guilty perhaps, sorry to repentance, but he didn't love her. How could he love her and not sense her need?

Carina cried harder. "Now I understand, Signore, how sins, even though forgiven, carry a price. How much better it would have been had I never left home, never tried to punish Flavio's infidelity, never sought my own way."

Oofa!

Only once or twice had Carina experienced God's direct chastisement, and the word in her mind sobered her now.

Daughter, I am sufficient. I Am.

Carina's breath heaved in her chest as the words sank in. The promise was so astounding. Here was God, the God of the universe, promising to be whatever she needed. And she could sulk?

Chastened, Carina crossed herself. "Forgive me, Signore! What a fool I am! Oh, Dio . . ." Peace permeated and surrounded her.

How long she sat and basked, feeling its healing power, she couldn't say, only that when Quillan came back through the door, she smiled so sincerely, he stopped and stared at her.

"What?" His stance was defensive, and sensing that, Sam circled him, then faced her as well, eyes earnest.

"Do you think something is wrong because I smile at my husband?"

Quillan stood silently, then, "Have you changed your mind?"

"Yes. No. Actually, God has."

He raised his brows. "God has what?"

"Changed my mind and my heart. I'm not angry."

Quillan advanced and stood beside the bed. When he was gone, she would picture him there, looking exactly as he looked now. "Then you're not upset I'm going?"

She shook her head, thankful she could give him that. He would not have to stew over her while he made the treacherous trip to Fairplay.

He stayed still and silent so long, her smile faded. "Don't you believe me?"

He nodded, still unspeaking.

Why was he upset? She could feel his tension. "What is it?"

Lowering his face, he said, "Nothing. I'm glad you don't mind. I'm sure you'll be fine."

Her laugh surprised even herself. "You're a terrible liar."

Quillan's face bristled suddenly, and again the air crackled between them. "What am I supposed to say? Do you think I didn't see Makepeace leaving?"

"Alex?" Her stupefaction was not feigned. "Leaving where?"

"Here. Leaving your door and walking away as though the devil were on his heels."

Now she understood. "Well, I don't know anything about that. I never saw him."

"You're saying he wasn't here with you?"

"If he was at my door I never heard him. I was praying."

Quillan's throat worked, and the volatile clouds churned in his eyes until they parted to show her a need so raw it hurt. "I can't stand the thought of him here with you."

"He's not."

"He will be."

"Not here." She pressed her hand over her heart. "Where it matters. It's not Alex Makepeace I love." She engaged his eyes, forcing him to see. She had told him once before that it wasn't Flavio she loved. How could he not see that it was he?

"Oh, Quillan, you *are* a pirate. You stole not only my earthly possessions, but my heart, as well. Don't you see? It's you—obstinate, impossible man that you are." She caught his face between her hands. "I love you."

For a moment she thought he would cry, and if he did, she had no idea what she would say or do. But instead he caught her own face between his hands and kissed her, kissed her so long and hungrily she could scarcely breathe. She clutched his hair in her fingers, his wild honey mane. His arms closed around her, and she felt his passion surging through the muscles. He was her husband, and he loved her. His body told her better than his words, his lack of words.

"Now I can't go." His voice was hoarse and pained.

Laughing softly, she kissed his cheek and whispered, "You have to."

His fingers dug into her back between her shoulder blades. "You always win, don't you?"

"Do you feel like you've lost?"

"Lost control, lost my mind." He kissed her again, groaning

softly. "I don't know how to love. I want to, but I don't know how."

"You know." She clasped his face and drew back. "You loved Cain, and you love D.C."

"An old man and a boy."

"You love Mae."

"Mae?" His brows rose abruptly.

"You helped save her life."

"That's not—"

"You saved mine. Three times." She drew him back and kissed his lips softly, then circled his neck and kissed him deeply. With Quillan's wall torn down, she couldn't restrain what she felt for him. God had promised to be sufficient, but in his grace He had added on to that the love of this man. And now she felt Quillan's tears on her cheek.

"Then you'll believe me if I say it?" It was hardly more than a whisper.

"Try." She spoke into the softless of his new mustache.

"I love you, Carina."

"I know."

He crushed her, but not even the pain of her bruises could make her pull away. It would be ten times more painful now to watch him walk out the door. But in some ways, less. She would not have to worry whether he would return.

Quillan tried to remember all the reasons he had to go to Fairplay. They mattered, he knew. Of course they did. He breathed the scent of Carina's hair, her wonderful cascade of rippling silk that hung over her shoulders and onto her back. *Silken threads of charcoal black, shimmering iridescent plumage, let them swallow me up, entangle and entwine, ensnare my restless feet and tether me like a hawk's jesses, let me drown, let me drown in her tresses.*

He slowly drew back, forcefully governing himself. Catching Carina's hands together at his chest, he looked into her face. She looked like an angel, peaked brows over dark melting eyes, lips the color of dawn, darker now from his kisses. He wanted more. He wanted to kiss and hold her all through the day and into the night. He wanted to board up the windows and bolt the door.

But he had to go. If he didn't leave early he'd never make it over the pass to Fairplay. So far the day was clear, and he should capitalize on that. He brought her fingers to his lips, held them there. "I have to go."

She nodded.

"I want to stay."

"I know." She opened her fingers and held them to his cheek. "Once this sale is finished, once you're able to travel—"

"Don't make promises you can't keep. Only God knows what happens next." Her smile was soft and sad. She was trying not to cry. If she cried he wouldn't go.

She stroked his cheek. "Take Sam with you."

"No. I want him here."

"I have people here. You need him. I need to know you're not alone on that road. If nothing else, he'll keep you warm."

Quillan glanced at the dog. Sam wanted to come. It was in the flapping of his tail, the arch of his neck, his readiness to spring up from his prone position before the door. "All right. I'll come back as soon as I can, as soon as I hear back from D.C."

She nodded again, and he guessed her throat was as full as his.

"Don't forget what I said."

"How could I?"

He gave her his rogue's smile, but only half managed it. Then he turned, whistled to Sam to follow, and left before he changed his mind. His step was unaccountably light as he cut through the congestion to the livery. His wagon stood outside, loaded with provisions and emergency tools: ax, shovel, firewood, tarps.

Alan sat outside in the winter sunshine soaping a harness. "You're off, then?"

Quillan nodded. "With Carina's blessing, if you can believe it."

Alan grinned. "I believe it, boyo."

"Then believe this: I can't court her anymore."

Alan's grin crumbled. "Are ye daft?"

"I can't court her because I already told her everything, made a soppy fool of myself all over her."

Alan slapped the lines against his thigh and laughed. "That's it, now! I dinna ken ye'd be so simple!" He shook his head, befuddled. "The courtin' never stops, Quillan. No matter how much ye love her."

Quillan stared. "What am I missing?"

Alan shook his head. "Love is sunshine to the rose. It can't stop shinin' just because the bud begins to bloom."

Quillan reached a hand to Alan's shoulder. "Thank you, Alan."

Alan patted his chest. "Follow your heart, Quillan. It understands more than your mind."

Quillan pulled himself into the box of his wagon as he had so many times over the past two years. His mind was no slackard. He used it prodigiously while he drove the long hours alone. But Alan was right. Intellect could only take him so far. What he needed now were things of the heart: trust, faith, love.

The waiting was easier when Èmie or Mae or Joe Turner stopped in to chat. Even Lucia had been loquacious, and Carina wondered if it was a conspiracy among her friends to cheer her in Quillan's absence. She mused how each one had come into her life. Èmie she'd met at the baths, a stiff, ghostly woman drained of joy. Berkley Beck had introduced her to Mae and vouchsafed a room in the boardinghouse Carina's first night in town. Had he intended even then to control and possess her? But Mae was a treasure for all her rough ways, and Carina had seen her soften like wax held between the palms.

Then Joe—sweet, funny Joe—who believed she'd made his fortune by stealing his room. He'd made her a legend: Lady Luck. Lucia, they'd found in desperate circumstances and hired into the restaurant. She was dogged in devotion to both Carina and Èmie. As were Celia and Elizabeth, twins brought to her attention by Alex. Their father was a rocked-up miner, no longer able to work. And then, of course, there was Alex.

Only there wasn't. Whatever he'd been doing at her door the morning Quillan left, he hadn't returned. How could he? Even that didn't matter as it had. Though day passed into day, she felt almost cheerful. She certainly felt stronger, her natural vigor returning. She could feel it. Or was it Quillan's love that healed and sustained her, the words he'd spoken at last?

She refused to dwell on his absence and focused instead on his confession. Yes, he loved her. And that thought kept her heart singing. That and the efforts of her dear friends. This afternoon her room had been invaded by one party after another. By the time Dr. Felden assessed her progress, she was almost punchy. She wasn't surprised when he ordered quiet for the rest of the evening.

And that was all right, too. She'd found a new and deeper solace in her time alone. Before it had chafed and frightened her to do nothing. Her forced quiescence had changed that, especially the day Quillan had spent silently with her. That had been special, though she hadn't seen it at the time. How many things she missed until after, when she could look back on them.

It had snowed two days after Quillan left, and she guessed he wouldn't be back soon. The road would be impassable with fresh powdered snow. It was one thing to come from Leadville over snowpack, another altogether to take Mosquito Pass after a storm. She prayed he wouldn't be impetuous enough to try. No, he knew that road too well and wouldn't risk his team.

She looked at the table where he'd sat only days ago engrossed in Cain's Bible and writing in his journal. She wished he'd left it. With his words, she would have felt him close. But she almost felt him anyway. Though they couldn't speak or see each other, she knew he was thinking of her as she thought of him almost incessantly. His shadowed face when they'd first met on the road. His mocking smile. His earnest smile. His eyes, gray orbs with charcoal rims. His hair worn long like his father's had been, though Quillan had never known his father.

The mystery of Wolf and Rose had drawn her, compelled her. In spite of Quillan's fury, she'd delved into their story and learned oh so much more than she'd expected. Though she'd never laid eyes on Quillan's parents, she loved them. And loved him better for it. *Ah, Signore.*

A knock came at the door between her room and the hall to Mae's kitchen.

"Come in." Carina smoothed the blankets over her knees. She had dressed that morning in a soft flannel dress of Èmie's that did nothing for her figure but did not require a corset. She was just too glad to be out of her nightgown and sat atop the covers.

Èmie peeked around the door, her long, plain face breaking into a smile. "Good, you're awake still. I've brought someone." She pushed the door wide.

Carina cried, "Father Antoine!" Another friend whom she'd wondered if she would see again. The priest followed Èmie into the room, smiling. He seemed to have found a peace Carina had not seen him possess since his brother Henri's death.

"Where have you been? I've asked and asked. Èmie didn't

know or wasn't saying, and I was ready to give up and believe you had abandoned us."

"I've been a hermit."

"Truly?"

He nodded.

"And you won't get any more from him than that." Èmie pulled a chair from the table and placed it near the bed for her uncle, then took the second for herself.

"I may need the seclusion again someday, and I don't want well-meaning people stomping up to find me." He said it with a mischievous grin. He had lost weight, a substantial amount, though he had little extra to lose. Where his muscles before had been those of a vigorous man, he was now lean, almost gaunt. Yet he didn't seem diminished in vigor.

"Well, sit and tell me everything else." Carina's joy in seeing him washed away all of Dr. Felden's advice. Besides, she'd slept enough these last days to make the very thought tedious.

Father Antoine spread his hands. "What's there to tell? I questioned my purpose, and God, in His mercy, restored my vision."

"How?"

"Prayer and silence."

Had he said that a few days ago, she would have scoffed, but her own spirit had been quickened lately by those very things, though not to the degree he must have practiced. He'd been gone months alone somewhere with God. On the mountain, surely. He'd given that much away with his "stomping up" comment. His only appearance had been to perform Èmie and Robert's wedding, and then he had vanished again. And that must prove Èmie knew where to find him. But Carina understood her silence.

"And peace?" she asked softly. "Have you found peace about Henri?"

His smile gentled. There was sadness, yes, but not despair. "I believe he is with God. Beyond that?" He shrugged. "Now tell me how you are. Mae and Èmie told me what happened, but I want to know what's happening here." He touched his chest over his heart.

Unexpectedly, tears sprang to her eyes. Why now, when she was so content? "Do you know about the baby?" She glanced briefly at Èmie, then back to the priest.

He nodded.

She pressed her own heart. "Then you know how I am here. But God gives me strength."

"And Quillan?"

She sank back with a soft laugh. "Quillan is healing, too." She suddenly sprang up. "Father, you must see something!"

"What?"

Carina glanced at Èmie.

Èmie said, "Do you want me to leave?"

Carina searched her friend's face, such a dear face, so trusted. "No. But I don't want anyone else to know." She turned to the priest. "For Wolf's sake." If anyone cared about safeguarding Wolf's memory, it was Father Antoine.

He wrinkled his brow. "What is it, Carina?"

"A cave. Under the shaft in the Rose Legacy. Wolf painted it all, Father. His whole life. It's very sad, but also ... triumphant. I don't know. I think seeing it helped Quillan, though it must have been terrible, too. I want you to see it, Father. You cared so."

The priest fingered the heavy cross that hung at his waist. "A painted cave." He smiled slowly. "That would be Wolf."

"But you understand why no one else can know? It's very ugly, some of it. It could easily be mistaken."

"No one will know from me."

"Nor me," Èmie murmured. "Though I wondered what you and Alex Makepeace had found up there."

"Alex Makepeace?" The priest looked from one to the other.

Realizing Father Antoine had been gone most of the time since her marriage, Carina said, "He is Quillan's mine engineer. And my friend." She chose her words carefully. "We found the cave together."

"That explains your grim faces." Èmie folded her hands. "I did wonder."

"Do you think others did as well?"

Èmie shrugged.

Carina turned to the priest. "I think it should be sealed off after Quillan and I leave."

"And where are you going?"

"He's taking me home, Father." She couldn't hide the emotion in that thought.

"To your family."

"Yes." Her voice lost some of its strength.

"And they know? About your marriage?"

She opened her mouth to answer, then closed it and shook her head. "I tried so many times to write, to tell them everything. Now I think it best I just go to them."

He cocked his head. "I've never taken you for a coward, Carina."

"You don't know Mamma."

"I'll pray for you and Quillan both." He smoothed his cassock. "And now I must let you sleep."

"Will you see the cave?"

The priest nodded. "I'll see it." He stopped at the door and moved his hand in blessing. "Good night, Carina."

Èmie stood, too, but Carina called her back. "Will you stay a moment?"

Èmie took her uncle's chair beside the bed. "So you really are leaving?"

"I have to, Èmie."

Èmie sighed. "I thought you and Quillan could be happy here. I guess this was too much for you." She reached out and touched the paling bruise on Carina's wrist.

"Even without this, Èmie, I need to see my family. I need to be near them. I was crazy to think otherwise. I love you and Mae, but..."

Èmie squeezed her hand. "I understand."

Covering Èmie's hand with her own, Carina drew her closer. "I want you to have the restaurant."

"What do you mean?"

"I mean this, all of this." Carina waved her hand to indicate the extent of her property.

"But, Carina..." Èmie shook her head, overwhelmed.

Carina shook her. "You don't want it? After all you've learned and mastered?"

"I ... of course, but..."

"Is it Robert? Won't he want you to continue? At least until he's successful?"

"It won't be the same without you, Carina. I can't be you."

Carina spread her hands. "It will be yours. Whatever you make it."

Èmie sat very still. Then, "You're kind, Carina. I know what this restaurant means to you, the good you've done with it. I'd be honored to carry on. I'll speak to Robert."

Carina squeezed her hand. "There's room to add a clinic on the other side by Fletchers."

Èmie grinned. "So there is."

Carina folded her hands together. "Signore, you know my friend Èmie of whom I've spoken many times before. I want her to have this restaurant, so would you kindly arrange it with her husband who's not too sure yet what he is or should be doing?"

Èmie laughed. "That's not fair, Carina. Even a doctor can be bitten with the mining bug."

"Oh, *sì*." Carina waved her hand. "And maybe he'll think twice about risking his life when he has the skills to save others."

"He already is."

"Then take this gift; add a clinic. If your cooking is bad, he'll have the treatment."

They laughed until Èmie suddenly threw her arms around Carina's neck. "You've changed my life."

Carina squeezed her back, too emotional to answer. It would not be easy to let go. As much as she wanted to go home, needed to, it would not be easy to let go.

Six

Take heed before you give your heart,
for given once, 'tis ere more lost.
And though it beats within your breast,
each steadfast beat now bears a cost.

— Quillan

QUILLAN ENTERED THE SHOP for the third time. Since there was still no reply from D.C., he would mark the day with another gift. This shop was down the street from the Italian market where he'd purchased Carina's supplies, but it was full of feminine fripperies. He vaguely recalled her pausing outside its window the one time they went to Fairplay together.

The first day of this trip he'd purchased a lace collar, the next a parasol, though it was definitely not parasol weather. He finagled a good price because of that. The third day he chose a different shop and bought a box of hand-decorated velum stationery. But today he was back to the first shop. He went straight to the glass case and eyed what he already knew he would purchase even though it was priced at a usurer's cost.

The clerk noticed him immediately. "So you've decided on it?"

Quillan frowned. Not even an offer to budge on the extravagant price. "Thought maybe you'd come to your senses and were ready to charge a realistic fee for a nice but certainly not irreplaceable item."

The man smiled. "Don't you think she's worth it?"

Quillan glared. "She's worth it, but the pin's not."

The clerk shrugged his beefy shoulders. "It's what it is." He knew he had Quillan trapped, and Quillan resented it. He'd looked in the other shops. There were trinkets plenty, but none so perfect for Carina as the amethyst stickpin in the case before him.

"All right, package it." Quillan pulled out his money, wishing he could wipe the grin off the storekeeper's face.

The man leaned close with a conspiratorial whisper. "Bitten bad, are you?"

Quillan didn't answer.

"Hoping to get somewhere with this one, I'd wager." He showed yellowed teeth the shape of stalactites.

Quillan said, "It's for my wife."

"Oh." The clerk tapped his nose. "Never hurts to lay it on thick." He wrapped the pin in tissue and handed it over.

Quillan snatched it. If any more days passed, he'd do his shopping elsewhere. But he knew Carina would love the things he'd purchased. If only D.C. would answer the telegram and the weather would clear. He went outside and looked into the sky, gray with more impending snow.

"Two things, Lord. A telegram and a blue sky." He brought his gaze down to a bearded man watching him. Was it so foolish to stand in the street and pray? Quillan tipped his hat, and the man walked past. Quillan went to the telegraph office.

The clerk looked up. "Nothing yet."

Quillan thanked him and went back out. What could be taking D.C. so long to answer? Was he upset Quillan would even consider selling? Couldn't he understand the position they were in? He went back to the hotel to secure Carina's gift in his pack with the others. The parasol, of course, stood in the corner.

Quillan walked over, picked it up, and opened it. He looked up through the ecru lace and imagined Carina standing beneath it. He closed it abruptly, before the longing for her became painful. He tore a sheet of paper from his journal and found his fountain pen, which he'd filled with ink from an eyedropper the night before. With it, he now wrote a letter to his foster father. Reverend Shepard would be ecstatic to know he was at last seeking the Lord's wisdom.

Quillan also inquired after his wife, Leona. He pictured her curled in her bed like a skeletal infant, bawling and picking at the covers. The image evoked a wrenching sympathy. Was she still alive? Frequently insanity left its victims physically tenacious, though she'd seemed so frail.

He would likely not receive a reply before he left the area with Carina. He wrote as much to the reverend. Then he thanked him for the years of care he'd been given in their home. He might never see the man again, and he wanted his foster father to know his gratitude, though those years had been the most painful of his life.

Setting the letter aside, Quillan took out his journal. He'd filled three pages with Scripture verses that had spoken to him in his reading, his own ramblings that had followed, and some poems he'd written to share with Carina. His most recent he read now.

Without you time escapes its rule and lingers overlong,
Yet were I there with you, my love, t'would skip and bound and leap.
The distance stills the hands of time, the days the hours prolong,
As one by one the minutes put the sun and moon to sleep.
But time, it cannot halt for long without the Lord take heed,
And God will spin it soon, my love, and set the earth aright,
Then to your waiting arms I'll run with haste and all due speed,
To set the stars adance again to brighten up your night.

Time had once had no hold on him. But now it seemed a force he battled daily. *It's only that I miss her, Lord.*

It is good for the heart to hunger. This time Quillan didn't wonder at the words. He'd grown accustomed to the answers coming to his mind. And he knew they were the Lord, especially when they weren't what he wanted to hear.

But he governed himself, using the time to write in his journal, long stretches of still time he'd never allowed himself before. Mae was right; it was something he should learn, though patience and peace were slow in coming.

It seemed a blessing straight from heaven when on the eighth day, the telegraph clerk reached into a cubby behind him and held out D.C.'s reply. Quillan paid the man and hurried out to the street. He unfolded the paper and found the text.

Sorry delay. On retreat. Sell mine. Treasure in heaven. D.C.

Quillan clutched the paper to his chest, picturing Cain's scapegrace son. From the sound of it, he'd matured, and his faith still upheld him. He'd make a fine preacher. Quillan wished he could tell him he'd found his own faith. Wished he could have found it before old Cain was killed. But he supposed Cain knew somehow. Maybe there was some portal through which Cain watched them both, knew that even if hard times were not behind them, at least they were on the right path.

He folded the telegram. Now he would take Carina home. He closed his eyes in silent gratitude, his sense of purpose keen. He went to the Italian market and purchased items they could stock in the wagon for their trip: jars of olives, dried spicy sausage called pepperoni and another named Genoa salami. Both beat jerky by a long shot. He bought her semolina flour and olive oil, a string of garlic, and pickled anchovies.

He carried the crate to the wagon, then loaded the other gifts he'd amassed for her. He gave his horses one last lookover. Jack and Jock, his leaders, were well rested and fresher from an eight-day rest than they'd been in years. His wheelers, Socrates and Homer, he'd leased to a driver for two short trips, but they were strong Clydesdale blood and were fresh enough after two days' rest to make the trip over the pass—supposing the weather held and the trip was indeed short. Quillan worried a little that the recent snow might have reached a depth and softness that would make the road a nightmare. But whatever the case, he was going.

Carina felt good to be out of bed and dressed in her blue chintz shirtwaist and full linen skirts. Her corset was tied, but bearably, and *Nonna*'s shawl warmed her shoulders. Ah, to stand and walk. It was ten days since Quillan had left her door, and her concern had risen. But it was out of her hands. So what good was fretting?

But fret she did. She walked to the table where he had sat and studied. She sat in the chair he had used. She took out her own journal, flipped to a new page, and wrote her frustration, her fears, her longing. Then she closed the journal. *Signore, have mercy.* Per piacere, *Signore. Have I not learned patience?* She rushed on before she could hear an answer to that. *You know I am trusting you. Is it so much to—* She jumped at the knock on the door and hurried to open it.

Nothing. No one. Then she realized it was the other door.

Sciocco! Chiding herself for a fool, she closed out the cold and went to the side door. Why would Quillan knock? Would he not let himself and Sam inside? She opened the door to find Mae and threw herself into the woman's arms. She felt Mae's laugh rumble inside her chest.

"Gracious, Carina. Is it as bad as that?"

Carina clung to Mae's softness. "I'm *pazzo* with waiting."

"A little cabin fever, too, no doubt. Well, I see the doc gave the go ahead for you to be up."

Carina drew back and waved a hand. "Standing and walking. No riding, no jostling, no overexcitement. Doesn't he know I'm dying of unexcitement?"

Again Mae laughed. "Well, sit yourself down and tell me what's all this about Èmie taking over for you."

"I can't sit." Carina crossed the room, wringing her hands. "But yes, isn't it wonderful? Robert agreed she should oversee the restaurant. He might attach a clinic to the side, and she'll be close to you, Mae."

"A lot I care about that."

Carina crossed back to her and snatched Mae's hands between her own. "You will be there for each other, won't you? I'll miss you both so much."

Mae's voice grew thick. "We managed fine before you, Carina."

The words were gruff, but Carina saw the pain behind them. "Oh, Mae." Once again she flung herself into Mae's arms.

"Land sakes." But Mae held her close and stroked the hair hanging down Carina's back. "Lot of fuss."

"I feel like I'm tearing part of myself away. I'll miss you. I'll think of you."

Mae softly peeled Carina's arms from her neck. "You're not gone yet."

"I already miss you."

Mae shook her head, laughing. "Well, I'll miss you, too, for what it's worth. You sure have livened things up. But I think it's right, you going with Quillan. He needs a new start somewhere himself. Outside of Crystal he can be his own man, not under the shadow of Wolf and Rose. Just the two of you starting fresh."

Carina walked anxiously to the window. "When will he come?"

"He'll come when he comes. He's Quillan." Mae chuckled softly. "Some things don't change."

Carina threw up one hand. "*That* will change if I have anything to say."

"And I'm sure you will. But remember, Carina, he'll tame better with honey than vinegar."

Carina spun. "Do you think me sharp tongued?"

"I've heard you draw blood."

Carina clutched her hands at her breast, feeling an agonizing ache.

"Not to say he doesn't need it sometimes, the way he goes on with that ne'er-do-well pose and that smile like a—"

"Pirate."

Mae paused, then laughed. "Never thought in those terms, but that is what it is. Oh, you two will be flint and steel. But I'm not sure that doesn't make for a better flame in the end."

"If only he'd come." Carina spoke more to herself, looking once again toward the window. And then it seemed as though she'd wished him there, for she watched Quillan climb the step, Sam at his heels. With a cry, she rushed forward, jerked open the door, and threw herself into his arms. "I was so wishing for you!"

Loaded down with his pack, he lost his balance, then recovered. "Carina, what are you doing out of bed?" His breath was white with every word.

"Is that all you can say?" She caught his cold cheeks between her palms.

Suddenly he crushed her into his embrace and buried his face in the crown of her hair. He groaned. "Oh, I missed you." He half carried, half swung her inside and kicked the door shut with Sam jumping around them in eager jubilation. He cupped her head, raised her face, and kissed her. Carina forgot everything else. What else was there?

When Mae left, she didn't know, but when they at last parted, Carina was alone with the man she loved with aching force. "What took you so long? Every day I looked for you. Every day I prayed, 'Signore, bring my husband home!'"

Quillan laughed. "I know. I'm sorry. I didn't hear from D.C. until two days ago. I tried to get back that very day, but the road was impassable. I had to dig through."

"Oh, Quillan." She clutched his hands, thinking how hard his work had been. She knew well that treacherous strip of road. "I'm glad I didn't know. I'd have been sick with worry."

He held her again, stroking her hair. "Are you well now?"

"I've never been better." She reached up and kissed his icy mustache.

"I mean healed." He pulled back. "Are you healed? What does Doc Felden say?"

She waved a hand. "No riding horseback or even carriage. No overexcitement." She laughed. "No doubt at this moment he'd be ordering me to bed."

Quillan reached out and stroked her face. "Don't tempt me, Carina." His mischievous eyes caught her breath. Then he turned away. "Wait till you see what I brought you."

"You brought me something?"

"Something! My pack is twice as heavy."

"Oh." She caught her hands beneath her chin. "Show me."

He paused. "Maybe I shouldn't. If Dr. Felden said no excitement . . ."

Carina pounded her fists into his chest.

He caught them, laughing. "All right, all right. Sit down and compose yourself. You can compose yourself, can't you?"

Carina thought she had never seen him so genuinely happy. Instead of responding to his barb, she sat on the side of the bed and folded her hands in her lap.

He cocked his head and stood a long moment, just looking. "Have I told you what a beautiful woman you are?"

"Once." On their wedding night.

He swallowed, as though to speak again, then turned and tugged his pack up onto the bed.

She didn't care that it was frosty with snow and would get the quilt wet. She felt like a child on Christmas morning. What had he brought her? She watched him tug open the ties and tried not to squirm. She leaned close when he reached in, but he raised his brows and paused until she settled back. Then he drew out a tissue-wrapped parcel, small and light. How could that make his pack heavy?

He held it out, and she took it from his hand. Carefully she opened the tissue to find an exquisite lace collar with a tiny pearl button fastening at the back. "Oh, Quillan, it's beautiful."

"That was the first day."

"The first?"

As an answer he reached in again, felt about, then brought out a flat box some six inches by eight wrapped in paper. "This was the third. Day two wouldn't fit in the pack. It's in my wagon."

"What are you talking about?" She reached for the box and untied the ribbon that held the paper closed about the box. The box held writing paper painted with a border of roses.

He said, "Every day I was gone I found you something."

She looked up from the paper to see him reaching once again into the pack. "Every day?"

"You'll like this one."

He handed her a tiny parcel, which she opened, finding a clear pinkish purple amethyst in a gold filigree setting on a thin gold stickpin. Her throat tightened with emotion. It was not even that the pin was beautiful, but that he had so carefully chosen each item he was presenting. She knew him, how he must have shopped about to find the right things, then haggled and paid. Tears filled her eyes as she looked up at him.

"Don't cry."

"I can't help it."

He bent down and raised her chin. "I can't give you the others if you cry, Carina." A tear dropped to her cheek, and he stroked it away with his thumb.

"It's too much," she said.

"How else could I show you—" he dropped to his knees, face earnest—"how much I care?"

She held the stickpin to her breast and closed her eyes. She felt his lips touch hers and eagerly replied. He eased her back on the bed and kissed her deeper, catching her hair in his fingers. All her being quickened to him, her husband. She brought her arms around his neck. The rest of the gifts would have to wait.

———

Quillan lay beside his wife, amazed and humbled. He hadn't intended it—probably the doctor would frown upon it—but he'd been so gentle, every touch, he hoped, erasing the hurtful ways he'd touched her before. And now with her curled in against him, his breathing matching hers, he knew what it was to be one. He felt incredibly whole.

Lord, don't let me hurt her ever again. He felt an overwhelming need to protect, to guard this woman who tried to seem so fierce and independent but was truly fragile, as all life was fragile. He fought the sleep coming over him, not wanting to surrender the intensity of emotion that coursed through him as he held Carina sleeping, or nearly so, in his arms. Love, unlooked for and utterly beyond his understanding, had a grip on his heart that pained him. Maybe if he'd learned it as a child, known it for years as others did, as Carina had, in a family—maybe then it would not be so terrifying.

But their union tonight intensified his fear of losing her. What if he couldn't be what he promised? What if he failed her again, hurt her again? She could be vindictive, but it wasn't that. It was his own failings that formed the nightmare. *God, help me. Teach me what I need to know.* He closed his eyes and buried them in Carina's hair. With his muscles strained from digging through the snow to her, his energy spent loving her, sleep came, and Quillan succumbed.

Seven

*As a snowflake, icy edged, unique in shape and kind,
so a soul traversing life, alone until it finds,
one to which it cleaves and forms, a new and wondrous thing.
God in perfect wisdom makes the human heart to sing.*

— Quillan

CARINA WOKE FOR THE FIRST TIME in Quillan's arms. At first she thought she dreamed him there, but his warmth, the prickling of his whiskered chin on the side of her neck, the sound of his breathing, were too real. Her heart swelled. *Signore!* Not once had Quillan stayed with her until the morning.

No, that wasn't true. They'd woken together in the mine, when he'd pulled her from the shaft. And once, again in the mine, after the vigilantes had tried to hang her. But those were not the same. Still, she suddenly felt a longing for the Rose Legacy, to be alone with Quillan on the mountain. It was impossible. She couldn't make the trip. Dr. Felden would never allow it. But if he didn't know . . . Turning slightly, she shook Quillan.

"No." He nestled his face deeper into her neck.

She laughed. "Wake up. I want to do something."

"So do I, but Doc Felden would have my hide."

Had he read her mind? Then she realized what he meant and blushed. Why was she blushing when there were no longer secrets between them?

Quillan kissed her behind the ear. "Let's hibernate till spring."

Her heart warmed. He wanted to stay! *Signore, at last!* But she

69

was restless for the mine, the square foundation that had been Quillan's parents' home, the shaft above the limestone cave that held the geode crystal cave and the painted chamber of Wolf's life. She wanted to go with Quillan.

"Hibernate?" She wiggled again, this time dislodging his arm enough that she could turn onto her back. "You're not a bear, though you growl like one when you're wakened. Come on. It's late, and I want to go out."

He raised himself to one elbow and hovered above her. "Not a bear, eh?" He plunged his face into her neck.

With a shriek, she fought him back, laughing. "Stop it. You'll wake Mae's entire boardinghouse."

"I'm not the one making all the noise."

"You're causing it." She could hardly believe him. He could play!

He closed her into his arms and settled her snugly against him. "There's no sense going out. It's going to snow today."

"How do you know?" She pushed his chest.

He said, "Sam was whining in his sleep."

"So?" She turned her face to see his expression.

"So that's how I know." His eyes had a half open languorous quality.

"A dog whines, and you know it will snow?"

"Not *a* dog. Sam—Second Samuel."

She waved a hand. "So he's a prophet, eh?"

"Do that again." His mouth quirked.

"Do what?"

"Wave your hand like that." He formed his rascal's grin.

Carina hid her hand beneath the covers. Quillan caught her face and kissed her. Again she marveled. Had this tenderness always been inside him, waiting to show? Or had it just germinated? Whichever it was, she thanked God for it now. Pushing gently away, she said, "I want to go to the Rose Legacy."

"Um-hmm."

"Now. Today."

"Ah." He kissed her again.

"Quillan. I want to go with you. Into the cave—"

Quillan covered her mouth with his palm. "You know the doctor won't allow it. No horseback, remember?"

"He wouldn't have to know." She spoke through his hand.

He took the hand away with a frown. "And you think I'd do that? Defy his orders to satisfy your whim?"

"It's not a whim, it's . . . I want to go. Here." She pressed her hand to her heart. "We could take Father Charboneau. He wants to see Wolf's pictures. Did you know they were friends?"

"From my mother's diary I guessed it." Quillan forked his hair back over his shoulder. "But it's out of the question, Carina. You're not fit to make the trip."

"But—"

A knock on the outside door stopped her argument. Quillan smiled smugly and rose, pulling on his pants over the long wool flannel drawers no mountain dweller would be without. He padded to the door and opened to Dr. Felden.

"Quillan. I hadn't heard you were back."

"I came in last night."

The doctor glanced at Carina. She had already wrapped herself in Nonna's shawl and straightened the bedcovers around her. Quillan pulled on his coat and boots and whistled softly to Sam.

"Coward," Carina wanted to holler as he slipped through the door, leaving her to answer for them. One look at Dr. Felden's scowl and she wanted to run, too.

"You understand, Mrs. Shepard, that your kidneys are not yet fit? That is, not fit yet to handle a delicate condition." A new pregnancy he meant. "That prudence requires patience."

Blood rushed to her face. *Tell that to my husband.* Having a physician for a father had rendered her immune to many of the embarrassments of her culture, and she was unflustered by the mention of body parts and ailments others found discomfiting. But having the doctor scold her as though she were responsible for Quillan's actions last night— She should not be surprised. He was a man.

"I feel well, Dr. Felden."

"Your feelings are not reliable." The doctor flung open his bag. He drew out his binaural stethoscope to hear her heart. Carina knew this morning it would race. How could it not? Quillan was home and he loved her. He loved her.

———

When Quillan returned, Carina was dressed in a cream-colored blouse with the new lace collar he'd brought her affixed to the upper edge with the amethyst stickpin. She sat at the table with a blank sheet of the new writing paper before her and pen upraised. Quillan walked through the door, laden with his suitcase and several other bundles that he had retrieved from his wagon. Sam slunk under Carina's chair, laid his chin on her lap, then slunk back. Why did the dog have to look so guilty?

Carina raised her chin, but before she could chastise him, Quillan held out a long parcel. Her eyes went to it, then back to him. "What is this?"

"For you. Day two. It was in my wagon, remember?"

Softening, she took it, unwrapped the cloth tied about it, and held the lace parasol across her knees. Quillan watched her open it, then study the pattern of the lace before at last raising it over her head and giving it a twirl. She cocked it against her shoulder, tipped her head like a coquette. "You are a coward." She smiled.

"Guilty." He might as well admit it.

She brought the parasol down with a flourish and laid it on the table. "It's very beautiful. You're going to spoil me."

"Guilty again." He glanced at the table. "A letter?"

She sighed. "I was writing to Papa."

"You haven't gotten very far." The page was blank.

She laid the pen down.

"Letting him know we're coming?" Did he imagine her flinch?

"Yes." But she made no move to take up her pen again.

"What did the doc say?"

Carina glared. "He said I'm so well you should take me to the mine."

Quillan reached across the table and took her hand. Staring straight into her face he said, "Tell me that again."

She bit her lower lip, then threw up her hands. "I'm tired of these walls!"

"That's easy enough." Quillan stood and took her coat from the hook. He raised her to her feet and slipped the coat up over her arms, covering her hair to the neck.

She tugged it closed in front and fastened the buttons. "You're taking me to the mine?" She seemed both surprised and eager.

"No horseback, remember?"

She frowned, almost a pout. But then she was Carina Maria, daughter of Angelo Pasquale DiGratia, friend of Count Camillo Benso di Cavour, prime minister to Victor Emmanuel II, king of

Sardinia-Piedmont. At this moment, she looked every bit of it. He opened the door, allowed Sam to whisk out before them, then scooped Carina into his arms.

She caught her hands around his neck. "What are you doing?"

"We're paying a call."

"To whom?"

"Alan Tavish. He's missed you, lass."

She laid her forehead on his jaw and laughed. "Very well. But so little way I could walk."

He pulled the door shut behind them. "It's slick. You don't need a fall."

She leaned over to examine the sheen on the snow-packed street. "And my two-legged steed is surefooted?"

"It'll be my back taking the brunt if we go down."

She nestled in against him. "It'll be good to see Alan and Daisy. Poor mare, she's been neglected."

"With Alan? Never." Quillan made his way to the livery, amazed how little it took to carry Carina the four blocks down and across. Again he sensed her fragility. And those men had beaten her with sticks. He forced back the hateful thoughts. He'd taken plenty of beatings in his life and found the strength to forgive. It was different when the victim was Carina.

Quillan heard voices when he entered with Carina still in his arms. Alan had company already, but whoever it was, they weren't perched near the front in Alan's normal spot. He returned Carina to her feet and looked down the first row of stalls. Alan was around the bend, and the voice speaking now was familiar. Quillan started that way with Carina on his arm. She seemed reluctant.

They rounded the corner and saw Alan in discourse with Alex Makepeace outside the stall of his huge steel-dust stallion. Both men turned. Both reacted to Carina's presence. Quillan wished it were Alan's reaction he noticed more. Beaming, Alan doffed his cap. Alex looked as though he'd buried his mother.

"You're a sight for these old eyes, lass. Up and well, ye are." Alan gripped her hand between his own.

"If you count being carried all the way here." Carina's tone was light, but Quillan sensed the tension in it.

Inside he cursed Makepeace for being there, for ruining his visit. Then he tried hard to find a charitable thought and failed.

If the man had any civility he'd excuse himself, but he seemed rooted to the spot. Alan was oblivious and chatted to Carina about the cold, the snow, and the mare stabled beside Makepeace's stallion. Daisy looked like a runt.

Makepeace drank in Carina's presence, though it was obvious he tried to hide it. "They're plenty warm, Carina," he interjected. "This new barn gives good shelter and warmth with the stoves." He patted his steed's muzzle. "Happy as horseflesh can be this season."

"Not that she doesn't miss your touch, lass. 'Tis grateful she is to see you." Alan's words were borne out by Daisy's whicker as she raised her snout toward Carina's stroking hand.

Makepeace's face matched the mare's. Quillan stiffened. "We shouldn't overdo it, Carina. Though it may be warm enough for horses in here, it's anything but snug."

"Come along by the stove, then." Alan angled past, thwarting Quillan's escape.

Maybe Makepeace would bow out now. But the man seemed stubbornly oblivious to the turmoil he was producing inside Quillan's belly. How had they spent hours alone together, when just moments in Carina's presence could bring Quillan to the point of blows? He caught Alan's glance and realized the old man was hardly oblivious. He knew, too, what Alan would say. Pray. Quillan may as well do it on his own.

Lord, help me here. You said love your enemies. Makepeace isn't even an enemy. Under other terms, I'd probably like the man. If it weren't for Carina. And . . . oh, hang it. He caught himself. Did one think so disrespectfully while praying to Almighty God? *Sorry, Master. Cleanse my thoughts. Make them right.* He took his place against the wall so close behind Carina her back rested against his hip as she sat on the barrel.

Alan had offered the rocker, but she had refused. It was so much the old ostler's chair it had taken on his shape. As he stood, Quillan felt the tension subside. He looked at Makepeace and realized what the man suffered. He hadn't asked the Lord to show him that, but it was there, almost as though he were reading the man's heart. He understood how it must be, how it would be for himself in Makepeace's shoes. How could anyone not love Carina?

Alan and Carina discussed the restaurant and Èmie's plans to take Carina's place. That was news to Quillan, and he tried to concentrate. He glanced across at Alex Makepeace and saw there the bitter resignation of a man who knows he's lost. Makepeace met his gaze, and in that moment, Quillan understood Christ's message. Wish no harm to any man. Return no evil. That was the way to inner peace.

Two hours passed as Alan and Carina talked with some minor interjections from Makepeace and Quillan himself. At last Quillan sensed Carina tiring. Even by the stove, the huge stable was not as warm as her cozy room. And as much as she might deny it, she still had healing to do. He touched her shoulder, and she turned, reading his concern.

She smiled. "My husband reminds me I'm not yet as strong as I was."

"Go home, lass." Alan took his pipe from his pocket. "I'll have a smoke with Alex, then see about me dinner."

Carina stood, and Quillan led her to the door, then took her once again into his arms. After leaving Carina to nap, Quillan made his way back down the street. He found Alex Makepeace leaving the livery. "Hold on a moment, Makepeace."

Makepeace turned, a little gun-shy.

Quillan slipped the telegram from his pocket. "D.C. wants to sell." He'd made no mention of it earlier with Alan and Carina.

Makepeace raised his brows. "Excellent. So we'll complete the matter?"

"The sooner the better. And with as little noise as possible." They walked together to the bank, where Alex produced the note drawn on Tabor's bank and signed by his own hand.

Had Makepeace carried the note inside his vest to be ready or for safekeeping? It didn't matter now. Their transaction was complete. They shook hands. Quillan said, "May it bring you good fortune."

Makepeace's grip was firm. "It already has."

Quillan turned to go.

"Quillan."

He turned back.

"Carina never faltered in devotion."

Quillan studied his face, his earnest message gallantly spoken. "I didn't think she had." He headed home. It wouldn't be home for long, though. Soon they'd be on their way. And now it was time to consider the one task that remained before they could leave Crystal. He turned back suddenly and called, "Makepeace."

The man had gone some distance, but stopped. Quillan changed direction and met him on the corner. "What would it take to seal off the cave?"

Makepeace frowned. "The whole cave?"

Quillan shook his head. "Just Wolf's chamber."

Makepeace rubbed his beard. He didn't ask why. Anyone who'd seen the pictures would understand. And Carina may have told him more than necessary. Makepeace dropped his hand. "Could wall it off, but that might attract attention. Collapse it with giant powder . . ."

Quillan didn't want it destroyed, just inaccessible. "What about rocks? Could we rock it off? Make it look like a natural slide?"

Makepeace shrugged. "Be a lot of work."

Quillan nodded. "But possible?"

"Certainly, if we blasted from the outside and lowered the rock through the shaft."

Quillan pictured it. The work would be hard and tedious. But he was up to it. "Will you arrange the materials—pulleys and whatnot?"

Makepeace nodded.

"I need to make one more trip before we close it up for good."

"Just give the word." Makepeace looked so solid, Quillan understood the comfort he'd been to Carina. Such unquestioning loyalty. Makepeace was a good man.

Now if Quillan could just find a way to get Carina to the mine. He went to Mae's and used her ax to fell twin saplings with three-inch trunks. He cleared their branches and hacked off the skinny tops to form six-foot lengths of strong wood. With rope and a canvas tarp from his wagon he fashioned a litter. Then he tied a woolly cot pad over that. Suspend it between Jack and Jock . . . It could work.

He spent the next hour contriving a harness and trying the litter between his leaders. The twin geldings seemed confused to be pulling together without a wagon, and with something strange between them. But they grew accustomed quickly enough.

He disconnected the litter and stored it in Jack's stall. Then he left without waking Alan from his nap. Carina was not in her room when he returned. Quillan found her directing activity in

Mae's kitchen. She glanced up briefly, daring him to shoo her
back to bed, but he didn't. Already men were lined up outside the
door, waiting for the first seating at Carina's tables.

Quillan slouched onto the bench near Mae's stove and
watched her show Elizabeth how to make the little pasta pillows
called ravioli. He hadn't realized she was teaching the younger
girls to cook. He'd only seen them clearing tables and washing
dishes.

"Now we put them to bed." Carina laid a sheet of dough over
the mounds of filling placed at even intervals.

Quillan recalled the first time he'd seen her do that ... and
fallen under her spell.

"Then cut them with the biscuit cutter." She pressed her hand
over Elizabeth's, encircling the cheese-and-spinach-stuffed mound
and leaving a circular cut.

Quillan responded physically. What was it with Carina and
food? She hadn't just fed him but had tantalized him with new
and exotic flavors. As she stepped back from the table to give Elizabeth room to pass by, he caught her hand, drew her into his lap.

She flushed, but with Elizabeth there he wouldn't kiss her. He
knew the limits of propriety even if she doubted it. Mae sauntered
in from her dining room, which came off the other side of the
kitchen. Already she was ladling out stewed beef to her boarders.
It had seemed a satisfactory meal to Quillan until he'd tried
Carina's fare.

Mae raised her brows at the two of them but didn't comment.
Her face had a red sheen from the escaping steam as she refilled
the serving pot. She grunted, lifting it, then went back out.

Carina started to rise, but Quillan held her in place with his
arm across her waist. She turned and met his eyes. Let her see the
fire there; he had no need to hide it now. *What freedom found in
love unveiled that lightens heart and limb; unshackled every hindrance be
that burning light could dim.* There was nothing dim in him right
now, but with an effort, he let her stand up.

Two hours more she stayed on her feet, overseeing now, in
both the kitchen and out among the tables. She didn't stay long
in the dining room, though, and Quillan wondered if it was
because he waited in the kitchen. He ate the portion she set before
him, but the food seemed secondary to her presence, and he
guessed more than one man in the dining room felt that way. It

didn't rankle as it had. Maybe the compassion he'd found for Alex Makepeace stretched to the hungry men Carina fed, as well.

He could see she was wearing down before she would admit it. But at last she allowed him to lead her, weary, to her bed. Carina was stronger, but Dr. Felden was right. She was not yet fit. For some reason he thought of his mother, Rose, never recovering from the tragedies of her life. *God, don't let that happen to Carina.* But she had strength and a will that had carried her all the way to Crystal. She was not like Rose.

In their room, he watched her undress. He supposed they could hang a curtain to dress behind, taking turns so neither would see the other indecent. But he couldn't see her as indecent. From the first glimpse he'd had of her shape under the spring at the Gold Creek Mine, he'd been mesmerized.

So he stood now and watched her and made no offer to turn away or leave her. Neither did she ask. She accepted his gaze without embarrassment or umbrage. And when his palm warmed her lower spine, she turned. No poetry could express it.

Eight

Majestic are these hills, O Lord, we humbly enter in.

In pine and aspen, creek and lake, your song of praise begin.

Draw nearer to your presence, God, ascend the highest place.

With eagle, bear, and lowly squirrel, we humbly seek your face.

— Quillan

CARINA STARED AT the contraption suspended between Quillan's blacks, Jack and Jock. He couldn't be serious, couldn't really expect her to ride there, lying on the woolen pad like some Egyptian princess.

"Once you're on, I'll wrap blankets over you. You'll be plenty warm." Quillan cupped her elbow. Sam pushed in between them.

She ignored his tail banging her leg. This was Quillan's surprise? "You don't really think—"

"You want to visit the mine, don't you?" There was no mocking amusement in his eyes. He must mean it.

She threw up her hands. "I will not ride through town like ... like some invalid with everyone watching and shaking their heads and saying, 'Poor Carina, she rides in a litter like an old woman, like a—'" She couldn't even think what else they might say.

Quillan hooked his thumbs in his waistband. "Who'd say a word?" Sam nudged Quillan's palm with his nose.

"To me, no one. To themselves and each other ..." She waved her hand. "I can't do it."

The dog sat on his haunches, grinning.

"Then we won't go through town. I'll take you down along the creek."

"Through all the tents." She turned that way.

"Hardly a one."

It was true. There were very few living in tents along the creek anymore. The cold was too bitter. But those who were knew Quillan well. She put her hands on her hips. "I won't do it."

Quillan shrugged. "All right." He walked around Jock with Sam dutiful now at his heels and started unfastening the litter.

"You'll saddle them now? We'll ride up together?"

He shot her a look sideways.

"We could both ride Jock, as we did after the flood. Do you remember?"

He walked around Jack and unfastened that side. The foot end of the litter dropped to the ground.

"Or Jack." She pulled her coat tighter at the neck and met him in front of Jack, halting his progress.

He hung his arm over Jack's withers and slacked his hip. "No."

She had a flash of memory; his hat brim shadow hiding his face on the road moments before he dumped her wagon and all her dear things down the slope to destruction. He'd had that same stance, that same stubborn tone.

She thrust her fists at his chest. "I will go. With or without you."

"Not unless you plan to hoof it."

She jutted her chin. "I'll take Daisy."

He caught her wrist. "Doc said no horseback."

"That was days ago."

"I haven't heard different." His voice was steady now.

"You've made *other* exceptions." She tugged against his grip.

If he was chagrined he didn't show it. "Doc Felden said you might be changeable these days. I guess this is how it looks."

She jerked her arm free. "How dare you patronize me!"

"Look, Carina, I found a way for you to go to the mine. If you don't want to do it, it's no skin off my nose. Just move over so I can finish here."

"I will not!" She planted herself directly before him. "You and your work! It's always first. Never mind what I want." She'd raised her voice higher than she'd intended. A clump of miners passing by all turned to look.

Quillan didn't answer, just stepped around her and started working the front strap loose.

"Did you ever think how humiliated, how helpless I would look lying there between the horses?"

"Actually I thought how smooth and joltless your ride would be." The third corner dropped free, and he moved over to the last.

Carina wanted to retort. His steady purpose brought back too clearly his execution of her wagon. She'd dreamed of it last night, only she'd been on the wagon plunging over the side with Nonna's rocker and Mamma's dishes and ... She closed her eyes and heard the pallet come loose. One pole scratched across the frozen ground, then Quillan must have lifted it. She looked and saw him carry it to the stoop and lean it against the front wall of her house like a sign: *Invalid here.*

Then she noticed how he'd tied it all together and padded it thickly. Three blankets lay folded across Jock's back. Her anger withered. She ran her fingers across Jock's chest as she passed under his neck and stepped up to the porch. Quillan leaned his hip against the post.

She took one step up and then another. He held a hand out, and she threaded her fingers with his.

Father Antoine rounded the corner. "Are we ready?"

She looked from Quillan to the priest. "Ready?"

"To see the cave." He looked from her to her husband.

Quillan had planned it all. Her transportation, the priest's chance to see Wolf's paintings, their chance to see the mine again. She swallowed past the tightening in her throat. She was the rogue this time. Dropping her head with a sigh, she said, "Quillan was just attaching the litter. We're following the creek up."

The corners of his mouth deepened, but Quillan said nothing as he took the litter from the wall and carried it back to the horses. Father Antoine caught the other end and helped fasten it in place between Quillan's blacks. Carina swallowed her pride and stepped onto Quillan's folded hands for a boost up, then lay down on the litter. Quillan tucked the blankets tightly over her. His fingers squeezed hers a moment. Sam whined, but Quillan shut him into the house, then he and Father Antoine each took charge of a horse and started up on foot.

She closed her eyes so that if anyone saw her she wouldn't know. The *clop-clop* of the horses' hooves on the frozen street

81

changed to thudding as they neared the creek and started up. The snow was deeper. It would be harder to plod through. Carina felt selfish. She pulled the blanket higher over her shoulder and settled into the rhythmic swaying. If Quillan would have just let her ride . . . But he was resolute.

No matter that her strength had returned, that her back hardly ached. The word of a doctor meant more than her obvious improvement. Yet, part of her appreciated the care. He had gone to great lengths to ensure her comfort.

She watched the sleek black muscles of Jack's shoulders, then gazed a little higher at the cold blue sky. She was glad for the blankets. The sun was shining, and Quillan and Father Antoine were no doubt warmer walking. But lying still, she would have been chilled. Quillan had thought of everything. What had caused her outburst?

Changeable. The doctor thought her changeable? Had warned Quillan? Beh! She tugged the blanket to her chin. Didn't she have reason? She caught Father Antoine glancing over Jack's back. Could he read her thoughts?

He dutifully held Jack's reins, but she knew it was to Quillan Jack responded, and to Jock, his twin. She remembered too well trying to control Jack separately. And landing in the creek for her trouble. And Quillan trying not to laugh—though not hard enough. Oh! And there again a glance from the priest.

She raised her head from the cocoon of blankets. "Èmie said you've been busy, Father."

"Four weddings, one last rites, and one baptism," he said. "And that was only yesterday."

She couldn't accustom herself to his gaunt smile. He needed "feeding up," as Nonna would say. Carina's chest tightened. Soon she would see Nonna. And Mamma and Papa, elegant Papa. But most of all old Giuseppe. She pressed her cheek into the woolly mat again. How thoughtful for Quillan to have attached it. She felt like a lamb pressed to a ewe's belly. She could smell the musky scent of lanolin in the fleece. He was a good man, her husband. She warmed at the thought.

It took an hour and more to reach the circular shelf outside the Rose Legacy mine. The burned-out foundation was buried in snow, nothing more than a vague outline. But the mine gaped as though surprised to see them climbing up through the snow, and roots formed eyes above the tunnel mouth.

Quillan brought his team to a halt, and Carina sat up. The ride had been as smooth and joltless as he'd predicted. He walked around Jock's rump as she slid toward the edge. Then he gripped her waist and swung her down.

"Thank you." She smoothed her coat.

He untied the coils of rope from Jock's side and hung them over his shoulder.

"Did you bring lanterns?" she asked.

"Miners' candles. In my pack." He gave her a hand over the snow. It dwindled to a thin coat of powder immediately inside the tunnel.

Carina felt a quiver of excitement. This was the first time she would go down to the cave without Alex. Yet it felt so right with Quillan. He'd saved her from the mineshaft before she even knew there was a cave beneath. The cave had been Alex's discovery. The painted chamber had been hers.

Quillan emptied a large lumpy bag of fodder and grain onto the ground for the horses. Carina watched them nose it eagerly. They wouldn't wander far on this steep snowy slope. Quillan unfastened the litter and leaned it inside the tunnel, tossing the blankets at its foot. He wouldn't leave the horses encumbered. That was the first good thing she'd noticed about him, how he cared for his animals.

Inside the tunnel, Quillan shrugged off his pack. He took out tin candle holders with a flap of metal at one edge to keep a draft away. He affixed one candle and handed it to Carina. The acrid smell of the match caught her breath, then the flame grabbed the wick and stretched upward, its thin light dancing across the low ceiling.

"We'll just use one until we're down." Quillan picked up a coil of rope and started working it into a harness. When he finished the knots and twists, he held it open for her to step into.

Carina handed the candle to Father Antoine. She had not thought to wear the pair of pants that she occasionally wore, and the rope harness caught her skirts up awkwardly. But it was dim and both men discreet in their gaze. She took the few steps to the edge of the shaft and looked down. Before God healed her fear of heights, the sight would have set her head spinning, her stomach surging to her throat. It was intimidating even now.

She clung to the rope as Quillan lowered her, using the spikes he'd attached to the beam as a pulley. Just the way Alex had let her down that first time when she'd sensed the darkness like a hostile force. She felt safe today with Quillan and Father Antoine, however. She reached the ledge, which had been the floor of Wolf's shaft, then gathering herself, swung into the hole where he'd broken through the roof of the limestone cave.

This was the worst part of the descent, dangling helplessly in the vast darkness of the first chamber. With no light at all she could hardly sense her downward motion. Maybe she was just hanging there in the void. She smelled the musty bodies of bats. Then her feet hit ground and slid on the pungent, slimy guano. She climbed out of the harness and tugged. She wouldn't yell and set the bats off in a cloud.

To her immediate left plunged a subterranean well. She knew it was there but could see nothing. Alex had sent her down with a candle in her pocket. Quillan had not thought to. He was not as accustomed to the underground as a mining engineer. Now, though she knew the cave held nothing evil, the darkness preyed on her mind. Her ears fixed on the soft *plink-plink* of water dripping somewhere. And the mouth of Wolf's chamber moaned. She would never forget that sound.

She heard someone, Father Antoine she guessed, directly above her and stepped aside. He landed with a grunt, and called, "I'm down."

Carina put a hand to his arm at the flutter overhead, but his words must not have been enough to frighten the bats en masse. "Bats," she said and felt him look up, though they were in pitch darkness. How ingrained their habits. "Step this way, Father. There's a well to your left. Did you bring a light?"

"Yes." He fumbled in his pockets, and she wondered if his mind felt muffled, like hers.

The end of the rope brushed the floor with Quillan's descent. She caught the end and held it firm. Soon she heard him straining and stepped out of his way. The snick of a match sounded loudly in the chamber, and she watched the tiny flame lick the candlewick. It caught easily.

Quillan landed and tugged the handle of a holder from his pocket. "Forgot to give you this."

She took it and lit the candle from Father Antoine's. Quillan lit his, as well, then all three held them out at arm's length and circled slowly. The light glanced over the closest stalactites, stalagmites, and a narrow sheet of tawny flowstone, only hinting at the size of the cavern.

Father Antoine said, "Wolf painted this?"

"Not this one." Quillan pointed his light away in the direction of the painted chamber. "It's over that way."

He started, and Carina followed closely with Father Antoine behind her. They felt the floor rise, and the men needed to duck their heads as they entered the narrow cave tunnel. Suddenly the floor dropped, and they entered the small chamber. It was the third time Carina had been there, but as her candle illuminated the pictures around her, she felt the same trembling emotion. Wolf's saga could not leave her unmoved.

She glanced at Quillan. He had fixed immediately on the final picture in the circular mural, where Wolf stood with his son raised over his head. Father Antoine circled slowly, studying each new image with a grim countenance. She knew well what he was feeling. He'd been a part of Wolf's life.

Wolf had told him of the slaughter of his family, shown him the scars of being a white slave among the tribes. But it was not the same as seeing the images Wolf had transferred from his mind. Without speaking, Carina joined Quillan and laced her fingers with his.

He kept his gaze to the wall. "I remember this." He spoke so low, she wasn't certain she'd heard.

"Remember?"

He nodded. "Impossible, I know." The opening in the teardrop-shaped ceiling moaned softly. He looked up. "That, too." His hand tightened its hold on hers. "The first time I heard that, I recognized it. That sound has been in my dreams all my life."

"But, Quillan..."

"I know. I was only an infant. But I'm sure Wolf brought me here." The candlelight flickered across his face.

"And this scene..." He stepped closer to the wall. "Carina, I remember it."

"Not impossible." Father Antoine joined them. "The mind is a tome, holding every image, every word. If you did see it, even in those early months before Rose sacrificed her good for yours, then surely it's locked away somewhere."

Quillan returned his gaze to the image on the wall. "I've always remembered easily. Words. Pictures."

Father Antoine asked, "Words spoken or written?"

"Both. But mainly written. When I was young I thought everyone did." His face hardened. "Then I learned otherwise."

Carina guessed it was a painful memory. He had so many of those. Quillan turned now, and together they circled the chamber, reading Wolf's life on the walls. Like his son, Wolf's life had not been easy. A fierce defensiveness rose up in her for Quillan. He may have had a joyless youth, but no more. She would make him happy.

He looked down, and she thought he had read her thoughts, but then she realized she was squeezing the blood from his fingers. She relaxed her grip. When they had completed the circle and stood once again at the final painting, Quillan asked, "Why would he show me this?"

Both Carina and the priest knew the question was much deeper. Why would Wolf take his infant son into the cave and show him his deepest secret when he couldn't bear to have the baby near? When Quillan's cries set off memories too painful, too present to bear? When Wolf's madness made Rose give their child to another to raise?

Father Antoine said, "Perhaps his mind was like yours, Quillan. He didn't read or write, but he remembered. How else could he depict those early scenes with such detail? He couldn't have been more than four or five at the time."

Quillan frowned. Carina bit her lip. Had Wolf passed on a gift to Quillan? Or a curse?

"Maybe," Father said softly, "he knew you would remember."

Quillan drew a slow breath. "I've asked Alex Makepeace to help me seal this off. I don't want others—"

"Quite right." The priest circled the cave with his eyes. "Wolf's borne enough."

His words brought a low rumbling. Some trick of wind through the angled opening above? It grew, and now Carina felt it in the ground. Did the earth shake? But no. It was like the flood, something rushing, crashing above them. Quillan tugged her as snow powder gushed through the small opening like sugar from a sack.

"Avalanche!" And he turned and rushed down the tunnel to the main cavern and the rope.

Carina's candle fluttered as she hurried after her husband. The bats beat the ceiling with their wings and swirled like a dark cloud above. But they must sense that their exit through Wolf's chamber was shut off. Quillan shimmied up the rope through the bats, his candle doused. Father Antoine joined Carina, holding the end of the rope with the harness swishing the floor. Quillan disappeared into darkness. She wondered if she should put on the harness, but the rope hung limp once he reached the top. Had he forgotten them?

Father Antoine took the rope firmly. "I'll go next and bring you up."

She didn't want to be left down there. What was wrong with Quillan, to rush up and abandon them? Father Antoine pushed back his sleeves and started to climb. He wasn't as swift, moving like an inchworm on the rope. But he doggedly climbed. Now there was only her candle lit, and she lost the priest in the dimness.

She was alone in the cave with the bats. What was happening? Could it really be an avalanche? The rope jerked and she caught it, climbed into the harness, and blew out her candle.

The first tug yanked her off her feet. The men must be pulling together. She was hoisted into the musty cloud of bats, but not one touched her. *Grazie, Signore!* She pushed through the hole in the ceiling, which was the floor of Wolf's shaft, used her legs against the wooden ties that formed the walls, and then she was up. But the tunnel was as dark as the cave. Where was the daylight?

Quillan caught her waist and helped her from the harness. She felt him shaking. Quillan shaking! *Dio!* "What is it? What's wrong?"

"We're buried." His voice was grim.

"What do you mean?"

"The avalanche has covered the mine." Quillan relit her candle. "Chunks of snow and ice like boulders and tons of powder."

She tried to picture it. The closest she could come was to imagine the flash flood that had torn away half the city of Crystal.

Quillan smashed his fist into his palm. "I should have known with the warming today."

"How could you? Could you know the flood was coming, too?"

He pressed his palm to his forehead and stared at the tunnel's mouth. "My team."

And now she knew why he trembled. Jack and Jock. *Oh, Signore*. She gripped his arm. "Maybe they ran. You left them free. Maybe they heard it and ran."

Quillan didn't answer, and she looked at Father Antoine. His grim face belied her. But couldn't they have? She thought of Dom, her own mule lost in the flood, carried away by a force beyond him. How Quillan loved his horses. She ached for him. "What do we do?"

Her question seemed to settle Quillan. Give him a task, let him work. He held his candle up and searched about. "Carina, in your trips here, did you ever see a shovel?"

She shook her head. The little alcove where Quillan had found candles held nothing but some rotted sacking. Her gaze fell on the litter. "What about the poles? Could you poke through with them?" She pointed.

Quillan blew his breath sharply. "We should be so lucky." He set his candle on the floor and pulled the litter from the wall. "With so little light showing through, there must be more than six feet of snow piled out there. But . . ." He started untying the corner of the litter.

Father Antoine handed her his candle and joined Quillan. "How can I help?"

Quillan handed him the other end. They worked at it together. Carina held both candles to give them light. Once they had the poles free, Quillan plowed through the snow that had settled inside. He thrust the pole into the center of the opening. When he drew it out a cascade of powder erased the hole. He tried again, higher, but the same thing happened.

Carina stood the candles on the floor, then tugged the blankets out from under the falling snow and shook them out. Father Antoine and Quillan tried again and again to poke through the snow mass. She folded the blankets and laid them atop the wooly mat and canvas tarp. She tugged Quillan's pack loose and set it beside the other things. There was also the empty sacking in which he'd brought the horses' fodder. She tucked it along the wall where it would be less obvious.

Quillan banged his pole on the floor. "It's no use. Until the snow packs, we're rearranging powder."

If it was only powder, maybe the horses were all right. How much damage could powder do? Then she imagined the depth and mass of it. Their six-foot poles made no difference at all. What if it were twelve or twenty feet deep? No horse could survive that.

Quillan laid his pole against the wall. "We'll have to wait until it melts and freezes. Then it'll clump when we dig."

She nodded. "How long will that take?"

"If it's clear outside and the sun works on it deeply enough, maybe a day, maybe two."

"Two days! *Madonna mia!*" The walls closed in. Two days in the dark? Had they candles enough? Had they food? Water?

Quillan walked over, pulled out his pack. "I had Mae pack us some lunch. Not much for several meals, but better than nothing."

Carina sank down onto the mat. Just now she didn't feel hungry, she felt trapped. *Oh, Signore, there must be some way.* "Tomorrow, or the next day, then you can dig through?"

"With a pole? Maybe." Quillan unwrapped the paper from a slab of stewed beef between two thick slices of brown bread. "If we divide this three ways . . ."

Why was he insisting on food? Wasn't there something else to be doing?

"Cut it two ways," Father Antoine said. "I'm used to going without."

Quillan glanced up. "You'll need strength to help me dig."

But the priest only waved his hand. "God will give me strength."

"Oh, sì!" Carina jolted. "We must pray!"

She folded her hands at chin level, head tipped back. "Signore! You have promised where two or more are gathered, you are there, too." That thought brought comfort. "Help us now. Help us know what to do. Help us do it." She hoped no one but God heard her rising panic.

Father Antoine said, "Lord God, you ordained that we should have dominion of the earth. Give us courage and wisdom."

Father Antoine had heard. Why else pray for courage? She must not show her fear. It would only add to their burden.

Quillan had bowed his head, but he stayed silent so long Carina thought he would say nothing. Then he did. "Help my poor beasts. Amen."

Quillan unsheathed the knife that hung at his belt and sliced the sandwich in two. She wasn't hungry, but Carina took her half. It mattered to Quillan. Maybe he believed they would be out soon. Maybe he needed to act as though they would.

She bit into the crumbly bread and stiff meat. It brought Mae so vividly to mind. Would she worry? Would she send help? Did she know where the mine was? She'd lived in upper Placerville once. Surely she'd remember. But could anyone get through the snow?

Carina chewed reflectively. They must make the most of what food they had. And water? Snow, she supposed. But Quillan drew a canteen from the pack. He offered it, and she drank. Father Antoine, also. Then Quillan drank deeply. He'd worked up a thirst, no doubt. It would be hardest for those who worked. She would do what she could, but what would that be?

When she finished eating, she lay down on the woolly mat, pillowing her cheek with her arm. Quillan covered her with a blanket and sat down at her head. His palm rested there, warm and comforting. He no longer shook. He was in control. He would do what he could.

Father Antoine also sat against the wall. "At least we have air. Many's the miner caught below ground without air. I wouldn't want to go that way. Unless it were God's will."

Quillan looked at him. "Feels a bit tight, though."

Carina looked at her husband, a man so accustomed to the road he preferred it to house and hearth. Well, here was a test. Like her climbing up to the mine time after time when she first discovered it to conquer her fear of heights. How would being closed in work on Quillan's mind? It wasn't doing too well with hers.

His fingers sank into her hair, cupping the back of her skull. "Ever played crambo?"

She raised her head. "What?"

Father Antoine smiled. "A rhyming game. But we haven't any paper."

Quillan shrugged. "We'll do it without. You ask the question, Father; Carina, give a noun."

Father Antoine cocked his head, then said, "Do you wear pomade?"

Carina sat up straighter. "Any noun at all?"

Quillan smiled. "Whatever comes to mind."

"Toad."

He raised his eyebrows. "Now I'll make four lines of rhyme that answer the question using your ... interesting noun."

"You said anything."

"Mm-hmm." He sat for a few moments. "If with something sweet and smelly, I should coat my hair with a jelly, when I took me down the road, dust would coat me like a toad."

Carina clapped her hands and laughed. "That's why you never wore your hair like Mr. Beck."

"That, Carina, is not the only reason."

She sat up fully, locked her arms around her knees, and leaned the small of her back to the wall. "Now Father takes a turn. I'll name the question."

They sat and played until her stomach told her dinnertime had come. She said nothing, though, and when neither man mentioned food, she guessed they would need it more tomorrow. *Per piacere, Signore, let us get out tomorrow.*

Quillan got up and extinguished all but one of the candles. "Need to save what we have." They talked in the near dark, Father Antoine telling about Placerville and other camps in the early days of his wandering. Carina grew weary and lay down again on the mat.

Father Antoine sat wrapped in a blanket, arms crossed above his knees, head resting on his arms. It looked as though he'd folded up, but she didn't think he was asleep. His lips moved silently, and his closed eyelids shifted. In a while Quillan lay down on the mine floor beside her, his back to hers. The three blankets Quillan had brought gave them one apiece, but the cold grew steadily.

"We could light the timbers and melt our way out." Carina said drowsily, expecting no answer.

But Quillan said, "It might come to that." Then he pressed his back closer.

She drifted into sleep thinking this was the third time she'd slept in a mine. Once in the shaft where she'd fallen during the flood, once after the vigilantes hung Berkley Beck and all the roughs, and now under a massive blanket of snow. *Signore, is there something I should know?*

Nine

*W*alls of stone, iron bands, rope around my mind. Air that thins, darkness deep, reasoning confined. Fear, fear, fear.

— *Quillan*

QUILLAN LAY STIFFLY ALERT. Carina's breath sounded like a soft breeze, Father Antoine's a leather bellows. But he couldn't get anywhere near sleep. He kept picturing Jack and Jock on the circular shelf outside the mine with a mountain of snow rushing down on them like a train. He prayed their demise had been swift—a broken neck, a blow to the head. But he guessed they'd been pummeled down the slope, then suffocated where they stopped, the powder more deadly than the icy boulders that carried it.

He pressed his hand to his eyes. How could he have known? Could he have? The day had been so clear and promising. He'd thought they'd spend an hour or two in the cave, then go back out to lunch by the horses and be home again before the sun set. Nature never considered his plans.

His team had survived the flood, both Jack and Jock swimming to safety. Was that only months ago? He pressed closer to Carina. He had thought he'd lost her then. It was the first time he realized how much she mattered.

His plan to escape was a good one—to wait until he could delve the snow. And he'd tried to make the waiting as easy as he could. He'd sensed Carina's fear, and the word games had helped. Yes, his plan was sound. But what if the snow didn't pack? What if it was too deep to get through with nothing but poles? How

93

long could they stretch one lunch? Would someone come? Alex Makepeace? Possibly. He forced his eyes to close. It did no good to ponder it now.

Could they burn the timbers and melt the snow? They'd likely bring the tunnel down on their heads. Was there another way? Quillan couldn't think. Had the horses seen it coming? Had they run? Why hadn't he put them inside? They'd have been safe inside. There was just room for them all in the short tunnel before the shaft. He groaned. If he'd only brought them inside.

His thoughts circled again. They were driving him crazy. Crazy like Leona Shepard? His foster mother spent her days trapped in a mind that had lost touch with reality. His mother, too. Would his do the same? How long could he stay in here before he cracked?

Quillan rubbed his neck and searched the space around him. Something was different. Was it morning? The darkness was not so complete. If he moved his hand in front of his face, he could almost see it shift. Or did he imagine it? He raised up on one elbow. No. There was an almost imperceptible lightening.

Now if the day dawned clear and the sun could penetrate . . . He folded his blanket over Carina and felt for the candle he had used last night. He shuffled on his knees to his pack and took the box of matches from the outer pocket. He struck a flame and lit the candle. Neither Carina nor the priest woke up.

Quillan stood and studied the wall of snow by the dim light of the candle. Trying to melt the snow would be futile. And if they didn't get out soon, they might need to burn the timbers to keep from freezing. What if they pulled the snow inward and pushed it down the shaft? How much would they have to move? And what if it rushed in and covered them?

He turned back and surveyed his father's mine. Wolf had hewn and timbered these walls. Why? What would he want with a mine? Was it greed, as Leona Shepard claimed, or was he trying to find himself, as Rose suspected? Either way, it had ended tragically, both his parents dying in the flames that left only the burned-out foundation outside.

Outside. Would they ever get out? Quillan paced to the edge of the shaft and back to the wall of snow, to the edge and back again, then stopped as Father Antoine stood up. He looked old.

He'd be as old as Wolf would have been or older. Fifty? Sixty? Older?

The priest joined him. "Is it morning?"

Quillan nodded. "I think so."

Father Antoine carefully tugged each sleeve of his coat at the wrist, then pulled it closed at the neck. His breath formed a cloud. "We need to consider a certain matter of hygiene."

Quillan glanced at Carina, who had not yet stirred. Now that the priest mentioned it, his own bladder needed attention. "Any ideas?"

Father Antoine shrugged. "We've no container, so a space will have to do. Your wife will need privacy. We could hang a blanket."

The thought was infuriating, that a basic human function would soon make their space unbearable. Trapped and contaminated, like animals. He felt the nerves fuzz up his back and shook his head. "I'm getting us out of here."

Quillan grabbed a pole and thrust it deeply into the snow outside the opening. Powder still, and something hard. A chunk of ice. But ice wouldn't pack either. He thrust again and again, harder and harder. Powder flew. He almost lost the pole, pawed frantically at its end and yanked it back.

"Don't break it." Father Antoine spoke softly. "Nothing we have is expendable."

Quillan turned, teeth bared. He threw the pole to the floor with a loud smack, then *whama-whama-whama* as it rolled to the wall.

Carina jerked her head up. "What is it? What's wrong?"

Her face, still softened by sleep, sent a poignant stab to Quillan's ribs. He hadn't meant to wake her. He pressed his palms to the splintered, spongy timbers of the entrance and dropped his forehead to his arms. His chest heaved.

Father Antoine gripped his shoulder. "Be calm. With God all things are possible."

Quillan tensed. Did he believe or didn't he? If God was in control, what was his part? He forked his fingers into his hair. He needed air, needed space. The cave. There was more room in the cave below. Thoughts of the spacious cavern set his heart rushing. He turned. "We'll move down to the cave."

Carina sat up, pulling the blanket around her. The priest neither moved nor spoke.

Quillan grabbed the candle and held it over the shaft. "There's more room down there." He shot the priest a glance. "Room to accommodate needs. I'll climb up hourly and check the snow." He hoped no one would argue. He was set on moving them down. If nothing else it gave him something to do.

"How are we for food and light?" The priest gathered his blanket and folded it.

Quillan frowned. "Not as comfortable as I'd like. Two more sandwiches, some dried apples and plums. A dozen candles and a full box of matches."

"I wonder . . ." Father Antoine hung the blanket over his arm. "Are bats edible?"

Carina missed the humor and shuddered.

Quillan quirked an eyebrow. "Pray that we don't have to find out."

Carina watched Quillan bundle together the tarp, blankets, empty sack, and extra coils of rope. How would moving down to the cave help them get out? It was pazzo. But she didn't say so. Quillan's tension was visible. She'd been right. Her husband needed to get out worse than she.

But how, Signore? She stood up and realized something much more pressing. Suddenly the cave seemed a very good idea. *Che buono!* "I'll go down first. You can send the bundle to me when it's ready." She took her candle holder from the wall. Its candle was only a stump, but it would give her time to find a private place.

Quillan laid what he'd bundled onto the mat and pulled the rope up. She climbed into the harness, avoiding both men's eyes. Were their bladders made of steel? With Quillan wielding the rope, she worked her way down the timbered side of the shaft and into the hole at the bottom, almost used to it now, though the dangling still brought her heart to her throat. Then she was down and quickly freed herself of the harness.

She pulled her candle holder from her skirt waist and lit the stump, then started immediately for a far end of the cavern opposite the tunnel to Wolf's cave. She and Alex had not gone that way, at least not together, though he had spent time alone taking samples and whatever else he did with his geological instruments. She reached a small alcove and hiked up her skirts. The sooner this was over with the better, and a torn edge of petticoat was better than nothing.

How basic life became. Relieved, she headed back toward the center of the cavern. The rope was nearly down, holding the tied-up mat and blankets and extra rope. She hurried over to catch it. Setting down her candle, she untied the bundle, then jerked the rope. Quillan drew it up. Soon she would not be alone.

Knowing they would have the same need she had upon their descent, she picked up the bundle and candle and started for the tunnel to Wolf's chamber. That would give them privacy. Though Quillan had tied it tightly, the bundle was ungainly, and she had to squeeze through one part of the passage. Her candle was very low by the time she reached the chamber.

As she stepped down she realized the light was better, nowhere near the pitch darkness of the outer cavern. She looked up. The opening angled so she could not see the actual hole through which the bats had flown the first time she and Alex found the chamber. But what if—

"Carina!" Quillan's voice echoed from the cavern.

She shrank immediately into one wall, and a second later the chamber swarmed with bats. She dropped the bundle and held the candle in front of her face. The bats shied away, whirling and frustrated, before flying back to the cavern. Slowly she lowered the candle. Was he pazzo? She stalked back to the cavern.

Quillan turned. "There you are."

"I'll thank you not to send the bats my way again." She tossed her hair back, shivering at the thought of those musty bodies and reptilian wings.

"I didn't know where you were." He looked as though every ligament in his body were drawn up short.

She reached for his arm. "Are you all right?"

He stiffened. "No. I have to get out of here."

"Quillan, what about Wolf's chamber?"

He stared into her face. "What do you mean?"

"There's an opening at the top. Could we try that way?"

He looked off toward the passage.

Carina searched the chamber. "Where's Father Antoine?"

"He'll be with us shortly." Quillan caught her arm and pulled her with him.

Some of the bats still circled the ceiling, and Carina shot a glance over her shoulder before entering the narrow passageway. With both their candles it was bright enough, but again she noticed more light in the chamber.

Quillan said, "There's daylight coming through."

"Can you see the hole?"

"Not with that angle. Get the priest."

Carina left the chamber, but Father Antoine was already in the passageway. "Quillan needs you. I think we might get out through Wolf's chamber." Turning back, she and Father Antoine found Quillan studying the ceiling from beneath. Carina leaned against the wall. She could tell it was too high. What was he planning?

"I can't tell if it's open up there, but there's certainly more light. Maybe this exit is not buried as deeply as the other one."

Father Antoine studied the ceiling. "What does it matter, if we can't reach it?"

Quillan turned. "Can you sit on my shoulders?"

The priest raised his brows. "Can you hold me?"

For answer, Quillan crouched. Carina crossed her arms, saying nothing as Father Antoine hiked his cassock and climbed onto Quillan's shoulders. Even with the weight he'd lost, he was not insubstantial, as tall as Quillan and heavy-boned. How could this work?

With the priest sitting on his shoulders, Quillan strained, his muscles roping and bunching as his fingertips left the floor and he straightened slowly. Father Antoine stretched up, but they were still a good distance from the ceiling.

Carina brought one hand to her mouth as Quillan almost lost his footing on the slippery floor, and he braced a leg as they steadied themselves. "Can you see out?" Quillan's voice was tight with strain.

"There's a slanted chimney. I can't see the end."

"Is it large enough to fit through?"

"At this end, yes. I can't quite—" he pulled himself taller from the waist—"I'm not high enough to see."

"Come down." Quillan spoke with clenched teeth. His face was red and his arms shook.

"Be careful." It was out before Carina thought. Of course they were careful. But her nerves tightened just watching. Father Antoine was not young. And bearing that much weight, Quillan could be injured. Quillan bent, catching the priest piggyback.

Father Antoine slid to the floor, and Carina breathed her relief.

They were no closer to escape, but at least neither man had broken his neck. Quillan crouched, rubbing one shoulder and hanging his head. He breathed heavily, in pain most likely. To hold a man his own weight like that . . . She wanted to comfort him, but his tension kept her back.

Father Antoine stretched his own joints. "Five feet more, at least, to reach it." He circled beneath the hole. "If I stood on your shoulders . . ."

Still crouching, Quillan looked up. "I couldn't hold you standing."

"There's nothing for it, then. Unless . . ." Father Antoine stopped pacing. "Carina . . ."

Quillan stood slowly, pressed his elbows back and stretched his chest. "Carina can't do it. She shouldn't even be in here."

"Do what?" She stepped away from the wall.

Father Antoine turned. "If you stood on his shoulders, and he—"

"No." Quillan shook his head. "It's out of the question."

The priest didn't argue, and Carina sighed her relief. Did Father think her an acrobat? She would not perch at the top of a human ladder even if God had healed her fear of heights.

Quillan narrowed his eyes at the ceiling. "Come with me, Father. I'm going back up for the poles."

Father Antoine followed Quillan out, and rather than stay alone in the chamber, Carina followed, too. Candle raised, she wandered to the edge of the well while Quillan climbed and then pulled the rope up after him. Father Antoine waited at the bottom, and soon the poles of her litter were coming down tied to the rope. How handy that litter was proving to be. A good thing she had decided to ride it. But then if she hadn't, they would not be there at all.

Father Antoine grasped the poles and untied them. She held the light for him to see, but it was guttering now. They would have to get a fresh candle out of Quillan's pack.

Her candle went out, leaving only Father Antoine's candle sitting on the floor to light the enormous cavern. Strangely, it didn't frighten her. She thought—no, she believed—God would get them out. Hope had grown from the comfort of their first prayer, and she had added others since. Father Antoine laid the poles down, and Quillan came back down the rope.

Carina wanted to tell him it would be all right, but she saw he was working it out in his own way. Physical and mental exertion. He and the priest started for the passageway. She called, "Wait. I need a new candle."

Quillan half turned, and she dug into his pack. Father's light was low and guttering, and she did not want to be fumbling in the dark. Quillan seemed unconcerned, almost oblivious now, his one focus the opening in Wolf's chamber. "Come on." He started on, not bothering with a candle of his own. But he carried the poles and coils of rope.

Inside the chamber, he lashed the poles together, then fixed a rope at the center and knotted it tightly. Then he eyed the ceiling, circling as Father Antoine had done earlier, though when Quillan paced there was almost an animal tension in the motion. He held the tied poles like a javelin, but she could see frustration in his features. Finally he lowered them. "It's no use. That angle blocks my throw from any side."

The priest merely nodded, no doubt having reached the same conclusion. Though still very dim, the chamber had brightened even more, taunting them with hope. Quillan looked ready to snap. Carina sucked her upper lip.

He turned to her abruptly. "How do you feel?"

"I'm fine, Quillan." She wouldn't add her own fears to his.

"Do you hurt?"

She shook her head. What was his intention?

Once again he displayed that intensity that had frightened her before she knew his true nature. "Can you do it, Carina?"

"Do what?"

"Stand on my shoulders as Father said."

She backed away. "That's pazzo."

Quillan drew himself up. "It's the only way, or I wouldn't ask it. I'll do all the work. You only have to stand up and get the poles into the chimney. I'll hold you."

He couldn't be serious. But he was. As serious as she'd ever seen him. He spread his hands. "I won't let you fall."

Her head swam. She could almost believe she wasn't healed of that old fear. But surely anyone would dread what he proposed. How could he ask it? She could tell him no, she wasn't strong enough. "If I don't?"

"Then we wait."

The priest folded his arms. "The snow cover is thinner up there, or we wouldn't have this much light."

"I already know that." She waved her hand. "So I perch on his shoulders like a monkey and . . . and what?"

Quillan demonstrated with the poles. "Push them up through the chimney, hard like this. Throw them even. They have to get all the way through the opening so they'll catch on it and we can climb the rope."

Carina only stared at him.

"I will bear all the weight. Try to grab that jut beneath the opening and balance yourself."

She looked upward, finding the jutting edge of the ceiling he meant for her to hold on to. Why wasn't this small chamber wet like the outer cave? The she might have stalactites to hold instead. But then the ceiling might have towered above instead of rising just out of reach. Oh, Dio . . . Why couldn't the opening be in the lower part? Why the very highest point?

As though he'd read her thoughts, Father Antoine folded his hands. "Maybe we should pray." He began, *"Pater noster, qui es in caelis . . ."*

Soothed, Carina murmured in Italian, *"Sia santificato il tuo nome . . ."*

Quillan joined in. "Thy kingdom come, thy will be done . . ."

Their voices rose, joined, and strengthened. And when they finished, Carina looked up at her husband. His eyes were already on her. Could she trust him to hold her safely? She knew his strength, had seen it when he worked. She looked from him to the priest, then sighed.

Quillan took that as acceptance. He crouched.

"What do I do?"

"Step here." He patted his shoulders.

"Wait a minute." She unlaced her boots and tugged them off, trying not to step in the guano, then hiked up her skirts and stepped where he told her. "What do I hold?"

"Hold my head to get on."

She remembered Father Antoine doing the same, but he hadn't been standing. She put her second foot up and perched, froglike, on his shoulders, gripping his forehead. "Now what?"

"Hold on."

He grabbed her ankles and started to stand. She felt Father Antoine's hands holding her steady on her waist. She fought the urge to jump off and focused on not falling. When he was fully upright, she said, still clinging to his head, "Now what?"

"Now you stand and reach for that jut."

"Madonna mia. I don't think I can."

"Carina, if you could slide down that mountain after your wagon goods, you can stand up now. I won't drop you."

She closed her eyes for a quick moment, drew two deep breaths, then tried to push herself up from his shoulders. Her legs would not straighten. *Oh, Dio.* She drew up her chest and balanced her fingertips on Quillan's head, then pressed again with her legs, wobbling as her hands left their rest. Under her skirts, Quillan's hands came up her calves, strong and steady as she straightened her legs, then unbent at the waist.

Arms stretched upward, her fingers found the jut in the ceiling, enough to balance with, if not hold on to. Quillan swayed slightly, and she gasped. "Don't move!"

"I'm trying not to." He slid his hands behind her knees and tightened his grip. "Give her the poles, Father."

Father Antoine lifted them, thinner end first. Wobbling a little, she reached with one hand and grabbed the poles. They were heavy and awkward. She gripped them tightly, trying not to hit Quillan in the head.

"Now get them through the shaft, Carina."

Oh sì. Throw them in the shaft. She'd be lucky if she held on to them at all. She raised the poles, but the angle would not allow them in. She was too low. *Signore, why did you make me so short?* She tried raising the poles over her head as high as she could stretch, but it wasn't enough. "I can't get them in. We're not high enough."

"On your knees, Father." Quillan's voice was tight, and she realized he was straining worse than she. Physically, he had the worst of it, though it was no picnic balancing. But he thought Father's prayers would raise them two more feet?

Glancing down, she stopped her breath completely as Father Antoine dropped not only to his knees, but to all fours. They couldn't mean to . . . But they did!

She gripped the jut with all the strength in her fingers. Quillan raised one foot, leg shaking as he lodged it onto the priest's back. She couldn't watch, focused only on clinging to the rough ceiling. With a rush, she rose a couple feet higher and the poles swung at her side.

"Ow."

The thump told her she had done as she feared and bumped the ends into Quillan's head. What did he expect? Her own head was bent against the top of the cave now. She could see through the shaft to the snow. But how deep was the snow?

She drew the poles up nearly parallel to the ceiling. Her arms shook. So did her legs. Quillan shifted his hold, and Father Antoine gasped, "Quickly, Carina."

She gathered herself. With all her might, she thrust the poles into the shaft. The motion threw her forward to the edge of the shaft. She caught it and held on.

The poles had lodged in the snow. What if it were too deep? "Can you move one step forward, Father?" What was she saying? Move? They would fall!

But, uncomplaining, he slowly inched forward, and she clung to the edge of the shaft. She pulled the poles back, then reaching deeper, shoved the poles as hard as she could. Daylight. She saw blue sky. "They're through! The poles broke through the snow!"

"Can you get them all the way through?" Quillan's strain was evident in his breathless tone.

"I can't reach them again. They're in too far."

"But they're not through? Not all the way to hook over the shaft?"

She shook her head, then realized he couldn't see her. "No. They're still lengthwise in the shaft."

"We need them all the way through. Father?"

Oh, Dio? He couldn't be thinking . . . Carina clung to the opening as Quillan moved again beneath her. Slowly he began to rise, and she knew Father Antoine now had Quillan's feet on his shoulders. He couldn't manage more than that, but it was enough to raise her halfway into the shaft.

She gripped the poles and shoved. They flew out the end of the shaft, and snow fluttered in around her face. She blew it from her mouth. "They're out."

Catching her legs in a new grip, Quillan grunted with the strain. "Now's the tricky part."

Now? What did he call the rest of it?

Quillan said, "Pull on the rope. Slowly. Don't let the end of the poles come back in. They have to catch sideways."

And how was she to manage that? He wobbled underneath her as she reached for the rope. *Per piacere, Signore* . . . She pulled more rope. So far no ends of the poles. She pulled again and it caught fast. The poles must have turned on their own. She gave it a tug to be sure. "The rope is tight."

"Great! Good. Now come on down."

"Down?" Carina's legs watered at the thought. "You think I'm pazzo?" She took hold of the rope and drew her knee up into the opening. "Push."

Quillan shoved her into the shaft, cushioned with leaves and debris. She was only thankful the freezing temperatures would have killed any insect or other life. The chimney wasn't long, and it slanted so to require little strength. If it had been straight up, she could not have done it. But as it was, she braced herself and crawled the last couple feet, then pushed her head through the snow, chilling her neck with frosted crystals. She shook it free, blinking in the brightness. The air was keen and brittle. She pushed with her elbows, brought one knee out and then the other, and crawled onto the mountainside.

Her breath came in one exultant puff. *Grazie, Dio!* Her muscles shook from strain and relief, but she didn't hurt more than she might have pulling that stunt at any time. She figured she was healed. And she was out! Then she noticed she had no boots. She called down the chimney, "Send up my boots, if you don't mind."

Their cheers sounded below. After a moment, the rope wobbled and she pulled. It was heavier than she expected, and she saw that the bundle of blankets, as well as her boots, had been attached. Well, why waste effort? She pulled the rope until the bundle came free, then unfastened it and her boots and sent the rope back down.

She shook her boots free of snow and debris and pulled them on, lacing them tightly. Her hands burned across her palms from the rope. She pulled her gloves from the pockets of her coat, the soft kidskin gloves Quillan had bought her, and put them on.

"Take her up again, Carina," Quillan called.

She reached for the rope. This time it was his pack she brought up. Once again she untied it and tossed the rope back down the chimney. She looked out at the periwinkle sky, the sunshine brilliant on the snow. Upward to her right would be the entrance to Wolf's mine, but it was nothing but a white wave now, the entire mountainside changed.

She rubbed her arms against the cold, then heard a grunt as Father Antoine pushed up through the opening, his shoulders curved and angled to fit out. She moved aside to give him room. "God's handiwork looks fine today." She waved her arm over the vista.

He laughed, pulled himself the rest of the way free, and sank down beside her. "Indeed it does." He drew in a deep, satisfied breath.

In a short time Quillan came through the hole in the mountainside, an even tighter fit for his muscled shoulders, but thankfully it was just wide enough. He pulled himself up and stood. With hardly a glance about him, he rocked his neck and rubbed it with one hand. Then he stooped, lifted the poles, and untied the rope around them. He stood them upright in the snow and reached for the tarp bundle.

Carina raised her brows. "Can't you stop for one minute? Look around you. See what you've been given." She couldn't get enough of the scene —white-flocked trees and jagged granite faces as far as she could see. To the west a mackerel sky ... It was mostly the sky she reveled in. Spacious, bright, colorful. Everything she'd been deprived of in the dark cavernous hollow. Her soul sang.

He worked the bundle free and shook the tarp out. "We have a long walk home."

And then she remembered ... the horses. Of course he was upset. She got to her feet as Quillan reattached the tarp to the poles. "What are you doing?"

He didn't answer, just kept wrapping and tying. He was making the litter again? Didn't he see she was healed? And what good would it do without Jack and Jock? Oh no. She brought her hands to her hips. "What do you think you're doing with that?"

"Father and I can—"

"Oh no, you can't. I'll not be carried about like an Egyptian princess. I can walk."

Again he ignored her. She turned to the priest. "Father, talk sense to him. Didn't I climb through a shaft just now? Didn't I balance like an acrobat? Does he think me an invalid still?"

Father Antoine raised his hands. "I make it a point never to interfere between husband and wife."

With smaller twine, Quillan was now attaching the woolly mat. Carina fumed. Hadn't she just proved her strength? Were they all pazzo—the doctor, the priest, and her stubborn husband? He thought she would lie there and let Father Antoine and him carry her down the mountain?

Quillan shrugged into his pack. Father Antoine scooped up the blankets. Carina's hands fisted at her sides. Quillan motioned with one hand toward the litter lying between them. She shook her head. His jaw tightened.

"Carina, I have enough on my mind already. Lie down and stop being foolish."

Hah! Foolish? That was what she would look on the litter.

"I am perfectly capable of walking."

"And one slip could set you back."

She crossed her arms at her chest. "You didn't worry about that when I stood on your shoulders."

"I knew I could hold you. You're nowhere near Father Antoine's weight."

"That's not the point."

With an exasperated sigh, Quillan bent and scooped her into his arms. Blood rushed to her face and words to her mouth. "Omaccio! Put me down!"

And he did. On the litter. With a pirate face he told her, "I have more rope."

Oh! He would tie her down? She squirmed, but he caught her wrists and stared so intently, she knew he would stop at nothing. He was a tyrant, her husband, when he felt strongly about something. She felt the strength of his feelings now. He would not let her walk. She slumped down with a huff. Bene. If they wanted to carry her, let them. She had put on enough of a show for Father Antoine.

Quillan nodded to the priest and they lifted her. "Stay to the edge here." He started down. "Avalanche only came this far. We should have tried this exit yesterday."

"We didn't think of it yesterday." The obviousness of her statement made no difference to him. He kept on like a man possessed.

Since Quillan went down first, Father Antoine carried the end of the litter near her head. That gave her a view of Quillan's back, and she watched his head turning side to side. What did he search for? The horses? She hoped they would not find the corpses. She'd seen enough during the flood. But Quillan searched the slope all the way. The new piled snow must be twenty feet deep, and much of it was chunks and slabs. Were his blacks under there somewhere?

Then she heard it. A snort. A terrified snort and whinny. She froze, but Quillan lowered the poles to the ground and bolted through the frozen terrain toward the black head just showing above the surface. He fell, floundered up, and thrashed through to the horse. Carina couldn't tell if it was Jack or Jock. Whichever one, it was alive.

She stood up from the tilted litter, and Father Antoine dropped his end and went to help. With his arms, Quillan flung the snow away from the beast, freeing its neck by the time Father Antoine reached him. In her skirts, Carina didn't cross the snow. She would only get in their way. She folded her arms and waited. *Oh, Signore, let it be all right.* If the horse were injured, if a leg were broken ... It would kill Quillan to have to shoot it after finding it like that.

She sat down on Quillan's pack and waited. The men worked methodically now, careful to free the horse in a way that would not allow it to panic and injure itself further. They had to be careful not to sink in over their own heads. At one point they lay prone to work the snow away from the beast. It must be powder underneath.

The horse heaved and lunged. Quillan caught its head. Part of the bridle and reins remained, and he gripped them and subdued the animal. Then carefully, rising now to his knees in the snow, Quillan backed and pulled the horse forward. It lunged. Quillan fell back, and Carina shot to her feet. Would he be trampled in his effort?

But Father Antoine caught the horse around the neck and held it back while Quillan recovered his position. Together they worked the horse—she thought it was Jock—over the broken surface. Slowly they plowed through in leaping lunges, cleared a path, then another lunge and another.

Jock didn't seem to be injured. Certainly its legs worked. Carina clasped her hands when they plowed the last distance through waist-high drifts. Jock looked fine, if a little frightened. *Grazie, Signore!* What an unlooked-for boon.

She turned to Quillan. "Should we look for Jack?"

Quillan's expression changed. "I already found him."

She searched his face. "Found him? Where?"

"Under Jock. His warmth must have kept Jock from freezing."

Carina stood a moment, absorbing that. So they'd fallen together, but one, though trapped, wasn't buried alive. The other was not so lucky. Had Jock known Jack was dying beneath him? Did animals think that way? She reached out to pat the horse. He shied.

Quillan stroked Jock's shoulder. "There, Jock. There now." He soothed the horse with his hands.

Her stomach growled, and she realized that with all the excitement of trying to escape the cave, they had eaten nothing. Surely they could rest and let the horse calm down. She reached for Quillan's pack and tugged it open. The remainder of the lunch was on top as well as the canteen. She took both out and Quillan nodded.

"Good idea, Carina." He gave her a softened look. Repentant? He should be. Tie her down, indeed.

Jock stood quivering as they ate the crumbling bread and beef. Quillan palmed the dried plums and apples and held them out to the horse, who lipped them noisily out of his hand. Carina could almost feel the love pass between them, and a surge of her own love for Quillan washed over her. That, and the food soothing the lion in her belly, made her almost cheerful until Quillan stood, brushed the crumbs from his thighs, and eyed the litter.

"I'm not riding it again, Quillan. It's mostly level here, and only a gentle slope into town. I can walk."

He tugged a rope from his pack. "You'll be tired."

She shrugged. "Then let me ride Jock."

"Doctor—"

"Felden would never have allowed me to perform acrobatics and climb that chimney. But I did it." She untied the woolly mat from the litter, threw it over Jock's back, and turned to Quillan. "Your hand, please."

Quillan looked from her to the horse, then to the priest. Father Charboneau's expression was carefully neutral. Quillan turned back to her. "Not so fast." He wound the rope around the front and back of the mat to hold it in place and gave it a tug to be sure. Then he took out his knife and cut the remainder of the rope. The rest, he tied to the broken but usable bridle.

Carina's heart swelled when he turned, caught her at the waist, and swung her into a sidesaddle position on Jock. Quillan eyed her. "Satisfied?"

She smiled. "Grazie."

His mouth quirked up, almost roguish. "What's the response?"

"*Prego.*"

"Prego, Carina." He cupped her knee, then turned, untied the tarp, and left the poles lying in the snow. He rolled the tarp tightly and stuffed it into his pack, then took hold of Jock and started on. Father Antoine gathered the blankets, sent Carina a quick grin, and came up beside her. Carina felt strong and capable, no longer prisoner to her injuries or anyone else's opinion. Now surely they could go home.

Ten

....

As a dove from a cage spreads its wings to the draft,

so my hands on the reins in the freighter man's craft.

As the dove winging higher up into the sky,

so the plodding of hooves, crack of whip say good-bye.

— Quillan

QUILLAN WAITED WHILE Carina made yet another tearful farewell. She had an amazing reservoir of both tears and words. As for him, the sooner they were on the road, the better. Well, he'd had one difficult parting. Alan Tavish. Which was why he'd picked up the team and wagon without Carina, had those few moments alone with a friend he would likely never see again. And that was why he had given Sam to Alan, so the old man would not be alone.

Beyond that, Quillan could leave Crystal without regret. Carina, it seemed, could not. He leaned back against the wagon, crossed his arms and his ankles. Already they'd added half again as much as he had planned to haul, parting gifts from all who couldn't let her go without some token. Finally she disentangled from Èmie. No, one more hug for Mae. He leaned back again. Ah, for real this time?

Down the first stair, down the second. He straightened as she kept coming. He waved a hand to Mae, farewell to a woman he respected, to Èmie whom he hardly knew. And there was Carina, her waist between his hands. He swung her up onto the spring-loaded carriage seat he'd fashioned in place of the ordinary box

111

he'd ridden for two years. It was even cushioned and covered in leather. Impractical, but he had her comfort to think of.

"All set?" He half expected her to say no, there were dozens more people she must bid adieu, or rather *arrivederci*. "How many ways are there to say good-bye, Carina?" He climbed up beside her.

"Too many." She sniffed.

He took up the lines and released the brake. She turned and waved furiously as he slapped the traces on the team's rumps. He felt a pang seeing Jock pulling beside a chestnut gelding. His Clydesdales, Socrates and Homer, in the wheeler positions, didn't seem to care, but Quillan could swear Jock missed Jack. Still, it was good to be off.

"It's breaking my heart." Carina clutched her throat with a limp handkerchief as they passed Father Antoine Charboneau.

Quillan raised a hand. He had the priest's word and Alex Makepeace's that they would block off Wolf's chamber once weather allowed. As to the rest of the cave, Makepeace had plans to lead guided tours for adventurers. Bully for him. He'd have his hands full between that and the New Boundless. Too full to miss Carina, Quillan hoped, though his wife had said a private and prolonged good-bye there, too.

Her breath sucked into a sob, and he cupped her knee. "It'll be all right."

"Why can't we take them all?"

He pulled with his left hand to bring the team around the corner. "They have their lives."

"And they'll go on without me, and I won't see Èmie's restaurant, and Mae . . . she started out so prickly and—"

"You made her into mush."

She slapped her gloves across his thigh. "Stop it."

"Sorry."

She reached into her pocket and pulled out a lump of silver the size of a caterpillar. "And this from Joe Turner, the first silver nugget he got from the Carina DiGratia mine shaft. He's afraid all his mines will stop producing now."

"Unhealthy superstition."

"He made me a legend." She dabbed her nose with the handkerchief.

"You made yourself one." And that was the truth. Crystal

would not forget Carina. She didn't know it, but her mystique would only grow in her absence. Carina DiGratia belonged in the stories of Crystal, the same as Wolf and Rose, but Carina Shepard belonged to him. He reached an arm around her shoulders and pulled her close to his side.

They passed the end of Main Street and left the buildings of Crystal behind. Quillan didn't look back, though Carina turned and watched until the town disappeared behind a curve. He didn't remind her it was she who wanted to go home, nor that she'd despised the town for most of her time there. He just let her grieve.

The road was hard-packed snow. If the weather held, they would cross Mosquito Pass into Fairplay and stay there tonight. If they got a very early start, the next day should bring them into Morrison, possibly even Denver. How long they spent there depended. Carina was excited, thrilled at the prospect of meeting Rose's family. He was uncertain what to feel.

"How long do you suppose a letter would take between Sonoma and Crystal?" Carina stuffed the handkerchief into her pocket.

"How long's it been taking?"

She shrugged under his arm. "I sent two letters at the start. Then everything turned upside down and . . ." She waved her hand and sniffed. Back out came the handkerchief. She dabbed one eye, then the other. "Mamma sent one reply. 'So glad you're safe and happy.' When, of course, I was neither. I couldn't keep deceiving them. So I stopped writing."

He felt a dim foreboding. "You haven't written your family since?"

She shook her head. "But I must write Mae and Èmie and Father Antoine." She threw up her hands. "Oh, so many others!"

He glanced sidelong. If she hadn't written since the start, her family knew nothing about him. His knowledge of women might be vague, but wasn't that unusual?

"I miss them already."

"Why don't we just stay?" He threw it out flippantly.

She spun under his arm. "You know it's impossible. You've sold the mine; I've given everything to Èmie. What would we do?"

He shrugged. "Still have my wagon and my tent."

She pushed him in the ribs. "Don't be ugly."

"That was ugly?"

"You're mocking me."

Well, maybe a little, he conceded. "There's only two choices, Carina. Stay or go."

"Of course we'll go! But it's so hard. You'd see, if you had a heart at all." Again she smacked his thigh. This time he kept quiet. Somehow he doubted Mae was flailing anyone, or Èmie either. They'd miss Carina, he was sure. He just doubted it would be so animated. They began a short climb, and he removed his arm from her shoulders to use both hands on the reins.

"How can I want two opposite things so much?" She started to cry again.

Quillan shook his head. "Enough, Carina. How many tears can you cry?"

"As many as I need to." Her pout proved it.

He knew better than to say more, but her crying gave him a helpless feeling he didn't like. Would she keep it up all the way to Sonoma?

"Besides, tears are natural, necessary."

"Necessary?"

In answer, she dug through the bag at her feet and took out a small volume. "Here." She flipped through the pages, sniffed, and cleared her throat.

"Tears, idle tears, I know not what they mean,
Tears from the depth of some divine despair
Rise in the heart, and gather to the eyes,
In looking on the happy autumn-fields,
And thinking of the days that are no more."

She swiped at her eyes. "You see? Tears for the days that are no more. Our days here are done, and our friends . . ." She folded the book cover over her hand to hold the place while she pressed the handkerchief to her eyes.

Quillan glanced at the spine. Tennyson. There was one man who agreed with her. But tears were not in Quillan's nature.

She dabbed the handkerchief to her nose. "What is it the French say? *Partir, c'est mourir un peu.*"

Quillan glanced over his shoulder, startled to hear French from her lips. He shouldn't be surprised. Nothing should surprise him anymore. "What does that mean?"

"To leave is to die a little. That's how I feel."

Dying a little. He understood that. He died a little with Cain. And leaving Alan, too, he supposed. It did feel like death of a sort. He just couldn't express it in tears.

She patted the book. "Tennyson knows how it is."

"He's a poet."

She turned. "So are you. But you have no idea how I'm feeling."

Quillan cocked his jaw, staring straight ahead. Words came unbidden. "Like footprints in damp sand on the creek bed of the mind, so the ripples on your soul from the friends you leave behind." Yes, it hurt to leave Alan.

She slapped the book shut and flung her arms around him. "Oh, Quillan, I'm sorry. I've been unfair."

He raised his elbows to keep hold of the team as her head lodged between his upper arm and side.

She sniffed. "But don't you feel bad for leaving anyone?"

"I'll miss Alan." The tightening in his throat proved it, but he shoved it back and focused on the road.

She settled her arms around his ribs. "Only Alan?"

His elbows were going to get very tired.

She stroked his chest. "You don't make many friends."

"Don't want many."

"You'd be surprised how many think well of you." She locked her fingers again, settling in. Good thing she was little.

"That's the difference between friendship and respect. I think well of lots of people I won't miss at all."

She pressed her face to his chest and laughed, then ducked out under his arm and picked up the book, which had slid to the floor. Quillan dropped his arms before she could wiggle back in. It could be worse, though, for a long cold drive than Carina reading Tennyson. A smile tugged his lips. Could be a lot worse.

———

Carina had not seen Denver since she had passed through on her way to Crystal. She had been too distressed to notice much as she rode the train through to the railhead in Gunnison, where she had purchased her ill-fated wagon and driven up to the city that called itself the Diamond of the Rockies. In truth Crystal was hardly more now than it had been then, a rough camp trying to make a name.

But they had left the snowy mountains behind, staying one night in Fairplay and one in Morrison. The land they'd covered into Denver was tawny brown and nearly treeless. But Denver was a true city; gas lights along real streets lined with buildings that didn't look as though they'd been thrown together with whatever was at hand, shop windows filled with more than picks and shovels. No work-weary men teeming the streets and wagons dodging stumps in the road. Men in top hats, fashionable ladies on their arms, strolled the timbered walkways.

Perhaps the whole city was not so fair, but to her eye, Denver was a long sight better than Crystal. As Quillan drove the wagon through the streets with a knowing confidence, excitement pushed aside the aching for her friends. She was with Quillan. And he was fine company. "Where are we staying?"

"The hotel's about six blocks down."

She looked at the buildings around them. "There are hotels right here." Imposing buildings with ornate trims and moldings. She looked up the tall brick face of one that especially appealed to her. "What about this one? Why not stay here?"

He maneuvered their huge wagon past the hotel's entrance. "Because that one's a bordello."

Carina jerked her head around to scrutinize it. There was no tinny music, no women dangling from the balcony. It looked perfectly elegant. The windows were draped in sheers and velvet with leaded panes, some of them stained lovely colors. She could not believe it a house of ill repute. "But it's beautiful."

He quirked his mouth. "Not all iniquity is ugly, Carina."

She pulled her gaze away, stung. From her first day in Crystal she had judged by appearances. Hadn't she thought Mr. Beck kind and upright? And Quillan a rogue pirate? Well, he was a little that. But she was gullible. Even before she fled Sonoma, she'd seen only the surface. Flavio's charm and *bello volto*, handsome face, and *eleganza*.

She moistened her lips with her tongue. How would she see him now? Would she see past all that to the unfaithful heart? And what would Flavio see? Not the trusting woman she'd been. And what did it matter? She had a husband. Flavio would think nothing of her at all. *Buono!*

But what about Quillan? What would her family think about him? She glanced over. He'd shaved before they left Crystal, all but his mustache, which rivaled the late General Custer's. Now he was on his second day of beard, and his hair hung loose in soft shaggy layers. Her heart jumped. She loved the sight of him. But what would Papa think?

She sent her gaze ahead to the stone building Quillan angled toward. It lacked the color and glow of the bordello, but seemed a solid, comfortable place. Quillan eased the wagon off the road and into the drive. He pulled on the reins and called, "Whoa," then set the brake and jumped down.

She felt stiff behind the knees and sore everywhere else as he swung her to the ground. A doorman opened the door for them, and she glimpsed a tasteful elegance surrounding the long mahogany desk to which Quillan led her.

The clerk had an elongated neck with a pointed larynx that bobbed above his stiff collar and satin vest. "Good afternoon, Mr. Shepard," he said in a low, respectful voice. She hadn't expected him to address Quillan by name. Her husband was known in a city this size?

She looked around the lobby with its brass chandeliers and cut-glass globes. The portieres hanging inside the doorways were olive-toned green, tied with gold tassels, the carpet red and gold. The clerk smiled graciously. She suddenly remembered Mr. Barton looking through his fish spectacles, thinking her wanton. But then she'd been with Berkley Beck, and all Crystal knew before she did what kind of man he was.

Quillan signed the ledger, then handed another man a coin. "Would you show my wife to the room while I take our wagon to the livery?"

"Certainly, sir." The man took their key from the clerk. "This way, madam."

She followed the man up the stairs to the second floor landing, then down the long hall to the room with a brass number twenty-five nailed to the door. He unlocked the door and handed her the key. "The dining room is open, madam, if you and your husband desire a late luncheon. Bath and water closet are at the end of the hall."

"Thank you." She went inside. The walls were gentian blue, the fireplace painted white, very like the room in which they'd spent their wedding night. Her heart quickened. She crossed the room to the window. It looked directly on the brick wall of the building next door. No stubbled ground and mountain creek. No view of slopes climbing majestic peaks. No valley beckoning her to come, to seek the secrets of a mine returned to the mountain or a spring gushing forth over frigid tiers of ice, or a cavern painted with a man's life.

And now she was missing it all again. *Dio, what is wrong with me? Will I never be satisfied?*

But maybe it was natural to miss it all, even though she was going home. In a large way Crystal had formed her. It would always be there in her heart. But home beckoned more strongly. She dabbed a renegade tear, then turned back and took in the room. Comfortable indeed.

Quillan must have done well to stay there often enough to be known by name. But one had only to consider the prices he charged for his goods. How strange that he'd lived in a tent in Crystal. He was certainly a man of contradictions. She fingered the amethyst pin. He didn't look like a wealthy man, didn't act like one. But was he? Funny not to know.

If he were a man of substance, if he had wealth ... She stopped that thought. She had fallen in love with the rogue freighter. That was enough for her. But would it be for Papa?

She took off her coat and hung it on the brass tree. Then she went down the hall and used the water closet. It was luxury after Crystal, even if it was shared by every room on the floor. She washed her hands and face, then went back to the room.

She had just opened the door when Quillan climbed the stairs, followed by the same man with their bags. She turned and smiled. Four weeks ago, in pain and grief, she had despaired of hope. Now Quillan looked at her with such love it stopped her breath. *Dio, you are good.* She stepped aside as the porter deposited their bags, received another coin from Quillan, then left.

Quillan motioned her in and closed the door behind them. "Do you like it?"

"It's lovely."

He slipped out of his coat. "Not as elegant as your first choice."

"I'm certain they wouldn't know you there."

He opened his cuffs and rolled his sleeves. "*Are* you?"

"Yes." She remembered too well the disdain he'd shown for his mother, Rose, until he had read her diary. He would never cross the door of a bordello, but he no longer hated the unfortunate women inside.

He hung the coat, then crossed to the fireplace and rested his hand on the high-back chair angled there. After a moment he said, "This is where I read my mother's diary."

"In this room?" She crossed to him.

"In this chair." He turned and took her in his arms. "Thank you, Carina." He bent, and it was a long while before she was free to answer. When he released her, she stroked her fingers over his scratchy jaw.

"Sorry." He scraped his palm over it. "Guess I'll shave before dining."

She smiled, cocking her head to the side. "You prefer that look."

He touched the skin beside her mouth. "I don't want to chafe you."

"At luncheon?" She raised her brows.

"After."

One word could set her heart pounding? She would not let on so easily. "Should we see the DeMornays after?" That was their purpose, after all. And she could hardly wait to meet Rose's family, Quillan's family.

He hung his thumbs in his pants waist. "I don't know." He walked to the fireplace, poured coal into the brazier. Then he added kindling and flicked a match. Warmth and light kindled, and he held a palm to it. Firelight played over his features as he squatted there.

She sensed his hesitance, but didn't understand it. "You haven't changed your mind?"

He glanced up. "Not altogether." He stood and dusted off his hands.

She touched his arm. "Quillan, what is it?"

"I'm not sure what good it will do."

"Good?" She turned him toward her. "To know they have a grandson, to learn what became of their daughter!"

He winced.

"Knowing is better than wondering. And you! You'll see your family, know here"—she pressed her hand to her heart—"from whom you came. You have to go, Quillan."

"They have their lives, Carina."

"And you're part of them. They just don't know it yet." She caught his hands between hers. "Family, Quillan, is the most important thing."

He expelled a slow breath. "Guess I'll clean up, then."

Carina smiled. He would take it head on. "We should send a runner, requesting a visit. Do you have Mr. Tabor's introduction?"

He took it from his vest.

"Good. We'll send that, too."

His mouth quirked up.

She put her hands on her hips. "What?"

"Good thing I have you to soften the blow."

She slipped her arms around his waist. How natural it seemed to touch him. Was it only weeks ago she thought she didn't know him? He hooked his hands behind her neck, resting his arms on her shoulders. They were hard and heavy, working arms, lean and strong. "Keep the *mustachio*. It's perfect."

He rubbed it across her forehead, kissed her there, then let go.

Two hours later they rode a hired rig to the DeMornays' home in an elite neighborhood. Though not among the original founders, they had an enviable niche in Denver society, and their location demonstrated that. Carina looked up at the trim red-brick house as Quillan lifted her from the carriage. She felt daunted but hid it for his sake.

In his wedding suit, hair tied back, Quillan looked fine and jaunty, his mustache bold, his eyes subdued. Surely they would welcome him. He hadn't explained their visit, only requested it on grounds of mutual importance. He'd stared a long time at the reply, William DeMornay's card and a brief inscription: *On Mr. Tabor's recommendation, I can spare a moment at four o'clock today.*

Not exactly warm, but then, Mr. DeMornay had no idea it was his grandson he was corresponding with. A maid answered their knock and led them to a parlor. "Wait here, please."

Carina felt Quillan's unease. He stood very still—to a casual eye, contained. But to her . . . So much rested on this, so much of who he was. *Signore, give him courage.*

He held a packet in one hand. Carina knew its contents. Rose's diary and a deed to the Rose Legacy mine. He had made his claim official before leaving Crystal, and the land agent had issued him a fresh deed based on the claim. It included only the information Rose and Wolf had given the first time. No surnames.

The door opened, and the DeMornays came in together. Carina was glad for that. They had requested an audience with both, but William had worded his reply in the singular, and she didn't know whether that would include Quillan's grandmother, as well.

"Good afternoon." Mrs. DeMornay motioned them toward a pair of blue leaf-patterned chairs. "Please sit."

Carina and Quillan took their places. Mrs. DeMornay sat across from them on an amber tufted-velvet chair. William DeMornay remained standing. He said, "I know Horace Tabor more by reputation than acquaintance."

Quillan nodded. "He said as much." Then he stood and extended his hand. "I'm Quillan Shepard. My wife, Carina."

William's handshake was dry and peremptory. "How do you do." He turned back to Quillan. "You have a matter of importance to discuss?"

Quillan reluctantly regained his chair. Carina guessed he didn't relish being put on a lower plane by this coldly indifferent man. He said, "Mr. DeMornay, it might be good if you sat."

Carina glanced at Mrs. DeMornay. She was a feathery woman with very narrow teeth that protruded in a slight overbite that, surprisingly, did not diminish her beauty. Even at her age she had a graceful bearing, and her silvery hair, swept upward from her face, was full and lustrous.

William DeMornay sat down in a green leather chair, eschewing the matching footstool. He folded his leathery fingers across one knee. "Now then?"

Carina had no idea how Quillan would handle this. But it was his to handle. She silently started to pray.

"Mr. and Mrs. DeMornay, are you acquainted with Rose Annelise DeMornay?"

They both visibly stiffened. William said, "Why do you ask?"

"Because if you're not, the reason for my visit is irrelevant."

William stayed silent a long moment, then, "Our daughter was named Rose Annelise."

So the relationship was what Carina suspected. She was looking at Rose's parents, the ones Rose couldn't bear to shame. But before either she or Quillan could respond, William added tightly,

"She is dead." He knew? Had Rose contacted them? Had word reached them from tiny Placerville?

Quillan said, "I know. But Rose Annelise DeMornay was my mother."

Very slowly Mrs. DeMornay's hand rose to her throat.

William DeMornay made no sound, just stiffly rose from his chair. "I think you had better leave."

Quillan reached into the packet, drew out the deed. "This is the mine my father staked in Placerville."

William DeMornay's features pulled tightly. "Whoever your father was, he had nothing to do with my daughter."

Quillan brought out the diary, laid it atop the deed on his knee. Mrs. DeMornay gasped softly.

William's hands clenched at his sides. He drew himself up. "Our daughter Rose died at the age of nineteen. She's buried in the churchyard. There is no possible way she is your mother." Before Quillan could answer, the old man's mouth twisted. "What are you after? Money?"

Quillan looked as though he'd lost his breath. Then Carina saw cold rage come into his eyes. He stood up abruptly. "I didn't come here for money." He stared Mr. DeMornay in the face until the older man looked down. Then he put the diary and deed back into the packet and folded it into his hand. He looked at Carina, and she stood up.

That was all? He would leave without making them see? She wanted to stomp her foot, tell them all to consider Rose and stop acting so stubborn. How could they refuse to acknowledge the truth? Mrs. DeMornay recognized the diary. Carina had seen that clearly. Didn't she want to know what the pages contained? What her daughter's words could tell her?

Quillan put a hand to her elbow. Did he suspect she might blurt out all she thought? She turned to Mrs. DeMornay. "Thank you for meeting with us. I'm sorry for your loss." She looked the woman sharply in the eye. Her loss was greater now that it included her grandson as well, and she wanted the woman to know it.

Mrs. DeMornay looked up from her to Quillan. Was it longing in her eyes, or age and sorrow? She said nothing.

William opened the door himself to end their audience. Carina pulled her coat closely about her, the cold emanating from

Mr. DeMornay as she passed him. *What hatred.* The maid showed them out, handing Quillan his hat. He put it on his head silently. They walked down to the carriage.

The cabby hustled to open the door. "Where to now, sir?"

Quillan said, "The cemetery."

Carina jerked her face up.

"Which one?" The man gave Carina a hand in.

"Where's the DeMornay plot?"

"Oh, that'n. Not far."

Quillan climbed in beside her. Carina felt him shaking. Was it rage or disappointment? And either way, what was he doing? Why would he visit an empty grave? No matter what the DeMornays said, she knew the truth and Quillan did, too. They rode in silence until they entered the churchyard, and the cabby drew up at the cemetery gate.

"Here you are, then. Shall I wait?"

Quillan nodded. He helped Carina down with none of his usual flourish, then headed through the gates. They walked along rows of impressive family plots, Quillan silent and purposeful.

Oh, Signore, how he must hurt. Would he always be rejected?

The DeMornay plot held one grave, a tall monument with a wreath of roses carved around the nameplate. *Rose Annelise DeMornay, beloved daughter.* And only nineteen years spanned the dates. Had she been so young when she slipped away and fled, carrying her secret, her shame? But what of the other years, those that brought her to Wolf, that gave her Quillan and took him away? What about the part of her life in her diary? Was it nothing?

She thought of the grave where Rose actually lay, interred with her husband, Wolf, who died with her in love. That grave was marked by a stone on the mountain above the Rose Legacy and covered with wild flowers in the summer. Carina had sat beside that grave and read Rose's diary and wept for a woman she never knew, yet loved.

Quillan put his hands in his pockets. "They spared no expense." His tone set her teeth on edge. His hip was slack, his eyes narrowed.

She wished she'd never convinced him to talk to them. "Why would they make her this grave?"

He walked around the wrought iron fencing to the back of

the stone tower, staring up at its pristine point. "To create the illusion. The grief-stricken parents of the unsullied daughter. Better dead than disgraced."

"But what if she'd come back?"

Quillan didn't answer.

She tried to imagine it. Would they have turned her away, pretended they didn't know her, either? Impossible. Had they known so well she wouldn't try? Or had they believed her dead, truly grieved their daughter, and at last built a monument to her memory? "Maybe they knew in their hearts she was dead."

Again he didn't answer. She felt him withdrawing. *Signore, don't let him close me out.* She wanted to touch him, but he stood too separately. He was fighting, but what?

She rested her hand on the iron fence. "It doesn't matter what they think. You've seen them now."

"And they've seen me." He gripped two of the posts until his knuckles whitened. Then suddenly he let go. "Come on." He started for the carriage.

She hurried behind. What was he thinking? Was there something they could do? His stride made her lift her skirts to keep up. "Where are we going?"

He reached the carriage and opened the door before the cabby could climb down from his box. Carina got in.

"Take us back to the hotel," Quillan called up and pushed in behind her.

She could almost taste his disappointment. What had seemed irresolution, she now knew was self-protection. If she had not argued for the meeting, he might have decided against it. What had he gained? The knowledge that his only family didn't want him, wouldn't even believe him.

"They don't matter." She reached over and took his hand, felt him stiffen. She expected no answer and got none. It wasn't true. They had mattered, more than she would have believed. He said nothing the entire drive back. When they reached the room, she expected the same, but though he didn't speak, he took her hand and led her to the bed, closing the door behind. And that, though the sun had yet to set.

Quillan needed to feel alive. It was as though he'd been snuffed from existence. Seeing his mother's grave dated before he was born, hearing, *"There is no possible way she is your mother."* He knew it was lies, but it hit him anyway. He was nothing, no one.

He kissed Carina. He didn't want her to talk. Her platitudes changed nothing. He wanted the primal affirmation he found only with her. But when he was through, he felt empty. Carina stroked his head, kissed his brow. She knew him. She knew what he was feeling. But he turned away and stared at the wall.

"Don't go away." Her voice was thick and husky.

"You think I'd leave?" He spoke to the wall.

"Here." She tapped his temple.

She knew him all right. He was closing up. She wanted him to turn, to talk. But he felt like stone. When he didn't move, she got up and dressed. He heard the door close behind her, and he was glad to be alone. It was familiar territory. His mind wandered over the episode. There was no question he'd found his mother's people. Nor did he question their obvious disregard.

That was expected, and it no longer hurt. The hard part was learning they had put Rose to death without knowing, maybe without caring where or how she truly was, interred her memory rather than praying for her return. Why? He couldn't fathom it. He felt an aching tenderness for his mother, wanting to shield her from them, take her where their judgment couldn't hurt her.

He shook his head. That was foolish. She was beyond all human condemnation. Only God in His mercy had charge of her soul. Not the DeMornays. What had he hoped to accomplish? Certainly not some grand reunion, some open-arm welcome to their long lost progeny. If he was truly honest, he'd hoped to recognize them, to see something of himself, some extension beyond his own being.

Had he looked hard enough he might have found it. Had they conversed he might have seen mannerisms, intonation, expressions. Maybe he had. He closed his eyes and pictured William DeMornay, as stiff and unyielding and silently furious as Quillan felt right now. Strange to think the harder part of his nature came through his mother.

Well, it was done now. But their accusation that he wanted money rankled. As though money were paramount to family and belonging. What had Carina said? Family was the most important thing. For that he'd pursued it, not for any financial gain. His anger surged. That, at least, he could feel.

Oh, God, help me make sense of it. But he couldn't. He rolled from the bed and put his pants on, then sat down atop the covers. He'd hardly settled in when Carina came through the door with a tray. Her beauty hit him physically. Had she gone down to the dining room looking so ravishing?

Two plates of pork seasoned with apples, buttered potatoes, and winter squash steamed up as she set the tray on stands across his legs. He looked from it to her. "Did you go down for this?"

"I ordered it up and charged it to your bill." She settled onto the bed beside him.

He'd never eaten in bed in his life. Unless you counted sitting on the edge of his cot in his tent with a heated can of beans or potatoes. But then the cot had been the only thing to sit on.

She took a napkin from the tray, unfolded it, and laid it against his chest, which he had yet to cover in a shirt. Carina didn't seem to care. She tucked her hair back behind her ear where it had fallen forward as she leaned toward the tray. With one finger he flicked it loose again.

She turned, suffocated him with the warmth in her eyes. "Do you want to eat or not?"

Unfortunately he did. He blessed the food, saying the prayer Reverend Shepard had taught him as a boy. Then he took the fork and knife and made short work of the meal. He could see Carina's amusement as she ate hers with more delicacy. When they finished he moved the tray to the floor and turned to her. "What made you do that?"

"At home, when I was sick or peevish, Mamma would bring me a tray in bed. I always felt like a princess." She waved her hand in the way that fascinated him.

"So I'm the prince?" He pulled up the side of his mouth. "Far cry from a pirate, isn't it?"

"Not so far." She shrugged. "If you consider all the despot rulers."

Amused, he tucked his arms behind his head and studied her. "I must be wicked, with all my kin against me."

"Your kin don't know what they're missing." She set the tray on the table beside the bed, then sat again and shook her hair back. Did she know what that hair did to him? "Soon you'll have more kin than you can stand."

Carina's family. And she hadn't told them about him. He

raised her hand and kissed her fingers. "Ever been to Alaska?"

"Alaska!"

"Great salmon fishing." He stroked her fingers.

She tugged her hand away. "What are you saying?"

"With my wagon I could haul for the canneries. The cost of goods is astounding."

"You want to go to Alaska?"

Did he? He'd thrown it out as a joke, but just now the thought was mighty appealing. Her face was stricken, though she didn't say what was obvious to see. She wanted her family, her most important thing.

"Well, maybe we'll go by way of California."

She eased. "And maybe we'll like Sonoma so well, your wandering feet will stop clamoring."

He smiled. "Well, now. Wandering feet." He looked down at his gray woolen stockings and curled his toes back.

She settled against him, and he brought his arm down to circle her shoulders. No, wandering was not on his mind.

Eleven

What stench is in a tainted soul that righteous men recoil,
some fetid, darksome malady which makes their blood to boil.
Why not instead a cleansing balm to wash away the stain,
and let men see as God has seen the weariness and pain.

— Quillan

WITH QUILLAN GONE to get the wagon, Carina took one
last look around the lobby. They were leaving Denver after just
one night, and she wasn't sure how to feel. If things had gone well
yesterday, they might have stayed awhile and gotten acquainted
with the DeMornays—Rose's parents. Carina felt a keen disappointment. And though Quillan wouldn't show it, she knew he
stung still.

But now they would go to Sonoma. Oh, how she longed to
see her home, her own mamma, her dear papa. Everyone, even
Divina. She could almost feel their arms around her. Of course
they would love Quillan. Why did she doubt it? They were not
DeMornays; they were DiGratias!

She turned, and there was Mrs. DeMornay coming through
the door with a quick darting step, glancing back once at the
door, then proceeding to the counter. She stopped short when she
saw Carina. "Oh. Oh, you're here."

Carina drew herself up almost to a height with the older
woman. Before she could speak, however, Mrs. DeMornay caught
her hand and drew her into the alcove by the front window. "I've
been forbidden to speak further with your husband, in case he

tried to pursue things again. But nothing was said about you."

Carina was startled. This seemed so out of character from the woman who had sat so prim and stately, offering no word yesterday when Quillan said his piece.

"Please, I have only a moment."

Carina caught the woman's hands. "Tell me."

"Mr. DeMornay needs to believe . . . I'm certain he does believe . . ."

"That Rose lies in that grave?"

Mrs. DeMornay shuddered. "You can't know how it was. We did what we had to, at first to protect Rose, then all of us. Judge me kindly."

As they had judged Rose? And Quillan? Carina stayed silent.

Mrs. DeMornay's liquid eyes were nearly aqua, perhaps paled a little with years, but Carina wondered if Rose's eyes had been the same. Wolf had painted dark hair on the cave wall. Rose would have been a beauty indeed. The older woman dampened her gathered lips. "The diary . . ."

"It is Rose's diary." Carina stooped and drew it from her satchel. She had kept it close this morning, unable to pack it dispassionately into the trunk for the wagon. She pressed it to her heart. "My husband's mother's words."

Mrs. DeMornay nodded slowly. "It was my gift to her on her nineteenth birthday." Tears wet her eyes. "Your husband . . . was he, is he the product of a certain liaison? One which she fled . . ."

Surprised, Carina shook her head. Mrs. DeMornay knew of Rose's seduction? "That child miscarried." The word brought a pang to her heart, recalling Rose's anguish. "Quillan is Rose's son by Wolf, her husband."

"Wolf." Mrs. DeMornay shook her head. "Wolf?"

"The Sioux named him Cries Like a Wolf." Carina thought the woman would faint she turned so pale and trembling.

"He was a savage?"

"He was a white captive who left the tribe and made his way to Placerville. A brave and wonderful man. Mrs. DeMornay, Wolf loved your daughter fiercely." Loved her unto death. Slowly Carina drew the diary from her breast. She held it out. "It's all in here."

"No, I can't." Mrs. DeMornay shunned it with her hands. "If William saw . . . But here." She reached into her purse, drew out a locket on a chain. "This is mine, so I can give it."

It was large and gold, valuable in that alone. But Carina sensed more. Mrs. DeMornay opened it. Carina drew her breath in sharply. A photograph of a girl with dark curls and pale eyes.

Mrs. DeMornay pressed it into her hands. "I want your husband to have this."

Carina covered it with her palm. "He will treasure it."

Mrs. DeMornay's lips trembled. "My daughter is . . . truly dead?"

Slowly Carina nodded. "Quillan was raised by another couple." She sensed the woman would not bear more of the truth than that. "He only wanted to meet Rose's people."

Mrs. DeMornay dropped her gaze. "I'm sorry."

"I know."

"I have to go." The woman's eyes flicked to the doorway. "I was going to leave the locket at the desk. I can't defy William. If I were to see your husband . . ."

"Go then. He's fetching the wagon."

But she hesitated. "He has her mouth. Wide and generous. Too generous. Rose . . . No, I won't say it."

"She loved deeply."

Tears filled Rose's mother's eyes. "Yes . . . impetuously." She pressed Carina's hands. "As you do, I surmise."

Did she guess that from their short encounter? Did she wear her love for Quillan so blatantly?

"Don't sacrifice that." Mrs. DeMornay released her.

Carina shook her head. "I won't."

"Give Quillan the locket and . . . my love." Mrs. DeMornay's voice shook.

Carina nodded, a lump stopping her speech. She looked down at the photograph in the locket as Mrs. DeMornay passed out the door. Quillan did have his mother's mouth. She closed the locket and folded it into her handkerchief, then put it in her satchel. Straightening her skirts, she went to wait at the door.

When Quillan pulled up in the wagon, she went out. He lifted her up and tucked the satchel behind the seat, exactly as he had the first time they'd met. His expression, too, was reminiscently grim. He had slept poorly, even groaning softly in his sleep. The DeMornays had opened old wounds. She considered the locket tucked secretly in the satchel. Should she give it to him now?

But Mrs. DeMornay's concern had been palpable. And in his current mood Quillan was too unpredictable. He might confront Mr. DeMornay, and where would that leave his grandmother? So Carina said nothing.

Quillan climbed in beside her. "I'm putting you on the train, Carina."

He would start that again? They had argued it last night, but she had not changed her mind. "I want to travel with you."

"The train makes more sense."

And she would arrive home without him. "Then sell your wagon and come with me."

He shook his head. "I need it."

She tossed her hands. "Then drive."

He took up the lines. "At least let me inquire."

"What's to inquire? We can take the train or we can drive. I am not doing either without you."

He stayed silent until they reached the station. Bene. If he would be stubborn, she would, too. She refused to leave the wagon seat when he dismounted and walked to the ticket counter. He would have to bodily remove her.

But when he came back, he eyed her squarely. "How about a compromise?"

She clutched the seat in case it were a ruse. "What compromise?"

"Train's got a car for hauling carriages and such. They'll take the wagon and horses while we ride in the passenger car— together."

Suddenly exuberant, she clasped her hands at her throat. "Then yes! Of course yes!"

He flicked his hat with the tips of his fingers and leaned his elbows on the wagon side with the closest thing to a smile he could manage. "Glad I don't have to pry your hands off that seat."

She tossed her chin. "You only needed to be reasonable." She held out her hand.

Instead of taking it, he caught her waist and swung her down. "It wouldn't have taken much." His grin pulled sideways. "Even with your best grip."

"I would have made a horrible scene."

He cocked his head. "A shame I missed it."

She started to retort, but he sobered and went about readying the wagon. She swallowed her gall. After all, they were taking the train, and that meant she'd be home in days, rather than weeks.

They surrendered the full wagon and horses to a Union Pacific railroad man loading the flatcars and stock cars. She waited while Quillan instructed him pointedly about the horses, then a porter took the bags they would have onboard. Following him, Carina glanced back at the wagon as its wheels were lashed to the car and rendered immobile. She had a brief flash of her own wagon tumbling down the side of the mountain. Quillan's freighter held gifts and reminders as precious as the things she had carried east.

But now they were heading west. She had traveled first class from San Francisco with Guido and Antonnia Mollica, then second class with the maiden aunts Anna and Francesca Bordolino, who thought it sinful to bask in such extravagance and probably couldn't afford it. The second-class car, while not the squalid illness incubator of the emigrant cars, tested one's capacity for discomfort.

She didn't know which tickets Quillan had purchased. Would he think the best extravagant also? They passed the emigrant cars, bleak and stark. Already a smell emanated from the passengers who had been westward bound from the Atlantic coast. Poor people—how could they bear it? But then she thought of herself at Mae's in the beginning. One adapted she supposed, as one must.

Carina breathed a sigh of relief as they passed the shabby third-class coaches interspersed with the baggage cars. She glanced at Quillan as they also passed the second-class day coaches to the elegantly appointed Pullman Palace cars. She raised her brows as he held out a hand for her to mount the stairs. So they would travel first class. Her husband quirked a smile. Was her face so revealing?

They found a pair of plush seats facing each other, and Quillan motioned for the porter to relieve himself of their load. With a night's growth of beard, his buckskin coat, and his hair loose, Quillan drew curious glances from the other passengers. And some not merely curious. The gentlemen at large appraised him, but the ladies seemed to think him an exciting spectacle. In their eastern titters they discreetly pointed him out to each other.

Carina sat down and smiled. Maybe they would think her a daring partner to this western pirate. But she dismissed the thought when she noticed one red-whiskered gentleman perusing her boldly. Suddenly she resented the scrutiny of these coddled sophisticates out for a lark. She had seen them before, well-heeled adventurers traveling west for an excursion. The transcontinental rails of the Union and Central Pacific Railroads joined a decade ago at Promontory Point had made her home their playground.

With hardly any delay, the train headed out of the station. Across from her, Quillan looked out the window, seemingly unaware of the scrutiny—a fact that made him all the more mysterious to the women in their car. Carina couldn't help but see what they saw: a man unlike any other.

Quillan chafed on the train as he hadn't with his own reins in his hands, even though their speed tripled anything his horse-drawn wagon could manage and traveled where he could never have pressed his team. He looked across at his wife, lost in a periodical. She had been reading aloud from *Harper's Weekly*, then had noticed his slack attention and fallen silent.

He rubbed his hands over his knees, unable to catch the pace, the rhythm of the train. Would he rather be traveling the rough stage road that paralleled the iron rails across the land? Rather see Carina with road dust and weariness in her face? At least he'd have that sense of connection. They'd be alone together.

Though the Pullman car allowed space and comfort, he squirmed under the curious gaze of the passengers around them. Carina seemed oblivious, though not a man aboard was oblivious of her. What could he expect? He could hardly go around gouging eyes. At least people gave them space. His visage, no doubt.

Carina glanced up. *"Agitato."*

"What?"

"You're restless. Agitato."

He shrugged.

She closed the magazine. "I thought you liked hours and hours of traveling."

"Alone on my wagon, in the open, with my hands on the reins."

She waved her hand. "Ask the engineer to let you drive."

"No thanks." He stretched his legs out under her seat and crossed his ankles. "Only live animals."

"Antiquato."

"There you go, calling names."

She laid the magazine on the seat beside her. "I said you're old-fashioned."

"Maybe." He uncrossed his ankles and hunched up in his seat. Had his hindquarters ever plagued him so on the box? "But I would be in control."

"Relax for a change. Let life happen."

"I don't like it when life happens."

"*Testardo.*"

He glared. "At least insult me in a language I understand."

"Testardo—stubborn."

"Testardo. Now that one I could use back."

"Then it would be testarda."

He straightened slightly. "So adjectives change form."

She nodded. "To match the noun. Some nouns are feminine, like *saggezza*, wisdom. Others masculine: *disturbo*. Annoyance."

He crooked his brow. "Is there a point?"

She laughed.

He straightened the rest of the way, pressing his back to the seat cushion. "How do you say contrary?"

"Contrario."

"And contraria?"

She waved her hand. "It would never be used that way, of course."

"I sense biased instruction."

"You want to learn?" She flicked her fingers toward him.

He folded his arms across his chest again. "Okay."

She said, *"Buon giorno."*

He repeated it.

She tapped her ear lobe. "You have a good ear."

"Buon giorno means good ear?"

She laughed much harder than his error could have warranted. "It means good day. A polite hello or good-bye."

"Buon giorno." He committed it to memory.

She said, *"Come stai?* How are you?"

Come stai? That, too, went into recall. "And what do I answer?"

The corners of her mouth twitched. "At the moment?"

"Watch it."

Again she laughed. "You say, *Bene.* Fine."

"And all this time I thought you were cursing me."

"It can also mean, *Fine!* or *Well!*" She threw up her hands.

He nodded. "And if I'm not fine?"

"*Male!*"

"Very descriptive."

"Italiano is a beautiful language. *Bella lingua!* And easy. Much more regular than English."

He leaned forward. "In words maybe. But the inflection and sign language . . ." He shook his head.

"What are you talking about, sign language?"

"The hand motions." He caught her hand as it flew by. "I don't think I'll ever get the hand motions."

She tugged, but he held on, laughing. "And the fire of it. Every sentence is exclaimed." He threw up both hands. "Buon giorno! Come stai! Isn't life incredible! I just met you on the street!"

She slapped his knee. "I won't teach you, then."

He settled back. "You can't help it."

"What do you mean?" Her lower lip pouted in pure prima donna irk.

He should stop before she really got mad, but he couldn't resist. "I'll learn whether you intend it or not. It just slips out."

"What slips out?" Her hands formed fists atop her knees.

"Your language." The train wobbled over a rough portion of track. His hat dropped off the hook and landed on the seat. He hung it back up.

"It does not."

"Sure it does. That time in the mine shaft? You talked all night in Italian. And provoke you? Whew! There must be a switch. Gather enough emotion, out comes Italian."

"Omaccio!"

He laughed. "Un gross'uomo."

She slapped the magazine across his knee.

"And that's another thing. Are all the women in your family slappers?"

Her mouth fell open with a huff. Then she snapped it shut and glared.

"Not that I mind. You can't damage this tanned hide. But—"

"Oh!" She threw the magazine flapping into his face.

"And throwing things. I suppose I'll get used to that."

She jumped to her feet just as the train took a sharp turn. Quillan leaped up and caught her waist as she swayed. "It's all right." He addressed the startled faces around them. "Just a cramp." He settled her back down to the seat, looking all fired to spit nails. "Careful, now. Don't want to tumble into some gentleman's lap."

"Certainly not yours!"

"Now, Carina." He laughed.

She crossed her arms and pouted.

He nudged her knee with his. "How do you say *I'm sorry*?"

She looked to the window and clamped her mouth shut.

He leaned across. "Pardon me? Forgive me? Anything like that in Italiano?"

"Mi dispiace." She spoke without looking.

"Mi dispiace for having hurt you." He took her hand. "I deserved the violence."

She sniffed.

"Let's see . . . *bella signora*."

She turned. "What are you trying to say?"

"My wife is the most beautiful woman on the train."

She waved him off with her hand.

"The most wonderful woman I know." He pulled a wry smile.

"You can count on one hand the women you know."

He imitated her gesture. Her eyes flashed. He caught her hand before she could slide to the corner. "Carina, you may not realize it, but your hands are more communicative than words. It's the first thing I loved about you."

"It is?" She softened.

"It is. Your gestures mesmerize me."

"They do?" But now she looked suspicious.

He laughed. "I mean it."

She threw both her hands up. "How would I know? One minute you tease, the next—"

"It's in the eyes, Carina. You have to watch the eyes."

"It's more in your mouth. Sometimes you make your eyes like plates, but your mouth, that's what gives you away." She paused.

Quillan wondered what she was thinking. She reached under her seat for the satchel, drew it up, and plunked it into her lap. Carina reached in and took out a handkerchief. Was she going to cry? Surely he hadn't upset her that much. But she unfolded it and cradled something in her palm.

"What's that?"

She held it out. "It's for you."

"You bought me a locket?" He took the chain and dangled the heavy gold necklace.

"I didn't buy it. Look inside."

He rested the locket on his knee and worked the catch. The lid flipped open. He stared at the photograph inside.

"It's your mother."

He jolted, then shot his gaze to Carina. "Where did you get it?"

"Mrs. DeMornay. She was forbidden to see you, but she risked bringing it to me. She wanted you to have it . . . with her love."

Quillan's hand started to shake. He pressed the back of it to his knee. "I don't understand." Why would the woman give him a picture of his mother when she wouldn't even admit they were related, wouldn't say a word of acknowledgment when her husband denied the possibility, then sent her . . . love? Fury wrapped his heart like a boa constrictor, tightening until there was pain in his chest.

Carina's words rushed on. "The locket was hers. She gave it to you, her grandson. She said you have your mother's mouth."

So she believed him, but wouldn't tell him to his face. Throat tightening, he looked at the photograph. Even allowing for fuzziness in the image, his mother was lovely. And he knew her. Again his infantile mind had captured something and gave it back to him now as memory. He said, "Her eyes were blue. No, green. Something in between, very bright."

Carina smiled.

"And I remember her hair, the feel of it. Like yours." He looked across at his wife. "How can I remember that?"

"It's a gift."

Holding his mother's face in his palm, he searched his mind. "I wish there were more."

"But you have more than you might. You have her picture, and some memory. And your grandmother knows you."

"My grandfather doesn't." Fury flared afresh.

"Mrs. DeMornay said he has to believe Rose died. He deceives himself. Maybe he doesn't know the truth. Or it hurts too much. Maybe it isn't judgment but pain that traps him."

Carina was naïve if she believed that. A man like William DeMornay didn't delude himself. But he might easily delude others. Quillan closed the locket. "When did she give you this?"

"This morning."

"You didn't tell me?" How could Carina keep something like that silent? He hadn't thought she could hide anything, yet he'd had no idea.

Carina waved a hand. "She risked too much bringing it. If you got angry, confronted William DeMornay . . ."

His hand clenched around the locket. He might have done so. Just as he had confronted his foster father, he might have forced DeMornay's hand. "So you reined me in."

She shrugged one shoulder, a girlish gesture that softened his mood. He slid the locket into his coat pocket and sat back in silence.

At last Carina spoke. "Are you angry?"

He shook his head. "No." He could be—with Carina for withholding, his grandmother for conniving, his grandfather for outright rejection—but right now he sensed his mother. Anger would get in the way. He didn't want to lose the feel of her.

Carina sighed. "Maybe I was wrong."

"I'm not angry."

She waved her hand. "I should have told you."

"Carina." He met her eyes. "Could we not talk right now?"

Her hand dropped to her lap. "You are angry."

He dropped his head back. "I just don't want to talk. That's all."

She grabbed the periodical and flipped it open to the page she'd hit him with.

Quillan watched her stare at that page a long while. He felt the weight of the locket against him, the weight of his thoughts, of Carina's concern, and his own hurt that could overwhelm him if he let it. How could he hold it back? He took Cain's Bible from the pack at his feet, held it, then opened to a page Cain had dog-eared in the Psalms. How Cain had loved the Psalms. Quillan read down to the line: *Cast thy burden upon the Lord, and he shall sustain thee.* Again he felt that sense that it was written for him. Was God speaking to him?

Quillan considered the text. It seemed so simple. Just turn over the bad thoughts, the hard feelings, the rage and disappointment. Cast it all on the Lord. But how? He had a beautiful wife and a new life ahead, with more good fortune in his pockets than he deserved, yet the hurt inside him gnawed. They refused to recognize him, and Mrs. DeMornay—Quillan didn't even know her first name—she knew he'd spoken the truth. What was it in him that people spurned? What flaw did they see?

Cast thy burden upon the Lord, and he shall sustain thee. Did he want to turn over the hurt? He'd nursed it so long it was part of him. Most of him. Who was he without it? It drove him, made him fight, made him work, made him succeed. It steeled him for the next rejection. It was all he knew.

Carina gave up pretending to read and watched him. Did she see his resolve to keep the hurt like a grain in his belly, coating and coating it like a treasure forming inside? Was it wrong? Hadn't he surrendered to God in the cave, given over his life? But the Lord had enough burdens from those who couldn't carry them. Quillan would carry his own. As his mother and Wolf had before him. He had a vague sense that those burdens had destroyed them. But he pushed that thought away. His trouble made him strong. He had to be strong.

Twelve

Of all iniquities and sins, judgment I despise.
Enthroned, the self on dais raised, looks down with jaundiced eyes.

— Quillan

CARINA SAW THE HOODED LOOK in Quillan's eyes. He was closed into himself again. Every hurt, it seemed, put him back inside that place she couldn't reach. She should have told him at once, let him handle it as he needed to. Why had she protected Mrs. DeMornay when it was Quillan who mattered?

He brooded now—over her duplicity? She hadn't intended it that way, but how did it appear to Quillan? Why else would he close her out? She had wounded him without thinking, and he withdrew. She sighed. *Signore, make me wise to the ways of my husband.*

He refused to look when a woman approached from one of the other seats, her cheeks pale but with two pink splotches of excitement. "Good morning. Or is it afternoon? I lose all track of time on the rails."

Carina formed a polite smile. "Hello."

The woman rested her hand atop Quillan's seat to balance. "My name is Priscilla Preston." She held out a gloved hand.

Carina clasped it briefly. "I'm Carina DiGratia Shepard."

"Charmed to make your acquaintance." Miss Preston glanced at Quillan, but Carina didn't introduce him. He didn't want to talk. She could sense the storm inside him. In a different mood he would rise and introduce himself, at least attend the conversation for politeness' sake. Not in his current frame of mind; at least that's what his scowl said.

Miss Preston seemed to realize he wasn't going to look her way. "I'm traveling with my aunt to San Francisco."

"My husband and I are going to my home in Sonoma Valley. To my family."

"I'm traveling to a relative, as well." Priscilla brushed at the dust on her sleeve. "Now that Father's gone, I have only Aunt Prudence and a cousin I detest. It's unfortunately to him that we're bound. He's dreadfully dull. Is your family dull?"

Carina raised her brows. Even if she detested a member of her family, she would not tell a stranger such. "No. My family could never be called dull. Numbers alone would prevent that: parents, grandparents, uncles, aunts, and cousins, some so distantly related I don't believe they really are." She smiled. "My papa is a great man. Everyone wants to be family to Angelo Pasquale DiGratia."

Priscilla's lips parted, showing two front teeth turned out like a couple on promenade, the other teeth crowded close behind. "My father was a doctor."

Carina clapped her hands together. "Mine is as well!"

"Really?" Priscilla put her fingers to her cheek. "Father's practice was phrenology. Are you familiar with it?"

Carina bit her lip, searching the things Papa had discussed with her. "It seems . . . did it have to do with the mind?"

"The brain and the skull—certain organs in the brain compelling behaviors, identifiable by physical characteristics." Again she glanced at Quillan. "Father often lectured on Dr. Gall's methodology. He could look at a person on the street and tell you his inclinations and temperament, as well as physical weaknesses and strengths. It's scarcely disputed anywhere now. But, of course, not many are well versed in it."

Carina didn't think Papa was. At least he didn't treat anyone according to that science as far as she knew. He treated what he saw in the body. But it was interesting to think you could tell one's inclinations just by looking. "What characteristics did he look for?"

"May I?" Priscilla waved at the edge of Quillan's seat, then sat daintily when Carina nodded. If Quillan objected, he could have said so. As long as he was being silent and withdrawn, she may as well converse with someone else.

"Well, you see, once you know where certain organs are

located, you can tell by the bumps of the head the strengths and weaknesses in character. For instance, just above the external opening of the ear and extending a little forward and backward above the upper flap of the ear is the organ of destructiveness. If the organ is large, the opening of the ear is depressed. Such a person has the impulse to kill and destroy." Her eyelids fluttered quickly with the words. "A small endowment there causes a soft character. Combativeness is right about here." She touched the side of her head. "Hindus are especially lacking in that organ."

Carina had certainly not heard this before. If Papa was versed in phrenology, it was not something he discussed. She folded her hands across her knee. "Tell me more."

"In the back of the head is the organ responsible for philoprogenitiveness."

"Philo—"

"A love of one's offspring. It causes the bulge in the skull for those well endowed. People with flat perpendicular heads are annoyed, rather than delighted, by children."

Carina noticed Priscilla's flat head partly disguised by the wrapping of her thin blond hair. Did that mean she disdained children? How strange to think you knew someone by the shape of her head. She glanced at Quillan. If he heard the conversation he showed no sign.

Miss Preston was still talking. "Beneath the posterior edge of the parietal bone is found adhesiveness, the faculty which prompts—"

"Wait now." Carina waved her hand. "How do they know what's in the brain beneath the skull?"

"By studying the brain, of course. As I was saying, that's where you'll find the faculty of adhesiveness, the desire to embrace, to find joy in friendship and constancy in marriage."

Carina said, "What does it look like?"

Priscilla paused. "Well, I can't exactly say. It took years for Father to develop his expertise. I only understand the idea and recognize some of the more outstanding characteristics."

Carina sat back. Was there validity in this woman's suppositions?

Priscilla shrugged. "How else do you account for the differences in types?"

"What types do you mean?" And now Carina was curious

again. She was sure Papa had not spoken in such terms.

"Why the bilious, the nervous, sanguine, and lymphatic. Doesn't your father gauge his treatments by these temperaments?"

"I don't know."

"Surely he must if he's any kind of reputable doctor." She took a scented handkerchief from her pocket and sniffed daintily, then dabbed her throat. "The four types were identified years ago. But Dr. Bell's phrenology was the key, you see."

Carina didn't see, but she was willing to listen.

"The types are manifested not only by which body systems predominate, as was formerly believed, but by which faculties in the brain are preeminent."

"But how do you know these types?"

"That's simple. The nervous temperament is marked by silky thin hair, thin skin and muscles, paleness, and often, delicate health. Due to a less robust physique, the mind is vitally active. It is the temperament of genius and refinement."

Carina noted Priscilla was describing herself. "And the others?"

"The bilious temperament has a determined disposition, black hair, dark eyes and skin, firmness of flesh. An energetic brain manifestation suited to enduring much mental and bodily labor."

The physical characteristics were her own, Carina mused, but did that mean she was a workhorse?

"The sanguine are moderately plump, red haired, ruddy. Fond of outdoor exercise. The lymphatic: corpulent, fair skinned, weak, and slow. The brain is also feeble in function."

Carina thought of Mae. There was nothing feeble in her brain, and she was as strong and vital as anyone Carina knew. She settled back against the seat, certain now she'd been served a dose of quackery.

"Then, of course, there are any number of combinations."

But Carina had heard enough. "What happened to your father?"

"Yellow fever. His temperament, of course, was the nervous type. He lacked the constitution to battle the disease as a more hardy, less brilliant type might have." She sighed. "So I must travel to my cousin and place myself under his protection. Aunt

Prudence and I can hardly hope to support ourselves as we're accustomed."

Carina supposed Priscilla was lacking in adhesiveness as well as philo ... whatever that word was that meant she didn't like children, or she might consider marrying.

"Well." Priscilla straightened. "Auntie's getting agitated." She indicated a thin woman with equally bulging eyes. "I'd better go." She hesitated, as though expecting to be retained, then whisked back to her seat.

Carina looked at Quillan. "What did you think of that business?"

He frowned. "I wonder which bump governs gab."

So he had been listening. Carina smiled. "It must go along with genius in the nervous type."

He leaned forward to take her hand in his. "I prefer my bilious wife. I'll get more work from her."

Carina snatched her hand away. "The very thought! No wonder some people think they can lord it over others. Because someone is heavy or dark—why, if she knew how silly and patronizing she sounded—"

"She wouldn't care. She has it all figured out. There's no changing that sort's mind. Trust me." Quillan settled back, again wearing his surly scowl. Carina read his mood, felt him withdraw. Would that always be his way? She sighed.

But before they could settle into silence, another woman approached, perhaps emboldened by Miss Preston's attempt to draw them into the social interaction of the Pullman crowd. She made no pretense at Carina, but spoke directly to Quillan. "How do you do, sir. Are you a sporting man?"

Carina looked over the small-framed woman and wondered what sport she could possibly mean. After the last conversation she would be surprised at nothing.

Quillan turned, and that was all the invitation the woman needed, apparently. She took out a deck of cards and raised her eyebrows. "Poker or vingt-et-un?"

Quillan's mouth quirked. "Neither, thank you. My wife and I are conversing."

The woman glanced Carina's way, shrugged, and passed on to the next seats.

Carina said, "Conversing? I thought you didn't want to talk."

Quillan returned his attention to Carina. "I certainly don't want to squander cash on a lady cardsharp."

So that was it. The three gentlemen in the next seat didn't seem to have such qualms. The woman had insinuated herself among them and was shuffling with agile, dainty fingers. For the next half hour Carina watched her win hand after hand as the men's faces grew longer and darker with each.

Carina scrutinized her husband. "How did you know she would win?"

"She cheats."

"What do you mean?"

"No sharp is without a marked deck or extra cards in a lacy sleeve or any number of tricks. Only a fool would accept that offer."

"Or three."

The woman was being asked to leave. Not so politely, either. A moment later another game started in the back corner of the car, near the retiring room located behind the curtain. A corpulent man brushed aside the curtain and joined the game, adjusting the waist of his breeches. Several curious parties looked on. Were they all gullible? How did Quillan know the woman was a cheat?

"Can you see her tricks?"

Quillan shook his head. "I've never spent enough time at the tables to learn them, nor do I suppose I'd catch on quickly. I only know enough not to be taken in."

"It comes from a distrustful nature."

He declined his head in agreement. "Guilty. But why should I trust before someone proves trustworthy?"

Carina smiled. "I should take lessons from you. Trusting everyone leads to trouble."

The train whistle blew, and Quillan stretched, then looked out the window. "Cheyenne station. We need to change trains." They had headed almost due north from Denver. Now they would go west. He started gathering their things for the porter. "I'll need to see that the wagon is transferred. Are you hungry?"

She nodded, looking out the window as the train pulled to a stop. Though the largest and most important city in the Wyoming territory, the ramshackle town of Cheyenne looked as though it had blown in from the vast, windswept land and snagged like tumbleweeds along the tracks.

"Come on." Quillan took her arm and angled her through the other disembarking passengers. Carina headed for the public diner while Quillan made arrangements for the horses and wagon.

As she walked toward the station, she watched the other passengers rush to transfer their baggage, take care of any other needs, and grab food in the scant time allotted. The stops, she was learning, were orchestrated to cause the most panic in the least amount of time. The crowd around the rectangular counter that surrounded the servers was a hive, people darting in between bodies to place and snatch their orders, paying before the food was transferred to their hands.

She tried twice to gain the counter, then pressed her arms to her sides in frustration. A moment later Quillan touched the small of her back. "Step away, Carina." He shouldered his way through, then raised two plates of food over the heads of those seated. He found for her a stool at a tall side table and stood beside her with his plate in hand.

Carina examined the fare. It was boiled eggs with a strip of beefsteak and fried potatoes. There was no time to consider quality. First-class passenger or not, if she didn't gulp it down in the remaining ten minutes, she'd go hungry. The food was not bad, but as one accustomed to savoring her meals, the experience left her giddy. Quillan had barely acquired them a cup of coffee each when the train whistle blew. It was too hot to gulp, so Carina sucked a few desperate sips from the top, then left the rest.

"I feel like I'm riding a tornado." She hurried behind him to a larger train even more elegantly appointed with brass trim and fittings. It shrilled its whistle as they approached. Carina choked in the smoke and cinders that wafted from its smokestack on a gust of wind. She caught a glimpse of the Miss Prestons likewise switching trains. With her wrap billowing out and her skirts flapping against her legs, the elder aunt looked like a bewildered prairie fowl. No doubt Priscilla would have a reason for that, some bump on her poor aunt's head. Another gust blasted. Carina tasted dust and felt it on her teeth. That was one thing about traveling by train. One never escaped the dust.

The Pullman coach was arranged much as the last had been, though the seat pairs were separated by curtains, and she noticed that this one had upper berths that pulled out for sleeping. The wood ceiling was polished as shiny as a mirror and ornamented with moldings, with a stained-glass design in the center. Carina took it all in at a glance as Quillan vouchsafed their seats.

Once settled, she dug into her valise for toothbrush and powder, though she'd scarcely had time to chew her meal. She headed for the curtained retiring room at the back of the car. When her teeth were scrubbed clean, she scrutinized them and mentally pronounced them strong, white, and well aligned. She meant to keep them that way. Whatever other travails she faced, losing her teeth would not be one. She was just bilious enough to make sure of it.

Carina returned to Quillan. He was watching Priscilla Preston carry on across the aisle with a new audience. As he listened to a new list of brain organs and their corresponding characteristics, his face changed from bemused to irritated. He turned. "How widely held is that phrenology, do you think?"

Carina shrugged. "I'd heard of it only."

Quillan seemed disproportionately irked. He frowned. "If people judge so easily by the outward appearance of someone's head or any other such nonsense . . ." He frowned and didn't finish.

But she knew what he meant. Glancing down, she saw his mother's locket in his palm. He was still stinging. And wondering. Did people look at him and find something undesirable? Impossible! But she herself had done so. She'd seen a rogue—a handsome, heartless blackguard. But inside he was vulnerable, caring. Why couldn't he show it?

She said, "We all judge by what we see. Maybe not head bumps or complexion, but expression, perhaps, or comportment."

Quillan shook his head. "It shouldn't be that way. People shouldn't judge without knowing."

"But, Quillan, God gave us the capacity to discern, to intuit." She leaned toward him. "And we choose the face we want to show."

He looked at her. "Not you."

"What do you mean?"

"You show it all," he said. "Everything you think, everything you feel, everything you want is right there for all the world to see. You're so real it . . . it hurts."

She squeezed his hand holding the locket. "I don't want it to hurt."

He said nothing more. After a while he turned back to the

window, which left her vulnerable when Priscilla Preston returned.

She looked toward Quillan, though she spoke to Carina. "Do you think we'll see bandits?"

"Bandits?" Carina raised her brows. The woman certainly chose the strangest topics.

"You know, train robbers, highwaymen. Like Black Bart, the poet? Or Sam . . . Oh, what was his name? I never can remember his last name."

"Bass. Like the fish."

"Yes, that's it. Anyway what are the chances someone will rob the express box, do you think?" Miss Preston's eyes took on a queer glow.

"Not high, I think." Carina had seen enough lawlessness to last a lifetime. The last thing she wanted was a notorious outlaw keeping her from home. Dime stories of gunfighters and robbers like Black Bart who left a poem in place of the contents of the express box might thrill someone like Priscilla Preston, but having had her own pockets pinched and nearly ending up in a noose for her involvement with Berkley Beck, a man as unscrupulous as any train robber, Carina was not intrigued with the thought.

"What about Indians? They've been known to derail trains."

Where was she getting her information? "It's been a long time since that has happened."

"Can't you envision anything thrilling to break the monotony of this bleak landscape?" Miss Preston stared disdainfully at the never-ending plains of Wyoming passing at a tedious pace. "Why go west if it's as tame as anywhere else?"

"I'm sure you'll find plenty of excitement in San Francisco."

"Oh, balls and galas, I know." Miss Preston tossed her head. "I want something dangerous."

"Try walking the streets after dark."

Miss Preston turned to her, one eyelid lowered. "I'm not stupid." And now she looked at Quillan. "I'm certain if anything does happen to the train, Mr. Shepard will protect us."

Quillan turned slowly and leveled his gaze. "What makes you sure of that, Miss Preston?"

She tipped her head, obviously pleased to have drawn him out at last. "I've heard about you western men. Not smart and natty like our swells, but rough and ready to the quick. Am I right?"

Quillan eyed her so long, she started to fidget. Carina knew how it felt. He said, "What do the bumps on my head show?"

"Well . . ." Her eyes traveled up his face. "It's hard to say with all that hair." The tip of her tongue moistened her lips. "But I'd guess at a certain lack of restraint. A small propensity for violence, perhaps. Am I right?"

His eyes turned to flint, and Carina trembled. Would he do something rash? He was irked enough, she was sure. Had Miss Preston singled him out as the most dangerous and therefore interesting potential of the moment? Was she intentionally baiting him?

"Someone of your genius need ask?"

Carina winced at his sarcasm, but Miss Preston merely basked. She didn't understand Quillan's caustic nature, another mark against her theory. If it were so obvious, wouldn't she see Quillan was baiting her back?

"What do you do, Mr. Shepard?" Her eyes darted quickly down the length of his frame. "Buffalo hunter? Indian agent? No, wait, your wife said you were from a mining town. I bet you were a hired gun."

Quillan didn't answer.

"Oh, there's no need for embarrassment. That's simply thrilling. Did you ever kill a man?"

Had her morbid curiosity no limit? Without a flicker of emotion Quillan said, "Only women . . . who talk too much."

Carina caught her breath.

Miss Preston's eyelids parted, the whole of her blue irises slightly bulging, but she laughed. "Well! Maybe I'll see something more interesting, after all, than the polygamists in Salt Lake. Are you taking the train from Ogden into the Mormon city?"

Carina shook her head. "We weren't planning on it."

But Quillan said, "Why should I see another man's wives when I've plenty of my own?"

"You haven't." Miss Preston's finger just touched her out-turned teeth.

Quillan shrugged. "Of course they're all squaws."

Miss Preston stared, obviously doubtful, yet not certain he was in jest. Carina could almost hear her thoughts. Would he, could he, be serious? Indian wives. Well, wasn't he just the sort? And then she shivered. Perhaps even Miss Preston had her limits.

"You'll have to excuse me now. I must see to my aunt. I've left her too long."

Carina watched her hasten back to her seat, then turned to Quillan. "Omaccio."

His rogue's smile. "Indeed."

Thirteen

Fair play: Conformity to established rules, no matter how unfair.

— *Quillan*

SPARRING WITH MISS PRESTON had annoyed Quillan enough that he could not slip back into his reverie. He felt no stake in the conflict as he had with Carina in their early skirmishes, but the woman's ideas had gotten under his skin. He didn't realize he was brooding until Carina mentioned dinner and he noticed the time had passed. He should apologize for being such poor company, but Carina seemed to understand as he stood and led her through the cars.

He pushed opened the final door. One look told him the Pullman Hotel Express dining car was an extreme improvement over the station diners. With his stomach signaling anticipation, Quillan seated Carina at a flower-adorned table with damask cloth. The aromas rivaled even Carina's cooking. Almost as soon as he'd seated his wife, Quillan found a white-jacketed server at his elbow.

The man handed them menus. "Wine list, mistuh?"

Quillan shook his head. "Just something to fill the space between my ribs and backbone."

But Carina looked eagerly over the list and said, "Look. Here is one of Haraszthy's wines."

"Someone you know?" He looked over the fancy printing of the page.

"A very famous viticulturist. One of the first in Sonoma. We must try a bottle."

"Choose what you like." Quillan looked over the food selections, finding few with which he was readily acquainted. He read the frilled offers of blue-winged teal, antelope steaks, boiled ham and tongue, fresh trout. There was pheasant and plover in a choice of sauces. Corn on the cob and fresh fruit. Filling his space would be a pleasure.

He glanced up at Carina. Was she used to such finery? She certainly looked the part, though his lace collar and amethyst pin contributed. Not that she needed ornamentation. Next to Carina, Miss Priscilla Preston was limp lettuce. But he didn't want to kill his appetite thinking of that one.

They ordered, and the food was everything it claimed. Carina took dainty bites of her browned trout with hardly a bone to be found. Quillan's pheasant in caper sauce was tender and savory, the corn kernels plump and buttery on the cob. He just might enjoy himself and forget the cloud of rejection and unease, the brooding over the DeMornay's treatment of his mother.

A young gentleman approached the table, hands in his silk-embroidered vest. "May I make your acquaintance, sir? I'm William Scott Bennet, assistant prosecuting attorney, Boston."

Quillan stood and shook the man's hand. Even beyond the discrepancy in dress, there was no question of the disparity in their stations. What could this young man want with him? "Quillan Shepard at your service."

"I understand you're a bit of a hand with a gun, sir."

Quillan hardly needed to guess where that information came from. But what was the man's point?

"Several of us are putting together a shoot in the morning. Care to join in?"

"What's your target?"

"Prairie fowl, antelope, and buffalo, if luck is with us." He took one hand from his vest and balanced himself on the back of Carina's seat for the turn. "We'll be shooting from the parlor car."

Quillan eyed the popinjay. "How will you retrieve your plunder?"

The man smiled. "That would be a trick, wouldn't it? But join us, won't you? We'd like to make it a contest, try our hands against a gunman."

Quillan stiffened. Miss Prescott had obviously been prolific of tongue. He should not have misled her. Though he did have his gun in the travel bag, he had no intention of becoming a spectacle. "I'm afraid I must decline."

"But, sir, it will be the high point of our jaunt. How better to test our sportsman's abilities than with a master? And surely we'll give you a bit of a run."

Quillan glanced at Carina, then back. "I'm afraid you've been misled."

Mr. Bennet laughed. "No need to be bashful, sir. I'm young, but astute. Part of the job, you know, reading character."

Quillan tensed. There it was again. Judged by appearances. He had a sudden desire to put this upstart in his place. "What time?"

"Eight o'clock on the nose."

Quillan nodded, then turned back to Carina.

She raised her brows. "You're doing it?"

He shrugged.

"What if you lose?"

"Then Mr. William Scott Bennet will have a story to tell."

She sat back and eyed him. "But you won't lose, will you?"

Quillan picked up his knife and ran the blade through the sauce pooled at the edge of his plate. "I haven't seen them shoot."

"But I've seen you. You took the head off a rattlesnake with one bullet shooting from the holster."

"Reflex."

She looked askance. "Another might have shot off his own foot. How did you learn?"

Quillan stared down at his plate. "After I left home, I realized how vulnerable I was, a boy of fourteen with little muscle and less experience. I'd been taken in by someone just a little older, a little wilier. I knew I wouldn't let that happen again, but what of someone stronger, deadlier? So I purchased a side arm and taught myself to use it."

"To use it well."

"Came fairly naturally." He gave her a quick grin. "Just like for you."

"Beh." She flicked her chin with her fingers.

He definitely needed to learn that gesture. It was so descriptive. "Have you finished eating?"

"Yes."

"Then I suggest we retire." He led her back to their seats, reached up and pulled down the upper berth and fixed it into place, then rearranged the two facing seats to make a lower berth. Neither would hold both of them, and even with the curtains it would be uncouth. "Have you a preference?"

Carina looked up at the berth over her head. "I'll take the lower."

He unfolded the blankets provided, tossed one up for himself, then arranged hers. He pulled the curtains closed around them, drew her into his arms and kissed her. Then he climbed to the upper berth and removed his coat and vest and shirt. He laid them carefully beside him, then settled down onto the pillow. Looking up he saw his own face clearly, and that of the woman in the next berth over. It was the elderly Miss Preston, and she obviously had no notion of his view in the polished ceiling. She read a small book, *Fireside Tales*, her bespectacled eyes straining to read the print in the insufficient light.

Quillan turned discreetly to his side, thankful Carina was not atop where the man at footside would glimpse her. Something to remember if he ever traveled the Pullman Palace car again.

The air was brisk, the wind gusty as the party opened the side doors of the parlor car and assembled along the narrow balcony for the shoot. Carina counted four men armed for the sport, but many others had collected to watch. Quillan was in his buckskin, with another day's growth on his face. Rogue pirate, indeed.

Miss Preston pushed in close to her. "Isn't this fun? I hope they find enough game to make a good contest. Will your husband win, do you think?"

Carina shrugged. "I don't know the rules."

"First to spot, first to shoot claims the prize. If they hit it, of course. That man in the brown chesterfield and gaiters is keeping the score."

Carina eyed the sandy-haired man with a pad of paper ready, wearing white pantaloons covered to the knee in leather gaiters. He seemed a bit of a popinjay.

"He's a newspaperman." Miss Preston said. "I wouldn't be surprised if you see your husband's name in print. Supposing he wins, of course." She licked her finger and held it up. "Wind is from the west."

Carina didn't point out that the train's own motion caused

that eastward breeze, and the gusts buffeted the side of the cars from the north. Not quite the genius she thought herself, that Miss Preston. Quillan stood ready with the others, armed with his Colt .45, his Winchester rifle leaning on the wall beside him. The side arm hung holstered at his hip as she'd seen it first. He hadn't worn it since the demise of the roughs made his passage in and out of Crystal less dangerous. But she knew he carried it with him.

The crowd chattered until a yell of fowl and a shot rang out. It was William Scott Bennet who took aim and fired at a plover that took to the sky at the train's passing. He must have failed to account for the train's motion, for his shot missed. A moment later Quillan took down a second plover that plummeted from its startled ascent. Bennet frowned, but the crowd cheered.

"Waste of good meat," Quillan said.

Miss Preston tittered. "Did you see him draw? He drew from his holster faster than I could see."

Carina nodded. "He once shot the head from a striking rattle-snake." Perhaps it wasn't striking, but it might have been.

Miss Preston's eyes did their spread and bulge. She turned swiftly and fixated on Quillan once again. In a short while someone hollered again and fired at a dusty brown blob not far from the train.

Quillan turned with a scowl. "There's no sport in prairie dogs."

But the scorekeeper counted it, so there were four more shots before the rest ducked underground. Quillan refused to shoot. A kestrel darted up from a ravine and Quillan hollered, "Falcon," and shot. Both it and the mouse in its talons crashed to the ground.

"That should count for two," someone hollered. "Brought down two with one shot."

The scorekeeper agreed. Now Quillan was tied with the youth who'd shot three of the prairie dogs. The train was approaching a trellis over the same ravine, and everyone stopped for a moment to watch. It seemed such a rickety contrivance could never support the mighty, chugging steel monster, but it did. Directly beyond the ravine a herd of antelope bounded, their delicate white and tawny forms leaping.

Quillan shouted, "Antelope," and brought one down with his Winchester rifle.

The others started shooting randomly, decimating the herd trapped between the tracks and the ravine.

The scorekeeper raised his hands. "No credit without acknowledging the target."

Quillan jerked the rifle from one young man's hands. "Enough!"

"I say." Bennet got between them. "What's the harm?"

"People depend on those animals for food."

"People?" Bennet raised his brows.

One woman laughed. "Didn't you see it on the menu last night?"

"That's not what he means." The speaker was the short, round-headed fourth man of the shooting party. "He means Mr. Lo, the noble savage."

"He's concerned about Indians?"

Carina saw the warning signs in Quillan's face. Whether he spoke for the Indian tribes or not, the sport had gone too far. He would not participate in slaughter. He reached for his rifle and started toward her when more shots came.

The scorekeeper looked bewildered. "Who fired?"

But at that moment Carina realized the shots had not come from the train. A half dozen horsemen galloped toward them. Two split off toward the engine, and the others came alongside the caboose. The first rider caught hold and jumped aboard. Quillan pushed his way inside, but it was not haven he sought.

Carina rushed toward him. "Don't go, Quillan. There are too many."

He didn't answer, just pressed her hand, then turned to the others. "If you want to put your shooting to better use, come now."

"That's crazy!" The young man who'd shot the prairie dogs balked. "They'll take the Express and leave us in peace."

"No guarantees of that." A hefty bearded man reached into his coat for a Sharps four-barrel pepperbox similar to the one Quillan had bought Carina. She recognized the shape and grip. "The last time this happened they went through each one of us, women included. Took everything valuable we had."

That sobered the whole group.

Miss Preston's gaze intensified. "Would they?"

Even as she spoke the train began grinding to a halt. Grabbing hold of the posts as they were swept forward against one another, everyone started talking at once. This gang apparently would not be satisfied with the Express car. Otherwise why stop the train?

Quillan nodded to the man with the Sharps. "Anyone else with me?"

Bennet and his three friends looked at each other, then stepped forward. Quillan reloaded his Colt as he spoke. "We'll split up. There's a Wells Fargo agent in the Express car. He'll be armed and ready, but he's only one man. We'll need someone to go forward and cover the ones holding the engineer and fireman. If they're complying, they probably won't be hurt, but we can't take that chance."

Bennet said, "I'll go," raised his rifle, and pressed through the crowd.

A gunshot sounded from the back of the train, and Quillan's face hardened. "Let's go!" He holstered the Colt and snatched up his Winchester.

"But what are we doing?" The balking youth caught his arm.

"We'll contain them to the Express car or take them out from there."

"Take them out?"

But Quillan was already moving into the small space between cars. Carina watched him go, her heart turning to lead. This couldn't be happening. Quillan would take on armed outlaws? His sense of justice had already been piqued. Now it sought release. But at what cost?

The newspaperman in the chesterfield coat was unarmed but hurried after those who were. Carina felt paralyzed, one hand to her heart. *Oh, Signore.* But before she could finish her prayer, Miss Preston clutched her arm.

"Will he stop them? Will he keep them from coming in?"

At last she was showing a healthy fear. "I don't know."

Miss Preston's eyelids pulled wide. "Did you get a look at them? At any of them?"

"Not closely." And now Carina realized it wasn't fear but excitement on Miss Preston's face.

"Come on." The woman pulled her forward.

"What are you doing?"

"I want to see for myself."

Carina tugged free. "This is not a show." She wanted to slap the woman. "People could die. My husband could die."

But whatever macabre curiosity held Priscilla Preston compelled her forward. Carina shivered. Her desire for excitement could endanger them all. Carina hurried after her.

Quillan led his companions through the first passenger car where people sat, white-faced, having heard the gunshots. At the end of the second car, he pressed close to the wall beside the door, gun at the ready, listening to the quiet that followed the shots. The other men divided up on both sides.

Quillan chafed. He had good horses and a wagon that held far more than Carina's trinkets. His life's work in the form of cash and bank notes was in a strongbox nailed to the underside. He wasn't about to lose any of it. More than that, lives were at stake. "That Wells Fargo man can't stand alone."

The men shared glances. Quillan read their fear. "Keep guard here at the door. I'm going through."

"I'm with you." It was the man with the Sharps.

Quillan looked at him. "What's your name?"

"Sam Tillory."

"Someone give Sam a rifle."

The contestant with sandy lamb chop whiskers handed his over, and he took the Sharps. Quillan raised his own Winchester. His Colt was loaded at his hip, but nothing spoke as loudly as a rifle aimed at the chest.

"There are four of them." The young man who'd shot the prairie dogs raised his own Remington rifle. "I'll come, too."

"Are you sure?" Quillan searched the man's eyes. Though he saw fear and insecurity, he also saw determination. "All right." Quillan started through the door. One of the outlaws rode alongside the train, probably communicating between those holding the engineer and the others robbing the freight. At the moment he was passing forward away from them.

Quillan crept from one car to the other with Sam Tillory and the other, whose name he'd neglected to learn, right behind. Two of the gunmen had worked the side doors of the freight car open. Probably the gunshot they'd heard. A third was in there also.

Quillan cracked the end door just enough to see what was happening inside.

"There's no way I'm turning over this box." The Wells Fargo man stood with a rifle poised.

"Don't be stupid. We've four guns to your one."

Quillan jolted at the voice. He couldn't see the speaker, who must be the one mounted outside the car. But he knew him. He left the door and eased over to the edge of the car. Removing his hat, he peeked around the side. The black kerchief over mouth and nose only enhanced his recognition—Shane Dennison, looking exactly as he'd seen him last, half a lifetime ago.

Quillan's heart pounded. What were the odds of meeting up with his "friend" who'd staged the bank robbery and left him, a fourteen-year-old fool, to take the fall? But then, was it such a long way from robbing banks in Laramie to robbing trains on the Wyoming plains? His hands tightened on the rifle. His Winchester '73 was a .44-40 with a center-fire cartridge. Powerful and accurate. Swallowing the tightness in his throat, he moved back toward the door, then pushed it open with the barrel of his rifle.

One of the outlaws saw the motion and jerked his gun from the Wells Fargo agent toward Quillan. "Stop right there!" he hollered.

Quillan stopped but pushed the door fully open with his foot to let his partners be seen, guns at the ready. "What we have here is a Mexican standoff." Quillan said it loudly enough to be heard by the man outside the train car. And now he had full view of Shane Dennison.

The man stared up in disbelief. "Quillan?"

Quillan didn't answer, mostly because his fury and disgust were choking him.

Dennison's eyes smiled above the kerchief. "Well, I'll be hog-swallowed. Here I thought we were in trouble."

"No trouble if you take your men and go. Or do you still leave them behind?"

Dennison cocked his head. "Now, that was not my fault. If you'd have followed orders—"

"I'm giving them now." Quillan saw Dennison's eyes spark, and he slid his finger to the trigger. "Clear out before people get hurt."

"Are you threatening me?" Dennison's own finger twitched.

He'd been a terrible shot, but that was fourteen years ago, when Quillan had been impressed by his august age of eighteen and every honeyed word that proceeded from his mouth. Fourteen years was time enough to develop skill with a weapon, especially when it appeared he used it for his livelihood.

The other men were looking tense and uncertain. Quillan knew the longer they waited the tighter the nerves would get. He glanced quickly at the agent, who seemed relieved to have backup but not sure where to go from there.

"This is not your day, Shane. Call off your men and go." Quillan wasn't sure why he assumed Dennison was in control, except that his was the bully personality always taking the fore.

"Why don't you step over and disarm that agent? We could use another hand. Give me a chance to make up for the last time." Dennison made his voice reasonable, but Quillan almost laughed. Two parts gall, one part stupidity—that was Shane Dennison.

"There's payroll in that box, Quillan." Again the eyes smiled.

"Pay that other men have earned."

One of Dennison's party laughed, but Shane didn't. "So you're a bleeding heart now. Sure a long way from the reverend's personal devil."

Quillan heard hooves. In a moment there'd be another gun to face. He stepped inside the car and aimed his rifle at Dennison's chest. "Time to move on."

"To move you on—to the next life." Dennison raised his gun and fired.

Carina's heart seized like a fist clenched as gunfire exploded in the next car. *Per favore, Signore, per piacere, keep my husband safe, keep them all safe.*

Miss Preston rushed between the seats to the window. The outlaws' horses stood empty-saddled, except the one man galloping from the front. "Yoo-hoo." Miss Preston tapped the window, waving at the outlaw on horseback. "Hey, look over here. I want to see your face."

The man spun and fired, splintering the wood beside the window. Carina flung herself at Miss Preston, slamming her into the wall, then dragging her down. "Are you crazy? *Pazzesca?* You want to get someone killed?"

Priscilla Preston's skin flushed fiery red. Her eyes bulged farther than ever. "Get off me this instant. I want to see his face."

Carina looked at her aghast. "Come to your senses!"

But Miss Preston struggled free and ran for the door and through it. Carina stared in disbelief. As the outlaws scrambled to their horses and galloped away, one last gunman emerged from the freight car and leaped to his horse, firing wildly. He took a bullet in the chest and fell, but not before Miss Preston crumpled on the tiny balcony. Two men reached out and dragged her inside. Her shoulder was bloody, and she shrieked, then flipped her head side to side, moaning.

Reluctantly, Carina knelt and took Miss Preston's head in her lap. "Is anyone a doctor? See if there's a doctor on board."

A man rushed to check the other cars. Carina wanted to scold and scream at Miss Preston. Genius indeed. How could anyone be so stupid? But Carina had no emotion to spare. Where was Quillan? *Signore!* She stared at the door flapping open and shut. The one opposite on the Express car was splintered. She could see motion inside, but little more.

A man pressed in to where she knelt, and Carina recognized a doctor's authority. "Hold her head up," he said.

Carina adjusted it in her lap. He pulled on Miss Preston's eyelids and felt her pulse. Then he tore her dress at the shoulder seam and checked the wound. Carina looked on with no squeamishness. She'd seen plenty of blood. The bullet looked to have entered beneath the clavicle, but whether it had lodged against the scapula or passed through she couldn't tell.

Carina had a desperate urge to drop Miss Preston and find her husband. But she held on as the doctor urged the shoulder up and searched for an exit wound. Finding none he said, "I'll have to cut." He looked into Carina's face. "Perhaps someone else . . ."

"I have assisted surgeries." She could hardly believe she had said it. Why should she succor Priscilla Preston? And where was Quillan? What if he, too, lay injured . . . or dead? She started to shake, but it wasn't at the thought of the doctor's knife.

Miss Preston began to thrash, and the doctor ordered, "Hold her while I prepare." He went to his bag and began assembling instruments.

There was a commotion behind her, and Carina turned. Quillan entered with his companions. He supported the groundhog shooter, whose leg was bloody above the knee, but whose face was kindled with pride. Quillan's own sleeve was bloody and torn, but he was alive. *Grazie, Signore!*

Quillan eased his injured man onto a seat. Then he looked down at Miss Preston and frowned. "How—"

"She went outside to watch." Carina tried not to sound as disdainful as she felt. It was not for her to judge.

A minute later Bennet rushed in from the other end of the car. "They got away. I fired some shots, but the two at the front rode away."

Quillan looked out the window. "One fell. But I think he's past the doctor's help."

"What about the agent?" someone asked.

Quillan glanced back at the Express car. "He's standing. But I don't think he would have been for long. He wouldn't turn over the box. It's a cinch they'd have shot him."

Carina's heart swelled. Quillan had saved the man's life. There seemed three types of men: those who took life, those who saved it, and those who wouldn't risk either.

The older Miss Preston rushed into the car with a handkerchief to her mouth. "Oh! My niece!"

A portly matron circled her with an arm. "There, now. The doctor's tending her."

As she spoke, the doctor held a cloth dampened with chloroform to Priscilla Preston's nose and mouth. Carina recognized the odor and held her breath, then felt the woman slacken. Then the doctor brought out his scalpel and the probe with a tiny scooplike shape at the end to remove the slug. It took only a few minutes. Then he treated the wound against infection with carbolic acid. Again Carina recognized the odor and the process. She doubted this doctor wasted his time reading the bumps on people's heads. After he had bound the wound with clean bandages, two men lifted Miss Preston to a berth and closed the curtains around her and her aunt.

Next the doctor moved his operation to Quillan's companion. "What's your name, son?"

"Miles Chapen Smith."

"Well, Mr. Smith, it appears the bullet passed through the muscle of your thigh, exiting here."

The man winced. "Then at least I'm spared the surgery."

"You are indeed. And you're a lucky man. Farther to the left it might have severed an artery."

The man blanched. "Well, we gave those rascals the rout, didn't we?" He looked up at Quillan with adulation.

Quillan quirked his mouth. "We did."

He suddenly gripped Quillan's hand. "Thank you. For pushing me aside."

Bennet shook his head. "And I thought I was taking the dangerous assignment."

Quillan met his gaze. "We all did our part. Maybe they'll think twice before hitting this line again."

The Wells Fargo agent came in behind them. "I've secured the car, but I want to personally thank you men." He looked at Quillan and lowered his brows. "You know the gang?"

Carina startled. How could Quillan know those men?

"Just the one. A long time ago."

The agent eyed him a long moment. "When we get to the station, I'll need your statement for my report. Can you make an identification?"

"His name is Shane Dennison. I don't know if he goes by it still."

"They might have papers on him. They might not. Anything you can tell us will help." The agent glanced at Quillan's bloody arm. "Hit bad?"

"Grazed."

Carina sighed her relief. She hadn't wanted to see the doctor dig a bullet from Quillan's flesh. She had already imagined too many horrors. The train began to move as the doctor disinfected and bound Mr. Smith and Quillan's wounds.

Then Carina took her seat once again across from her husband. "Does your arm hurt?"

"Burns a little." Quillan eyed the bandage over the slit the slug had dug through the side of his arm.

"You could have been killed."

"I wasn't."

Carina saw defiance in his eyes. Not the morbid affection Miss Preston bore danger, but akin to it, as though he willingly pitted himself against death, accepting either outcome. She shivered. There were depths to her husband she could not fathom.

"Go ahead." His voice was low.

"What?"

"Ask." He shifted his seat.

Had he read her thoughts? "How did you know him?"

"He's the one who left me to take the fall for his robbery at the bank in Laramie."

Carina raised her brows, recalling the brief angry explanation he'd given her before, how as a boy he'd been taken in and betrayed. Another rejection.

"I was impressed by him once. Now he's just a worm."

Carina sighed. "To people like Miss Preston he's a hero."

He was quiet a long moment. "If she still feels that way when she wakes up, then she's more disturbed than I thought. People imbue some Robin Hood image on those brave enough to threaten the powerful and unscrupulous railroad barons. But they're nothing but thieves and scoundrels, just like the roughs, preying on those weaker or more virtuous."

But Quillan had stopped them. At his own risk, he had stopped the outlaws victimizing the train. Her heart swelled. Quillan was wise. And he was safe. And he had done a wonderful thing. *Grazie, Signore.*

Quillan stared out the window of the train. Shane Dennison. The sight, the sound of his voice, even the wheedling words he'd used to try once again to draw Quillan into his spell; all of it brought him back to that part of his life of which he was least proud. Had needing human approbation made him so susceptible to influence that even someone of Dennison's ilk could seem heroic?

What was this need in him to be accepted, and at the same time make himself so difficult to accept? Hadn't he tried to push Carina away with everything in him, all the while desperate for her love? It was a war inside. And the Shepards—had he been partly responsible for Leona Shepard's accusations? Hadn't he defiantly kept silent, even brazenly misled her at times?

Shane Dennison. Why had God crossed their paths again? Shane Dennison, to whom Quillan had once confided his unhappiness, his anger toward the reverend, his hatred of the reverend's wife. Yes, he had prided himself in becoming a thorn to Reverend Shepard, called himself the reverend's personal demon. Dennison remembered that? After fourteen years?

As for his "friend," Dennison seemed to have stayed the course he set for himself. From that first robbery, how many others had followed until now they met up again, on opposite sides of this shootout? Quillan shook his head. It could have gone the other way. One of these days he'd get in over his head defending the underdog or standing for justice in an unjust world. But like so many other things, it seemed a tenacious part of his nature.

He'd hardly finished the thought when a man came forward, hand extended. It was the one who'd been keeping score for the shooting contest. "Mr. Shepard, may I offer my thanks." His grip was firm, confident. "Roderick Pierce is the name. I'm in the newspaper business. I'd like to write up our little episode."

Quillan shifted, aware of the burning wound in his arm. "The more print you give it, the better he'll like it."

"He?"

"Shane Dennison, the leader of the band."

Pierce pulled out a notebook. "Dennison, you say? Friend of yours?"

Quillan didn't answer. He trusted reporters on a level with lawyers like Beck. The man raised a questioning brow. Quillan shook his head. "Not a friend."

"But you are acquainted?"

"I knew him once."

The man scribbled. "How long ago?"

"Long."

The pencil paused. Pierce looked up. "One, five, ten years?"

Still Quillan didn't answer. He began to feel invaded. What if he told the man the year, the city, the connection he'd had with Shane Dennison. How would the story be twisted? Just as Wolf's life—and death—had been twisted into some macabre tale.

Carina leaned forward. Immediately Pierce took notice. "Ma'am?"

"My husband is injured. He needs to rest."

"Certainly. This will only take a moment." He turned back to Quillan. "If you could—"

Carina laid her hand on his arm. "Thank you for understanding."

Pierce paused, looked from her to Quillan and back. Quillan felt Pierce's reluctance crumble against Carina's resolve. He should speak for himself, but one corner of his mouth twitched as he held his silence. Carina's lips parted in a soft smile.

Pierce tipped his head. "As you like, ma'am. Mr. Shepard, I'll speak with you again." He turned crisply, glanced once more at Carina, lingering, in Quillan's assessment, a moment overlong. Then he left.

Quillan closed his eyes, but even as he did, William Scott Bennet spoke his name. Wearily, Quillan opened his eyes again.

"Mr. Shepard..."

"Quillan." It was habit, even if he no longer disdained the name of Shepard as he once had.

"Quillan." Bennet held out his hand.

Quillan shook it.

"Some of the fellows would like to buy you a drink, sir. Would you do us the honor?"

Quillan glanced at Carina, but it seemed she wouldn't come to his rescue this time. Now that she'd mentioned it, he was tired, but he couldn't refuse the companions who'd stood with him. Quillan got up from his seat. "All right." He just touched Carina's shoulder as he left her.

Carina watched her husband be carried off by his exuberant admirers. It was fitting they should honor him. If not for his insistence, this entire episode could have—would have—ended differently. Yet she knew he was uncomfortable. He was not used to acclaim and acceptance, nor even companionship. Her heart jumped. Maybe now he would learn. Then she caught sight of Roderick Pierce hurrying after them.

She sighed. Quillan would reveal no more than he liked. But what would the newsman make of Quillan's reluctance? Would he think her husband had something to hide?

Fourteen

How weak the man, bone and blood, felled by flying lead.
How glad my hand was not the one by which he now lies dead.

— *Quillan*

AT GRANGER STATION, Quillan took leave of Carina and
followed the Wells Fargo agent off the train to make a report.
Carina and the others who had witnessed the incident would be
questioned and shown posters, but railroad officials took Quillan
into a small office with walls lined with charts and maps.

He waited there with the Wells Fargo agent until three other
men joined them. One of these men, unremarkable but for the
width between his eyes, motioned him to sit. There were only two
chairs, so the other men remained standing. A certain unease settled on Quillan as he glanced about.

The wide-eyed man said, "I'm Detective Bittering. I understand you have some acquaintance with the outlaws who held up
the Union Pacific?"

Quillan nodded. "I recognized one of the men."

The detective spoke slowly and deliberately. "How could you
recognize him if he was masked?"

Quillan sensed an antagonism he hadn't expected. Hadn't he
just acted to save their interests at the risk of his own life? "I knew
him."

"When?"

"Fourteen or fifteen years ago." Quillan's throat felt tight.

The man jotted that down on a sheet of paper. "That's a long
time. Have you seen him since?"

169

"No."

"Yet you knew him with only his eyes showing."

"Eyes, forehead, voice."

"You must have known him very well."

Quillan shifted in his chair. "Several months."

The detective stood and walked across the room. "You knew him for several months; you haven't seen him in fifteen years; yet you knew who it was."

Quillan stiffened. Was he on trial?

Bittering glanced over his shoulder. "Forgive me, Mr. Shepard, if I seem skeptical. Comes with the territory."

Quillan nodded slightly.

"At what point did you know the leader of this gang was your friend?"

"He's not my friend."

"Must have made quite an impression." Bittering tapped his pencil on the edge of the oak desk. "You knew him only a few months."

"I have a keen memory."

"Have you?" Bittering walked to the wall and studied a schedule chart.

There was a knock at the door, and Bittering motioned one of the other two men to open it.

Pierce stood outside. "Detective Bittering, I'm Roderick Pierce, *Rocky Mountain News*, Denver. I'd like to be present as you speak with Mr. Shepard here. I'm covering the story."

Quillan tensed, certain Bittering saw his unease.

"Don't mind if you listen," Bittering said. "But don't interrupt or ask questions of your own." He fixed the man with his wide stare. Quillan suspected he did not ordinarily let pressmen in on his investigations. Did he do it now to intimidate? Mr. Pierce gave Quillan a smug smile. Quillan had been less than forthcoming on the train, and even less polite. Now there was no way to keep the man from knowing whatever the detective pried loose. He felt sweat on the back of his neck.

Bittering turned back to Quillan. "Mr. Shepard, how did you know this . . . What did you say your friend's name was?"

Quillan's jaw tensed. The detective was baiting him. "I didn't say." He didn't argue the term *friend* again. He wouldn't dignify the tactic. But he added, "His name is Shane Dennison. I knew him when I was a boy in Laramie."

"A boy of eight, nine?"

"Fourteen."

"Almost a man."

"Almost." Quillan's hands tightened on the edge of his chair.

"Was this Shane Dennison your companion?"

Quillan thought back to those days when Dennison had taken a liking to Quillan, taken him under his wing and championed him to the other difficult boys. He nodded. "For several months."

"Why did you part company?"

"I left town."

"Your family moved?"

Quillan pictured himself walking out of Laramie without even a horse. He'd hitched a ride on one wagon or another until the dust of Laramie was covered by so many other layers it was no longer recognizable. "No. I did."

"Mind telling me why?"

Yes, he minded. But he knew from that first clash with the law that it mattered little what he minded or didn't. "Personal reasons."

"Unhappy at home?"

"Sure."

Bittering gave him a quick stare. "And you never saw Dennison since."

"That's what I said." Quillan glanced at the agent. Why didn't he speak up, tell the detective how it had been? Without Quillan's interference both the Express box and the man's life would have been lost.

Bittering laughed lightly. "Yet your keen memory recognized him at once."

"That's right." They had covered this already. The detective was crossing back, trying to confuse him.

"Are you wondering why a detective is here in a small whistle-stop like Granger to take your report?"

Quillan hadn't, but now he did.

"I'll tell you. This is the third time in four weeks the train's been hit in almost that same spot. We believe this gang could have an inside man, someone aboard who signals when there's a ripe payload on the Express, relays any delays, that sort of thing."

Quillan took that in without showing any emotion. Didn't

they realize a man like Dennison could stake out a track and learn its patterns as easily as he studied the flow of a bank? Then another thought occurred. They thought he was the inside man. "Then why would I rouse the others to fight off the outlaws?" His frank assessment startled the detective, but he recovered quickly.

"Jealousy? Struggle for command? Any number of reasons. I have many accounts from fellow passengers of your aloofness, unwillingness to mingle." He raised his brows at Pierce, who nodded heartily.

"I don't mingle by nature." Quillan's voice sounded tight to his own ears.

"Don't you. Well. You seem to have mingled with Shane Dennison. You knew him, and from what I surmise, he knew you, too. Seemed surprised you'd stand against him." This time he glanced at the agent.

"He was surprised I was there at all. It's been so many years."

The detective turned. "That's right. Fifteen years, yet you knew Dennison by his eyes alone."

Quillan didn't repeat the other details that had clued him in. He looked at a short stack of books atop the oak file cabinet. "Will you hand me a book?"

Again raising his brows, which gave his wide forehead a singularly unpleasant appearance, Bittering reached for the top book and handed it over. It was a survey written longhand by a man named Eustace Washington. Quillan opened randomly and silently read the first two paragraphs of the page. He turned the book around and held it out to Bittering. Pierce leaned closer, pencil poised. Quillan recited word for word what he had just read.

Bittering followed the page, then looked up.

Quillan met his eyes. "I recall things well."

Bittering stood a long moment. He'd felt certain he had it all figured out. Now Quillan saw disappointment take shape and soften the hard line of his mouth, the wide gaze of his eyes. Quillan stood up. "I'm not your man. Now if you'll excuse me—"

"Mr. Shepard!" Pierce fairly leaped from his corner. "May we try another example, for the sake of authentication?"

Quillan looked at him. "Authentication?"

Pierce whisked a paper from the desk. It held a diagram of the spurs and lines running to and around Ogden, the next major hub. Quillan studied the diagram. "So what?"

Pierce tore a paper from his pad. "Can you reproduce it?" He held out the pencil.

Quillan stared from it to him, then took the pencil and scribbled what he recalled from the diagram. Pierce laid the two papers on the desk. Except for slight differences in length and direction, his drawing was very near the other. The other men stepped close to see.

Bittering said, "Will you give us a description of your ... of Dennison?"

"Don't you have him on a poster? His career has spanned fifteen years." Quillan met Bittering's eyes. Let him realize the nature of that first relationship. Quillan no longer cared.

"He's never been pictured without the mask."

Quillan hesitated, then took the pencil again from Pierce. He was not an artist. Recalling words or a diagram was one thing. He thought of Wolf's cave. Unlike his father, he'd never spent much energy on pictures. But he stared at the paper and recalled Shane Dennison's face. It wasn't artistic ability that mattered, but attention to detail, the shape and placement of the mouth, the roman nose, the way the chin caved in toward the neck. He turned over the page and drew Shane Dennison as he remembered him. "He's no doubt filled out some. Has a mole here at the edge of his lip." Quillan swallowed, pushed the paper across to Detective Bittering. "I hope you find him."

Bittering held out his hand, but Quillan turned and left the room. Once again, every man had assumed the worst of him. Even the agent whose life he'd saved.

Carina watched them carry Miss Preston from the train on a litter not unlike the one Quillan had made for her ride up the mountain. Priscilla Preston would be kept in town to heal from her injuries. The doctor strode purposefully beside his patient. He must be staying, too, as the town could hardly support a physician of its own. Miss Preston's aunt walked alongside the litter like a lost soul, but Carina was not sorry to see them go. Shaking her head, she recalled the younger woman's foolishness. If the bullet had been six inches lower, she would never have opened her eyes again.

She looked again down the hall toward the room where

Quillan was being questioned. How long could it take to get his statement? Then she saw him coming toward her, his stride long and forced. Angry? No, it wasn't anger so much as defiance. Why was he defiant, defensive, on guard? He took her arm without a word and led her back aboard their coach and to their seats.

She turned. "Are you finished? They took your statement?"

With a half laugh, he smirked. "Sure."

She caught his hand. "What is it, Quillan? What happened?"

"They made assumptions. I proved them wrong."

She pressed his hand to her cheek. "What assumptions? Tell me!"

He turned and jerked the curtains closed around them. She was not surprised to then be jerked tightly to his chest. His mouth on hers told her he'd been hurt and was seeking solace, as always, in her physical love. She kissed him deeply. "Don't let it bother you, *caro mio.*" She stroked his face. "What do they know?"

"Am I so wretched, Carina? Do I . . . do I look evil?"

"No, my darling."

His fingers dug into her back. "I must."

"No. Not evil, just different. People distrust what they can't understand."

He grabbed her arms and held her out. "Do you trust me?"

The violence of his question frightened her. "Yes. Of course I do."

"Why?"

"Because I love you."

He dropped his forehead to the crown of her head. "How can you?"

"I just do." She smoothed his thick, wonderful hair and felt the violence leave him. "Don't let them hurt you."

"I don't know what God's doing. Cain said He had plans for me, but I don't see it. I don't understand."

"Don't try to. Just wait."

He sagged. "For what?"

"God will show you. *Gesù Cristo.* He will."

Quillan's breath came easily now as he enveloped her gently into his arms. "Don't ever leave me, Carina."

"No. I promise."

He sighed. "They thought I was one of the gang."

"What? How could they? You *stopped* the outlaws—you didn't help them!"

He rubbed his hand over his jaw. She heard the sandpaper scrape of his whiskers. He did look rather wild.

She touched his face with her fingertips. "You could shave."

"I don't want people to judge me by how I look."

She sighed. "But they do."

His jaw grew tight. "Then let them. I am what I am."

She smiled. "Oh, Quillan."

He tipped her chin up and stared into her eyes. "You don't want a pirate husband?"

"I want you any way at all." She heard other passengers coming aboard. The whistle blew, and more voices sounded outside their curtain.

He looked at the flimsy barrier and whispered, "You know what I wish? That you and I could have this train all to ourselves, with no one else."

She pressed her hands to his chest. "Others would love and trust you if you gave them the chance."

He shrugged one shoulder. "I don't seem to know how."

She stepped back from him as the train made a small lurch forward. "You'll learn."

"You're supremely confident of that."

She nodded, drawing the curtain back behind their seats to reveal the rest of the car. Then they sat down across from each other, eyes held unswerving. His mouth pulled slightly up at one edge. "God's got his work, taming me."

Something smoldered inside her. Did she want him tame? Or was it his difference that made him so irresistible?

They were scarcely on their way when one group after another came to shake Quillan's hand, to comment on his courage. Mr. Pierce appeared, pad and pencil in hand. "If you don't mind, Mr. Shepard, I'd like to follow up on that demonstration. It'll make a great angle for the story."

"What demonstration?" Carina looked from one to the other.

Mr. Pierce described Quillan's reproduction of text and diagram. She looked at her husband. How had he felt, forced to perform such things to prove his innocence? But then she knew how he'd felt. "Mr. Pierce, my husband—"

"It's all right, Carina." Quillan motioned the newsman to sit beside her. "What would you like to know?"

For the next half hour Mr. Pierce questioned and Quillan demonstrated his mental capacities, reciting portions of books he'd committed to memory, explaining that it had been an ability he'd discovered early on, and how he even had infant memories of his mother's face and hair. Carina was amazed he would share something so intimate. Was he trying to trust? To be trusted?

"It's amazing, Mr. Shepard. "

"Quillan."

Pierce nodded. "Quillan, you realize this is a remarkable gift. To what do you attribute it?"

"To God."

Pierce raised his brows.

"That surprises you?" Quillan half smiled.

"You don't look the God-fearing sort." Pierce shifted uneasily. "And the agent said Dennison called you the 'reverend's personal demon.' "

Quillan sat back and crossed his arms over his chest. "So I was. But every man can be redeemed if he's willing. Don't you believe that?"

Carina watched the newsman search for an answer. Mr. Pierce seemed nonplussed, and she was certain Quillan had intended that.

"I . . . well, I suppose. If he's willing."

"Are you willing, Mr. Pierce? Do you serve God with your pen?" Quillan made his face innocently curious. Knowing him as she did, Carina recognized his effort.

The newsman flushed. "Well, I certainly don't thwart him."

"Fence-sitter, are you?" Quillan seemed to enjoy turning the tables on Mr. Roderick Pierce, even phrasing the question in the tone and manner of the other man's speech.

"My experience hasn't led me one way or another. I'm a reporter. I depend on my eyes and ears. So far they've not seen or heard God. Which doesn't mean I discount him completely. Too much starch in my early spine for that. Only I'm lacking sufficient evidence to make a secure declaration."

Quillan nodded. "Well, my experience is, the longer you resist, the harder it gets. Best make your peace before the going gets rough."

Pierce eyed him. "And I imagine you'd be one to know."

Carina glanced at Quillan, who didn't answer, leaving Pierce to his imaginings.

Pierce said, "Care to illuminate your relationship with Dennison?"

Quillan shook his head. "No."

"Off the record?"

Quillan smiled, but still said nothing.

"Waltzed a while with the wicked, did you?" Pierce said it conspiratorially.

Quillan glanced to the window and back. "Mr. Pierce . . ."

"Oh, I understand the lure, Quillan. I've raised some dust myself. Were you one of the gang?"

Quillan narrowed his eyes. Carina saw the hooding that made them flat as pewter plates, revealing nothing. She didn't know what the newsman was trying to do, but Quillan suspected something. He said, "Bittering put you up to this?"

Mr. Pierce sat back abruptly. "I don't quite follow."

"Did he put the bird in your ear to feel me out, make sure he didn't misfire when he let me walk away?"

Carina felt Quillan's fury, tightly contained, yet evidenced in the taut tendons of his neck.

Pierce spread his hands. "Bittering?"

"Or are you just a dog on a scent?"

Mr. Pierce frowned. "No need to get testy. Curious, is all."

"Mr. Pierce, this book is closed. Write your story and color it any way you like. I'll never read it anyway."

"I'll send you a copy. Staying in San Francisco, are you?"

Carina said, "Sonoma. Send it to the DiGratias of Sonoma, California."

When Quillan said nothing, Mr. Pierce turned to her. "Your family, ma'am?"

"That's right. I'll read your story, Mr. Pierce. So tell it right. My husband is a hero."

"Carina." Quillan's voice was tight.

"Three times he saved my life, not counting the risk he took today."

Mr. Pierce smiled, sizing her up with his eyes. "Well, I wish I had more than a column or two, Mrs. Shepard, to truly do it justice."

"Just tell the truth, Mr. Pierce. Tales have a way of growing on their own."

He laughed. "That they have. Thank you for the reminder."

"You're welcome."

The newsman stood, bowed slightly to Carina, then held out a hand to Quillan. "No hard feelings?"

Quillan shook his hand. Carina watched him as Mr. Pierce left. He was no longer coiled like a snake ready to spring, but neither did he seem reposed. He turned to her. "Carina, I don't need you to defend me. I can speak for myself."

"Well, you don't."

"If I want to crow, I'll crow. If not, I would appreciate your not doing it in my stead."

"Why don't you defend yourself? Tell him you had nothing to do with that bank robbery?"

Quillan winced. Too late she saw Mr. Pierce on his way back through the car. She brought her hand to her lips as he descended once again.

"Mrs. Shepard, you cannot refuse me now. It would be nothing short of cruel, the like of which I might not survive."

Carina frowned. "You should be ashamed of eavesdropping."

He flashed a smile. "Ashamed? It's how I earn my bread. Everywhere there's a story if you just have ears to catch it. Now tell me about this bank robbery." He glanced at Quillan, realized that was not his best chance, and turned back to her.

"I'll tell you nothing except that my husband was in no way responsible. Even the judge pardoned him."

"Went before the judge, did he?"

"Well, he had to, to get out of jail, didn't he?"

Again she saw Quillan wince.

"Of course. Was he jailed long?"

"I don't know. He was fourteen. I only met him last year."

Mr. Pierce turned to Quillan. "That's what you meant about Dennison leaving men behind? Let you take the fall, did he?"

Quillan scowled. "It's not your business."

"But you'd better give it to me right, or as Mrs. Shepard says, the tale might grow."

"Is that a threat?" Quillan's voice stayed flat.

"Mr. Shepard, I'm trying to be fair."

"You're trying to get what I don't want to give."

Mr. Pierce sat back. "All right, so I am. I'm nothing if not thorough. But given that, I am fair. Tell me your story."

Quillan shook his head. "I don't want it in the papers."

"Dennison bamboozled you, continued a life in crime while you went straight, and here, fifteen years later, you have your reward. Why, there might even *be* a reward if your efforts lead to his capture. He's been a thorn to the railroad for two years."

Quillan shook his head. "I didn't do it for any reward. I didn't even know it was Shane until I heard and saw him."

"What went through your head when you knew?"

Carina looked at Quillan. His throat worked, and she thought he would refuse to answer. Then he said, "Disgust that I could ever have looked up to him."

Mr. Pierce sat quiet a moment. "May I quote you on that?"

Quillan hesitated. "Mr. Pierce, I'd prefer none of it found print, but it seems you're set on putting it down. Quote me if you like."

"Thank you, sir. It's been an honor making your acquaintance." Again he stood.

Quillan cracked a wry smile. "Dare I hope this departure permanent? Or need I muzzle my wife?"

Roderick Pierce laughed heartily. "I could never be the cause of your covering any one of your wife's features. As I said, I've only a column or two. Though I guess there'd be more to print if I looked."

Quillan didn't answer. With another laugh, Mr. Pierce took his leave, and Carina met Quillan's sardonic stare.

"I'm sorry. I didn't mean to tell."

"You never do. But somehow the whole world learns my business anyway."

He was right. Through her, Crystal had rekindled the story of Wolf and Rose and suspected Quillan of the brutal murder of William Evans by family association alone. Now Mr. Pierce knew one of Quillan's secrets, which every reader would soon know, too.

"I'm sorry."

Quillan smiled darkly, his eyes searching over her face.

"What are you doing?"

He cocked his head. "Picturing you with a muzzle."

"Oh!" She threw up her hands. "I said I was sorry. What more do you want?"

"Dare I hope for restraint?"

She frowned. "I'm not secretive by nature."

"No?" His brows rose, mocking her.

She tossed her lace gloves for want of a better weapon.

He caught the gloves, laughing. "There you go again."

"And why not, when you provoke me so?"

He folded the gloves together and handed them back.

She snatched them from his hand and turned to the window, sulking. Why did he make such a row about nothing? Nothing? How would she like her misdeeds paraded out for all to read? *Oh, Signore, why must you always make me see?* She turned back to Quillan and made her face meek. "I was wrong. In my family we talk. We tell stories about each other, even embarrassing stories."

"You certainly have none of those."

"Oh, yes. The time I kicked Tony when he beat me in a foot race is a great favorite—Carina's temper a fine theme."

"Kicked Tony, eh?"

She rolled her eyes. "I grew out of it."

"I think I'll guard my shins, nonetheless."

She raised her chin. "There have been plenty of times I could have kicked you, wanted badly to. Have I?"

"Not specifically."

"So there." She waved a dismissing hand.

"And these stories are told to . . ." He spread his fingers.

"Us. Ourselves. The family."

"Your parents and brothers and sister."

She shook her head. "Everyone. Aunts, cousins, godparents. The stories—" she searched for the right description—"they hold us together."

Quillan seemed to consider that. He grew pensive, and she tried to imagine him with her boisterous brothers telling tales and laughing over misdeeds and mishaps. She felt a deep misgiving. Quillan was not like them. He would be a dove among crows. How strange to think of Quillan as a dove, but the image stuck.

"You'll see," she said. But would he? Could he change his very nature? Did she want him to?

Fifteen

Why men seek fame I cannot see; 'tis but a call "Come feed on me."

— *Quillan*

FOR THE REMAINDER of the trip, Quillan could not avoid attention. The men wanted to shake his hand. A photographer took his picture. The women found him more fascinating than ever, and he was surprisingly charming. Carina watched with admiration and amusement. Her husband was a hero. And he suffered it well.

Two days later they arrived in San Francisco. Carina's heart rushed as they detrained near the wharf. The late afternoon was bright and cool with a breeze off the water. But unlike the snow-covered realms of Crystal, the green of spring was starting in the trees. Sonoma would be just awakening. Her heart fluttered.

She stared out past the piers as Quillan oversaw the unloading of his wagon. He tethered the four horses to a rail with the wagon beside them. Joining her, Quillan seemed dazed as he looked out over the water. Hands behind his back, he stared out. "That's the ocean?"

"The bay."

"I've never seen so much water." He studied with interest the mighty steam-powered vessels anchored along the piers with some masted ships among them.

Carina half expected his wanderlust to sweep them aboard. And then to Alaska? He hadn't mentioned it since that once. Maybe he'd teased only. But it wasn't beyond him.

"Never been on a ship."

"Well, we'll be taking a ferry tomorrow. That one there—the *James M. Donahue*." She waved a hand. "It has made its final run today, but tomorrow we'll take it across the bay."

"How far?"

She shrugged. "Thirty miles, I think."

"Thirty miles of water."

"That's only the bay." She waved her hand to the west. "Out that way is the Pacific Ocean. It goes forever." She said it with a jesting smile. "Come on, before the sea lust gets hold of you."

She led him along the wharf where vendors sold live crabs and lobsters and thick bowls of chowder from stalls steaming with a tangy fish smell. San Francisco wasn't Sonoma. The briny air clamored with the bustle and purpose of ocean trade. Quillan watched the stevedores along the piers, and she could almost hear him considering the possibilities of such labor. How would he find the rhythmic life of Sonoma, lives so connected to the land the people grew sleepy when the vines were dormant, then came alive with the bloom. Could Quillan ever stay put until harvest?

Not that it meant sitting still. There was much work. Even for Papa, the *dottore*. Though he tended all who sought him, especially his own people, there were too few in Sonoma to support a surgeon of Papa's caliber. So he spent hours with a microscope, shipped from New York, studying tissues and creatures too small to see. His studies engrossed him, but he could have done that anywhere.

It was for the land that he'd come to Sonoma. Horticulture became a passion. Of course the grapes, but also herbs and plants for food and medicinal use. Papa loved his land and what it could produce. The climate was perfect. Where else was such a perfect climate, except maybe Sardinia? Papa had known that and chosen his land with care.

"What are you thinking about?"

She startled, glanced up at Quillan with the setting sun sending a glow over his shoulder. "My papa."

"Care to enlighten me?"

"Oh." She waved her hand. "You'll meet him soon enough."

"Wouldn't hurt to know a little in advance." Putting a hand to her elbow, Quillan assisted her up onto the timbered walk.

No, it wouldn't hurt for him to know something of her papa, but she felt reluctant to elaborate. She stopped before a vendor's stall. With his pipe between his teeth, the gnarled vendor reminded her of Alan Tavish in a crusty seaman sort of way. Did Quillan see it, too, and was he missing Alan? It freshened her own pang for the friends she had left.

She nodded to the old man. "What do you have fresh?"

"Crabs just boiled, ma'am."

"We'll take one. A large one."

From a pile of red- and white-shelled crustaceans, he pulled one monstrous crab complete with legs and eyes, laid it on a square of paper, and handed it over with a small wooden mallet. "Two bits."

Quillan paid, eyeing the creature askance. "You don't really intend to eat that?"

Carina smiled. "Haven't you had crab from the shell?"

"If I ever had, I'd know."

She walked to a bench and sat, placing the crab on the paper between them. Holding one pincer, she struck the shell with the mallet, then pulled it apart to reveal the meat. "Try it."

Quillan pulled the white fleshy fish from the claw, held it up a moment, then put it into his mouth. He ate it, then nodded. "It is good. Though you'd never know to look at it."

"It's wonderful. *Meraviglioso.*"

"Meraviglioso. How do you say crab?"

"*Granchio.*" She held it up by a claw.

"Meraviglioso granchio." Quillan hammered the shell and slid a long chunk of crabmeat off the thin, pliant cartilage. "How do you say bay?"

"*Baia.*"

He looked out over the water. "The closest I've gotten to crossing something like that was on a river ferry once. Mostly I just splash through on my wagon."

"Don't try it here." She waved at the bay. "Or you'll meet these face to face." She held up the crab.

He laughed, then looked back over the water. "Tomorrow we cross. Then what?"

"Then we drive north."

"How long?"

She considered. "Four hours, maybe three." The very thought brought her heart rushing to her throat. She looked out across the water. Just north of San Pablo Bay lay her home. Tomorrow they would go there. She wished they could start now! She fairly throbbed with excitement. "Tomorrow we'll be home." She squeezed his arm. "You don't know what this means to me."

He studied her face, then smiled. "Yes, I do."

"I don't care if the whole world can see. I'm going home to Mamma and Papa. To everyone! *Mia famiglia.*"

He looked down at his hands.

She reached out and grasped them. "And yours." But the niggling thought returned. What would they think of Quillan? Maybe Father Antoine was right. She should have written. Well, it was too late for that now. And tomorrow . . . tomorrow she'd be home!

The next morning Quillan held the rail of the *James M. Donahue* steamer. He looked out at the huge expanse of blue salty water that held them afloat. At his side, Carina had become a scintillating creature, as though the sea air or the California shore had quickened some magic in her. Or maybe it was that she would soon be home with her family. He felt singularly unsure of his own place in all of it.

Carina was reluctant to discuss the individuals in her family. She spoke of them all as a group, giving him a broad brush of the whole picture but saying little in particular except that he would see for himself soon. Too soon. Yet she wouldn't be so eager, so animated if she didn't believe it would all come right. Would she?

There was that part of her that was remarkably credulous, truly astonished by the ugliness of the world. She'd been protected from it so well. Crystal had come as a shock, and so had he. But that was before he loved her. Now he would do anything to preserve her innocence. He did not want to be a source of disillusionment. He shook his head. Maybe he had it all wrong, but he had reason to be gun-shy.

After they docked, they would take the wagon road to her home. What happened there remained to be seen, but he'd feel a sight more comfortable if her family knew he was coming. The DeMornays had not been inspiring.

Why hadn't Carina written? Surely a woman as close to her family as she was would want them to know she had married. Yes, she had spent months fraught with uncertainty. But she'd been steadfast in her commitment, never entertaining his offers of divorce. Thank God. Yet her family knew nothing of it. He frowned, felt her nudge on his elbow, and turned.

"How can you look so dour with the sun gleaming on the water and the shore drawing nigh? Why are you frowning?"

"Carina . . ." But then the whistle shrilled three times, drowning out his question.

"Look! There's Sonoma landing." Carina gripped his arm. "Oh, Quillan, soon!"

He sighed. Why spoil her excitement? Maybe it would be all right. Maybe it was his own experience that made him doubt where nothing warranted doubt. After all, she knew her family.

The steamer chugged up to the wharf. One of the huge paddle wheels reversed and brought the boat alongside. Men rushed to toss ropes as the steamer eased to a stop and the boilers were shut down. The black smoke stopped belching from the stacks.

Quillan watched as the gangplank was stretched across the gap of water, then turned to Carina. "Go on ashore while I oversee the wagon and team."

She nodded, half oblivious to him already. He had loaded all their gear into the wagon before it was loaded onto the steamer, so she carried nothing but her lace parasol and a small valise. She had exchanged her brown woolen coat for a violet duster she purchased in San Francisco with money from her own pouch. How much had she actually made running that restaurant of hers?

Carina looked elegant and fresh, with such color to her cheeks he wanted to kiss them. But he refrained. As he watched her cross the gangplank and go ashore, he felt a fierce pride. He went down and helped the sweating black man take his balking horses ashore, pulling the wagon behind. On the wharf, he inspected the wagon and found everything in order.

He lifted Carina to the spring seat. It seemed a waste now that they hadn't ridden all the way from Crystal. But he was glad for the springs once they started along the road. The deep mud ruts had hardened, and the wheels jolted unmercifully. Carina would not have stood it long, though to look at her you'd never know she had recently been battered.

She breathed deeply, hands clasped at her breast, and murmured, "Come bella."

It was a lovely scene: gently swelling hills just starting to green with patches of bare oaks. Here and there a stand of redwoods, and along the creeks grew rust-colored willows and bushes that he guessed would berry. At rare distances, they passed farmhouses. All about, cattle grazed—white, black, brown, and marbled. There were flocks of sheep and geese and goats. A pastoral landscape. If ever a land was of milk and honey, this was it.

Quillan felt something stir inside. This was a place to settle, to put down roots. Hadn't Cain said every man needed roots? Was it possible? An ache started in his throat. Did he dare hope to find a home, to make a home? He could live here with Carina. He felt it.

Though the air on the bay had been chilled with wind, it now waxed warm with a balmy scent. As they rode farther from the shore and deeper into the hills, the sun warmed the land, and him with it. Farming. He had never considered it. He'd been fleet of foot and restless, never trusting one place to stand him for long. Now...

Lord, is this it? What you planned for me? A home, land, a family?

Carina pointed out properties and landmarks, saying many of the words in Italian. Did she realize...? But he committed them to memory as she talked. Some of the land was quilted with what looked like dark gnarled stalks tied to wooden crosses with arms reaching out, between them a froth of bright yellow.

Carina caught his gaze. "Those are the grapes. They've had winter pruning but no buds yet. The fava beans are in bloom."

"Beans between the grapes?" Then the tough dark stumps must be the grapevines. They looked dead compared to the bright yellow of the bean plants.

She nodded. "Fava, orchard grass, clover—to hold the soil against the winter rains."

Fog clung in the low areas over the creeks, though the hills were bright with sunshine and breeze-tossed grasses. Quillan realized how little he knew about such a life. Was he dreaming? Could he settle down and learn?

"And there." Carina pointed. "You can just see Sonoma."

Ahead, a cluster of buildings stood closer together than the farms, but still orderly. The road went straight into what seemed a large central square. Quillan eyed it with curiosity. They were coming in at midafternoon, but the town seemed sleepy even so.

"That's the plaza. General Vallejo laid it out and plotted the streets around it. Cattle used to graze there along a white picket fence. Now with the train through, it's not pretty anymore."

Quillan eyed the dirt square, gauging it some six square acres or more. The tracks ran along one side, lined by stores and businesses and ending in a turntable at one corner of the plaza. He said, "Who's General Vallejo?"

"Mariano Vallejo. He was sent here by the Mexican president. A great man for the community and a friend of Papa's. He gave us our fountain."

"Fountain?"

"In the courtyard. You'll see it. A lovely white swan."

Quillan's belly tightened. A fountained courtyard. High connections. What did he know about any of that?

Carina motioned. "Turn here."

They had not entered the plaza, were still some blocks from it as he brought the wagon onto a smaller road that started off east.

"Over that way is Lachryma Montis, General Vallejo's home. He has a spring-fed reservoir that provides water for his gardens. He sells some to the town." She dropped her hand to her lap. "Papa's land is ahead about a mile and a half."

With every sentence Quillan felt less sure of his chances. Had that quickening inside at the sight and scent of the land, at the thought of settling down, been God's urging or his own desires? He'd know soon enough. He snapped the lines, and the horses picked up their pace.

Carina's heart swelled at the sight of Papa's white palatial home surrounded by vine-covered hills and rows upon rows of shapely apple and orange trees. After Crystal it seemed everything fine and marvelous. The walls of the courtyard welcomed her with the wrought iron gates standing open. Voices and laughter came from inside. Male voices. Her brothers were playing bocce along the west wall where a strip of sand had been laid out for the game. As the wagon entered the yard, hooves *clop-clopping* on the cobbles, the rumble of the huge wheels echoing on the stucco walls, her brothers stopped and turned.

"Carina Maria!" Vittorio's call sent her heart leaping. How long had it been since she'd heard and seen them? Too long!

"Hello, hello, I'm home." She held out her arms as Angelo reached up for her waist.

He swung her down. "Where have you been? Why no word for so long? You nearly put Mamma in her grave." His tone was not what she had hoped for. Weren't they happy to see her?

"It's Papa who's been a dead man." Joseph snatched her satchel from behind the seat as soon as the wheels ground to a halt. "Do you have more? Anything in the back?" He eyed the tarp-covered load.

"Yes . . ."

"Do you owe the driver money?" Vittorio hollered up to Quillan, "What does she owe you?"

"I don't—" But every time she turned to answer, Angelo pushed her farther from the wagon, and Lorenzo and Tony had placed themselves between her and Quillan. She was too small to resist, and they were too many; all her brothers, her twin cousins Matteo and Benny, and—

Then she saw Flavio, his white shirt sleeves rolled above the wrist, his vest open over loose-fitting pants. He stood with another cousin, Nicolo, one hand on his hip. His mouth was firm, accusing, but his eyes darkly melting. Her heart jumped, but she wasn't sure with what. She had known she would see him; how could she not? But she hadn't expected it so soon.

"Look who's home!" Catching her arm, Tony tugged her toward Flavio, but Angelo stopped them.

"No, she's going inside."

"But Flavio—"

"Flavio can wait."

It wasn't Flavio she was concerned with. She tugged against them both as they steered her toward the house. "Wait." If they would just let her talk!

"We'll take care of things out here." Lorenzo swung open the large wooden door.

"You don't un—"

Angelo pushed her through. Carina stomped and pushed back, but they fenced her in with their arms, doing their duty, protecting the hapless woman from a strange man—who happened to be her husband! "Stop it, Angelo. Tony, let me go!" She thrashed her way back out the door and slapped at Lorenzo. "Stop it now and listen."

Lorenzo caught both her arms and pinned them to her sides, speaking in Italian. "What were you thinking riding in like that without a chaperone? Have you no decency?"

She struggled. "If you would let me talk for one minute—"

"Talk inside." He lifted her off her feet.

She kicked his shin hard. "Stop it!" Now Flavio was grinning, and that sent a rush of fury through her. She kicked Lorenzo again. "Stop treating me like a child!"

He dropped her to grip his shin. "You are acting like one!"

She straightened her skirts with a huff and found Quillan with her eyes. He had dismounted the wagon and come around to the near side. His hair was loose, his face shaven, the mustache full across his upper lip and down to his jaw. His face showed her nothing, but there was an animal wariness in his stance. No wonder, with her brothers behaving like madmen.

She pushed past Lorenzo, but Flavio blocked her way, both hands on his hips. He looked her up and down with a smug smile. "So you've come to your senses."

She raised her chin. "I never left them."

He switched to Italian. "I knew you'd come back."

He was so self-satisfied, she wished she hadn't. She switched to Italian to answer. "Gross'uomo. You think you know everything. You're so smart, so macho. Get out of my way."

"Your brothers can get your things. You come with me." He reached for her arm.

She shook him off. "My husband might have something to say about that."

The courtyard fell silent. To a man, they turned to look at Quillan. He strode over and held out his hand. She reached for it and pressed in to his side.

"This is my husband, Quillan Shepard. Quillan, my brothers: Angelo, Vittorio, Lorenzo, Joseph, and Tony. These are my cousins Matt, Benny, Nicolo, and Flavio." She had actually struck them dumb. No one spoke; no one moved. Then they all started hollering at once.

"What is all this commotion?" Mamma came through the door. "Carina!"

Carina ran to her, threw her arms around her neck, and kissed her cheeks again and again. "Oh, Mamma, Mamma."

"Carina, my angel. God has brought you back from the grave."

She shook her head. "Not from the grave, Mamma. Oh,

Mamma." Carina squeezed her again. Then she looked up and saw Papa.

He spread his arms, and she went to him, kissing him and pressing her face into his chest. "Papa."

They swayed back and forth in their embrace. "Carina, Carina. You're home." Then he saw Quillan and paused his rocking. "Who is this?"

Carina felt a quaking inside. Now it came to it. She turned. "Papa, this is my husband, Quillan Shepard."

He stood very still as his face darkened; his blue eyes hardened to rocks. "What do you mean?" His voice was flat and still.

She swallowed her fear. "We were married in Crystal, Papa."

"Impossible. Married without courting? Who chaperoned? Who gave his blessing in place of your papa?"

Mamma wrung her hands. "What have you done, Carina?" She gripped her cheeks. "Oh, I knew you should never have gone. You were only a baby. How could I have let you go?"

"I was not a baby. And I'm not now. I'm a grown woman, and this man is my husband." Carina saw Quillan's jaw tighten, as though someone took a winch and drew the tendons taut. She stomped her foot. "Where is your hospitality?"

It was a valid reprimand, but Papa wasn't swayed. "I'll give no hospitality to a thief." He looked directly at Quillan, drew himself up to a height with him, arms stiffening. "Who do you think you are, to marry my daughter without my permission?"

Before Quillan could answer, Carina blurted, "It was my choice, Papa."

"Your choice? Who are you to choose?" He threw up his hands. "Bene. You have no need of a papa." He turned for the house.

"Stop it, Papa. You dishonor me."

He stopped and stiffened. "I . . . dishonor you? You have taken away my right, my privilege. You married without my blessing."

"What of Flavio?" Mamma started to cry. "You were promised to him. A good match. A fine match. You love him."

Carina quailed. This was not the time for that, not in front of Quillan and Flavio both. Not with the way Flavio had shamed her, hurt her. How could it hurt still? But it did. She looked up defiantly. "I don't want to talk about that now."

"You don't want." Papa shook his head.

Carina's heart ached. She had disappointed him, wounded him. If he would just hear her! "Listen, Papa. I bring you a son, and you act as though someone has died." She waved her arm to include them all. "I bring you a brother."

"Were you married by a priest?" Mamma gripped her shawl beneath her throat.

"Yes." What did Mamma think? But at the time Carina had been so dazed it could have been a judge or anyone else.

Mamma was mumbling. "Then it's done." She pressed her hands to her face.

Carina caught Flavio's fiery gaze. What right had he to be angry? "Where is Divina?"

Mamma wrapped herself in her arms. "Married. Four months now. And expecting."

"Married?" Then what was the fuss?

Nicolo stood straighter. "To me."

Carina's mouth fell open. Nicolo had married Divina? She had never shown the least interest in Nicolo. And what about Flavio? Carina pictured them together as she'd seen them in the barn. Flavio had not married Divina? Her breath suspended as things came clear. Divina married to Nicolo and expecting . . . She looked again at Flavio, his face insolent and furious. She knew that mood. She knew all his moods.

Heart pounding, she walked to Quillan's side. "We've come a long way. Do you have room for us or not?"

Mamma bit her knuckles, crying.

Papa straightened slowly. "There is room." But his tone was far from warm.

"Come in, come in." Mamma waved them through the door. "You can unpack later. Come in."

Carina preceded Quillan, catching the look of pure hatred in Flavio's eyes as her husband passed. What had she done? She had forgiven Flavio, forgiven Divina. She had put her trust in the Lord and put the past behind her. But there was no forgiveness in Flavio's face. And he had not married Divina. Why?

She passed into the stately villa. What would Quillan think of it? But he had more on his mind than that. Another rejection. This time by her family. Had she thought it would be otherwise? She had fooled herself. The little voice inside had warned her, but her need to see her family had hushed it.

Mamma led them up to Carina's old room, then passed it and brought them to a guest room. "You'll have more space here." By that she meant a bigger bed. It was a room for married guests, and of course it made sense, but Carina felt strange going in. She was a guest now? Not family?

Mamma wouldn't look at Quillan. With her hand covering her mouth, she passed by him into the small room in back that held a maple commode and drain sink. She took the pitcher from the bowl and said, "Tia Marta will bring you water. The boys can bring your bags." The boys. Mamma thought of them all as children, though Angelo was thirty-four this spring.

Carina nodded. When the door closed, she turned to Quillan. He wore his rascal's smile. He could smile? "What?" She threw wide her hands.

He shrugged. "What did you expect, bringing home a rogue pirate?"

She stomped across the room and back. "My brothers are fools! I could have handled it better if they hadn't interfered."

"They were protecting you."

She stopped and looked at her husband. Did he look so disreputable? He wore his yoked shirt, having shed his buckskin coat on the drive. His pants were worn, his boots scuffed. Yet for all that, to her eye he looked strong and wonderful. Was it because she knew him to be? Couldn't they see him as he was, accept him as he was?

She threw her arms down at her sides. "They treat me like a child. I could have explained. Then Papa—"

"It wouldn't have mattered. He's right."

She knew it. From the very start. That was why she couldn't write, couldn't tell them. She had violated a trust deeply ingrained for generations, maybe forever. Though Papa would never have forced her to marry someone, he had the right, the privilege, of permitting or denying her choice. It was an affront to deeply ingrained traditions to show up with Quillan as she had. But what if she had written and they had told her not to come home? Could she have borne it?

She went to the window and looked over the hills stitched with grapevines in long straight rows. They had been pruned of their twisted arms and tangled manes and stood starkly against the wooden crosses that held each stalk. The sky hung misty blue, not brilliant as the mountain sky. Fuzzy green and frothy yellow filled the spaces between. The land was awakening, but not yet the vines.

Quillan joined her there, his palm warm against the small of her back. Carina couldn't tell what he was feeling. Her own feelings overwhelmed her. What had she done? How had it come to this? She thought of that day when Quillan had suggested they marry. So much fear had driven her, she never stopped to think of consequences outside of Crystal. In Crystal one lived by the edge of one's teeth. Here . . .

The door opened behind them. Tia Marta carried the pitcher to the washstand and placed it in the bowl. Then she came out of the anteroom. She did not avoid Quillan but stared pointedly. He gave a slight nod, which she returned, then rushed to Carina and held her. "Ah, Carina, ever the tiger. I told your Mamma . . ." She shook her head. "Ah, but you're back, eh? She's crying her eyes out in the kitchen. But she'll see."

Carina felt bleak. Mamma crying in the kitchen? Why? Because her daughter made a poor match? How could she tell? She knew nothing of Quillan. Nothing of what they'd shared, suffered, accomplished. Nothing of his own battles. But there was no reasoning with Mamma. "Where's Nonna?"

Tia's face jerked up, tears shining. She gripped her hands. "Oh, Carina. Nonna's in the grave, God rest her soul."

"No!" Carina's legs gave way, but Quillan caught her waist and kept her upright. Tears stung her eyes. This was the punishment she'd dreaded.

Tia Marta swiped at her eyes. "She passed two months after you left. In her sleep." She crossed herself.

Carina's chest heaved. She sagged against Quillan as Tia Marta went out and closed the door behind her. Nonna gone? Carina gasped for breath. And she hadn't said good-bye, hadn't prayed for Nonna's passing, hadn't even been there to ease her final hours. She spun and gripped Quillan's chest. "It's my fault. She was so worried, so—"

Quillan caught her hands. "It's not your fault." He circled her in his arms.

But it was, just as it had been with her baby. If she hadn't provoked the men, they would not have beaten her child to death inside her. And Nonna had been overwrought at her leaving.

She'd seen more than Mamma had. *You'll regret it, Carina. It's yourself you'll punish, not Flavio.* But she hadn't listened, and now Nonna was gone.

"Why didn't they tell me? How could they not tell me?" She poured her tears onto Quillan's chest.

His voice stayed low, gentle. "What good would it have done? You were too far to do anything."

"Don't tell me that!" She cried harder. It didn't matter that it was true. Nonna had died while she was gone. And it was her fault. She knew Nonna's heart was not strong, and she had broken it. This loss brought back the other, and Carina cried for the baby and Nonna together. Oh, why had she gone away?

Quillan held her in silence. He stroked her back and let her beat against his chest. This was not how she'd imagined it, not the way she'd wanted it. Had she thought they would welcome her with smiles and laughter, taking Quillan to their breasts and kissing his cheeks? Had she thought Nonna would be standing there, arms wide to welcome her home? She cried harder, shaking with sobs.

Now her whole family resented her, resented Quillan. She had come home, but it was not the refuge she had sought. *Oh, Signore.* She sniffed painfully. "What will I do? How can I face them?"

"They can't blame you, Carina. It's not your fault."

But he didn't know how it was, how their lives were intertwined like the very vines in their fields. If something killed one, the others sickened. What weakened one threatened the rest. She was like the insect destroying vineyard after vineyard while Papa worked furiously to keep it from his own vines.

There was a tap on the door, and Tony poked his head inside. "Giuseppe is asking for you, Carina."

She pushed back from Quillan. Giuseppe. Oh yes, she must see him, now especially. Tony glanced at Quillan, then shut the door without another word. Carina hurried into the anteroom and poured water from the pitcher into the sink. She plunged her hands into the warm, lemon-scented water and splashed it over her tear-streaked cheeks.

Quillan held the towel, and she pressed it to her face, slowing her breath and containing the awful emotion. *Help me, Signore!* As she prayed, she had a clear vision of Nonna rocking a baby in her arms. Carina gasped and opened her eyes. "She's in heaven with the baby."

Quillan furrowed his brow.

Dropping the towel, Carina grasped his hands. "Our baby, Quillan. Our baby's with Nonna. Maybe she knew, maybe God knew they must be together."

His expression showed he was not certain she was in her right mind, but she didn't care. She hurried out to the bedroom. "Come with me." She tugged him through the door and down the stairs. Women's voices came from the kitchen, some loud and angry, others trying to hush. Carina ignored them.

Outside they crossed the courtyard where their wagon stood unattended. Quillan hesitated. Carina knew he wanted to see to the horses. But she tugged him by the hand. "It's over here. By the barn." She took him through the courtyard gate and over across the yard. The mules would be out to pasture, though the winter grasses were thin. She passed the barn to the cottage beside it, a small whitened structure with a clay tile roof.

She didn't knock, just burst through the door and found Ti'Giuseppe sitting by his fire. No stove for Giuseppe. He filled the alcove with wood each morning and poked at it through the day. He turned in time to catch her, and she clung to his bony shoulders, kissing his cheeks with tears again streaking her own. He had shrunk. She felt his bones through his shirt, gathered and tied at the neck. "Tio?"

His lips parted on bare gums as his cheeks pulled into myriad lines, forming the smile she loved so dearly. "Bella Carina." His tongue formed the words, but it was his eyes that spoke them.

Carina knelt at his side. "Tio, this is Quillan."

Ti'Giuseppe squinted and reached out his hand.

Quillan gripped it, then covered it with his other. *"Il piacere è il mio."* The pleasure is mine. Quillan said it with perfect pronunciation, and she could see Ti'Giuseppe appreciated it.

She pulled up a chair beside Giuseppe for Quillan, then settled at his feet. "How are you, Tio?" She had to know he was well.

"I am better now to have you home." He cradled her shoulder.

Voice shaking, she said, "Tell me about Nonna," and covered his hand with hers.

His eyes stared away. "Nonna went with the angels. Very peaceful."

"Was she ill?"

He shook his head. "Only age. And there's no cure for that. Not even your papa, the dottore, can claim one."

Her throat tightened. "She had no pain, no suffering?"

Giuseppe's face softened. "There is always pain when you're old. She has none now."

Carina sighed. "I wasn't here."

He squeezed her shoulder. "You are now. And you've brought this man."

"My husband, Tio."

"I heard. You caused a fuss?"

Carina nodded.

"Your mamma?"

"Papa, too." She sank back against Quillan's legs.

"And Flavio." Giuseppe spread his papery hands.

She shrugged. "What do I care?" But she felt Quillan stiffen.

Giuseppe shook his head. "He will not take it lightly. The insult."

"The insult was his," she snapped.

Giuseppe looked at Quillan. "You watch your back, eh? They will avenge an affront to Flavio's honor."

Carina jerked up. "Flavio? With all his peace talk?" Did he not argue the evils of violence, decry physical force? It was his banner, yet underneath . . . No, Flavio would not—surely he would not . . .

Giuseppe spread his hands. "Talk is easy until it touches here." He tapped a finger to his chest.

Quillan rested his hand on Carina's shoulder. "Is Carina in danger?"

Old Giuseppe shook his head. "No. But you . . ." He pointed one finger at Quillan's face. "You have enemies. Not only her *fidanzato*, but her brothers, as well."

Carina knew that was true. Nevermind Flavio's unfaithfulness. They were blood brothers inside. Still she couldn't believe it would come to violence. "What can they do? Quillan is my husband. Will they make me a widow?"

Giuseppe sat back without answering. She looked up at Quillan. He met her gaze, defiant. She wet her lips. "We shouldn't have come."

"It's your home."

She shook her head. "Not if they're going to be ugly."

Quillan rested his hand on her head. "Don't worry about me."

"But you heard Tio."

"I heard." He stood up. "Now I need to see about my horses."
He went out.

Carina knelt before Ti'Giuseppe. "What do I do?"

He spread his hands. "Pray for God's will."

Sixteen

What lies a man believes to guard his feeble pride;
illusions fill his mind to succor him inside.

— Quillan

QUILLAN HAD UNHARNESSED the horses and led them to the trough by the time old Giuseppe came out with an oat bag. As he walked around the swan fountain trickling water from its upraised beak, Quillan gauged him older than Alan Tavish by a decade perhaps. He was bent but not gnarled, stiff though not arthritic. Life was kinder to some.

But there was a tremor in the old man's hand as Quillan handed the reins over, and he had lost all his teeth. Maybe the calamity of time just manifested differently. As Giuseppe led the horses to the barn, Carina came and stood at the gate; she looked lovely and exotic even with her features drawn in grief. Had he seen her in this environment, Quillan would never have dared to love her. Now that he saw what she was, what she came from, what she stood to lose—he would never have dared. But since he did, he was not going to back down because of any threats from her brothers. Or Flavio.

He hadn't arrived with any mental picture of the man. In fact, he'd forgotten him until this morning when Carina's face grew fierce. Flavio had wounded her, sent her running to Crystal with the hope he would come after her, prove his love, his regret. One look and Quillan knew that would never happen. Flavio was not that kind of man.

He had that melancholic beauty women gasped over, and

199

probably the changeable nature to match. But he was not one to lose face gracefully. Quillan believed Giuseppe's warning. His stomach twisted, but not with fear. He had thought he was through with the dragon, but what he'd felt for Alex Makepeace was nothing to this.

And he'd seen Carina's face. She might deny caring with all the bravado she could muster, but there was something between them still. Fine. Let Flavio come. He would release the wrath of Wolf's son. Quillan felt a check in his spirit. He looked up. What did God expect?

Then he thought of Carina's own words. *"Family is the most important thing."* Quillan's chest tightened painfully. He couldn't be an agent of destruction in her family, couldn't threaten what Carina held most dear.

What then? Leave? Never. He'd given his word. He watched her wander now over to the fountain and sit on the stone rim of the base. Her grief was apparent, but not eruptive at the moment. He untied and pulled the tarp from the back of the wagon. The furniture would need to be stored as long as they stayed in her father's house. But how long would that be? Anyway, there were things they would need now. Quillan opened the back, climbed up, and slid the trunk to the end of the bed. The sooner they found a place of their own, the better.

Quillan looked out through the courtyard gate to the land beyond—terraced and lined with vines, smelling of damp earth and sunshine ... Something stirred again like a tug inside his chest. He slid the trunk down and laid it on the cobblestones. Carina sighed. "What now?"

He straightened. "I don't know."

Carina's brother Lorenzo, he thought, came into the yard and stood, arms crossed. Quillan gave him a nod. "Lend a hand?" He took one trunk handle.

Lorenzo just stood. Quillan couldn't manage the trunk up the stairs by himself, so he set his end down and climbed into the wagon. He filled his arms with smaller bundles and bags, then jumped down. He passed Lorenzo near enough to sense the combative aura. Ignoring it, Quillan carried the bundles to the room, then returned.

Another brother had joined Lorenzo. Quillan wasn't sure which one; Tony, he guessed, the youngest. Together they carried

Carina's trunk past him and up the stairs. Quillan took a crate that held books and met the two brothers coming down the stairs. They neither turned nor retreated, so he backed down and let them pass, then started up again, every tendon tense. He hoped Carina appreciated his restraint. But then he realized that wasn't why he did it. Not for her approbation, but just because it was right.

She was still sitting at the fountain when he went back out. Both Tony and Lorenzo went up with a crate of books. Between Carina's collection and his own, there were several trips' worth. Quillan followed them up with another. They worked silently, emptying the wagon of all but the furniture—Carina's bed, lamp, washstand, and table.

"Bring the mules, Vittorio," Lorenzo called.

Quillan noted which brother that was and waited while he brought a pair of mules to pull the wagon. Quillan covered the bed again with the tarp, then tied it securely. He didn't want any moisture to damage the wooden furnishings. He felt as protective of Carina's things now as he'd been careless before. She didn't seem to care. Her tears had left her listless.

When Vittorio led the mules and wagon to the barn, Quillan sat down beside her at the fountain. Even that much made Lorenzo bristle. Couldn't a man sit beside his wife? Not if the man didn't belong, was a usurper, an outsider. That was what Lorenzo's glare said.

"Is all this land your father's?" Quillan spoke as naturally as he could manage.

Carina stood up. "Come. I'll show you." She walked stiffly toward the gate.

Angelo materialized there. "The ground is wet."

"We won't go into the vineyard."

"Go into the house. See what Mamma needs."

Carina drew herself up. "Get out of my way. I want to show my husband our land."

"It's not his land."

Carina's hands tightened at her sides. Though he had enjoyed seeing her kick Lorenzo, Quillan touched her shoulder now. "Another time, Carina."

"No." She stamped her foot. "This is my home. I will go where I please."

Angelo moved aside enough that Carina could pass if she wished, but Quillan was blocked. She turned and stalked to the house. Quillan held Angelo's gaze a full ten seconds before following. He found Carina in their room. She had opened the trunk and thrown her clothing over the bed. "They are insufferable! They think—"

"I'm after what you have."

She spun. "That's the only way you would marry me? Is that what they think?"

"I doubt they've gone as far as rape and pillage. But they don't put me past plundering."

"It's not funny, Quillan!" She stamped her foot again.

"I'm not laughing." He pulled her into his arms, dismayed when she started to cry again. "I'm sorry."

"Oh!" She threw up her hands.

Quillan caught them. "Give it time. They're shocked and angry." Especially Flavio, whom he noticed Carina avoided mentioning. "They'll get used to me."

"Oh, you don't know." She turned away and picked up a blouse from the bed. "Bearing a grudge is an art around here."

Quillan raised her chin. "They can't hate me forever."

"This life and the next."

Quillan reached for the blouse, draped it under her chin. "Isn't this the one we fetched off the mountain?"

She nodded.

"You hated me then. But see, I've brought you clean around."

She slid her arms around his waist.

He kissed her, whispering, *"T'amo."* Saying "I love you" in her language gave him a warmth that smothered all other concerns. If emotion brought forth Italian, Italian definitely brought emotion. But now was not the time. "I think I'll wash up."

"How can you do this?" Her fists came up between them.

"Do what?" He caught her fists in his palms.

"Act as though nothing is wrong?"

What could he tell her? He'd spent most of his life acting as though things didn't hurt, hiding his fear, his feelings. He wanted to be real with her, as she was with him, but he didn't know how. He kissed the crown of her head and released her. Then he gathered up his suit and went into the water closet.

Carina stared at the closed door behind which her husband disappeared. Had she missed something? Failed to understand the brutal looks from her brothers, Ti'Giuseppe's warning? Why did Quillan think this a lark? She had brought him into danger.

She spun and paced the room. She had thought Papa would be gracious even though she had insulted him by not seeking his blessing. She had thought Mamma might be difficult but would come around when she saw their love. She had imagined her brothers playful and adoring as they used to be. Had she changed everything so much?

And then she considered the heart of it. Flavio. She had expected him to marry Divina. Hadn't she? Or had she known bringing Quillan would be a slap to him? She searched inside, trying to see if there was a motive she had ignored. Yes, she had left with impure intentions. But the Lord had bought her for a price. He had brought her through more than she wanted to think. Even now, when her mind touched all she'd suffered, the hurt was fresh and raw.

No, she hadn't come home to punish Flavio, hadn't brought a husband to flaunt in his face. She had only wanted the safety and love of her people. But she *had* taken wicked delight in Flavio's shock. "Signore, forgive me."

One wrong thought now could bring everything down on their heads. God would root out and reveal her darkness. And it was there. A deep-seated satisfaction that she had hurt Flavio as much as he'd hurt her. He might be home right now, brooding on his loss. His fury would have seeped away, leaving the bald pain of love spurned. Despondency would overwhelm him, and he would know that he had caused it. His unfaithfulness had caused it.

"Signore, help me." She dropped to her knees beside the bed. "I should not gloat, not feel such satisfaction. Let me not take pleasure in his pain. Don't let me increase it." For even now thoughts of twisting the knife came to mind. "Am I so wicked? Don't I know what it is to lose what I love?" She pressed a hand to her belly where she had felt the life of her child and was seized with fear for Quillan. "Signore, protect my husband. Per favore, Dio."

Quillan then came out looking very presentable. His hair was tied back, revealing the fine bones of his facial features. His broad-cloth vest and frock coat did not hide his strong shoulders and muscular form. How handsome and good he was! Surely they would see!

Carina got up from her knees. Now she would dress. Dinner was always formal, but tonight she must show them how right she and Quillan were. She wished her wedding dress had not been ruined but chose it anyway. She had replaced the original lace with an inferior grade and brushed and cleaned all the mud and dust from the sea green silk. She shook it out now from its folds in the trunk and remembered the look in Quillan's eyes when he'd first seen her in it. Her heart beat a sharp staccato. *Signore, I love him so much!*

She went into the water closet to change, though she had dressed before him countless times. Here, in her home, she felt shy and young. She brushed her hair and twisted it back at the nape of her neck. When she came out, Quillan caressed her with his eyes. He must know how important this was, this first meal together. He tucked her hand in the crook of his arm, but before they walked down together she said, "I'll be in the kitchen with Mamma and the others. You will have to wait with the men."

"All right."

She meant it as a warning, but he was trying hard to look unconcerned. Maybe nothing would happen. They went down and separated at the foot of the stairs. Already Carina heard her brothers in the smoking room. Papa would be there, too, but she didn't hear him. She went through the narrow walkway to the kitchen behind the house and tied a stiff white apron over her dress. "What can I do?"

Her sister-in-law Rosa handed her a knife and a bowl of peppers. Joseph's wife had been the first to marry into the family and had fought the battle of acceptance because Mamma thought she wasn't good enough for Joseph. Now, plump and familiar, she moved to a corner with two-year-old Giovanni on her hip and watched Carina as though she were the stranger.

The kitchen was warm with redwood beams and creamy plastered walls. The lamps that hung at regular intervals sent a glow to the ceiling, which reflected back over the long marble work-table and stove. An icebox and pastry safe stood at opposite ends, but most of the beige tile floor was open, making it easy for many women to work together. Even those not working, Nonna in her later years and the mothers of infants, gathered in the kitchen at mealtime.

"Gelsomina has taken a Chinese cook," Tia Marta said to break the awkward silence.

"No." Carina glanced from Tia Marta to Mamma, who had stopped crying in order to cook, but made no effort to hide her misery. *"Veramente?"*

Marta nodded. "It's true. A *male* Chinese."

Carina tried to picture one of the pigtailed men in Tia Gelsomina's kitchen. But then, her godmother had never liked to cook. She would think it a good joke on the rest of them. Carina would have to go and see for herself. Maybe Gelsomina could help with Quillan, as well. She was not as rigid as Mamma and Papa.

Angelo's wife, Renata, leaned close to Lorenzo's petite wife, Sophie, and murmured something. Those two had experienced an easier time since Rosa took the brunt of Mamma's disfavor, though neither was perfect. Maybe that's all it was with Quillan. A little disapproval for a while ... bene, a healthy disapproval. Then everyone would see he wasn't so different.

Or was he? Carina raised her head and listened. The voices from the back room carried, but they were moderate, tempered. Either they were ignoring Quillan, or he was holding his own.

Mamma sniffed loudly and carried a pan of meat pastries to the oven. Already a pot of marinara sauce steamed on the stove with spaghetti drying over the chair backs. Plump purple sausages lay ready to fry in olive oil with the peppers Carina was cutting. Renata floured carp filets and laid them in a skillet already popping with oil. The aroma of crusty bread came from the oven. Mamma may be upset, but she was preparing a feast.

Carina thought of Nonna. It brought a fresh ache to see the kitchen without her, but for the moment her tears were spent. She wondered what her grandmother's reaction would have been. No, she knew. Nonna would have been shocked and angry that Carina had thrown away her match with Flavio. She had been partial to him from his youth, as she'd been to Carina. Nonna would have wept for her lost chance, but she would have seen Carina's love for Quillan, would have accepted it. Wouldn't she? Carina had to believe someone would.

The back door opened, and there was Divina with a basket. A

red shawl crossed over her chest and tied around her waist over the white blouse tucked into a gathered gray skirt. Carina had spent so many nights in painful fury over Divina's betrayal, but now she felt only sisterly love. Spreading her arms, Carina went to hug her sister and felt the protruding stomach against her own empty womb. Divina seemed full for four months.

She kissed Divina's cheek. "Oh, Divina, I missed you."

Divina stepped back. "Nicolo says you're married."

"Yes." Carina released her.

Divina's face squinched up, and she hissed, "How could you?"

Carina froze. Surely Divina understood? But her sister stalked past her to the marble table, laid out the apples from her basket, and set it aside. What right had she to bitterness, when Carina had stripped off her own and forgiven Divina's betrayal? In what way had she hurt Divina? In what way caused the breach between them?

Flavio. It was there in Divina's face. Divina loved Flavio. Because he was the one she couldn't have? But she had! Carina had seen them together, confronted them, and Divina had laughed. Carina's heart seized with the memory. That was why she'd fled. And Flavio did not come after her. So there was Divina's chance, yet she married Nicolo—solid, stocky Nicolo with a face like a bear. Bene. It was not Carina's part to figure it out. She had her own troubles.

The voices from the house grew louder, but Nicolo would have joined them and maybe another brother or two. Carina went back to cutting. She sliced the peppers into long thin strips and removed the stems, thick with seeds.

"How are you feeling?" Mamma asked Divina.

"Sick in the mornings. Nicolo has to fetch me bread before I can sit up."

Carina could just picture it, Nicolo panting by the side of the bed as Sam used to, tail wagging. Sam. Carina understood why Quillan left him with Alan Tavish, but she missed the dog's warm eyes and wet nose. She carried the stems to the compost bowl but scraped the seeds into a bowl. They would be saved and planted in the garden.

Now one voice rose up in the other room. Angelo's, of course. The oldest son pushing his weight. He was always the loudest and most outspoken. What Ti'Giuseppe called a blusterer. His words sounded clearly through the open kitchen door. "How do you intend to support my sister?"

Quillan's answer was too soft to hear.

"And you'll live off the fat of our land until then?"

All hands in the kitchen stopped. Carina held the knife suspended over the cutting board over the compost bowl. Some of the women looked toward the door, others at her. Carina could discern Quillan's voice, but not his words.

Mamma held out a papery bulb. "Crush the garlic, Carina."

But Carina set down her utensils and pulled off her apron. Tia Marta put a hand to her shoulder, but Carina hurried through the door.

Angelo's tone was more insulting than angry. "Can you read? Can you write? Do you—" He broke off when Carina came into the room, fists to her hips.

"Of course he reads! And writes poetry. And memorizes books. *You* can't claim as much!"

Angelo reddened. He wasn't stupid by any account, but neither was he a stellar student. Her brothers looked at Quillan, seemed to reappraise him, then dismissed that for their original assessment. Angelo sneered, "What has he to show for it?"

Quillan looked wary, tense. She didn't think the others could tell, but in his charcoal-rimmed gray eyes she saw something of Wolf. Carina waited for him to tell them about his mine, his fortune. Surely he'd made something from the sale? If not, he must have done well enough freighting? But Quillan said nothing, only stood with one hand holding his lapel.

Papa leaned one elbow on the mantel, elegant in silk-embroidered vest and white sleeves, exactly as Carina had remembered him—except for his expression. He said softly, "Where is your family? Who are they?"

Carina started to answer, but Papa sent her a scathing glare. "Let him answer for himself."

She clutched her hands together. What would Quillan say? Surely not the truth.

"My parents are dead."

Papa waved his hand. "Grandparents, uncles, cousins?"

Quillan shook his head a little stiffly.

Papa frowned. "You have no relatives?"

Carina's breath caught. She pictured William DeMornay in his fine mansion, his slender fingers folded in his lap, his grim expression. *"What are you after . . . money?"*

Quillan said, "No."

Carina's breath returned. The DeMornays had denied him. Even though the locket proved otherwise—the diary, as well—in their minds, at least William's, Quillan did not exist.

"So you have nothing." Papa extended his fingers disdainfully.

For the first time Carina saw his arrogance, and Quillan saw it, too. She watched his fire ignite.

Papa's chin raised. "And you think you should live here with my daughter, with my blessing, when you bring nothing."

Quillan's jaw tightened; the tendons stood out under his flesh. "I bring myself. Judge me on that."

Papa's eyes locked with Quillan's. "Then you have already failed. You stole my daughter, disgraced her and me."

Quillan said, "I have never disgraced Carina."

Papa's fist came down on the mantel. Carina jumped. Never had Papa lost his temper publicly!

"You contradict me? In front of my family?" He swung his arm to include all his sons.

Quillan said, "I meant no disrespect."

The vein in Papa's temple pulsed, but he contained his anger. "You found my daughter vulnerable and forced your attentions—"

"It wasn't like that, Papa!" Carina's hands clenched at her sides. "He saved my life!" Now all eyes were on her. "In my letter I told you Crystal was lovely, but it wasn't. It was hard and terrible. I went to Quillan for help."

Papa's eyes narrowed. "And he used that to marry you?"

Carina spread her hands. "It was all he could do to stop a man who was truly worthy of your disdain. You should thank him, Papa, for saving me from shame. I was the foolish one. Not Quillan."

Papa's mouth pulled down. "You defend him, but that does not excuse—"

Quillan stepped forward. "I ask your pardon for marrying without your blessing. If circumstances had permitted, I would have asked it."

Papa looked him up and down without speaking. Would he

accept Quillan's apology? Fervently she hoped so. He said, "I would have refused."

Quillan's chin dropped just enough that Carina felt the blow.

"You're a stranger to our ways, our religion, our life. I would not have wished exile for my daughter."

"I can learn." Quillan drew himself up.

"He can, Papa. You should see how quickly he learns the language." Carina leaned forward earnestly.

"Then we'll have to watch what we say." Papa's words were cruel, brutal in impact. He would not accept Quillan, not give him a chance.

Carina looked around the room, every face hostile, judging. Her fists hardened again at her sides. "If you don't accept Quillan, you don't accept me."

Angelo exploded. "Be quiet, Carina. This is our father's business."

Carina looked at Quillan. He stood stiffly, too proud to show the hurt she knew was there. It wasn't Papa's business. It was theirs.

Quillan dropped his hands to his sides. "Thank you for your hospitality. I won't impinge further."

Carina caught her breath sharply. "If you go, I go, too."

Quillan shook his head. "You need to stay here with your family."

"I'd rather sleep on the street." She turned for the door.

Angelo caught her arm. "Don't you dare insult Papa." His fingers dug into her flesh.

"I won't stay without my husband." She shot her gaze to Papa.

Her father raised a hand. "It's your husband who leaves you."

The pain shot through her. Would he? Had Quillan brought her there only to leave again? She turned to him, beseeching. Quillan's gaze softened. He wanted her to understand . . . what? Why he would leave her? She struggled against Angelo's hold, but Lorenzo caught her other arm and held her firmly.

Her eyes followed Quillan as he walked through the door. She heard his steps on the stairs. He was going. He would pack his things and go. Her heart thumped inside her. "No!" She fought off Angelo and Lorenzo and ran for the stairs, holding her side where the corset made hard breathing painful. She rushed into the room. "I won't let you go."

Quillan straightened from the bag he had opened. She rushed to him, clasped him in her arms, and pressed her tear-streaked face to his chest.

He returned her embrace with desperate force, kissing her head. "It's only for a while, Carina, until I can find us a place or build one."

"No." She shook her head.

He caught her face. "I'm not leaving you. But I can't stay under this roof."

"Then let me come." She covered his hands, pressed his palms against her cheeks.

He shook his head. "If you came now, it would destroy any chance we have. Show your father the respect he demands."

Carina shook her head. "Where will you be?"

"In town somewhere. I'll let you know."

A sob caught in her throat. "This can't be right."

"You heard him, Carina. I have to prove that I'm no different, that I can be what you are."

"So prove it here!" She clung to his hand.

He stood back. "Do you really believe that's possible?"

She looked up into his face. He was no fool, her husband. But it broke her heart to watch him go. He stuffed the rest of his clothes from the trunk into the bag, took up his leather pack and another satchel. He bent and kissed her lips, then left the room. His steps going down were like blows. She threw herself onto the bed and sobbed.

How could they be so cruel? What had he done? Why must he always prove himself worthy? Would no one ever accept him? She punched her fists into the bed. She accepted him, loved him. But she was being denied even that.

Had she committed some unforgivable sin? She thought of all the things she had hoped Quillan wouldn't say, the things she wanted to keep hidden. Was she ashamed of him, of Rose and Wolf? Was she ashamed of the way their marriage had happened? Did she know inside it was wrong?

No! She thrust herself up. She almost ran after him, but he was right. They had to make her family see, and they couldn't do that if she made the breach so wide it couldn't be healed. So Papa was human. So he'd been insulted. She would show him her love, her respect. Then she'd show him all the reasons he should love and accept Quillan.

She snatched a handkerchief from the bed and wiped her face. Then one by one she hung her dresses in the wardrobe, then folded her blouses and undergarments into the drawers. She looked up at the knock. "Yes?"

Divina opened the door. "Dinner is ready."

Carina seethed. She should go down now and eat with them? "I'm not hungry."

Divina advanced. "You deserve it, Carina. You've caused no end to misery. Flavio—"

"What about him?" Carina clutched her gabardine camisole.

Divina's face was a knife. She had put on more weight than just the baby, but her face now looked sharp enough to cut. "You know he'll never love anyone but you."

Carina huffed out her breath at the absurdity. "You can say that?"

"You stupid baby." Divina brought her face up close. "You think because Flavio dallies he doesn't love you?"

"Dallies, Divina?" Carina questioned. "Whose child is in your belly?"

Divina's slap numbed Carina's ear and burned her cheek. Carina pressed her palm on the stinging flesh. She stood frozen as Divina stalked from the room, then she backed into the bed and sat down, covering her eyes with her hands. Could anything else go wrong?

It was as if some evil had pervaded her family while she was gone. Everything that had been safe and good was gone. Everyone had changed. Or did she just see them differently? Had she been so self-centered and arrogant herself that she couldn't see it in them? Had she been so coddled and petted that she blinded herself to reality?

No. There was good. There had to be. She had brought distress to her family, but even in that they held together, stood as one. They were loyal to each other. It was just that she was now outside it. She dropped to her knees. "Signore, tell me what to do. I love my family. They are my people, my life. This land, this place—the moment I saw it again, my heart jumped inside me. I want to live here with my husband, raising our children."

She swallowed the hard lump in her throat and pressed a

hand to her belly. No new life had replaced the other. Her cycles were irregular, and there were times she felt a weakness all through her. Maybe it was best no life took hold. What if she couldn't sustain it? She thought of Divina's belly full with child. Whether Nicolo's or Flavio's, it didn't matter. She would hold a baby in her arms, suckle it at her breast.

Carina's loss overwhelmed her. She climbed onto the bed and cried. When Mamma came in, sat down, and embraced her, she wished for one moment she were a little girl again, playing with her brothers, her cousins, even Divina, who didn't play fair. She wished she could go back in time before she knew such grief as this.

"Shh, shh." Mamma stroked her hair.

But all Carina could think was how Quillan's mother had done the same, and how he had remembered the feel of her hair from infancy. Mamma had to understand. "I love him, Mamma. As much as you love Papa. I had his baby inside me, but it's dead now. They beat it out of me." She crumpled into Mamma's arms.

"Dear God, dear God." Mamma rocked her.

"You have to help me. I can't live without him." She didn't want to.

Mamma said nothing, but held her.

Carina pulled away. "Papa has to see."

"It's not only Papa."

Carina swiped her tears. "The others will listen."

Mamma shook her head. "Tell me why, Carina. Flavio gave you his heart, you, out of everyone he could have chosen. You know it's true. He could have had any girl, but he loved you, loves you still."

Carina stiffened. "He wasn't faithful, Mamma."

She shrugged. "So he's young. He would settle down when his children came."

Carina bit her lip hard to keep from saying his child was on the way. Mamma was not stupid. She knew Divina's belly was not a four-month size. But was it possible she knew nothing of Flavio's part?

"Anyway, it doesn't matter. I have a husband."

Mamma dropped her eyes. "Did he force you? It could be annulled if—"

"No!" Quickly she told Mamma about Berkley Beck and how

Quillan had protected her from a terrible marriage. It sounded impossible, but Mamma had no experience of Crystal, of roughs, of vigilantes.

Mamma gathered her black lace shawl and tied it around her shoulders. "The marriage could be unlawful on grounds of coercion. You were forced by circumstances."

Carina stared at her. Had she heard nothing? "Mamma." She caught her mother's face, made her look at her. "Quillan is my husband under God. Nothing will sever that."

Mamma didn't answer. She stroked Carina's cheek, and a tear pooled in her eye. Fear filled Carina, fear of something in Mamma's thoughts. But her mother stood up. "Why don't you come down and eat?"

Just like that? Carina looked up. "I'm not hungry."

Mamma shrugged. "As you like." Willowy and graceful, she left the room.

Carina stared after her. If she had agreed to annul the marriage, would Quillan now be safe?

Seventeen

Hatred: Forged in the heart, like poisoned air it seeps, from lips and eyes finding escape. And I? I am the smith who hammers it into the hearts of those I would esteem, those I wish esteemed me.

— Quillan

QUILLAN LAID ASIDE the journal. The room he'd found in the Union Hotel was suitable. But looking around it, he almost felt homesick for the simplicity of his tent on the creek in Crystal when he was answerable to no one but himself. He thought over the words he'd written, bitter words borne of yet another rejection. This time he had tainted Carina, as well. He closed his eyes, but her tear-streaked face was in his mind. Eyes open or closed, he saw her.

Because of him, her family resented her. How far would they go? He slammed his fist into his palm. His first thought was to run, to desert her. Wasn't desertion grounds for annulment? Then he realized it was impossible. He had made a covenant before God. He intended to keep it.

So the only thing to do was what he said before. He had to learn to be Italian. The thought sent a flicker of amusement, which was quickly quenched. Too much rested on it. But then, how did he know he wasn't? Wolf's people could have been from Italy. What's to say they weren't? Carina's father was fair, blue eyed. Joseph and Lorenzo, as well. Maybe Wolf's golden hair and gray eyes came from the same stock. But he was being fanciful.

Quillan stretched his legs out on the bed and thought of Carina and her family. How had he seemed to them? He was educated, yes; possessed extraordinary memory. And he had money, plenty of it. But the flood had taught him that didn't make the man. And he knew that even if he had named the amount, Carina's family would have rejected him. He was flawed. He must be.

Quillan lay back and stared at the ceiling. Maybe Mrs. Shepard had it right. She had seen his deficiency. No matter what he did, it would be there. The DeMornays had seen it, the railroad detectives, too. And now the DiGratias. But that would not stop him. Quillan closed his eyes and pictured the room full of DiGratia men, Carina's father and brothers. One day he would stand among them, if not welcome then respected. His chest rose and fell. He owed Carina that much.

Sitting up he dug into his pack for Cain's Bible, his Bible now. He'd committed large portions of the first three gospels to memory. The Shepards had forced him to learn verses as a child; now he devoured the text by his own desire. He opened to the fourth gospel, Saint John's, chapter fifteen. *I am the true vine, and my Father is the husbandman.*

Quillan pictured the fields he and Carina had passed through, lined with root-shaped trunks cloaking the hills between squares of wheat and oats. Pale green, gold, and vibrant yellow amid the stark brown vines that looked more dead than alive. Those were the vineyards, those rows of gnarled blackish stumps. He looked back at the text, sensing a message he was meant to grasp, but not understanding.

Every branch in me that beareth not fruit he taketh away: and every branch that beareth fruit, he purgeth it, that it may bring forth more fruit. Quillan looked up at the ceiling. Did he bear fruit? He was trying to. So that put him in the next category. He certainly felt that some of his old behaviors had been purged. "All right, Lord. You've been working on me. Now what?"

Abide in me, and I in you. As the branch cannot bear fruit of itself, except it abide in the vine; no more can ye, except ye abide in me.

Those were Jesus' words, but what was He saying to the people who had gathered? What was He saying to Quillan now? Abide in Him, though everything else be stripped away? That only through the Lord's help would he keep the covenant he had made? Become what he was expected to become?

I am the vine, ye are the branches. He that abideth in me, and I in him, the same bringeth forth much fruit; for without me ye can do nothing.

Quillan felt the truth of it. For all the years he'd fought God, there was little to show. A moderate fortune made by the sweat of his labor and blind luck. A few friends, but also enemies. And Carina. Carina had seen his flaws, suffered the worst he had to give, but loved him still. That was a wonder he could scarcely comprehend. But it sustained him as he committed the first ten verses of the fifteenth chapter to memory, then closed the book and went to sleep.

The next morning he went out. The first order of business was employment. The hotel clerk had suggested the imposing store on the northeast corner of the plaza, so he headed that way, assessing the building he approached. It had an attractive Victorian front complete with cupola and porch and looked nothing like the adobe barracks the man assured him it had been.

His view was blocked abruptly by Flavio and Nicolo, emerging from a narrow gap between two buildings. At the sight of him, they stopped talking and moving. Pausing his stride, Quillan stepped to his right. They stepped the same way, confused or contrary he couldn't tell. Quillan moved to his left as a third man came up a little behind them. Three to one. Not good odds if they meant to get ugly.

Quillan hesitated then stepped off the sidewalk and went around, not as much of an issue as it would have been in Crystal with the streets clogged with people and either rushing mud or choking dust. Quillan returned to the walkway near enough to hear the smug guffaws. If that was the worst Flavio could do, Quillan had dealt with it every day in primary school. He found a man unlocking the doors of the store.

"Good morning." The man spoke pleasantly enough.

"Good morning. My name's Quillan. I'm looking for employment."

The man turned the knob and pocketed his keys. "Solomon Schocken. What are you looking to do?"

"Well, if you're Mr. Schocken, the clerk at the Union Hotel said you had several interests I might consider. I have a freight wagon and team of four."

Schocken opened the door and admitted him. "This is my store."

Quillan looked about, noting the orderly, well-stocked shelves and tables. "Successful enterprise by the looks of it."

That obviously pleased him, but Schocken wasn't puffed up. "I have several such."

Quillan cocked his head. "I'm versatile."

Schocken appraised him, seemingly undaunted by whatever the DiGratias had found offensive. But Quillan had fit easily with working men, businessmen, even those like Horace Tabor who had come into better times. It was only personal acceptance he seemed to fend off without trying.

Schocken said, "I could take you on in the store. I've been looking to save myself some hours. But that seems a waste of your wagon and team. I've not much need for that sort of hauling here, with the railroad passing directly before as it does. Of course there'd be occasional transportation of furniture and such. But I've another enterprise you might consider."

Quillan waited while Schocken removed his coat and tied on an apron. "A basalt quarry. You might have seen it on your way in. We supply cobbles for San Francisco, Petaluma, San Jose. Quite an operation. I need wagons to haul the stones down Schocken Hill to the depot here at the plaza."

Quillan pictured it. Not so different from hauling ore, though he'd eschewed that out of preference. "What do you blast with?"

"What blasting we do is with nitro sticks. Dynamite. Safer than powder and far more stable."

"Until it freezes." At Schocken's surprise, Quillan added, "I've had some experience there. Hauled for the Leadville mines. Those white crystals of frozen nitro are no picnic."

Schocken reassessed him. "True. But we're not contending with mountain climes. Still, your experience would be helpful. What do you say?"

Quillan considered the offer. It could serve to get him established.

Schocken pulled open the window shades. "I've got a good crew. Mainly Italians. I import them."

Italians. That should prove interesting. And now his pluck quickened. "All right. Do you have anything for the evenings?"

Schocken turned with the feather duster he'd lifted from the corner socket. "The evenings?"

"I don't like much slack time."

For a moment Schocken seemed without an answer, then said, "How about stocking the shelves here at the store?"

Quillan looked around again. The store was long and filled with groceries and provisions, furnishings, dry goods, and yard goods. He saw racks of clothing, boots, and shoes. Shallow crates held cutlery, tin ware, and hardware. That should just about keep him busy enough to stave off the ache for his wife. At least until he figured out what to do about that. "Okay."

"You're an enterprising one. I admire that."

"When do I start?"

Schocken tapped the duster against his palm. "As soon as my clerk arrives, we'll go out to the quarry. Mr. Marconi is the foreman. He'll direct you from there."

Quillan nodded. "I'll set up my team." He went out and surveyed the plaza. The narrow gauge tracks ran along Vallejo Street on the corner of which sat Schocken's store. The cross street alongside the store was named easily enough First Street East.

Across the plaza, he saw two other general merchandise stores, a hardware store, and a couple blacksmiths and bakeries—one named Union like the hotel and livery; it wasn't hard to tell where the sympathies of these folks lay. There was a meat market, druggist, and stationer. He also counted several Chinese stores around the plaza. They included two laundries, three restaurants, a grocery, and one establishment that said simply *Chinese Store* and listed fireworks for sale. Sonoma was like any another town except for its pleasing layout around the square and what seemed regular quadrants flanking that. Very neat, though the pressed dirt streets were none too clean. Was there no provision for waste?

As he stood catching his bearings, a diminutive Chinese man stepped from the grocery and started down the street calling, "Fluit, cabbagie, ladish, splouts. Allie same plice."

Quillan's ear twisted around the pronunciation as the man in a shiny dresslike getup pushed his small wheeled cart past.

"Fushie and slimps. Vely flesh. Allie flesh. Allie same plice." The little man looked at him, then passed by, no doubt pegging him for a stranger not likely to buy. The man's braided hair reached almost to the street. Quillan was duly impressed.

He started for the Union Livery and Feed, where he'd left his wagon and team after removing them from Giuseppe's care. The furniture remained covered with a tarp in the DiGratia's barn. It was Carina's, after all. But he had to stop thinking like that. It wasn't his wagon and her furniture. It was all theirs. He couldn't allow division in his thoughts or the division in their lives could take root.

The livery was right next to his hotel, and after calling for his team and wagon, he went up to his room, donned the buckskin coat to protect against stones kicked up by the horses, and his broad-brimmed hat for the sun. He felt like a freighter again, and the familiarity settled him. It may not be his final vocation, but for now it was one familiar thing among so much strange.

He met Solomon Schocken in front of the store. Schocken climbed up beside him. "Fine rig."

Quillan nodded.

"Are the horses heavy shod? The stone in the quarry can be sharp and troublesome."

Quillan hadn't thought of that. They were shod for long hauls on rough roads, though. "I think they'll do. I'll check them over tonight."

They shared small talk on their way to the quarry, Quillan revealing as little of his situation as possible, partly because he didn't understand it himself. He had brought Carina home, but what did that mean for him?

———

Carina's eyes ached from weeping, but she could pursue sleep no longer, so she forced them open. The morning was well advanced, but no one had wakened her. She sat up groggily, reminiscent of the effects of laudanum. This time it was only grief and worry that made her heavy and slow. She sighed.

Pulling herself up, she washed and dressed. The morning sun was muted as always by the haze that lingered on the valley though the sky was clear. Much of the rain for the season was past. Now the slow warming would begin, the awakening of the land, the waking of the vines. She twisted the front strands of her hair back over her ears and plaited them together, leaving the bulk of her hair hanging down her back.

She saw in the looking glass that she had lost weight. With

her corset merely snug, the side seams of her dress were no longer tightly fitted. She put a hand to her flat belly. Was it possible she'd never bear a child? She vaguely recalled Mae asking Dr. Felden about that, and his nebulous reply. He had cautioned her again before she and Quillan left, cautioned that her kidneys might not support a pregnancy.

And anyway, with Quillan gone how would she conceive? She quickly shook the gloomy thought away. Quillan was not gone. He had promised to stay in town. She would make some excuse to find him there today. To see him, to touch him, to hear his voice.

She dropped to her knees. "Grazie, Signore, for this day. All things are in your hands. Melt my will to yours, but . . . per favore, give me back my husband." That had to be God's will. How could He will otherwise when He had given her Quillan before? Surely God did not give only to take away.

She might have believed that once—had believed it. But not anymore. The God she came to know on the mountains of Colorado was not a capricious God, playing with her heart. He was faithful and true. Goodness and grace. If she must suffer separation now, it was somehow for her good and Quillan's. "But how, Signore? I don't understand."

And maybe she wasn't meant to. Maybe she had only to trust. She stood up and smoothed her skirts. She might not be plump and soft, and her eyes were red and dry, but she would not sulk. Somehow she must make peace between her family and her husband. She went out.

Mamma was in the conservatory dribbling water over the newly sprouted tomato plants that would go into the garden after all chance of frost was past. Carina watched her with pride and fury. She'd always been proud of Mamma, so capable and lovely, so fiercely protective of her own. Was that it now? Did she feel threatened by Quillan?

Carina walked in, watched Mamma test the soil in the little clay pots with her finger, then drip water over the plants. She imagined the round red tomatoes that would make rich chunky sauces pungent with herbs and garlic. She looked over the other plants, squashes and eggplant and peppers, melons and beans, and then the herbs on shelves along the glass wall, tended all year. The conservatory carried their fragrance through deepest winter, which of course, was nothing to Crystal's snow-covered freeze. Nonetheless, the greenhouse gave Mamma an advantage over other wives in the area.

Papa used herbs for his medicines, also. His area of the greenhouse had plants arranged and labeled according to phylum, order, and species. Carina remembered him teaching her how to recognize and use them. She wandered over. Buttercup for asthma, arnica for sprains, slippery elm, aloe, chamomile, and clover for burns. Colds called for mullein plant made into candy. Coughs: onion syrup, unless they were severe, then Papa used paregoric, which he made from opium and camphor. She knew so many of his remedies, had applied them herself.

Thinking of Papa made her heart ache afresh. How could he have been so cruel, so cold and unyielding? That was not the Papa she knew. Yes, she had hurt him, but . . . Again she sighed.

Mamma looked up, watched her a long moment, their eyes holding each other with mingled hurt and love. Then Mamma said, "Good morning, Carina."

"Good morning, Mamma."

"There is tea and sugar in the kitchen. I know you didn't sleep." From the look of Mamma's eyes, she had not slept either.

Carina nodded. "Thank you, Mamma." She went out to the kitchen where the kettle was held just below boiling and the strainer filled with tea leaves over a cup. Carina steeped the tea, poured in some fresh cream, and spooned sugar into the cup. She slowly stirred, noting the small way Mamma had shown her love. On a cloth-covered dish stood a miniature panettone, baked only for special occasions.

Breathing the wonderful candied fruit aroma, Carina carried it with her tea to the marble table and sat down. Closing her eyes, she blessed the food, then cut and took the first wonderful bite. Oh, how she wished Quillan were there to experience it with her. Her lip quivered, and she sniffed back tears that once again threatened. Would they love and pamper her into forgetting this man they would not accept?

Carefully she wrapped the round, sweet loaf in the cloth and fit it into her pocket. She finished her tea, then went out of the kitchen through the back door. She passed the conservatory, saw Mamma watching through the glass. She didn't care. She would find Quillan and share the sweet.

But then she saw Papa. His pose and what he held stopped her. He stood at the edge of the vineyard, one entire grape stalk in his arms, its hairy roots dangling. Slowly she approached. "Papa?"

He turned.

"What is it, Papa?" But she saw the powdery yellow roots, knew already what he would say. "Phylloxera?"

He nodded. For over ten years the Sonoma vineyards had been plagued, whole fields destroyed by the parasitic insect that looked like sulfur powder on the roots of the vines. Papa had battled to keep his vines producing, trying one remedy after another. She looked at the rows of vines. Soon budbreak would begin, but the stalks looked sickly and weak. Could they even produce?

Papa sighed. "I think it's time."

"Time, Papa?"

He had resisted plowing the vines under, laying his fields to waste as so many others had been forced to do. "They will not survive another season. It's no use."

Carina's spirit sagged. All their work, their heart, their care—for nothing. No wonder Papa had little patience for insults. She saw two of her brothers scattered among the vines, checking the wood with little pruning knives and shaking their heads. The financial loss would be substantial, the emotional loss far worse.

Growing grapes was not the same as growing wheat or corn. It required nurture and individual attention to each vine. Every pruning was gauged by the particular plant's energy. How many canes were left and how many buds per cane would determine how that vine's strength would be directed. The more wood that was removed, the fewer buds that vine would produce. Fewer grapes made deeper flavor, but less wine. It was a delicate balance.

Then there was weeding, suckering, and tying up the cordons, the care given to the fragile white blooms that came out in May and filled the fields with an intense sweet honey smell, turned pink, then brown, then fell to the ground like weightless snow-flakes. The vines must make it through May without heavy rain or wind or the blooms would be lost.

Then the long, warm summer days would produce the fruit, appearing first beneath the leaves like tiny baby peas. At least a hundred days were needed from bloom to harvest for the fruit to swell. Sometimes in Sonoma they were blessed with more, even a month more in the best years. The vine grower must be patient and closely attuned.

And harvest. Harvest took the most toll on the emotions. The vine grower must guess the weather, eking every possible day from the season to give the grapes time. Only time on the vine allowed the grapes to sweeten. Her papa went out every day in August, walked among the vines, "bowing" to the grapes as he bent to see the developing fruit underneath the leaves. By taste he would determine the day, waiting for the last possible moment.

Then he would give the word, and suddenly the urgency to get the grapes in would sweep the family and what helpers they had amassed. Grapes would be grasped, sliced at the stem with a sharp curved blade, and dropped to the bins dragged along from vine to vine. Then the men would swoop up the filled bin atop their heads and, whooping and hollering, run to the wagon to unload. Even the thought filled Carina with fervor.

How could Papa bear it? If he was truly certain, all the roots would be yanked up and left flat on their sides in the dust, then gathered up and burned. They would have to start over with new root stock, hoping it would prove resistant. Even if it did, it was two years of tending the new vines before they would be allowed to fruit, and the wine from young vines was light and fragile, less complex, and unable to stand much oak from the barrels.

All this, she knew, was in her papa's heart as he looked over his trellised field. She put a hand to his arm. "I'm sorry, Papa." And as she said the words, she was sorrier still that she had wounded him, as well. If he felt defeated by his fields, how much more her insult must sting.

He turned only slightly. "It's life," he said.

She started to respond, but Angelo stalked up from the field with a face so self-righteous and belligerent she turned away. "Mamma needs you inside, Carina."

"For what?" She bristled as he caught her arm.

"I'll walk you in."

She could have wiggled free, but not without making a scene. And that she would not do. Not with Papa standing so silently. She walked with her brother, then couldn't resist asking, "How bad is it? Is Papa right that it's all lost to the pest?"

"The vines could maybe struggle on, but for what? The roots are decayed. No fruit will flourish. It'll only get worse."

"Papa was so sure he'd find a remedy."

"There is none." Angelo's face darkened as he stopped her at the door. "Leave Papa alone. He has enough to deal with."

Carina opened her mouth, but Angelo had turned away. He wouldn't listen to anything she had to say. He'd made up his mind. They all had. Throughout the day as she helped Mamma and Tia Marta with the spring cleaning in the house, she caught one or another brother watching from outside. To keep her in? What did they think to accomplish?

Quillan felt every one of the days he'd slacked off work—the days in Crystal before they left and the days on the train. Now, having loaded and hauled stone a full eight hours, his muscles had the familiar, though exaggerated, ache of a day spent in labor. Mr. Marconi was thorough and insistent the work be done swiftly and well. The Italian workers were diligent and talkative, though not to him since they preferred their own language.

Some words he picked up as their jobs intersected, some more as they sat to their lunches, which he had neglected to secure for himself before heading out to the quarry. His stomach rumbled now as he left the team to the liveryman's ministrations. But he was covered in rock dust, and before he could acquire vittles, he needed to wash. The sun was sinking in the sky when he finished scrubbing himself and had changed into a clean shirt, vest, and pantaloons.

Though there was a pub in the hotel, he went out to see what else the town offered. He had tucked several bills inside his vest pocket, but by the menus posted in the windows of the first two eateries he passed, the prices in Sonoma were lower than Crystal by plenty. Of course, the location and railroad made the transfer of goods more economical. He would grab a bite, then report to the store for his second shift of the day.

Rounding the corner, he caught sight of Carina. In the last of the sun's rays, her hair hung like a rippling shawl over her shoulders. Her step was quick, her expression earnest, her waist impossibly small. His heart jumped inside him as he imagined clasping it between his hands and swinging her into the air. The feeling was so intense he could almost be falling in love with her for the first time again.

She caught sight of him, and her face lit as she hurried over. "I was hoping to find you!" She held a basket over one arm, while the other hand touched his. He hadn't realized he'd held his out. It must have moved without any effort from his brain. But they got no closer than that.

"How's your family?" He cracked a half smile.

She huffed. "*Impossibile*. Angelo watches me like a dog on point. He has all my brothers on guard. Papa will hardly talk to me, and Mamma—" Carina looked away—"Mamma looks as though her heart is broken."

Quillan felt a surge of protective anger. Couldn't they be decent to her, at least?

Carina sighed. "Did we do the wrong thing?"

His heart clutched. Had they made her doubt already?

"Should we have stayed in Crystal?"

His chest eased. "We did the right thing. You needed to see them, and they needed to know, whether they like it or not."

She dropped her chin. "They're so—" her hands fisted at her sides—"old country! Don't they know this is America? Everyone created equal? Papa thinks on two levels. Mamma shouldn't. Didn't Papa choose beneath him? Because he loved her!"

Quillan's mouth quirked at her unintentional insult. "It only works one way."

"What do you mean?" Carina's face was fierce.

"It's one thing for a young woman to better herself by marrying the famous dottore. It's another altogether for her daughter to marry a scoundrel."

Carina stamped her foot. "You're not a scoundrel!"

Quillan cocked his head. "Your first impression was pirate. Is theirs so far off?"

"But you—"

"What? Cleaned up? You think that's what they see?"

She threw out her hand. "What do they see?"

He took her hand and led her away from the plaza, behind the buildings clustered around it, into the fields beyond. He stopped and turned her chin up. "They see their dreams for you ruined."

Her eyes showed him the truth of it. "What about *my* dreams?"

He cupped her cheek, feeling a poignant stab. What were her

dreams? He didn't even know. "The best I can do is earn their approval."

Now it was doubt in her dark luminous eyes. She pressed his hand to her cheek. "We could leave. Go to Alaska."

She had so little faith in him? "I've spent my life without family, Carina. You were eight months away and needing yours."

She didn't argue. "Why can't I have both?"

He slid his hand to the nape of her neck beneath her luxurious veil. "I'm trying." A wagon rumbled by on the road. It reminded him of the first time he'd taken her in his arms, when she'd told him about Berkley Beck's ledger and he'd feigned an amorous relationship rather than let the driver suspect her complicity in Beck's business. She looked up, anticipating his kiss, but he didn't kiss her. It seemed wrong until ... until he had the right? She was his wife under God, which no man could put asunder. But it didn't feel that way. He let her go.

Tears glassed her eyes. "It's not right."

Maybe not. But that's how it was. Quillan wished he had something he could say, something that could change it all. But to earn her family's esteem, he could only work and prove himself.

She sniffed. "What now?"

"I go back to work."

"Where are you working?" Her fingers were feathers on his sleeve.

"So far, the basalt quarry, hauling stone."

Her eyes widened. "You're working at the quarry?"

"During the day."

"But they'll all know. In a few days they'll all know Flavio's feelings about you. It won't be safe."

Quillan pictured the young virile men he'd worked with. They had been clannish naturally, but not pugnacious. Could Flavio provoke them against him? So far as Carina imagined? He was hoping to learn as much from them as he could just by watching and listening. And if he were honest, he hoped also to earn their esteem. Surely not every Italian in town could be under Flavio's sway. Who was this beau of Carina's anyway?

"Don't worry about me. Now I have to eat something before I start my second job."

"Second?"

"I'm working two jobs for Solomon Schocken. First at the quarry, then at his store."

"But you'll be exhausted."

Quillan smiled. "I better be, or there's no way I'll stand it." He deepened his gaze, roving with his eyes to her lips, then away quickly, the intensity of his desire too much. "But I went without lunch and—"

"Here. I brought you this." Carina held out the basket.

He caught the aroma, lifted the cloth, and feasted his eyes on the browned chicken with a mushroom sauce wrapped in paper. There was a chunk of crusty bread and some sort of black-skinned squash, breaded and fried.

"And this." From her pocket, Carina drew a cloth-wrapped ball. She opened it to reveal a small fruited loaf that smelled even better than the rest, if that were possible. She smiled. "Panettone."

He looked into her face. "How'd you acquire all this contraband?"

She laughed. "I packed the basket with twice what Ti'Giuseppe could eat, left him his portion, and escaped through the barn."

"With his knowledge?"

"Of course. He's the only one with any sense."

Quillan smiled. Why was it always the old men who accepted him? "What about your brothers?"

She waved her hand. "I always visit a while with Tio. They won't miss me."

"It's a mile and a half back to the house."

She shrugged.

Quillan could stand it no longer. He hunched down in the field and set the basket before him. With the fork Carina had thoughtfully included, he wolfed down the meal, too hungry to savor it as it deserved, though the panettone made an impression in spite of his haste. He wiped his mouth with the cloth and sighed.

Carina stood over him, smiling. "Where are you staying?"

"Union Hotel." He stood up and handed the basket back.

She hung it over her arm. "I'll try to get out every day."

"Carina . . ."

"If I leave a note at the desk, can you meet me?"

"I'll be at the quarry. Then I report to the store."

She stepped closer. "But in between?"

He slid his fingers into her hair. His heart set up a clamor. "You don't have to bring food. I can catch something in town." Eating would take up too much of their time. If her brothers were truly keeping guard on her, their meetings would be brief. "Where can we meet?"

"Behind the mission there's a wall."

"The mission?"

"The church across First East, right by Schocken's store. Listen, there's a patch of cactus higher than your head along the wall behind the mission yard where the Indians work. Flavio—" She stopped. "Well, Flavio kissed me once between the cactus and adobe walls. No one can see in there and try to interfere."

Quillan frowned. He had no desire to tryst with his wife where she once lingered with that dark-eyed darling. But since he had no better plan ... "All right. I'll check for a note when I go in to clean up."

She touched his cheek. "Now kiss me before I die of wanting it."

Eighteen

Oh sweet and painful love, thou needle in my heart;
should I draw you forth and let the bleeding start?

— Quillan

CARINA WATCHED UNTIL her husband was lost between the buildings. His kiss was warm on her lips, but it still remained that he went his way and now she must go hers. What had she thought, that everything would be different? That somehow he would have solved it overnight?

And she was far from certain that she could sneak away every evening using Ti'Giuseppe as a decoy. It wouldn't work for long. But maybe in a few days it wouldn't matter. Her brothers would relax. Papa would forgive. She quickened her stride. God would make a way. *Per favore, Signore.*

She started back through the fields along the road leading to Papa's farm. Dusk was deepening when she heard a horse trotting and looked up, startled. Flavio reined in as he caught sight of her. The fiery stallion tossed its head, back-stepping a pace. Flavio swung down with the fluid grace she knew so well, then led the horse off the road toward her. She stopped walking.

He came and stood over her, not so tall as Quillan, but the force of his nature had always made her feel small. She raised her chin defiantly. "What do you want?"

"I came to find you."

She started to walk. "So you found me."

He fell in step beside her. "It's getting dark for a walk."

"I don't care."

"Let me give you a ride, *tesora mia*." His voice turned to velvet.

She stopped, fists at her sides. "I'm not your darling."

He reached into her hair. "You will always be, your sham husband notwithstanding."

She jerked away. "He's not a sham."

"He left you."

Her fury ignited. "Because of you! And Papa! And my *imbecile* brothers." She stalked forward, but he caught her arm, pulled her around.

"Tia Franchesca says the marriage is invalid."

"Mamma knows nothing." But Carina started to shake. Mamma had told Flavio that? After seeing her weep, hearing her plea? Would they try to cause an annulment in spite of her? Could they?

Flavio caught her other arm. "I love you, Carina Maria." He spoke it with fervor.

Could he mean it, after everything he'd done? She remembered the first time he had said that, when she was only fourteen years old. How thrilled she'd been. Even now it was intoxicating that he wanted her still. But that was dangerous and terrible. "I am already married."

His fingers tightened. His lips formed a tight line. "Get on the horse." He spoke softly, but as always his tone compelled. Like Papa, Flavio did not holler, did not need to. Was she a little girl again to be controlled by his strings?

"Grazie, no." She tried to pull away.

He nudged her toward the animal. It shied, but Flavio tugged the reins. "Get on, tesora." An edge now in his voice.

She could hardly outrun him. It would be humiliating to try. Seething, she took hold of the animal's back and swung up onto the saddle, which was hardly more than a shaped and padded blanket. Flavio had always preferred bareback riding. Her skirts caught up around her knees, but she had worn her high leather boots to walk to town. What did she care if it looked less than ladylike? Did she care to impress Flavio? Beh!

He removed her foot from the stirrup and replaced it with his own. Carina quaked at the thought of him behind her. She recalled Quillan's chest against her back after he had saved her from the mine shaft, his arm holding her steady.

Flavio put his weight into the stirrup. At the same moment,

Carina kicked the stallion in the soft area between its flank and belly. The animal reared, and Flavio fell. Then she was flying across the field upon an enraged beast. But she knew as she flew that the stallion's fury was nothing to what Flavio's would be.

With effort, she gained control of the animal and steered it toward the road. It had been a long time since she'd ridden astride, and the jarring chattered her teeth, especially with one foot out of the stirrup. Her back ached. She yanked on the reins and at last brought the horse to a walk. Flavio was out of sight.

Arriving home, she tethered the horse in Papa's courtyard and started toward the house. She had half a mind to pack her trunk and go. But now her fighting spirit was kindled. She would not run, and they would not win. If Quillan was willing to earn their approval, she would give him the chance.

Tony suddenly blocked her way. "That's Flavio's horse."

"He lent it to me."

"Where is he?" Tony looked out through the gate.

She shrugged.

"Carina." He caught her arm. Of them all, Tony was closest in age and spirit. "Be careful."

She looked into her brother's face. "I shouldn't have to be." She walked by and went inside.

Strained with fury and frustration, she slept poorly and awoke in a temper. The mission bells were ringing at five o'clock Sunday morning, and she rose automatically and dressed. Without breaking their fast, the family filled two large carriages. Since Lorenzo still lived at home with Sophie, he drove one carriage with Ti'Giuseppe and Tia Marta, and Divina and Nicolo, who had walked over from their villa on Papa's land, which Nicolo earned by working the fields.

Vittorio drove the second with the rest of them, and a third carryall rattled behind with the servants, driven by Jerome. It was almost a parade, Carina thought, who had never considered it before. Here we come, the DiGratias. She disembarked sullenly and approached the large wooden doors of the adobe Mission Chapel of St. Francis de Solano.

Its red-tiled roof was lined with pigeons that the huge bell, suspended out front from a massive timber arch, had failed to dislodge. She smelled the sweet scent of the prickly pear whose gnarled woody roots and flat thorny leaves stood as tall as she, copious with cone-shaped fruits from which the Indians made many dishes. Then there was the more pungent scent of the blue flowering rosemary—low, dusty green bushes planted the length of the front porch. And then the mellow, mysterious scent of the incense as she entered the chapel.

With her head veiled in black lace, Carina dipped her fingers into the black metal font on the back wall, genuflected, then started down the narrow aisle between the benches. The lower portion of the white plastered walls were striped in ochre, maroon, and turquoise, ornamented with simple geometric and plant designs. The altar rail and five-stepped pulpit were painted a variant green.

They were among the first to arrive, and the silence welcomed her. She closed her eyes for a moment and let its peace enter her. She opened her eyes to gaze at a Spanish painting of Gesù being stripped and mocked. A painting on the opposite wall showed men nailing him to the cross. As she sat between the scenes, Carina's heart quailed.

She had seen these pictures day after day as she'd attended Mass with her family. But they had never touched her so deeply. Christ's pain and humiliation. Was there any hardship she could complain of that He had not borne? So she was scorned by her family, in disgrace. Had Gesù not been taunted and spat upon? So her heart longed to be united with Quillan. Had Gesù not wept for Jerusalem to be united with God?

Her temper fell from her like discarded rags as she knelt and folded her hands in prayer. Once it had been only form, but then Gesù had revealed himself, taken her into himself. *I am sufficient.* He was asking her to trust.

There was a rustling as the Lanzas took their place in the pew opposite the DiGratias, and Carina saw Flavio, stone faced among them. How angry he must be, but he didn't look her way. He forced a casualness that mocked the carved suffering of the eighth station of the cross above him on the wall. He was trying to look as though he hadn't a care in the world.

Carina sighed, then lost herself in the ageless words of the Mass, chanted by the mission brothers and the priest. After Mass they went home to breakfast with everyone: Angelo and Renata with six-year-old Carlo, Joseph and Sophie with their daughter Marta and two-year-old Giovanni, Nicolo and Divina, and Sophie and Lorenzo. Tony had asked young Marianna Rossi to join them, and she shyly agreed. Carina looked at them all gathered around the long table, the young ones at a low table of their own. It could have been any Sunday of her life, except that somewhere her husband ate alone.

Outside the peace of the chapel, she was again besieged by fears and longing. If only Quillan sat beside her now, her life would be complete. Mamma made a fuss over Marianna as she hadn't before. Was Marianna so much better a choice than the others had been, or was Mamma trying to show Carina how good it could be if she had looked closer to home?

Not only was she out of favor, she was watched even more closely. All day Mamma found things for her to do, or her brothers warded her off. Flavio had, no doubt, told them of her escape, and they were determined not to make the same mistake. She should put her foot down and demand an end to the absurdity, but that could mean complete ostracism, and she was not willing to give up yet.

For four days there was no note at the desk, and Quillan went from the quarry to the store, grabbing a bite in between. Was he crazy? Why didn't he go fetch his wife and take her away? She had offered Alaska the last time they spoke, and the thought was heady now as his ache for her grew.

But he knew she hadn't meant it. If he tore her away, she might never heal. Her family was the most important thing; she'd said so herself. He had to find a way to win their acceptance, to prove himself worthy. Wasn't he trying, working every day with her people to learn their ways, their language, even their gestures and mannerisms?

He threw himself down on the bed and took up the Italian grammar book he had procured. In just four days of studying it, he understood more of his quarry companions' speech. But now he couldn't concentrate. His body had adjusted too easily to the workload, not so different from what he had shouldered before. It wasn't enough to distract him from Carina.

Where was she? What was she doing? And with whom? It was driving him crazy. He reached for the Bible on the bed stand. But even before he opened it, the words of Jesus came to his mind: *I am the vine, ye are the branches.* That phrase persisted. But what did it mean?

Quillan knew the entire chapter by memory. He understood, or thought he did, the promises therein. *If ye abide in me, and my words abide in you, ye shall ask what ye will, and it shall be done unto you.* But wasn't he asking? Why, whenever he thought of that one phrase, *I am the vine, ye are the branches,* did he feel that he was missing something?

God had a purpose, yes, and Quillan was trying to accomplish it. Wasn't he? If he could just prove that he deserved Carina ... but that was the rub. He didn't deserve her. He was flawed. Something inherently wrong inside made him know that he didn't deserve her. But he was trying. Surely God would bless that?

Quillan slumped down on the bed, returning the Bible to the stand, unopened. Discouragement ate him, fury as well. What had he done to earn the ire of Carina's father? Yes, they'd married without his permission, but this was hardly the dark ages. And circumstances had forced it, hadn't they?

Could he have whisked her safely from Crystal and sent her home to her family? His chest contracted. He'd have never known her as his wife, never felt the healing balm of her love, her acceptance in spite of his flaw. Was that it? Did he have no right to that acceptance? He could hear Leona Shepard's words: *"You have no right to the care we give you. You're a devil from the pit of hell."* Did her illness let her see more truly than sane minds?

Quillan thought of Carina's father, so like William DeMornay. You are not my son, not my grandson. You don't exist. You couldn't be my daughter's son, my daughter's husband. He pulled the locket out from inside his shirt where he wore it next to his heart. He popped open the lid and stared at his mother's lovely face. He saw some of his own features there and certainly parts of his nature as well.

What would it take for him to prove himself and earn their respect, their acknowledgment? Was he a bastard soul? He'd lived with the epithet his whole life, everyone assuming the worst of his conception.

Was he a bastard son of the Most High?

———

Carina stood, arm snaked around the trunk of the young

almond in the courtyard, head gazing up to the foamy blossoms faintly pink against the beauty of the evening sky. If only things were as peaceful as it looked up there in the heavens. *Signore, I thank you for your grace.* Without it, she would be reduced by now to rage and despair.

Even so, she felt fractious and worried. What must Quillan think when she had promised to meet him, then not come even once? Mamma had insisted Giuseppe take his meals with the family. *"It's not good for him to be so much alone."* How right and kind it had sounded, but Carina knew it was only so she couldn't use that way of escape again.

It was absurd. They could not legally separate her from her husband. If she walked away today, they couldn't stop her. But she would lose them. And Quillan would lose his chance for family. He wanted her to stay; he had said so. Why couldn't they see his goodness?

Someone touched her from behind, and she cried out and spun.

Smiling, Flavio slid his hand along the small of her back. "I'm sorry, tesora. I didn't mean to startle you."

She tried to back away, but he locked the fingers of his other hand with the first, trapping her waist. "Your papa said I'd find you here."

"What do you want?"

"You know what I want." His voice softened. "And I know what you want."

She stared into his face. If he really knew, would he persist in tormenting her? If he just said the word, maybe her family would relent. Engagement promises were broken. If both parties were willing. What could he possibly gain by continuing his suit with her already married?

He sobered, dropping his chin just enough. "I was wrong."

Her breath caught. Had he finally seen? Could they make their peace and be done with it?

"But you have to know Divina never meant anything to me."

What? What was he saying? What had Divina to do with it?

"It's always been you, tesora. Don't you know that? I told you in every letter, every kiss." He pulled her closer.

She put her fists up between them, heart rushing. "What are you doing?"

"You want me to apologize. Very well. I deeply apologize for wounding you. It was foolish and . . . unfaithful."

Carina bristled. "Who told you to say that? Mamma?" She struggled, but he held on. "Did she think if you admitted your fault I would fall back into your arms and swoon?"

His eyes flashed. "You've grown a tongue like Divina's."

"Can you blame her, the way you used her?"

"Me?" He raised his brows with a snort. "It was she who came to me."

Carina glared. "And you merely accommodated."

He pressed her into the tree. "I've apologized, Carina. Now you must pardon me."

She stiffened. "I forgave you already."

He raised one hand to cup her face. "Yes?"

She swallowed the tightness in her throat. This was Flavio, whom she had loved most of her life, with whom she would always have a connection. Could she make him see? "I left here to hurt you, to make you pay for hurting me. A thousand miles I wanted you to come and beg my forgiveness. But in Crystal, I learned another way. I forgave you without an apology because the bitterness would have destroyed me. And I no longer wanted to hurt you."

He dampened his lips. "Then why did you marry *him*?"

Had Quillan no name to Flavio? He could not honor him even so far? "Because I love him."

She saw stark hurt in Flavio's eyes, and it saddened her to put it there. It wasn't what she wanted after all. There was no joy in breaking his heart. Then his face changed, and he went to that place inside himself where she couldn't follow. His breath thinned, and his hand tightened on her jaw. Something savage came from inside him, something she had never seen before. His voice rasped, "For that, I will destroy him."

She trembled. Flavio's hands left her abruptly, but she stayed pressed to the tree until he had left the courtyard and stalked away into the deepening dusk. She must go to Quillan, warn him. She gathered her shawl. Outside the walls of the courtyard, the wind was cold. Spring had not yet gained control, and she shivered as she hurried through the deepening darkness. No brother stopped her, likely because they had given Flavio his privacy. And they wouldn't guess her foolish enough to go out so late afoot.

There was enough of a moon to show her the road, little more. But she knew the way. Her chest heaved inside her corset as she all but ran. What if Flavio had gone directly? But that would be murder. Flavio could not, would not ... She had time, she tried to tell herself, but her feet wouldn't listen.

At last she reached the plaza. Unlike Crystal, where music blared and hollers and gunshots broke the night, Sonoma was merely pleasantly lively. People enjoyed themselves at the hotels and restaurants, but there was a lazy quality to their passing. In contrast, Carina's pace was frantic.

Where would she find him? The store? No, it was all closed up and dark. She rushed to the Union Hotel and passed through its front doors.

The clerk looked up from his book. "Good evening, Miss DiGratia."

She glared, then realized he had no way of knowing she was married. "Good evening, Mr. Renault. I must see one of your guests. It's urgent."

"Who is it, miss?"

"Quillan Shepard."

The clerk looked at her a moment, then checked the register and said, "He's in room thirteen."

She hurried up the stairs and banged on number thirteen's door. In less than a breath it swung open and Quillan grabbed her inside.

"What is it, Carina? What's wrong?"

"I looked for you at the store."

"I haven't gone over yet."

She clutched his hands. "You can't go."

"What's the matter?"

His tone and expression were far too stoic. She had to make him see. Her words came in a rush. "It's Flavio. He's going to hurt you—destroy you, he said. We have to go. Now. Before it's too late."

Quillan stared into her face as though he hadn't heard.

"I don't care about my things. Let's take the wagon and leave."

He let go of her. "I can't run, Carina; don't ask me to."

"But—"

The side of his mouth twitched. "I thought you said he was a pacifist."

He would joke? "You heard Ti'Giuseppe. Whatever he believes, or thinks he does, is subject to his heart. And right now his heart is violent." She gripped his forearms. "You must believe me."

"I do. But I won't run away. I won't give him the satisfaction."

"Oh!" She shook him. "This is not the time for pride."

"It's all I have." He jerked his arms free. "If I can't think well of myself, who will? Your family? The DeMornays?" It was a bitter tone she'd not heard from him in some time. But that was less important than his danger.

She had to make him understand. "Flavio will do what he says. And he will have the whole community behind him."

Quillan didn't answer, just stood opening and closing his hands at his sides. "I won't run." He turned and walked to the fireplace, stared into the brazier.

"It's not running, Quillan. It's . . . starting over."

"It's admitting I don't belong."

He didn't belong! That was the point. He was not one of them and never would be. But she couldn't tell him that. She dropped her hands to her sides, tears sparkling in her eyes. "Please."

He came to her and held her shoulders. "I know you don't understand. But—" his voice thickened—"if I were driven away again, I don't think I could stand it."

She covered his hands with hers, seeing his pain. She hadn't known, hadn't realized the depth of his need to be accepted. He would rather die than fail again. And he might. "Signore, help us." She closed her eyes on her tears.

"Don't cry." His hands tightened.

"What are we going to do?" She clung to him.

He brought her gently into his arms. "I don't know."

Her hair fell over his hands, and she held onto his waist as though to a buoy at sea. She remembered the time in his tent when he had impulsively held her just so, trying to calm her hysterics. He'd been so solid, so convincing. She wanted nothing more than to hold him, to feel him warm and breathing and strong. "Don't make me go back."

"You have to."

"Not now." She clung tighter.

He rested his face in her hair, his breath warming her scalp. "No, not now." And he kissed her.

Quillan lay beside his wife, too agitated to sleep. Her breath was a warm mist on his arm, and he studied the fall of her eyelashes on her cheek, the curve of her lips. They were slack and slightly parted, just showing the edge of her white teeth. He would have to send her back. There would be no end to strife if he kept her at the hotel. And only from within the bosom of her family could she resolve her need.

He would not let her choose him out of desperation. But as he looked out at the heavy mist of the gray, dawning day, he felt desperate himself. Was he wrong? He forked his fingers into his hair. Carina stirred. Her eyes opened drowsily. She smiled.

He touched her smile, giving her one of his own. *Dear God, I love her.* He shifted his position to face her. Maybe he shouldn't have kept her last night. People would see her going out; the clerk would know when she came. But maybe it was time people knew. He was not going to skulk behind some cactus wall even if that was good enough for Flavio. Carina deserved better.

She raised up onto her elbow. "What are you thinking?"

"That I'm the luckiest man alive."

She shook her head. "You have every hand raised against you, and you're the luckiest man?"

"First, it's not every hand. There are more than Italians in Sonoma. Solomon Schocken said last night that he's very pleased with my work. Mr. Marconi, as well. And he's one of yours."

Carina gave him a sad smile.

"And secondly, I wasn't referring to anyone but you. If I had nothing but you, I'd still be luckiest."

She cupped his shoulder. "Then let's leave. This morning."

He looked down at her velvety skin. "All right. Never mind your mother's broken heart, the sorrow you'll give your father. They had their chance. And as for your brothers, they're hardly sentient beings; no reasoning with them. Ti'Giuseppe ... now it would have been nice to say good-bye, don't you think?" He looked back into her stricken face. He'd known what expression he'd find, but it cut him anyway. They were all still her most important thing.

He cradled her face in his palm. "No, Carina. We can't leave. We have to see it through."

She didn't argue. She knew she had shown him her feelings. "I've prayed and prayed for the Lord to make my family see. But they're blind and deaf to me. Is God, too?"

"I'm not the one to ask." He shook his head. "I keep trying to understand, to find His purpose." He smoothed his fingers over her hair. "I'm too green to have any answers."

Carina fingered the locket that hung at his neck against his bare skin and sighed. "So what do we do?"

He hated to say it, but knew he must. "You go home. I go to work."

"Quillan, why do you have to work so hard? Didn't you get money from the mine? Couldn't you buy . . . something?"

He looked down at the sheet. How could he explain that he didn't deem that money his, and even if it were, that he hesitated to use it. Mrs. Shepard had accused him and Wolf of greed so many times, he was afraid to consider himself a wealthy man. He said simply, "I have money."

She waited for more, and he shook his head. "It's not about money, Carina. It's about respect."

"You think my papa's not respected? Does he work himself to the bone?"

"I have to show that I've earned it."

"Why?" She sat up abruptly.

How could she possibly understand, aristocrat that she was? He didn't even understand except—except maybe he'd believed more of Leona Shepard's words than he should. *You're greedy and lazy and worthless. You'll never amount to anything. Idleness is the devil's tool, and you're the devil's spawn.* He knew better in his head, but in his soul?

"I just do, Carina."

She sighed. "So that's it? I go home, and you go back to work. Then what? Wait until Flavio makes good his threat?"

"Ah, yes, Flavio's threat."

She pushed his chest. "Don't scoff."

"I'm not." He stood up, walked to the washbasin, and poured water into the bowl. He tossed it onto his face and rubbed the back of his neck and his chest, then toweled dry and turned. "I'm not defenseless, Carina. I can protect myself." She should know that already.

She nodded. "But . . ."

"I need to know what he is to you."

She stared at him uncomprehending. "To me?"

Quillan grabbed his shirt and threw it on. He took her hands and stood her up from the bed. "What if self-defense becomes deadly force?"

Her jaw dropped softly as understanding dawned. She shook her head slightly. "I hadn't thought. I'd thought only of your safety."

At least he had that. She'd thought of him first. But now he saw the struggle inside her. "I don't ... I can't—Quillan, I can't have his death on my conscience. He's my ... I've known him forever." She turned away. "I don't condone his actions, but ..."

"That's all I needed to know." And the gun would stay stowed in his room. That limited his odds, but he would not harm someone who mattered to Carina. His gut twisted. Of course Flavio mattered. He was one of them. And he'd been more, much more to her than any of the others. For Flavio, she'd left her family. Quillan turned away and buttoned his shirt.

Carina walked listlessly to the basin and bathed her face and hands. She dug her finger into his toothpowder and ran it over her teeth.

He grinned. "You could have used the brush."

She shrugged, more crestfallen than he'd expected.

"Carina, it'll be all right."

She turned. "Oh sì. And chickens lay golden eggs."

"Well, if they did we'd not have scrambled or fried, would we?" He caught her hands. "Get dressed. I'm walking you back to the house."

"You are?"

"I am. And I'm asking permission to court you."

Her breath came out in a little huff. "Asking Papa?"

"Unless you think Giuseppe'll do. My chances are better there." He pulled on his pants.

She stamped her foot. "Stop making fun."

"I'm not." He sat on the bed and tied on his brogans.

It took Carina longer to dress, but she had more layers, ties, and buttons. When she was finished, they went out together. Quillan stopped at the desk. "If Mr. Schocken comes asking for me, tell him I've taken my wife home, and I'll be to the quarry directly."

The clerk raised his eyebrows. "I will." Then to Carina, "Good day, er, Mrs...."

Carina smiled. "Good day, Mr. Renault."

The mist was thick and chilly, collecting on Quillan's face like a mask. Carina's hair pearled with tiny droplets by the time they reached the livery just next door. Quillan shook the moisture from his own hair. "If I didn't know better, I'd say it was raining."

"It will be soon." Carina ran her hands back over her hair as they stepped inside.

"I don't have a cover."

"I can stand a little rain." She nudged him with her hip. "I won't melt."

Quillan called for his wagon and team. "It's not that you'll melt. I don't want to return you looking like a drowned kitten. Hold on a minute." He went back and helped the liveryman harness his team, checking the animals and giving Jock a pat as he crossed to the bed. He pulled out his extra tarp. It was an ungainly cover at best, but he'd used it a time or two.

"Fine animals." The man said.

"Yep." Quillan laid the canvas tarp on the seat. Once he had Carina seated he'd arrange it.

"What did you say your name was?"

Quillan turned. "Quillan Shepard."

"Well, Mr. Shepard, if you ever look to sell them, look here first." The man held out his hand. "Corbaley's the name."

Quillan shook. "Well, I don't imagine I'll be looking to sell. These animals have been with me awhile, except for the gelding. Picked that one up when I lost this black's twin."

"A real twin?"

Quillan nodded. "Lost him in an avalanche."

"Darn shame."

Quillan felt a twinge, but the ache had passed. Together they led horses and wagon to the doors where Carina waited.

"I'll be with you in a moment, Miss DiGratia," Corbaley said.

"Actually, she's with me." Quillan gave Carina a hand into the box that replaced the spring seat. "And it's Mrs. Shepard."

"Well." Corbaley smiled. "I hadn't heard. Felicitations."

Quillan had to smile. If only. He mounted the box and snapped the lines. They lurched forward and he remembered the canvas. "Pull that canvas up over you, Carina."

She did, and it tented her well enough. When they arrived at the DiGratia house, Quillan stopped outside the courtyard. The gates were closed, but he jumped down and unfastened the wrought-iron catch. Instead of taking the team and wagon in, he helped Carina down and gave her his arm. Together they walked through the courtyard to the door.

Dr. DiGratia opened it himself, reading the situation clearly enough. His frown was infused with indignation and grudging respect. He had to know Quillan could have kept her.

Quillan spoke first. "Dr. DiGratia, I'd like permission to see my wife."

"See?" He quirked one arched eyebrow.

"See." Let him read into that anything he liked.

Carina's father stood a long time without speaking. Then he said, "It was also for your sake that I denied you before. You're the cause of a broken contract."

"The contract was broken before me, with better cause."

"I know nothing of that." Dr. DiGratia turned his gaze briefly on Carina. "I only know that my daughter begged leave for a time, distraught, yes. Against my better judgment, I let her travel. But nothing was said about breaking a valid contract to which I gave permission. As far as I'm concerned, that's grounds to annul your claim."

Annul his claim? After last night, after all their nights, their days, their struggle, their love? Annul the fact that they were one flesh, inseparable, indivisible except by death? "I request permission to see my wife."

"I deny it. You have no business with her. I spoke with the priest. He's looking into it."

"Papa!" Carina's voice broke. "How could you?"

"It is my responsibility." He held himself stiffly, in firm control of his emotions.

Quillan admired his determination, and the irony was not lost on him. Hadn't he told Carina again and again that the marriage was flawed, as he was flawed? Here was yet more proof. Quillan dropped his chin. "I don't want to be at odds with you. But Carina is legally my wife."

"There are things beyond the law. Moral codes."

Quillan bristled. There was nothing immoral in his love for Carina, and it inflamed him to hear it.

Dr. DiGratia drew himself up imperiously. "I suggest you go."

"Why, Papa?" Carina caught her father's arm.

"Because you are my daughter. Now go inside."

Quillan saw Carina stiffen, knew she would refuse. He said softly, "Go, Carina. This isn't over yet."

She looked up at him, confused and torn. He didn't want her to be hurt. But for the life of him, he didn't know what else to do. Carina went inside. Dr. DiGratia only looked at him, then followed his daughter inside and closed the door.

I am the vine, ye are the branches.

"I don't understand," Quillan said to the closed door.

Nineteen

*Matthew 8:20: The foxes have holes, and the birds of the air have nests;
but the Son of man hath not where to lay his head. What man am I
to long for that which Christ himself denied? What right have I
to hearth and home when Jesus bled and died?*

— Quillan

FITFULLY, CARINA DRESSED. It was two days since Quillan had brought her home. Papa had willfully ignored her pleas and arguments, and now she was expected to accompany them to the Garibaldi Hotel for a ball in honor of some accomplishment of its namesake. Since everything Giuseppe Garibaldi, the unifier of Italy, had ever done was considered grounds for celebration, there was hardly a date that couldn't suffice for some gala.

She looked at the dress Mamma had lovingly provided. Carina had to admit its stylish cut and lace-flounced bustle would set her off elegantly. If she could walk in on Quillan's arm, she would be the happiest woman of all. But of course that was impossible.

Frustrated, she slid her arms into the dress, bowing inside it, then swooping up to let it descend over her in a white lacy cloud. She reached behind and started on the buttons. "Come in," she called at the tap on the door.

Maria, the maid Mamma had retained from the mission, came in. Silently, she finished the row of buttons to Carina's neck, then seated her at the maple vanity—no easy trick with the volume of her bustle. Then Maria brushed her hair, drawing out the tangles until it shone and crackled. Carina suffered it silently, upset by the attractive twists and rolls that Maria formed to enhance her beauty.

She didn't want to look beautiful if Quillan were not there to see. What did she care that the other men would find her so? The other men and Flavio. She burned at the thought. She had not spoken with him since he made his threat, but she knew he would be there tonight. Was there any chance she could avoid him?

It was all so absurd. She should leave. Yet the thought of losing all her family was more than she could bear. Quillan had said it; to know she had broken Mamma's heart, pained Papa, to never see Ti'Giuseppe, just as she had missed Nonna's last days ... She couldn't do it. They were too much a part of her.

But wasn't Quillan? Of course he was! And more. *Oh, Signore, it's too much for me.*

"Miss is unhappy?"

Maria's voice startled Carina. But she looked at her own face in the mirror. As Quillan said, it was there for all the world to see. She sighed. "Unhappy and frustrated and confused."

"I will pray for you." Simple words from a simple heart.

"Maybe God will hear you."

"God will hear." Maria's hands brought up the last strands of hair, worked them into a braid, and intertwined the braid with the roll on one side. She tucked it in with pearl hairpins. The effect was masterful and lovely.

Carina wanted to cry.

"It will be all right, miss."

Quillan's words. But it wasn't all right. She should be with her husband, and more and more she knew it.

Since Solomon Schocken had not needed him that evening, Quillan perched at the picnic pavilion in the plaza and watched the goings on at the Garibaldi House, the arrivals of the Italian powers-that-be. He was coming to realize they held more sway than he'd imagined. Tuscans and Sardinians, used to their elite roles in the old world, had set up their miniature kingdoms in the new.

He was feeling bitter. They weren't all that way, but unfortunately the others seemed cowed and followed their lead. The men at the quarry had turned distinctly cold and gave him dark glares when he tried to communicate. The men loaded his wagon sullenly, making his team stand longer and his loads fewer. He found himself doing the bulk of it himself, and he felt it now in his back. But it was better to work alone and be effective than stymied by the others.

He rubbed his back. So Carina was right. Flavio held sway with the men at the quarry. Or the community at large accommodated her father in refusing to acknowledge him. A depressing thought. Again rejection was becoming a goad.

Another carriage pulled up in front of the hotel. With a flourish, Flavio emerged, followed by a shorter man—Nicolo, wasn't it? They'd been together in the courtyard when Quillan first brought Carina home. Yes, because Nicolo now helped Carina's sister from the conveyance. Would Carina be next?

A rush of fire inside warned him he was at a dangerous point. But Carina did not get out of that carriage, and it was led away. The next held an older couple, very elegant in bearing, he in a black Prince Albert coat and walking stick, and she bearing so much fabric it was amazing her back didn't snap.

The next carriage to arrive came from First Street East. It was open to the air, and as it approached, he saw clearly Dr. DiGratia's head and shoulders. His wife was beside him, and Carina must have been facing backward, hidden by the driver and team.

What would they say if he walked up to greet them, took Carina on his arm, and went into the hotel? He wore the getup he'd assembled for his about-town times, beige ankle-length pantaloons, white shirt, green quilted vest and cravat, with a brown broadcloth coat over all. He looked passing fine, if he did say so. He'd tied his hair back, which in his opinion, looked as pirate as leaving it loose, but drew less attention. And though his mustache was as brazen as ever, he'd removed the beard that had accumulated over the last four days.

He stood up as the carriage halted before the doors of the imposing front of the Garibaldi House with its red, white, and green flag and the motto *Italia Unita* proudly across the front. United Italy. Yes, indeed, they knew how to unite. His throat tightened painfully as Mr. DiGratia handed Carina down. She looked like an angel in white lace.

As she lighted, she looked about . . . for him? He stepped out from the pavilion, and for a moment their eyes met. Then her father put his hand to her elbow, and they went inside the doors beneath the ornate balcony upon which several young men stood with mandolins and guitars, serenading the partygoers' entrance.

Stiffly Quillan sat back down. What had he expected? That she would run to him and desert all else—the trappings, the patriotic music that carried across the plaza and promised dancing within. His gut wrenched. What was God doing?

I am the vine, ye are the branches. He scowled, wishing he'd never committed that verse to memory. "Fine, Lord. You're the vine. What am I supposed to do with that?"

Every branch that beareth fruit, he purgeth it, that it may bring forth more fruit. How much more purging could he take? He'd been cut to the quick; if he lost Carina he'd be severed altogether. He stood up again, feeling more alone than ever. Before Carina, he'd been alone by choice. He didn't expect to be accepted, so he didn't try. He had learned that early.

"Keep him away from the others, or he'll be the apple that rots the barrel." And Mrs. Shepard was so convincing the headmaster had looked down his long chin and ostracized Quillan. With no chance for friendship, he'd built a wall, guarded himself, and learned to live that way.

I am the vine . . . Quillan slammed his fist into his palm, and two Chinese crossing the plaza jumped and grabbed each other instinctively. Their eyes searched him, and with a rush of sardonic amusement, he realized he had at last encountered a people as reviled as himself. Just like him, they anticipated the kick, the thrown rocks, the insults.

He spread his palms to show he meant them no harm. They spouted gibberish, bobbing like ducks, then hurried away. Quillan pressed his palm to his forehead, squinched his eyes shut, then tightened his jaw and looked once more at the Garibaldi House.

Somewhere in there his wife danced and mingled and drove men mad. And he was outside again, to avoid rotting the barrel. He stalked to his room in the Union Hotel, jerked the suitcase from under the bed, and threw in the clothes from the bureau drawers. He pulled out the heavy metal box that he had stowed under the seat of his wagon for long trips, and piled in his books until only his journal and Cain's Bible remained.

He raised the Bible, picturing it in Cain's veined and withered hands, resting on his stump of leg. *"What tickles me is how the Lord chooses his instruments. Not the high and mighty who think they deserve it, but the lowly, the motley, the old cripples like me."* Quillan swallowed. How God chooses his instruments. The lowly, the motley—that one had resonated.

Had God chosen this for him? Was this God's purpose, that he be separated from the one person who loved him, whose love he turned to in despair, whose love healed him? *I am the vine.* Quillan frowned. *What, Lord?* But God's voice was drowned by another.

You'll never amount to anything. You're the devil's spawn.

Something tore inside. No more! He belonged to Jesus Christ. He'd given himself over in the cave where his father had offered him to his best understanding of God, the eagle in the picture. He was no bastard son. Those were lies. But what was the truth? What did it mean that Jesus was the vine? Why did those words haunt him, provoke him?

Quillan dropped to his knees, dropped his face to his hands, and dropped his guard, letting tears wash the bitterness from inside him. *God, I only wanted a family. Only wanted love.* He had yearned for it from the Shepards, looked for it again from the DeMornays. His last hope had been the DiGratias.

He folded his arms, bent over the bed, and laid his face down. He was a grown man. But to never know a father's pride, a mother's love . . . to never be accepted into that loving circle, that devotion he saw in the DiGratias' fierce loyalty to each other. How would it feel to belong?

I am the vine.

He had turned twenty-nine today, with no one to mark the day, no one to even know. He was so terribly alone. He was worse for having known Carina's love. That one taste would forever haunt him. If Carina were lost to him, what would he have?

I am the vine, ye are the branches. Abide in me. Abide in me.

The tension left his neck. His fisted hands unclenched, the tears stopped. Quillan opened his eyes. He had God. He had Jesus. Cain was right. God called the lowly, the motley, the ones everyone else rejected. He gripped Cain's Bible and opened to the verses. *Now ye are clean through the word which I have spoken unto you. Abide in me, and I in you. As the branch cannot bear fruit of itself, except it abide in the vine; no more can ye, except ye abide in me.*

Quillan straightened on his knees and clasped his mother's

locket. He had been looking for approval from men, desperate for love and acceptance from people. But it was God's acceptance he'd received, God's approval he needed. As long as he fought for the DiGratias', the DeMornays', the Shepards' acclaim, he would not bear fruit. It was God he needed to please. God was the father who could look down with pride and say, "Well done, my son."

A powerful yearning filled him. More than anything this world could give, he wanted that. More than the forty thousand dollars in the concealed box beneath his wagon, more than the esteem of men, even more than Carina's love—he wanted to know he had done right in God's eyes.

Breathing deep gulps of air, he recalled the verses in his mind. *Herein is my Father glorified, that ye bear much fruit; so shall ye be my disciples. As the Father hath loved me, so have I loved you: continue ye in my love.* His body started to shake. The bitterness, the pride, the resentment, the hurt. He saw them all part of another creature, not himself.

"Thank you, Father." His voice was hoarse with tears, but they were no longer bitter. They were the tears Tennyson had written of, the tears Carina understood. They came and washed away his wall. He had a father who loved him. And his purpose was to do his Father's will, whatever it was, to accept his lot and be content because God willed it. Nothing mattered more. Christ was the vine, and he the branch. Only abiding in God would bring him peace and make him fruitful.

Now, on his knees, he didn't pray for God to show him His will; he prayed to be made worthy of it. Before, he had surrendered to a powerful God, knowing his fight was futile. Now he found God longing to draw him in, a loving, merciful God. If his Father meant him to lose Carina, then he would cling to the vine, a weak and damaged branch. But apart from the vine, he was nothing.

Carina watched the musicians play the Veronese melody on violin, mandolin, cello, and guitar. A tenor, whom she had not seen before, sang in full voice, and the timbre of it resonated inside her. He had a corpulent neck that vibrated like the throat of a bird when he sang, and she wondered if the beauty of the sound was enhanced by it.

Thankfully they were not intended to dance while the soloist entertained them. She could lose herself in the music and for a time forget. Closing her eyes she let the rising and falling notes surround her, until she focused on the words sung in Italian, words of love. And then suddenly all her thoughts went back to Quillan's face as he stood by the pavilion in the plaza.

How dashing he had looked. For a moment she had hoped he would come to her, sweep her out of Papa's grip, save her this humiliating farce. Would he truly wait for Papa's permission? It would never come. Never. Mamma made it worse every night as they ate, extolling Flavio's virtues.

So he was an artist. So what? So he came from an important family. So he painted like Botticelli and sang like an angel. So . . .

"Stop pouting, Carina. You look like a spoiled child," Divina hissed in her ear. "You insult Papa."

"How?"

Divina pinched her elbow. "Everyone knows you think you're wronged. You don't have to make it so obvious."

Carina tugged her arm free. "That's Papa's problem."

"How quickly we change." Divina's tone grated Carina's nerves. "Papa's little favorite, his *tigre*. She's grown claws and will use them the first time she doesn't get her way."

"Shut up, Divina."

"I know you." Divina pressed her lips so close her breath filled Carina's ear. "It's Flavio you want to hurt. And when you're done, you'll discard that handsome rascal you've used to torment him."

Carina spun. "You know nothing, Divina."

Divina laughed and splayed her hand across her belly. "Oh, but I do."

Shaking, Carina watched her sister walk away. Was it possible Divina hated her so much? And what about Papa? If he loved her could he do the things he was doing? Had they all turned on her? Even as she wondered, she saw Mamma with Tia Gelsomina, Carina's own godmother, heads together, sharing the same pained expression. Like Mamma, Gelsomina held her age well; an attractive woman, though shorter than Carina by inches. Widowed six years, she was much pursued, but Carina suspected she enjoyed the pursuit too much to choose a favorite suitor.

Carina could stand it no longer. She crossed over to them in spite of the discourtesy to the poor man singing at the front of the long room. She bent and kissed Gelsomina's cheeks. *"Madrina."*

"Look at you, so beautiful." Her godmother wrapped her tightly in her arms. "But, tesora, you're so thin!" she whispered. "You've been ill."

"Only for a while. I'm so much better now."

Gelsomina grasped her arms and held her out. "How can you be, this terrible business." There was true compassion in her eyes. Gelsomina understood, hurt for her. "But there, now. It will come right."

"How, Madrina?" She gave her mamma a sorrowful look. "Everyone is against me."

Gelsomina stroked her arm. "No, no."

"Only you understand."

"Of course." Gelsomina's eyes were clear blue skies. "I am your godmother. I love you."

Carina's heart soared. If Gelsomina could—

"As soon as this trouble is behind you—"

"Behind me?"

"Your papa will figure it out. He is wise."

Papa, wise? Didn't Gelsomina know it was his stubbornness that was causing all the trouble? "He is proud."

"Of course he is, friend to the king. Such an important man."

Carina frowned. Oh yes, Angelo Pasquale DiGratia, physician and advisor to Count Camillo Benso di Cavour, prime minister to Victor Emmanuel II, king of Sardinia-Piedmont. And now all of Italy. She knew it like a litany, had recited it herself often enough. Now it irked her. "There is no king in America, Madrina."

"In Italy, my love."

"We don't live in Italy."

Mamma said, "It lives in us. Forever our home."

The singer finished and all applauded except Carina. She fixed her gaze on Mamma. "Then why did Papa leave? If it meant so much and he was so important, why did Papa leave?" Carina had been a little girl when her family and entourage had left Italy for Argentina. She had thought it a great adventure. But if Papa were so important, why did he leave what he had?

Mamma and Gelsomina shared a glance, and Carina looked from one to the other. For all the stories bantered about, that one she hadn't heard. She had unintentionally hit on something. "Why, Mamma?"

Mamma waved her hand. "He wanted something better."

"Better than friend to the king?" She knew how it worked. There were those with pedigree and power, and others without.

"You were too little to remember. Things were hard, unstable."

Mamma was lying. Carina had seen it many times. Mamma colored the truth, brushed over it whenever it suited her.

Carina looked at Gelsomina. "Madrina?"

"In Argentina there was great opportunity."

Carina jutted her chin. "Then why did he leave there, too?"

Mamma said, "To be part of the great America. For you and Divina and your brothers especially."

Carina flung up her hand. "What is so great about America?"

"Two things." Mamma's expression intensified. "Freedom and land."

"Papa had land."

Mamma shook her head. "You don't understand."

They could go on in circles all night. Mamma did not want to tell her. If Gelsomina knew, she, too, would keep it secret. Why did it even matter? What did it have to do with her and Quillan? She felt a hand on her waist and knew without turning it was Flavio. Mamma's face had a beatific glow, and Gelsomina nodded knowingly.

The music started, and Flavio leaned his mouth to her ear. "Do you remember the first time we danced, tesora mia?" He took her hand in his. "At Joseph's wedding."

She remembered. How her heart had soared! They'd been playmates, but that, that had been a turning point. She turned, met his melting gaze. Why did he persist? She saw the people watching them. It would be a terrible insult to refuse. She would incite Flavio's wrath if she embarrassed him now, in front of everyone. So she allowed him to escort her to the floor. His hand on her waist was warm as they began the saltarello with a skipping step.

As they danced, his hands never left her, nor did his eyes. "You are beautiful tonight, my love."

She swallowed her retort. She must not make a scene. Had he not heard her, not understood? Did he forget she loved another? No, there was something dark and taunting in his gaze. She spun, trying to ignore the warmth of his touch, which once had left her dizzy with dreams. What was this magnetism he had over all her family?

"You are my angel tonight. My cupid. I am under your spell."

Words like that, from his lips, from his pen, had captivated her once. He took her into a twirl with his lips at her neck. She thought of Quillan in the plaza, alone.

"I love you, Carina. It consumes me."

Madonna mia! What am I to do?

"The flames burn my heart, and I am helpless to resist."

"Flavio..." Her voice broke. She didn't want to hurt him. What she had dreamed of once was painful now. *Signore, help me.* Had she set it all in motion with her vengeful desire to strike back, to make him pay? How far would he go, driven by such fire?

She said, "I don't want to hurt you."

"You are the death of me." He pulled her out onto the balcony. Had he maneuvered them across the floor to do so?

"Please, Flavio, try to understand."

He caught her face between his hands and kissed her with all the ardor and arrogance in him. Carina struggled. How dare he make a spectacle of her? Or was that his intention? Was Quillan in the plaza? She strained to see, but Flavio would not release her. He pinned her to the railing, his mouth stopping her breath.

She pressed her fists against him, but he wouldn't stop the kiss. She kicked him as hard as she could through her skirts. He staggered back holding his leg. Her breath came in gasps as she searched the plaza in the dark. She could not see far, but she was certain she could be seen in the festive lights.

Was Quillan out there? Then Flavio grabbed her arms. "You can fight all you want, but I will win. I have everyone with me."

"Why?"

He smiled a slow, melancholy smile and moved in to kiss her again.

She shoved him back. "I am a married woman."

"Sham marriage. Sham husband. And soon you will be a widow."

Her spine went cold. "That's how you win my love?"

"I already have your love. I always have."

She glowered. "Once maybe. But you disdained it."

"I guarded and protected it, waiting for you to grow up."

"Beh!" She expelled her breath with the gesture from her chin. "You did no waiting at all."

He closed in, catching her waist between his hands. "I waited for you. Do you think I could not have had you if I wanted? You were butter in my hands. If I had once tried, you would have surrendered, just as the others."

She flushed with anger. Did Papa know? Did Papa approve?

"But you I kept sacred. You, I would marry."

"For that I should be grateful?" His face was so close now she turned hers to the side.

"You will be grateful. You will thank me for the rest of your life."

"I will not."

His lips touched her neck. She stiffened. "If you don't let go this minute I will scream." Would Quillan come to her defense? Was he out there now, thinking she invited this amorous attack? She pictured Quillan the avenger. What would happen to him if he threatened Flavio now?

But Flavio drew back. "Play your games, Carina. It only makes my victory sweeter."

She didn't answer. Anything she might say would only draw his ire back to Quillan. With a supremely haughty smile, he held out his arm. She fought the revulsion as she slipped her hand into it. The dancing inside was gay and lively as ever. Would Flavio push for another time with her on the dance floor?

But he bowed slightly and released her arm. "Grazie, tesora mia. I will dream of your kiss tonight."

Instinctively her fingers went to her lips. He laughed, winked, and left her.

Omaccio! Cialtrone! All the names she had called Quillan when he was none of that rushed to her mind. She had to get out. She searched the room for her papa and found him in conversation with General Vallejo, the Mexican official welcomed as one of them. His pleasant face and lamb-chop whiskers nodded to Papa's comment.

She drew herself up and approached them. "Forgive me, Papa, General." She bowed her head to them in turn. "Papa, I'm not feeling well. I want to go home."

His physician's eye assessed her, no doubt seeing the flushed cheeks and quickened pulse. "Take some air, Carina. You're over-heated."

"I am not overheated, Papa. I want to go home."

How Papa's Roman nose nudged upward when he was challenged. "The evening is cool. Stand a minute on the balcony."

She turned with a huff. She'd had quite enough of the balcony!

"A spirited young woman." The general said behind her.

"My little tigre," Papa answered.

For a moment Carina wished she had claws to slice them both. Bene. If they would not take her home, she would take herself. Not immediately, when Papa's eyes would be on her. But at the first opportunity.

When Papa's attention was caught by a new soloist, a soprano in satin and feathers, Carina slipped out the door of the hall and hurried down the stairs. Let them miss her. She was leaving.

Stepping out into the night, she considered going to Quillan. She could not see him among those lingering around the pavilion. He must have gone to his room. She was at once relieved and disappointed. At least he would not have seen her with Flavio.

She looked toward the Union Hotel. No, if Papa sent a contingent after her, it would not be healthy for Quillan. She had no doubt Papa knew where Quillan stayed. His connections were deep.

She started toward home, holding her skirts slightly raised, though the train would be ruined. What did she care? There was a light inside Schocken's store. Could it be Quillan so late? She stopped outside the window and looked between the crack of the blinds. She just caught a glimpse of Solomon Schocken at his desk. Her heart sank.

She passed the Chinese laundry and started along the lane between it and the Swiss bakery. A sweet smell caught her nose as she neared the rear of the building. Three Chinese men sat in the darkness, smoke curling around their heads and the strange long pipes they smoked. Opium. She knew the odor now. They looked at her with half-dazed eyes as she hurried past.

The road was long and rough in her dancing slippers and heavy bustle. Carina half wished she had found Quillan. He could have lent her Jock or the gelding. Had he named the horse yet? Plato or Icarus or . . . Sam. She felt a pang. Poor old dog. Second

Samuel had been Cain's dog before theirs. And now he was Alan's.

Almost for the first time, Carina thought of the people in Crystal. She had thought she would be miserable missing them, but so much had happened, she'd hardly thought of them at all. Did Alex still go to the restaurant? Was Emie managing? Did Mae miss her?

Quillan was right. They seemed distant and somehow insubstantial. Another life that had briefly crossed her own. It was only because so much of her energy was drained now by this current trouble. *What are you doing, Signore? What am I doing?*

She stopped walking to catch her breath. The corset was tight and uncomfortable. Had they missed her yet? Whom would Papa send? Flavio? She shuddered, glancing swiftly over her shoulder. What if he found her here alone, in the dark? After his words tonight, she would put nothing past him.

What did he mean he kept her sacred, did not defile her as he had "the others." How many lovers had he had? She hurried on. *Dio, get me home.* But as she approached the house in the moonlight, saw its imposing gates, she didn't feel like she was home. She looked at the tall arched windows, the elegant eaves and pillars. It was Papa's home, as proud and unyielding as he.

But there was nothing else to do but go inside. She rapped on the door, and Jerome, their servant, admitted her. She went to the study to await her papa. He would be angry, and she would as soon settle it now as tomorrow. She sat down in his room, lined with medical texts and scientific writings from all the great men of history. Her favorite had been the book of diagrams by Leonardo da Vinci.

She smelled the slightly antiseptic smell that reminded her of her papa. This was his room. She had spent many hours there. She thought of Divina's words. *Papa's little favorite.* It was true. Papa had little patience for Divina's silliness. It was she he had coddled, teaching her his craft, or at least the understanding of what he did. He had admired her spunk. She reminded him of Mamma, especially in appearance. How many times he'd said, "You're so like your mamma."

But there were ways Divina was like Mamma, too. Slapping and pouting and manipulating with her tears. And saying whatever it took in spite of the truth. Carina raised her head at the sound of the carriage in the yard. They must have all come home.

She got up and stood in the doorway, where Papa would see her when he came in.

He was the first through the door. His gaze locked with hers as Mamma pushed in behind, hands to her mouth.

"You're here, Carina!" She spoke with scolding relief.

"I told Papa I needed to go home." She back-stepped into the study as Papa came in and closed the door behind them.

He walked to the desk and turned. "Why do you insist on defying me? What have I done to earn your disdain?"

"I don't disdain you, Papa."

He looked her down and up. "You are a woman, not a child, but I give you credit for more thought perhaps than you deserve. I know your nature makes you vulnerable to your emotions."

"It's not my emotions, Papa."

He removed his coat and hung it on the stand. Then he turned, his pleated sleeves full and immaculate. He came and took her hands. She looked up into his face. Her papa was tall, as tall as Quillan, though not as broad in the shoulders. But, she realized with surprise, possessing the same sinewy build. Their faces, too, were similar, strong and angular; Papa's blue eyes and Quillan's gray, both intense in scrutiny.

"You must trust me, Carina. I know what is best for you."

"Do you, Papa?"

"You would never have questioned me before." His face grew sad, and it broke her heart.

"I don't mean to hurt you. I just don't understand."

"Some day you will."

She shook her head, turning away. How many times tonight would she be told she couldn't understand? Thinking of that, she turned back. "Papa, why did you leave Italy?"

His brows drew together. "Why do you ask?"

"I've never thought to before. But you had so much. Land and power and esteem. Why would you leave that?"

"You know your history. Italy was many years in disarray. How solid was its unification? Parts were still warring."

"Not Sardinia. Not our Italy."

Her papa released her hands and walked to the window. Looking out into the night, he stayed quiet.

"Mamma said you wanted freedom and land."

He turned. "That's right."

"But you had land. And position."

He rested his fingers on the window sash. "Land and position. Even power. But not freedom."

"What do you mean?"

He returned to stand before her. "Carina, power has inherent dangers. There is always the chance of losing it."

She searched his face. What power had he lost?

"I don't speak of my own power, but of those I served."

She nodded, encouraging him to continue.

"In a country full of strife and rebellion, and you're wrong to think it didn't affect us in Sardinia, there are always those who pose a threat to the ones in power. Our stability had been hard fought and harder won."

This, too, she understood.

He sighed. "Because of this, as a loyal follower, I was asked to do something that betrayed my oath." She knew he meant his Hippocratic oath, to preserve life and cause no harm. He held it next to his devotion to God.

"You refused?"

Her papa looked away. "There was a man, particularly dangerous in his views and charisma. When he was injured in an altercation, I was summoned by the family, who were powerful enough to know the level of my skill and wealthy enough to appropriate it, though the mischief of this particular member threatened them."

She waited, almost breathless. Had her papa helped the man and been exiled for it?

"Before I went to him I was contacted by an official of the king. He suggested that it would be in the country's best interest if the man did not survive his injury."

Carina could not hide her dismay.

"I went to the house and saw that the man's situation was grave indeed. It would take all my skill to save him."

"But you did?"

Her papa's throat worked, and her heart sank.

"I did not. Perhaps I could not have anyway, but I withheld the skill God gave me. I worked on his body, but not thoroughly enough to sustain his life."

She stood silent, unable to believe that was the choice her papa had made.

He drew a breath and released it. "For that reason I could no longer remain in Italy. I could not serve a king by whose order I betrayed myself and my God."

Carina trembled. "Oh, Papa."

He lowered his face, his eyes filled with grief. "I had seen the man, heard him speak. He was a hothead, full of dreams. His own family was afraid of him, of what he would cost them. When they learned that I was leaving Italy, they brought me his son. The mother had died in childbirth, and they feared the boy was . . . a liability. Indeed, at six he had his father's beauty and nature."

She clasped his hands between hers. "Did you take him, Papa?"

"He is your 'cousin.' Flavio."

Her legs weakened. She gripped the desk. "Flavio?" It was Flavio's father her papa had not saved? *Signore, help me.* She felt the burden of his guilt.

Twenty

To be submitted, flesh and soul, that is my desire.
To give myself, my all, my whole, and ne'er in that to tire.

— Quillan

FLAVIO CARESSED the smooth wooden ball, then eyed the long gravel lane and the arrangement of the other wooden balls already thrown around the small metal bocce ball. He lowered his hand into position, hanging the ball beneath his palm. Then swinging his arm and flicking the wrist upward together, he sent the ball down the lane.

It struck Lorenzo's and knocked Tony's to the edge of the lane, stopping within inches of the target ball. His shot put him in the lead. But that did nothing to ease the awful strain inside him. It felt as though he were tearing apart, tendon from muscle, sinew from cartilage, organ from organ. Such a hatred he had not felt since the day they told him his father was dead.

He had only been six, and though thoughts of his papa evoked strong emotions, he could not remember him clearly. He had images, but when he tried to see his father in his mind, it was more a sensation than a picture. What he did picture was the man he'd first fixed his hatred upon: Angelo DiGratia. When the dottore came into the house where Papa lay dying, Flavio had felt awe.

This man had healing hands. Like Gesù. He had heard the others talking, knew he was the finest surgeon to be found. He would save Papa's life, and everything would be right again. Flavio had trembled, forgotten, against one wall, as Dr. DiGratia struggled to mend the damage.

Flavio stepped back for Vittorio to take his turn. He cared little for the outcome of this game, though normally his sense of competition was extreme. Especially against the DiGratia brothers. He hadn't known the doctor had a family, or else he might have seen him differently.

Flavio had never known his mother, since she died birthing him. But he had heard that if only a doctor had come in time she could have survived. Now that the dottore was there, surely his papa would live. But he had not. And Angelo DiGratia became the target of all Flavio's grief and despair.

The horrible hollowness had put him into that black place where he could scarcely lift his head from the pillow. Liquid grief filled his veins. When, some weeks later, he learned his family was going to send him out of Italy with the doctor, he ran and hid in the alley behind the house. He would rather die on the streets than see that man again. Unfortunately, they found him and gave him no choice in the matter.

Flavio leaned against the wall enclosing the bowling lanes, remembering his arrival in Argentina with the doctor's party. It was marked most strongly in his mind by the jungle smell of the air and the look of bafflement on the faces of his company. They were at their wits' end to discover how to handle the young animal placed in their charge. Wrapped in fear and horror, he had been scarcely less than savage.

Vittorio's next shot posed no threat to Flavio's, but Flavio was struggling to concentrate. He recalled how one of the families traveling with the DiGratias, some distant cousin on the signora's side, the Lanzas, adopted him, willing to do what they could for the difficult boy. But strangely enough, it was the doctor who healed him.

Day by day, Flavio would sneak out and spy on the man, wanting only to feed the terrible hatred. But day by day, watching the doctor apply his skills to anyone who asked, even the Indians who paid nothing but a pouch of corn or a handful of colorful feathers, he realized he might have been wrong in his judgment. Signore DiGratia was a good man, but he was not Gesù. Gesù was a fairy tale.

And so the devotion Flavio had once held for God, he now

gave to Angelo DiGratia. God could have saved his papa, but hadn't. At least the doctor had tried. Or had he? Even in his love, there was doubt.

And now he loved again—Ti'Angelo's daughter. And again it was in the doctor's hands to save or not save his heart.

Lorenzo nudged him. "Your turn, Flavio."

Flavio lifted his second ball and went to the end of the lane. What did he care for a small metal ball on a stretch of sand when his heart was tearing in two? There were two other lanes in the long narrow building, but no one was using them. A withered Chinaman with a thin gray queue hanging down his back swept loose gravel into the left lane with a straw broom. Flavio lined up and eyed the lay of the balls before him. His arm and hand knew what to do, but his thoughts were distracted by the Chinaman's motion, by the *scritch, scritch* of the broom. His strain grew until he was being racked, torn, limb from limb. He flung his arm back and sent the ball like a missile into the old man's back.

"Aiyee!" The Chinaman dropped his broom and fell to his knees as Flavio found another ball and hurtled it toward his head. It glanced off the man's silken hat, splitting open the top of his ear, and he collapsed, covering his head and squalling.

A hand gripped Flavio's wrist, though he couldn't make out the face. Then the red fury became Tony's features. Flavio stared at him, shocked and paralyzed by what he'd done, thinking of the missiles hurled at his papa in the riot. He hadn't seen it, but had heard the family talking before they sent him away. Violent people had killed his papa. Violence Flavio had always despised. But now . . . He jerked his arm away. "Doesn't he know better than to sweep when I'm trying to make my shot?"

Lorenzo and Vittorio were staring. Flavio knew what they thought. He'd lost his mind. Reversed himself in the cheapest way. All his ideals, his philosophy, lost in a moment of petty rage. And inside he wasn't sure he would have stopped until he'd stoned the man to death. Humiliated and terrified by what he had done without thinking, Flavio curled his lip. "Stupid Chinese," he muttered. "Go back to China, old man!" He brushed off his sleeves, looked once more at the DiGratia brothers, and walked out.

He felt sick, as though something poisoned him. He had betrayed his nature, and still the strain was not relieved. The

Chinaman wasn't the source. The source and target of his rage was Quillan Shepard. He had told Carina he would destroy him. It had been words, bravado, to terrify her, to hurt her for saying she loved the man. But now he trembled. Now he believed he could actually do it. And in that thought, at last, the tearing inside him eased.

———

Carina stared in surprise as her brothers brought the old Chinese man into Papa's medical room. They laid him, chattering and cringing, on the table. Tony raised a hand, pressing down against the air so the man would understand what he meant. "Stay here. Lie down."

Carina saw the blood streaming from the old man's ear. She couldn't tell if it was all from the split at the top of it or if some came from inside, indicating injury to the brain and the inner ear. She looked from the Chinaman to her brothers.

Vittorio said, "Go get Papa. I'll work on him, but I want Papa to have a look."

Carina hurried out to find her papa. He was in the field, overseeing the removal of the vines. They should have been yanked out in the winter when they were completely dormant. It seemed crueler, somehow, to destroy them when they were making a weak, desperate attempt to grow.

"Papa—" she called—"Papa, Vittorio needs you. He has an injured Chinese."

Her papa turned, started toward her. In a short time he reached her. "A Chinese, you say?"

"Yes, Papa. He must have been struck with something."

Papa shook his head and started for the house. "Where was he hit?"

"In the ear. There's lots of blood, but I couldn't see if it came from inside. He's an old man, Papa. Who would do such a thing?"

"Who wouldn't?" he said softly. "Was ever a people so despised?"

"They are strange, Papa. People don't like what they don't understand."

Papa frowned. "People understand less and less every day."

They reached the house and went inside. Vittorio had cleaned the blood from the ear and was attempting to stitch the edges of the top together. He had been watching and learning from his papa for years. Now they worked together in both medicine and viticulture.

Carina saw a fresh trickle of fluid from inside the man's ear. Trauma to the brain. There was swelling, too. She thought of D.C., Cain's son, who'd been nearly killed by a head blow. But he had been silent and comatose. This old man chattered and shrieked in Chinese without end.

Papa approached him, laid a hand on his chest. The man became still, looking at Papa from his black almond eyes. "A candle, Carina," was all Papa said.

Vittorio stitched furiously while the man lay still. Carina brought a candle, and Papa moved it across the old man's vision. Then he handed it back to her and raised the man's eyelids slightly with his thumb. Carina felt the familiar surge of pride and tenderness, watching her papa work. Only Papa could have eased the man's terror with a touch.

She stepped back next to Tony. "What happened? Where did you find him?"

Tony glanced from her to their father. "He was sweeping up the lanes. Flavio got angry."

Her mouth parted as she searched her brother's face. "Flavio struck him?" Impossible. Flavio would never raise his hand to injure. He hated physical confrontation, scorned it.

"He lost his temper. Threw the ball."

Her mind couldn't argue with what Tony had seen with his eyes. Carina looked back at the old man. Flavio could do that? To a helpless old man doing his job? Then he was not the Flavio she knew. What had he become?

Tony took her arm, spoke close beside her head. "It's not his fault. He's powder, waiting to explode. You must do something before—"

"Before what?" She stared into his face.

"Before you lose them both."

She swallowed the surge of fear and hissed, "Quillan is my husband. What would you have me do?"

Tony shook his head. "I don't know, Carina. I only know that when Flavio threw the balls, he was not—" Tony spread his hands—"he was not Flavio."

She looked back at the old man in Papa's hands.

Lorenzo leaned over, assisting. "He was also hit on his back. You might want to check him there."

Carina looked back at the Chinaman as Papa eased his shoulder up from the table. She said, "Flavio struck him twice?"

"Before I stopped him."

Carina chilled at the implication that Flavio might not have stopped himself. She couldn't fathom it. Yes, Flavio was temperamental, introspective, and emotional, his moods unpredictable. But murder? She had warned Quillan but had not really believed it, not deep inside as she did now. *Signore, is it possible?* She thought of Flavio as she knew him, as she had loved him, his hypnotic appeal due as much to his unpredictability as to his charm.

But there was no appeal to such lack of control. She thought how hard Quillan had tried to avoid violence, even toward the roughs who had terrorized Crystal. Quillan protected life, though no one had ever protected him. She ached inside for the man she loved.

And then she remembered begging for Flavio's life. *"What if self-defense becomes deadly force?"* And she had told him no. But now she saw what Flavio could do. What if Quillan couldn't defend himself without killing Flavio? Or God forbid, what if he were killed? She pressed her palms to her head. "Tony, what do I do?"

He lowered his eyes, then said, "Annul the marriage."

It was a hammer to her chest. Annul the marriage that was life to her? And what? Marry Flavio? To ease Papa's guilt? To save Quillan's life? Did she love him enough to release him? For his life's sake? She gripped a hand to her mouth and rushed outside.

Trembling and weeping, she ran out to the vineyard, stood among the vines ripped from the ground, their roots drying. She could almost hear them weeping with her. *Il Padre Eterno! Help me, please. How can I give him up? How can I lose what you have given? Would you strip him from me as you stripped the baby from my womb? Must I lose everything?*

She looked at the dying vines. Just so would she wither and die without Quillan. He was her life.

I am sufficient.

Spoken to her soul, the words reverberated. God had told her that before, but she had believed He added Quillan's love to His. And, God forgive her, she had delighted more in Quillan's. "Oh,

Signore." It was God she must love with all her being, Gesù she must love enough to surrender Quillan. She dropped, sobbing, to her knees. "I can't do it." Like Abraham she would hold the knife to Quillan's heart if she rejected him now. God couldn't ask it. Could He?

She dropped to the ground between the rows, her fists in the soil that had nourished but now killed the vines. She sobbed until she could cry no more, gripping the dirt into her hands, grinding it under her nails. "I can't. I can't." But then she knew she must. If God asked it, she must do it. Her love for Quillan must be wrong, or God would not take it from her.

She slowly raised up, turned dull eyes to the hazy sky. Then closing her eyes, she said, "Signore, if you require it, I will obey." There was no joy in that surrender, only pain and obedience. But obedience would have to be enough.

She dragged herself up from the dirt, turned, and trudged toward the house. A man stood at the gate to the courtyard, his natty dress and posture somehow familiar. He tapped a newspaper against his arm, seemingly unsure whether to open the gate and admit himself or wait to be acknowledged. He turned as she approached. "Mrs. Shepard!"

And now she recognized him. The man from the train, Roderick Pierce of the *Rocky Mountain News*. She sighed.

"Mrs. Shepard." He said less confidently when he drew close enough to see her condition. "Are you . . . is everything . . ."

"What do you want, Mr. Pierce?"

He held up the paper. "I brought the article."

Carina looked at the headline, entitled *A Hero for Today?*, feeling a sick ache in her stomach. An article about Quillan's heroism, as if she didn't know enough. "Could you not have sent it in the post?"

"I could have." He smiled. "But, well the short of it is, the article has sparked some good things. I've sold *Harper's Monthly* on a series of biographical sketches featuring your husband. I say, from what I learned in Crystal, it's as good as Wild Bill Hickok. They're crazy for it."

Carina could do nothing but stare through tear-streaked eyes in a face smudged with dirt. The sight was not lost on Mr. Pierce.

"But perhaps now is not a good time?"

She laughed bleakly. "Now is certainly not a good time, Mr.

Pierce. But as for the sketches, you'll have to ask Quillan."

"Is he ... Forgive me, Mrs. Shepard, are you in trouble? Can I assist you?"

She looked into his earnest face. "I'm such a sight, am I?"

"Please don't think me untoward."

Again she formed a weak smile. "At this time my husband ..." How much longer could she use that word to describe Quillan Shepard? How could he ever be anything else? "My husband will be at Schocken's quarry." Waving her arms, she told him how to get to the quarry.

"Shall I leave this?" He held out the paper. "I have another copy."

She looked at the extended paper, slowly took it in her hands. "Thank you."

He tipped his hat. "Until next time, ma'am. I hope it will be soon and under better circumstances."

She smiled. A likeable man, though he did show up at the worst of times.

———

Quillan eased the wagon into the shade of the rock bowl, from which they blasted and cut the basalt cobbles. He set the brake and jumped down. His right shoulder sent a twinge from having been slept on without moving—the sleep of emotional exhaustion. He had awoken missing Carina with everything in him, but almost as strong was the sense that he didn't suffer it alone.

The verses he had read that morning from the prophet Isaiah left him no doubt that God knew, that Jesus understood personally all his grief. *He is despised and rejected of men; a man of sorrows, and acquainted with grief: and we hid as it were our faces from him; he was despised, and we esteemed him not.* Quillan had dropped to his knees, thinking of his own rebellion, his own rejection of the Jesus Cain had tried to make him see. Then he'd read on.

Surely he hath borne our griefs, and carried our sorrows: yet we did esteem him stricken, smitten of God, and afflicted. Just as everyone had assumed Quillan's guilt, imagined wickedness where there was only want.

But He was wounded for our transgressions, he was bruised for our iniquities. Quillan didn't want to think how many wounds he had personally added to the Savior's pain. The hateful thoughts, the bitter self-absorption. He was all too aware of his failings. *The chastisement of our peace was upon him.* The chastisement of our peace. Quillan pondered those words. He had felt the peace of God's presence, an inner trust of complete abandonment he'd never known before. Because Christ had borne the chastisement.

And with his stripes we are healed. That verse had brought tears. Again. Why would God himself take the whippings Quillan deserved upon himself? Why would Jesus succumb for the likes of him? Before, Quillan had felt he owed nothing to anyone. He went his own way, living by what conscience he had, with a fierce ingrained need to protect the weak, the mistreated. But for himself he'd refused redemption. Now he basked in it. God understood his failings and suffered with him. An awesome and incomprehensible thought.

That was the vine to which he clung, the vine that gave him life. He needed nothing more, yet . . . human weakness still made him ache with thoughts of Carina. Would that ever end? Surely even a branch shuddered at the pruning knife.

Quillan had already watered the horses, so he took the feed bags from the bed and hooked them over each animal's head in turn, with a soft word and stroke to their necks. Jock nuzzled him affectionately, and Quillan held the horse's muzzle to his face, then gave him his feed. He reached up to the box for the flat leather bag that held his own bread and cheese and his journal.

He perched on a gray heap of basalt, away from where the others ate, talked, and sent him dark looks. It mattered less today than it had before. *He is despised and rejected of men.* At least he was in good company. Quillan wasn't even sure why he had shown up at the quarry, except that he had taken the job, and until he was certain he should leave it, he meant to do it.

He was a man of action. Sitting around undirected would make him crazy. At least at the quarry he could work the strain away, something he'd learned early and employed nearly every day of his life. Others might long for empty time, but that was Quillan's enemy. His body was strong, his mind active. Both required work. He suddenly thought of Mae telling him he must learn to be still. Not likely. He bit hard into his bread.

He was halfway through the bite when he saw Flavio. The instant tightening in his chest quelled any thoughts that he was delivered from this present strife. There was the man who stood between him and his wife. If not for Flavio, Dr. DiGratia might think more kindly on him. More than that, it was Carina's own lingering connection Quillan fretted over as he looked at the figure Flavio Caldrone cut.

There was something fine in both build and manner that made him starkly out of place among the sharp hewn rocks and rough hewn men. But Flavio walked among them with an easy grace, confident of both their acceptance and respect. What was his story, Quillan wondered. A rich aristocratic family? Plenty to eat, plenty to wear, all the blessings of God and man at his disposal?

He watched Flavio draw the laughter of the men and wave it off as his due. Oh, to be so confident of approval. Had he won his way back into Carina's heart? He'd possessed the better part of an evening to do it; the Garibaldi House had been loud with frolicking well into the night.

That thought hurt more than it should. But Carina was the sweetest grace he had experienced; her love had brought him from bitter solitude to joy. He couldn't keep his thoughts there or he would break down. He forced a subjective observation of Flavio, the disarming features seductive in their beauty. Flavio looked like a work of Italian artistry, a Greco-Roman hero. Not Herculean—perhaps more like Narcissus.

After some banter, of which Quillan could only catch the cadence since he was too far to decipher any of the words he had learned, Flavio drew one man away from the others. They talked together with much nodding and gesturing, then gripped each others' shoulders briefly and parted.

Before striding away, Flavio sent a pointed glance his direction. Quillan stiffened, surprised. Flavio knew he was there? And now he noted a distinct tightness in Flavio's gait, like a dueler stepping out his paces. Unconsciously, Quillan's hand dropped to his hip. No Colt. But neither was Flavio armed, as far as he could tell. Quillan slid his palm to his thigh.

The man slowly turned on his heel and sauntered away. Quillan wrapped up the rest of his cheese. He was no longer hungry. The men were openly studying him, discussing him, too, no doubt. What did Flavio want? Why had he come there? To sow more discord?

Was it some sort of challenge? A flame flickered inside—Quillan's natural instinct. If he knew he was supposed to fight for Carina, nothing would stop him, not the whole mass of them together. But he was no longer sure she wanted that. Her face had been pained when she begged him not to endanger Flavio's life. By now that concern for the man she had once loved could have been stoked into the passion Quillan knew too well.

Walled in by her family and fed a diet of Flavio's attention, why would she think twice about the rogue she once deigned to love? The pain was like a living being in his heart, draining him of hope. How must Jesus have felt when all those who loved him turned away? Quillan brought out his journal and lost himself in words. It was the best way he could think to keep the pain at bay.

Flavio left the rock yard with the strain once again reaching intensity. He had spent the night in a storm, gusts of regret for his violence sliced by bolts of fascination and a rumbling confusion. He had lain still and thought of his father. He didn't know much, only the sensation of the man's virility, his energy, and a vague sense of equally potent rage and gloom. Probably akin to Flavio's own.

His papa had been a republican—less kindly, a troublemaker. That trouble had cost him his life. Flavio had never discussed it with Dottore DiGratia, but it stood between them in spite of the kindness, the acceptance he'd found from the man. Once his misplaced hatred had faded, Flavio had gravitated to Angelo DiGratia like a bee to nectar, seeking sustenance of a kind he found nowhere else.

He had thought for a time to learn the man's skill, to become a doctor himself. But the tedium of the scientific study in which Dottore DiGratia excelled was too much for Flavio. He could not sit still behind a microscope, could not still his hands long enough to mend torn flesh and damaged tissue. His mind flew from the task at hand to other thoughts more commanding, more creative.

The doctor wanted to mend, but Flavio wanted to make. The arts—they were his passion. In pictures and in music he spent his soul. No, he was not meant to follow the doctor. But that did not mean he loved him less.

Dottore DiGratia had become the father he lost. Signore Lanza was all right; Flavio had nothing against him. The man had fed and clothed him and allowed him his way. But Angelo DiGratia had taken him to his heart. Was it because he had failed to save his father?

Flavio wondered if the doctor carried that guilt or if it was just part of his profession. What was monumental in Flavio's life might well have been forgotten in Dottore DiGratia's. Except that sometimes he caught on the doctor's face a look of regret and . . . shame. He felt a stirring of power and remembered one of the few things his papa had told him. *"When you see a man's weakness, use it."* Flavio had not understood the words as a child of six, but he did now.

Flavio thought with pride of the doctor's protection of his contract with Carina, in spite of his indiscretion—which the doctor may or may not know about. Either way, Dottore DiGratia did not accept Quillan Shepard's claim. Yet the man would not give up. Surely that justified the possibilities he had just set in motion. Quillan was a threat to the DiGratias, a threat to him, and most of all, a threat to Carina. If an accident should occur . . .

He reached his stallion and mounted. Flavio had not brought the animal into the quarry where the shards of rock could damage its hooves. He brought the animal around, remembering Carina's trick when she had sent him sprawling and galloped off on his horse. He'd been torn by fury but also moved to ecstasy at her spirit. She was the only woman who matched his passion.

But she was too softhearted, too easily won, her love given irrepressibly. She could be deeply hurt. He knew now how deeply, and he cursed his foolish liaison with Divina. For that moment's conquest, he'd lost Carina. For a time. But not forever. As long as Dottore DiGratia upheld his contract, he had a chance of redeeming it.

Maybe Carina would not marry him willingly, but once Quillan Shepard was removed, then carefully, so carefully, he would win her heart again. He knew the words she liked to hear, and he was a proficient lover, though at the moment she did not appreciate his experience.

He frowned. If only she hadn't walked in on them. How stupid to use the doctor's barn. Divina had not been worth it. He thought now of Nicolo, sick with love for Divina. Did Nicolo appreciate the seed Flavio had started that made her willing at last? Flavio felt a twinge. Was he a monster not to care that his child would be raised as another man's?

Was there something wrong with him that he cared so little for Divina's distress? When she came to him, sobbing her news, he had felt nothing. Surely there should have been something? Maybe it was walled off in that place inside where he stood sometimes, wanting to go in, but unable to. In there was the child whose papa lay dying, whose mamma gave her life for his, whose family discarded him.

But he couldn't go in. And what, he suspected, might make him human, stayed safely buried. His emotions stormed around it, but like the eye of a hurricane, that part remained still and untouched.

Anyone hearing his thoughts would be amazed. Flavio without feeling? Flavio, whose feelings were always evident—his love, his passion, his choler. But they were all on the outside. It had begun on the ship, when his dismay and terror made him savage and he learned what power such emotions could have on people. Had Signore Lanza once taken a belt to him? Never.

But Flavio knew he gained more through benevolence than rage. Oh, how he melted Signora Lanza. She was butter in his hands. And as soon as his body came to manhood, so were the girls. Flavio turned into the lane to the DiGratias. Yes, he would win back Carina's love. He had been a fool to wait. He should have shown her what a husband he would be.

The gates were closed, but he opened them with a sense of authority. He crossed the courtyard, seeing no one and expecting no one. They would be in the fields ripping out the vines, the unproductive struggling grapes that could no longer yield a productive harvest. Just so would he yank Quillan Shepard and replace him with a hearty root stock.

He knocked on the door, then entered. "Dottore?" Flavio walked toward the study where the doctor researched and read, adjoining the treatment room where he saw the patients who came to him. "Ti'Angelo, are you—"

The doctor emerged from the treatment room. His face was stern.

Flavio stopped. "Are you seeing someone, Dottore?"

Angelo DiGratia closed the door behind him. "Come with me, Flavio." He led him to the study with its walls lined with books, the sort Flavio shuddered to read. Nothing beautiful—only facts, details, theories.

"What is it, Tio?" Flavio read his concern, his consternation.

"Is it true you struck a man yesterday with bocce balls?"

Flavio felt a flush of shame. His sons had told him? "I lost my temper. The old Chinaman . . ." He spread his hands. His excuse sounded churlish. "I was infuriated by . . . by the things that are torturing me. It had nothing to do with the Chinaman."

"Nothing to do with him, yet he's in my treatment room." Angelo DiGratia indicated the door separating the rooms.

Flavio stared at the closed door. "Is he hurt badly?"

"He is old. His bones are brittle."

Flavio shuddered. "I didn't mean to hurt him."

"The concussion is hard to gauge since I cannot employ him in discussion. I don't even know if he has family to care for him. He is in and out of consciousness."

Flavio knew better than to say it was only a Chinaman. And again, he was deeply ashamed of his outburst and violence, the sort of violence that had killed his papa. What must Angelo DiGratia think of him now?

"I'm sorry. What can I do?"

"Do, Flavio? You think you are a doctor now?" Angelo's expression cut him. "I'm ashamed of you, to injure an old man."

Inside Flavio quailed. To have earned the doctor's disdain . . . "I'm ashamed of myself. But I'm so angry, Tio. It—" he spread his hands—"it's tearing me apart. I thought nothing could be worse than when Carina left. But worse by far is her coming back with this, this—"

"I am taking care of that. I've spoken with Father Esser."

"Father Esser is building a new church. What time does he have—"

"He will consider the validity of Carina's marriage. He gave me his word to look into it immediately."

"What if he finds it valid?" Flavio burst out with the words before he could stop them.

Angelo DiGratia looked at him with gentle concern. "We will consider that if we must. But until then I'm trusting the wisdom of the church."

Flavio could not bring himself to do the same. Ever since he decided the healing Gesù was nothing but a myth, he'd had little concern for the church. Angelo might put his trust in black-robed fathers, but Flavio would see for himself that Carina's marriage was ended.

He dared not even show a flicker of that thought, which he both hated and clung to. If the doctor's concern was so deep for a worthless Chinaman, how would he consider the new plans in Flavio's mind? Flavio trembled. He had felt brash and defiant an hour ago. Now...

"Flavio." Angelo's voice was soft, gentle. "I know you love my daughter. I watched you grow up together. You are like one of my sons."

Flavio drank it in.

"But listen to me now." His thin brows drew together. "You cannot be at the mercy of your temper. Your father . . ."

Flavio tensed. The doctor had never mentioned him.

"Your father was unwise in his moods. I don't want your death on my hands."

He didn't say *too*. Flavio waited, but he didn't acknowledge that his father's death was already on his hands. Could the doctor have saved him? Had he tried? What judge was a frightened six-year-old? Just the same, Flavio imagined he knew the moment when Dottore DiGratia had decided either that he wouldn't or couldn't save his papa. He had seen a shadow pass over the man's face, a shadow of death like a dark wing.

"If you do something rash, you will pay the price." The doctor turned to the room behind him. "If that old man dies . . ."

"You won't let him." Flavio's voice betrayed his desperation.

Angelo looked back at him. "I'm not God."

Flavio's chest tightened. "I thought you were once. When they brought you to the house to save my papa. I thought you had Gesù's healing hands."

"Ah, Flavio." The doctor spread his fingers before him. "My hands are human, but sometimes God heals through them."

And sometimes He doesn't. Flavio stared at the delicate fingers outstretched from Dottore DiGratia's fine hands. Then he looked into the man's face, saw pain and fear there mingled.

"Flavio, don't do something you'll pay for more dearly than you can afford."

Had he read his thoughts? Flavio spread his hands. "Do what?"

"You and Quillan Shepard both want Carina. Let God decide between you."

Flavio stared at him. Something opened, some small painful part. "The God who took my mother? My father, too?"

Angelo's face turned gray. He leaned slightly against the desk, his hands dropping to his sides. "Don't lay your father's death on God."

Now it would come. Flavio felt his breathing suspend. Now he would know once for all if that early hatred had been deserved.

But the doctor said, "Men killed your father, not God." His voice shook, and he folded his fingers together at his chest.

"And that makes it all right?"

"No, Flavio. Nothing condones that."

Flavio felt cheated. Men killed his father? Men including the doctor? *Tell me the truth!*

And now Angelo's voice strengthened. "Neither does that condone your own violence."

Flavio felt the sap leave his limbs, despondence descending like a parasite, sucking him dry. In his hurt, he searched the doctor's face. "I will do what I must."

"You do it without my consent." Angelo's face was both stern and entreating.

Flavio's hands clenched at his sides. "Would you take Carina from me?"

He didn't answer for a long moment. Then, "I want what you want. But I will submit to God."

"Then you don't want what I want." Flavio turned.

Angelo caught his arm. "Flavio. Beware your nature."

Flavio exploded. "My nature! My papa's nature? Is it so dangerous? Is that why your hands could not heal? Or was it your will?" He was shocked to have said it aloud.

The doctor looked stunned. Then he drew himself up. "Your father was gravely wounded, battered and crushed and cut. What do you think I could do?"

Flavio stepped up close until his face was just before Angelo's. He sent his gaze past the blue eyes, probing. "You tell me, Tio. Could you have saved my papa?"

Angelo DiGratia became very still. His eyes blinked slowly once. "I don't know."

Flavio swallowed that. How could he not know? If he had

done all he could the answer would be simply, *No, Flavio, I could not.* The tearing inside worsened. Now that he knew, he wished he didn't. Could he ever look at this man he loved and not know he had let his father die?

Angelo caught his shoulders. "I love you as my own son."

Flavio's throat closed too tightly to speak.

Angelo pulled him into a fierce embrace. Flavio wanted his arms to come around the man who had taught him gentleness, concern for others, the value of life. But it was all a lie. His limbs were slogged with mud. He could not lift them, not to hold, to validate this man. He pulled away, refusing to meet the doctor's eyes. He turned and walked out.

Twenty-one

What hold the flesh upon the soul that yearns for purity,
while mind and body clash and strive for human surety.
Ah, my spirit, be assured, your wait is nigh to done;
for soon I deem all earthly joy for me there will be none.

— Quillan

THE CRUNCH OF BOOT on stone brought Quillan's head up from his journal. The last person he expected or wanted to see was Roderick Pierce. Was this a day of trial? He squinted up with little welcome. What on earth was the man doing at Schocken's quarry?

Pierce ignored his scowl with a grin, though the climb up the hill had taxed him it seemed. "Hello." He fit the word between breaths.

Quillan nodded once, nothing more than base courtesy.

"Remember me?" Pierce swiped off his hat and dabbed his forehead with his sleeve.

"Like a blood-sucking gnat."

Pierce laughed heartily. "Charming as ever." He glanced down. "What's that there? Writer, are you?"

Quillan closed his journal. Dust still hung in the air from the charges he had set to break up the new surface, and he had loaded his wagon already with the rough stone. He would carry the stone down to the yard below to be shaped into cobbles by the Italian stone cutters. He was only giving the horses a chance to graze before he headed down.

"Freelance?"

"No."

"Mind if I have a look? One writer to another?" Pierce held out his hand.

Quillan's stare was answer enough.

Pierce pulled a newspaper from inside his fustian coat. "I brought the piece that's made you famous."

Famous? Quillan looked at him, mystified. He was past the hope of meaningful human acceptance. On the verge of losing Carina, on guard for his life—and Roderick Pierce spoke of fame? God had a very odd sense of humor. Quillan nodded at the rock pile beside him. "You can leave it there."

"Actually," Pierce sat down in the spot Quillan indicated, "I have a proposition to discuss."

"No."

"Now I know you're not quick on the bait, but I think when you've heard me out you'll appreciate my ideas."

Quillan took his journal and stood. "I need to get back to work."

"Now that's just the thing." Pierce got to his feet, as well. "Why is a man of your financial situation working in a rock quarry?"

Quillan said nothing. What would Pierce know of his financial situation?

"I would think the sale of your mine would have you sitting pretty."

If Pierce had stripped him of his pants and shirt, Quillan could hardly have felt more naked. "What mine?"

"New Boundless. Wasn't that the name?"

Quillan turned and started down toward his wagon.

"Now the figures I got weren't staggering, but certainly substantial."

Quillan spun. "Figures?" Had Alex Makepeace run off at the mouth? "From whom?"

"It took some digging, but one thing led to another until *whop!* I'd landed in Horace Tabor's lap. Friend of his, are you? He spoke fondly. Very curious about your wife. I assured him she was as lovely as any woman I've seen. You don't mind my saying so, do you?"

The tendons in Quillan's neck pulled tight. Yes, he minded

any man noticing and remarking on her beauty. It only made the pain sharper. "I don't appreciate you digging into my affairs." He glanced at the newspaper Pierce had snatched up when he stood. "It's all printed in there?"

"Oh no." Pierce waved the paper then held it out again. "See for yourself."

Quillan grabbed it, shoved it inside his shirt. Then he bent and removed the rocks he had placed to block the wagon's wheels from rolling.

"I only covered the train incident with the small details your wife added."

Small details like his involvement with Shane Dennison in the bank robbery, no doubt. Quillan pulled himself up to the box.

"Mind if I catch a ride?" Pierce grabbed hold of the edge of the box.

Quillan did mind, but by the time he'd released the brake and taken up the reins, Pierce was aboard.

"Now hear me out, Quillan. I've started, and I may as well go the whole hog before you tip me over the side." He laughed. "The fact is, people were considerably taken with this piece, with you, and it doesn't take a Philadelphia lawyer to see the opportunity. I've sold *Harper's Monthly* magazine on a series of biographical sketches featuring the hero of the Union Pacific."

Quillan kept his eyes straight ahead. "Did they catch Dennison?"

Nonplussed, Pierce regrouped. "Not that I've heard. But he hasn't hit another train along the line since you put him off. Now, as I was saying—"

"Two letters, Pierce: *N* and *O*."

"The world needs heroes, Quillan. People to respect for their fortitude, courage, and old-fashioned gumption."

Quillan shook his head, amazed by Pierce's own fortitude. He surmised that nothing short of tipping him over the side of his wagon would suffice. If he were such a hero, why did Carina's father refuse to acknowledge their marriage? Why did the quarry men shun him? Last night God had shown him that man's esteem was worthless and at any rate, beyond him. Now here was Roderick Pierce, laying out the kingdoms of the world before him.

Was it the enemy trying to steal the peace he'd found in God alone? To turn him back to groveling for acceptance among those who would never understand, never accept? Fame. The wagon rocked over a ridge and corresponding dip, but Pierce stayed in the box.

"Well, I know you're a private man, but in truth, I've gathered enough to make a start on the sketches from other sources."

That irked. "If it's Hod Tabor, he's got more gas than evidence. Might as well write a dime store version and be done."

"That's why I'm here. Mrs. Shepard charged me on the train to tell it right. She sent me here today."

Quillan jerked the reins and turned. "You saw Carina?"

"I did." Pierce sobered.

"How was she?" Quillan could have bitten his tongue, but he had to know.

"Well, now that you ask, she wasn't good, not good at all. Quite upset. She'd been crying."

Quillan's heart tore. By now he had thought her embraced by her family's love, imagined her wooed and comforted by the same. "Did she say anything?"

"Just that I'd find you here. Trouble, is there?"

Quillan looked into Pierce's face. An unlikely confessor for sure, but the one person who, however misguided, seemed to care. "Yes, there's trouble. Carina's father, the good dottore, wants no part of me as a son-in-law. Her betrothed, from whom she fled to Crystal, wants me dead. And just about every Italian in town bows to one or the other."

Quillan wasn't sure what he expected, but Pierce's measuring gaze surprised him. "I say."

Quillan quirked his mouth at one corner. "Better look elsewhere for your hero."

"And have you lost your fortune, then?"

"My fortune?"

"Come, Quillan. I have it from Horace Tabor's mouth. He did finance the deal, did he not?"

Quillan frowned.

"I see that he did. You're a wealthy man, unless that, too, has been muddled?"

Quillan glared. "It's none of your affair."

"Lost it gambling, did you?"

Quillan moistened his lips, restrained the urge to bodily remove Pierce from the wagon. "I did not lose it. I don't gamble."

And now Pierce's curiosity peaked. "If that's so, what has the family so all-fired?"

Quillan faced him squarely. "Just . . . me." He saw Pierce reappraising him, taking in his rough cut, stubbled features, stubborn jaw, gray stormy eyes, unruly hair.

"You do present a formidable front."

Quillan started the wagon again.

Pierce caught the side. "Pro patria, is it?"

Quillan flinched. Did he present a bristly front like a porcupine ready to protect his vulnerable identity?

"You know, I could help you."

"No thanks."

"Tell the real story." Pierce persisted.

The real story was worse than the front. But there, he was sinking into his former thoughts. Why did Pierce keep chipping away the fragile peace he'd found? Jesus was the vine, God the vine grower, and he . . . he had to cling or be cut away and burned.

"Mr. Pierce—"

"Call me Rod."

"Mr. Pierce, you're wasting your time." Quillan neared the yard where he would unload his haul to be carried by hand wagons to the cutters, then stacked as street cobbles and taken to the depot. Sometimes that fell to him when they had enough rough material blasted from the surface to spare him from the work higher up.

"You know the best attribute of a newsman?"

Quillan didn't want to hear. He was weary of the argument.

"The nose." Pierce tapped his own. "That's where you know when you have something newsworthy."

Quillan brought his team to a halt, set the brake, and wound the traces. "Mr. Pierce—Rod—I don't know what you think you smell, but if you look around, you'll see keeping company with me isn't the safest choice right now."

Pierce looked. The men had stopped their labors and glared as one body. "That is an oddity of Italians, I've noticed. Clannish. But I wouldn't guess they'd take it too far."

Quillan thought back to Flavio's appearance earlier, his consultation with one of the workers and the taunting glance that followed. As they came forward sullenly to empty his load, Quillan muttered, "I wouldn't stake your life on that."

"Well, I've seen you handle a gun." He looked down at Quillan's belt. "Have it concealed, have you?"

Quillan shook his head.

"I see." Pierce rubbed his chin. "So that's the state of affairs."

Quillan jumped down from the box and started around to open the back.

Pierce climbed down and met him there. "I'm staying at the Traveler's Home Hotel. Why don't you meet me for a drink?"

"I have duties in Schocken's store after this."

"Till when? Six, seven?"

Quillan pulled himself onto the wagon bed. "My hours are my own. I'll work till I turn in."

Looking up, Pierce squinted into the glare. "Maybe I'll come around anyway."

Quillan shrugged and reached for the first rock. As Roderick Pierce strode off for his rented buggy, Quillan tossed the rock to the ground, and the men closed in under Mr. Marconi's watchful eye. He paused for a moment. Marconi was in an awkward spot between the ire of the Italian workers toward Quillan and the acclaim of Solomon Schocken. Quillan saw to it he did his work well. He would give Schocken and Marconi no cause for complaint.

After bathing, Carina peeked in at the Chinese man sleeping in the single bed Papa kept for patients too sick to send home. He seemed peaceful now, no longer ranting, though Papa checked his eyes every hour or two. But no one was in the room just now, so she left the old man to his rest.

She went up to her room and sat listlessly on the bed. She could hear the women gathering. From the bathhouse, she had seen Divina crossing the fields from her villa to Mamma's kitchen. She would not go down to suffer Divina's cutting tongue. And the others ... their murmuring and nodding made her squirm. What did they know? They had wormed into the vacancy she left and did not want to leave it now. And Mamma, Mamma was the worst. Now that she no longer wept it was certainly worse. Was she so confident the marriage would be annulled? Why weep when you've gotten what you want?

Carina glanced at the newspaper lying where she had dropped

it. What had Mr. Pierce written about her husband? Would it hurt too much to read? Could it hurt more than she already did?

She took up the paper and unfolded the pages. There was the headline. *A Hero for Today?* She wanted to cry all over again. *Signore, why won't they see?* She gathered herself and read Mr. Pierce's account of their adventure aboard the Union Pacific. He had highlighted Quillan's role, and he did capture the essence of her husband, his straightforward, dauntless courage, his ability to lead by example.

Then she read the part she was responsible for, his previous association with Shane Dennison. Mr. Pierce had sensationalized it, but not scandalously. He told a story of a boy enamored with a man, then left with the stark truth of that man's nature, how the boy had redeemed himself and now taken action on the side of right against the very one who had shamed him.

It was a good story, with a sprinkling of Mr. Pierce's wit and humor. He had told it well. Did that mean Quillan would let him tell the rest? She couldn't fathom it. She read the story again as Quillan might, saw his wry smile at Mr. Pierce's description, *This stalwart man of doughty countenance.* She brought the paper to her breast, pressing it to her heartbeat. *Oh, Quillan.*

She ached to see him. But it could only make it worse. What she wanted and what God wanted were no longer aligned. She must force her heart away from the one she loved. But how? Surely not by reading of his doughty countenance. It only made her picture his face, every shadow and angle that she had come to know.

"Dio, how can I stop loving him?" She turned at the tap on the door.

Divina tucked her head inside. "May I come in?"

Carina wanted to refuse. She did not have the strength to ward off Divina's cruelty. But she nodded.

Divina came inside and closed the door behind her, then sat down on the bed with a frank, but not unkind, expression. She said, "Carina, I'm sorry."

Carina stared. Was this some trick to expose her for the barb? She shifted on the bed, bringing her knee over and settling the other beside it. "Sorry for what?"

"For the way I've been."

Carina still did not trust her. "Why are you saying this?"

"Because you're my sister, and I've been hateful."

Something in Divina's tone, in her earnestness, melted away Carina's resistance. "You were hurt." And she knew from her own ugliness what hurt could make one do.

Divina dropped her eyes and nodded. "I thought Flavio would love me in your place. I was glad to have his child." Her eyes flashed up. "Yes, Nicolo knows."

But that wasn't right! Carina thought. A child should have his own papa, a family united in love, not necessity. Could Divina ever love Nicolo, when she'd pined so long for Flavio?

"I wanted so much to take what you had."

Such bare honesty. Carina hadn't thought Divina capable of such. Her heart stirred as she laid a hand on her sister's knee. "I forgive you, Divina. You and Flavio both."

Divina moistened her lips. "Then you'll have him back?"

Carina shook her head. "I can't."

"But why?" Divina caught her hand between hers.

Carina drew herself up. "Even if my marriage is annulled, I will love Quillan forever. And he will love me, too."

Divina started to cry, buried her face in her hands. "Then I can't ever make it right."

Carina took her sister into her arms and held her a long time while she cried, stroking her hair and patting her back. "Divina, you must trust that God will make it right."

"I can't."

"Of course you can. He is always there, always willing to take a broken heart."

Again Divina sobbed, but Carina simply held her. How many times had she felt such woe herself? *But, Signore, you have borne our sorrows.* Even now, when He was asking her to surrender her marriage, she knew God suffered it with her. And somehow, though it didn't seem possible, He would bring good of it. "Divina, God works all things together for the good of those who love him."

"How can He?" Divina sniffed painfully. "Oh, Carina, I'm afraid for him."

Carina had to guess what Divina meant. "Flavio?"

Divina nodded, fresh tears starting.

"Why?"

Divina swiped the tears from her nose. "You heard what he did? To the old man?"

"Yes, I saw."

"You know how he hates violence. If he is so angry he could do that . . ." Divina gripped her hands tightly. "Carina, you must not push him further."

"It is my fault he has a temper?"

"No, no, of course not. But he's so desperately in love with you."

"No." Carina shook her head. "I know what real love is."

"Mamma mia, Carina. Can you persist?"

Carina stood up, walked to the mirror, and turned back. "I'm sorry for Flavio, for everything he's suffered, for what he suffers now." And she was. She thought of what Papa had told her, felt the weight of it. And she thought of the deep melancholy inside Flavio . . . the wrongful loss of a father. Did Flavio's spirit know his papa might have lived? Even so, that didn't excuse his cruelty, his arrogance, his violence. She had only to think what Quillan had suffered in his life, yet he had grown to champion the helpless.

Slowly she shook her head. "I am sorry. But I can never love him as I once did."

Divina hiccupped. "Then God help the man you do love."

Quillan climbed down from the wagon inside the livery. The paper crinkled inside his shirt, and he pulled the newspaper loose. He wished he didn't want to read it, but his eyes searched for and found the column at once. He could at least see how accurate Pierce had been. He read the article, cracking a wry grin at several turns of phrase, but Pierce hadn't laid it on as thick as he might. It was quality journalism, and he could see why it had found appraise.

Quillan tucked it under his arm and reached beneath the box for his journal. He felt about, farther back, then walked around and felt around the other side where it must have slid. He climbed back up and looked underneath, but the space was empty. Had he left it on the hill? No, he recalled putting it under the seat when he climbed in, before Pierce climbed in beside—

He clenched his jaw. Not even Pierce could be that low. Or could he? Quillan stalked from the livery to the Traveler's Home Hotel just across the street. He asked for Mr. Pierce's room.

The clerk searched the register. "That would be room four, but I believe he's at dinner. Just a short while ago he asked if anyone had inquired for him. Is he expecting you?"

"Without doubt." Quillan went into the adjoining dining room and searched the tables for Roderick Pierce. The man was seated by the window, dining alone. Quillan crossed the room and stopped. "Where is it?"

Pierce stood. "Have a seat, will you? The meal's on me."

Quillan held out his hand. "My journal."

Pierce smiled. "Sit first. Man alive, you're a hard nut."

"I'll take that from a cheat." But Quillan sat.

"Steak?" Pierce indicated his own plate. "It's passing fine."

"I didn't come here to eat."

Pierce waved his waiter over. "Another plate like mine for my friend."

The man bowed and backed away. Quillan crowded the table. "My journal, Pierce."

Pierce sighed, reached behind the half curtain along the window, and handed the journal over.

Quillan flicked the pages, swiftly noting his own handwriting, then laid it in his lap. "I suppose you'll tell me you didn't read a page."

"On the contrary, I devoured as much as I could. Incredible writing. I'd hoped for more time before you discovered the loss."

"You blackguard."

"Not entirely. But I say, I never would have pegged you for a poet."

"I hadn't pegged you for a thief."

Pierce smiled. "Thievery connotes intent to retain. I only guessed it would be one sure way to get you here tonight. And I was dying for a look at those pages."

"I ought to blacken your eyes."

"Maybe you ought, but I suspect you won't."

Quillan brought his fists to rest on the table. "Why not?"

Pierce nodded. "Because I read your journal."

Quillan wanted to reach over and squeeze his throat. He lifted the journal from his lap and waved it in the man's face. "Not even my wife has read this."

"Don't worry. I haven't your memory."

"I wouldn't doubt you've copied it somewhere."

Pierce held up both hands. "I give you my word."

Quillan snorted. "Your word?"

"My tactics may be suspect, but my word is good."

The waiter brought Quillan's meal. He sat back as the plate was set before him, then tucked the journal once again into his lap. He looked down at the plate, the beef aroma causing the juices in his mouth to flow.

"Well, eat," Pierce said, resuming his own meal.

Quillan took up his knife and fork, cut a bite, and chewed it slowly.

Pierce smiled, raising his brows and nodding. "Eh?" They spent their next minutes eating and washing it down with hot coffee.

Then Quillan pushed his plate away. It was the first hot meal he'd had in days, and it did sit well. "All right, you've got me here. What do you want?"

"The more I learn vis-à-vis your journal there, the more convinced I am these biographies will be a triumphant success. You read the article?"

Quillan wished he could say no. "I looked it over."

"Then you know what I can do."

It didn't matter what Pierce could do. "How do I make it clear to you I don't want my life in your pages?"

"In all fairness, Quillan, I could write them now. From what I've already collected—"

"And stolen."

"True, in a manner of speaking. But that's my job."

Quillan shook his head, spread his hands. "What do you find so fascinating you can't let it go?" He truly did not understand.

Pierce tapped his nose. "It's just here, Quillan."

"Then what do you need me for?"

Pierce bowed his head a little. "I'm a fair man. I want to split the fee."

"Why? You have what you need."

Pierce half smiled. "Well, I have enough to whet my interest, but not really to fulfill the contract. There are gaps."

Quillan sat back with a sardonic smile in return. "Patchy work, is it?"

Pierce held up his hands. "Don't start that."

Their waiter came and cleared their plates. He laid the bill beside Quillan, who slid it over to Pierce. With a quirk of his brows, Roderick Pierce paid it, then he took a pad from his pocket and eyed Quillan frankly. "I've contracted three short sketches. I'm envisioning a rework of the news article for the first, to hook them in with a flourish. A little more detail on the bank robbery and your subsequent departure from home. Being an eyewitness to the train sequence, I need only your own thoughts."

Quillan couldn't believe he was sitting there contemplating Pierce's request. "What do you envision for the others?"

"The movement you led to clear Crystal of its rough element. How and what transpired."

Quillan frowned. "And the third?"

Pierce cocked his head. "A love story. How you stood up to opposition and won back your wife."

Quillan's chest constricted. "That story's not been told."

"I'm on leave from the paper." Pierce waved his pad. "I've got time."

Quillan shook his head, suddenly tired of the fight. "You're more than half crazy."

Pierce shrugged. "Maybe so. But I cap the climax as a journalist. Say, can we use some of those poems?"

Quillan raised his eyes in disbelief.

Twenty-two

What fulfillment can contend with possibility?
What sufficiency compare with opportunity?
Take heart, you fool, whom joy has spurned.
In strife the greatest prize is earned.

— Quillan

FLAVIO PRESSED IN BETWEEN the warm, soft flanks and sides of the cows as he opened the door to let them out of the milking shed. They went out to his father's pasture with a rolling gait, and Flavio dragged his fingers along the bony back of one tawny cow before closing the door behind them.

His mother had looked dumbfounded when he offered to do the milking for her that morning. "Are you all right, Flavio?"

His eyes were burning from two nights with no sleep, and a sharp pain connected his ears across the top of his skull. "Go back to sleep, Mamma Lanza. I'll bring you the milk."

Six pails of it sat now on the wooden table in the center of the milking shed, milk and cream together, which Signora Lanza made into marvelous cheeses: creamy Bel Paese and mozzarella in soft white balls still moist with whey.

He took up two of the pails and carried them to Mamma's kitchen, then made two more trips with the others. No wonder his mother was surprised. When was the last time he had helped with the farm? Not since university, surely. He didn't want to damage his hands. He needed them soft and pliant for his art-work.

But this morning it had seemed an art to urge the milk from the teats of the cows, something so basic it eased a little of the strain inside him. He had to let it go or the cows would not release their milk easily; they would sense his tension. Now, though, he felt the grips across his chest, the ropes in his neck frayed and taut. How much longer could he bear the strain?

It had never been so bad. He must find release. But how? He thought of the old man he'd struck down with bocce balls. It was shameful and humiliating, horrifying, to go against everything he believed. Yet was that what it took? Must he hurt and destroy to find peace? The thought shook him.

There was another way; someone who had brought him joy in even his darkest times. Carina. He stepped out of his mother's kitchen and looked across the hills in the direction of the DiGratia's house. Dottore DiGratia's house. His chest tightened with hatred and love so intermixed he couldn't untangle them. But then, he had always believed the two were not opposites, but only a hair's breadth from one another. Like pain and pleasure.

He walked farther out into the morning, damp with mist but promising warmth. As he stood, the light intensified, and between the hills the yellow yolk of sun slid onto the plate of the sky. Was Carina awake to see it? *"A thousand miles I wanted you to come and beg my forgiveness."* What if he had? That thought was tearing him apart.

His pride had not allowed it. He could not have run after her like some lovesick whelp. He had wanted her to come back and find him waiting. Chase after her, beg her forgiveness? Beh! But if he had . . .

He closed his eyes, let the early sunrays warm their tired lids. The night before he hurt the Chinaman and the night he learned for certain Dottore DiGratia had let his papa die had both been entirely sleepless.

His feet started toward the DiGratias'. He had left there swearing to break off with them for good. How could he face the doctor without hating him again? How could he be near Carina knowing she loved this imposter instead of her own dear Flavio? If she would only stop and see him as she once had. He must make her see. He first went to his retreat and slung his mandolin across his back.

Then he went to the stable, saddled his stallion, from Angelo

DiGratia's own stock, and started at a canter for Carina's house. The horse was frothed when he leaped down and brought it to the trough. Its hooves on the cobbles of the courtyard brought Tony out to greet him.

"Good morning, Flavio. The old man is awake and as sensible as any Chinese. Papa is sending him back to town this morning."

Flavio felt a keen relief, but only shrugged. "Maybe he won't sweep when a man is making his shot."

Tony frowned but said, "Mamma is making sausages and eggs and bread. I just came from the kitchen. You'll stay?"

Again Flavio shrugged. "I want to see Carina."

Tony noted the mandolin knowingly. "She's awake. I saw her coming from the bathhouse."

"Will you ask her to come out?" He looked around the courtyard, the small fountain barely trickling with the lack of recent rainfall, the slender almond tree almost past its bloom, the stone troughs and benches. Too public. He didn't doubt for a moment that Tia Franchesca, Carina's mamma, would watch every word, every gesture. "Ask her to meet me at the gazebo." That small circular retreat between the vineyards and the hay fields would suit his needs well.

"I'll tell her."

Flavio led his horse to the railed octagonal gazebo and tethered him to graze on the spring grasses shooting up around it. He climbed the three steps and circled the open wooden structure. Each side opened on beauty.

Flavio appreciated his father's open pastures dotted with cattle and sheep. But he loved Dottore DiGratia's groomed vineyards and fields, his gardens and orchards, the orange trees heavy with fruit all year. He wanted a stock in this farm as Nicolo had. But if that were all he wanted, he could have had Nicolo's share.

He took the mandolin from his back and stroked the strings, then hummed a *cantilena*, adding his own words as he saw Carina approaching. Her face was shadowed, and it broke his heart to see it. The song took a melancholy tone as she climbed the stairs. "Tesora bella, my heart must sing in your presence. . . ."

She frowned. "Tony said you wanted to *talk* to me."

His fingers lightened on the strings. How many times they had sat together in this very place as the evening stars came out and his hand made a sweet melody. "I remember your face in the starlight, the curve of your lips when you smiled. . . ."

"Stop it, Flavio. What do you want?"

He stopped strumming, caught her hand, and drew her to him. "You know what I want. Carina mia, t'amo. *Ti voglio bene.*" Yes, he loved her. She must know it, must hear it in his voice, his fingertips. Only her love would heal him, take away the pressure that would destroy him. He felt her shaking. She would see; she would relent. She would love him again.

She looked up into his face, but with pity. It was like a knife severing his thin restraint. "I'm sorry, Flavio. I truly am."

The last threads that held him together snapped. "No!" He yanked the mandolin from his body and smashed it into the post, splintering wood and mother of pearl in a strident wail.

She cried out and gripped her hands together. "Please."

But he spun and slapped her across the face. Then, hand stinging, he leaped over the stairs and yanked the stallion's reins free. He threw himself onto its back, numb to Carina's crying, calling out to him. She was sorry? Not so sorry as she would be. No, not so sorry yet.

He kicked the horse, driving him through the softened fields and vineyards of his neighbors to the empty hills beyond. Insult spurred him like a brand in his flesh. He had put it all into place. Hoping he would not need to follow through, he had nonetheless prepared. Giocco should have done his part; yes, certainly he would have done his part, for Flavio had paid him well. He rode harder now, the horse laboring beneath him. Flavio felt the animal's strain as fierce as his own, but he kept kicking the flanks, eating up the ground that stood between him and his purpose. He reached the quarry but circled around, coming to it from the top of the hill behind.

Only a few men were beginning their work below. But he knew Quillan Shepard would be among them. Giocco had told him the man came early and stayed late. Flavio dismounted and searched for the bundle Giocco promised to leave for him, under the rock that looks like the Virgin. Flavio saw the tapering formation and searched its feet. Yes, there it was, a bundle in oilcloth.

Carefully he lifted and unwrapped it. A stick of dynamite. He balanced it in his hands, its fuse trailing over his fingers. He'd never held destruction before. His hands were made to create. But no longer. Nothing but the destruction of that man could satisfy him now.

And so he waited, lying at the top of the hill until he saw Quillan Shepard making his solitary climb up, his wagon pulled by two caramel-colored Clydesdale horses, a chestnut, and a black. Fine animals, a good strong wagon, clattering more with an empty bed than it would full of stone. And the driver, Carina's lover, her *husband*, sitting atop it like a king.

Flavio's heart pumped thunderously. Could he actually do it? And how? Quillan must be on the wagon, not have time to leap free and run. It must look like an accident, like a mischarge of his own explosives. He must have some with him to dislodge the face near the top where Giocco said he worked.

Flavio looked down at the single stick. He had asked for a bundle, but Giocco refused. Only small charges were set, he told him, to loosen the stone, not blow it to smithereens. No one would believe an accident of gross proportions. It was safer for him that way, too.

Flavio watched the wagon draw nearer. It must look like an accident, but he wanted Quillan Shepard to know, wanted him to see whose hand it was that threw the stick. He took out his knife and cut the fuse shorter. He only needed a moment to show himself, throw it, then dive for cover.

He'd chosen his spot well, thanks to Giocco's direction. Quillan brought the wagon within twenty feet, then reigned in. As Quillan raised his foot to set the break, Flavio lit the fuse. He stood up, and Quillan saw him, made an instinctive motion of his hand to his hip, then gripped the edge of the wagon to jump down.

With bocce accuracy, Flavio hurled the flaming stick of dynamite. It landed underneath the wagon bed at the moment it exploded. The wagon jumped into the air, tearing the horses from their feet and hurling Quillan Shepard to the ground. He screamed when the wagon crashed down on him.

A second explosion sounded, Quillan's own charges detonated by the first, and flame burst over the grasses. The horses thrashed in panic, trying to free themselves from the wreckage of the wagon, but they were tangled in the traces and couldn't stand. Trapped beneath the wagon, Quillan writhed. Flavio stood transfixed, terrified. He wanted to flee, but he couldn't.

Flames licked up from the ground to the wagon wheels and climbed toward the edge of the bed. Quillan twisted beneath the pile of wreckage that pinned him down. Smoke choked and swirled up. The horses screamed.

"Please!" Quillan hollered. "Cut my horses free!"

Flavio stared. Quillan begged for his horses, though he writhed in pain and couldn't stop the moans? Suddenly Flavio saw his papa writhing just so, his moans torturing Flavio's tender ears, tearing open his heart. His papa had been crushed and broken as Quillan was now. Violent men had cut him down in his strength and youth, and no one had saved him.

Flavio pressed his hands to the sides of his head. The near horse gained its feet and jerked against the toppled wagon. Quillan screamed in pain. Without thinking, Flavio rushed forward, pulling a knife from his pocket. Amid the spreading flames, he slashed the leather reins until the animals tore themselves loose and ran.

Quillan's chest heaved. He closed his eyes, gasped for breath, and moaned again. "Oh, God . . ."

Hating himself for what he had done, Flavio gripped the massive undercarriage that trapped Quillan. With all his strength, he strained against the weight. Through tight jaws Quillan hollered his pain as the wreckage shifted on him. The undercarriage raised up only inches.

"Pull!" Flavio shouted.

Quillan twisted, trying to get free. Flavio pressed his shoulder lower and lurched with a strength beyond his own. The undercarriage lifted. Quillan slid himself out and rolled, choking on the blood that gagged him. Flavio gagged, too, staring down at the man he had mangled. What should he do? The workers below must have seen the smoke, heard an explosion greater than it should have been. Flavio heard them coming up. Waves of horror washed over him. He ran for his horse and galloped down the back side of the hill.

Quillan pressed his face into the dirt, gasping with pain and choking as the smoke engulfed him. He would burn. He would burn! Mrs. Shepard's voice in his ear. *You'll burn like your demon parents burned. Burn in hell!* He tried to drag himself from the fire spreading over the ground. *God! Help me!* But though he was free of the wreckage he couldn't rise, couldn't crawl.

Smoke stung his eyes, and he smacked the flaming grass with one hand. He sucked an acrid breath and choked. Nightmare visions of his parents' charred bodies filled his eyes as the grass crackled with flame. Suddenly hands grabbed him, and he hollered in pain. Leg. Hip. One arm bent wrong and pain shooting from his shoulder to his neck until a hot numbness replaced it.

His cheek scraped across the rough wood of a hand wagon as someone slid him in. He was moving, rolling and bumping in the cart. He gritted his teeth against the jarring. The caustic smell of burnt grass stung his nostrils. He gagged on more blood, spit it out, and tried to think. Something he had to do . . .

He tried to raise himself up in the wobbling cart. Men scattered about beating and stamping the burning grass, arms across their faces. And there, in the midst of it, his wagon was turning to charcoal.

Quillan collapsed, groaning. He couldn't move one leg. His whole right side was awash in pain. He fought to stay conscious. He had to.

Where were they taking him? To finish him off? The fire could have done that. Suffocate or burn. Like his wagon. Like his money in the safely concealed box above the front axle. First flood, now fire. Quillan stopped struggling. What was the use?

Shaking with fear, Carina nudged Ti'Giuseppe aside. "Let me do it, Tio. I have to hurry." She cinched the saddle and flipped the stirrup down.

"Carina." Giuseppe caught her hand. "Be careful."

"It's not me, Tio, it's Quillan. Flavio has lost his mind." She swung onto the horse.

"Go." He nodded his head. "Warn your Quillan."

"Pray, Tio." She grabbed the reins.

"Yes." He moved aside as she urged the horse out of the barn.

Carina rode hard to Schocken's quarry. She didn't know what Flavio would do, but she had to warn Quillan. Yes, even if it took deadly force to defend himself. She should never have said no. Flavio was too unpredictable, too unstable. Her cheek burned with his slap. Though the pain had died, for him to strike her . . .

She kicked her heels. Papa's horses were fine stock, but this one felt like a plodder to her now. "Per piacere, Signore! Make this horse fly."

Her hair was a mass of tangles, her face flushed with the wind and her own anxiety when she reached the quarry. There was confusion already in the yard, and she looked up at the men fighting a fire on the hill. Fire was bad, but Quillan was her only concern.

She swung down, searching for his wagon and team. Maybe it was too early; he was still abed or in town on some errand. The quarry was large; he could be ... Then she saw a horse running panicked among the stone piles. Its bulk and huge shaggy hooves ... Her breath caught. Socrates? Or Homer?

Again she searched the yard, then the hillside with her eyes, frantic now to make sense of the scene. Something burned on the hill, some large charred mass. And what was that being wheeled down by two men in a long handcart? She looked again at the burning shape and made out wheels. A wagon? Quillan's?

With a cry, she rushed toward the men hurtling down the hill into the yard. Workers just arriving huddled around the cart, and Carina couldn't see. They spoke altogether, asking the same questions as hers. What happened? Is he alive?

She pushed through and saw Quillan, still and bloody, curled on the cart. "Quillan!" Her shriek startled the men, and they looked more confused than ever. She gripped his wrist, found a pulse, then searched one face and another. "Who did this? How did it happen?"

They shook their heads. "He must have set a charge wrong."

"There was an explosion." They waved their arms up the hill.

It broke her heart to see the charred remains of his wagon. She knew what it meant to him. Was it an accident? Or had Flavio done this? Could he?

They shook their heads. "We don't know what happened."

It didn't matter. Quillan needed help. Crumpled and bleeding and unconscious, blood trickling from his mouth ... Dear God, what if his injuries were too great? "Take him to Dottore DiGratia. Quickly!" She didn't know if he should be moved, but if he had survived the ride down the hill ...

Someone ran for a team and wagon that stood in readiness but had not been loaded yet with stone. Four men lifted Quillan from the cart to the wagon. A cry wrenched from his throat, straight to her heart, but he didn't open his eyes. Her whole body shook. "Send someone ahead to get Papa ready. Tell him what happened." Carina climbed in and cradled Quillan's head in her lap. "Go! Go!" she called to the driver.

The wagon lurched and bumped, and Quillan's face flinched. Once, he groaned, but he still didn't open his eyes. Carina's heart trembled. Quillan, so strong and able. Did he know she was there? She held his face sideways on her lap so he wouldn't choke on the blood. There must be internal damage. What had happened? An explosion they said, like the men in the mine? Every one of them had died.

No, no, no! Don't even think it! Papa would know what to do. Papa would—Her spine suddenly went cold. Would Papa do what was needed to save him? Or would Quillan's death be more expedient, as Flavio's father's had been? *Signore, the thought is too terrible. Please, you promised to work good for those who love you. You know I love you. Only save his life, and I'll let him go.*

Isn't that what everyone wanted? Papa and Mamma and ... Flavio. Was he capable of this cruelty?

Or was it Quillan's own carelessness? She had seen him challenge death on the train and in Crystal, flying in the face of danger as though he could not be touched. Had he taken one chance too many? The men at the quarry thought it an accident. But she could not forget the rage in Flavio's eyes. Had she driven him to this?

Quillan moaned, and she covered his forehead to ease the lines of pain. "There, caro, not long now. We're almost there." She stroked the hair back from his head. It was crusted with blood and twigs and dirt.

Signore, I don't know what to think. You know everything, see everything. You know what happened. But knowing didn't matter now. Only saving Quillan's life.

They pulled up to the open gates, and Lorenzo motioned them in. Papa stood with Vittorio by the front doors, which also stood open. He would admit Quillan now—Carina felt a flicker of fury—as he wouldn't the first time. If only he had accepted him! But that did no good. She must not let bitter thoughts get hold.

Lorenzo brought a litter to the end of the wagon bed. Vittorio climbed into the wagon. Carefully they eased the litter under Quillan's legs, speaking softly. "This one is bad; careful not to jog it. And the hip. His arm is broken."

"His spine seems sound," Vittorio said. "Lift." They got Quillan the rest of the way onto the litter, then Lorenzo jumped down.

Carina followed as they carried Quillan inside. The treatment room smelled fresh with herbs from Papa's physics garden. It had been scrubbed in preparation. They laid Quillan on the high leather table in the center of the room, where Papa did his surgeries. Would Quillan require the full extent of that skill? Again her chest constricted. Would Papa give it?

"His right side." Vittorio said. "Leg, arm, ribs. The opposite collarbone, and there's swelling in the left wrist."

"Yes." Papa nodded. "And internal damage by the blood from his mouth."

They spoke in Italian as they examined him. Carina watched with fear growing. Why didn't Quillan respond? He was less responsive than he'd been only minutes ago.

"Scissors."

At Papa's soft command, Vittorio brought them.

"That's all, Lorenzo. Take Tony and go. The fewer in here now, the better." He began to cut the pant leg, then glanced at Carina. "You ought to go, too."

Did he think she could leave Quillan even for a minute? "He's my husband, Papa. What do you think I haven't seen?"

Her papa and brother shared a glance. Vittorio unbuttoned Quillan's shirt and gently slid it from his arms. Together they stripped Quillan, and the sheet covering the table absorbed his blood. Carina went and stood at his head, covering his forehead with her palm. He made no response. He didn't know she was there.

She reached for his mother's locket lying in the hollow of his throat. The case was crushed and caked with dirt. She opened the clasp and took the chain from his neck, cupping it all into her palm. Maybe she could clean it. Maybe it could be repaired. It meant so much to him. A sob caught in her throat as she dropped it into her pocket.

Vittorio brought a pail of warm soapy water and washed the dirt and splinters from the wounds and all Quillan's skin, searching, she knew, for damage beneath. There was a gash on the side of Quillan's head that clotted his hair with blood and dirt. Vittorio held the scissors uncertainly.

Carina shook her head. "Don't cut it."

Vittorio dipped the cloth and soaked the wound. "He must have struck a sharp edge in falling, but it's not deep."

"Suture?" Papa asked without stopping his own examination.

"A bandage will do, I think."

"Then leave it." Papa swabbed the blood from Quillan's chin, then opened his mouth and washed inside. When his head was laid to the side, a trickle of fresh blood seeped out again. Papa frowned, probing Quillan's abdomen.

"What is it?" Carina asked.

"Heat. Swelling. Something damaged. It will need surgery." Papa met her eyes, knowing the terror those words would give.

Carina swallowed the terrible tightness in her throat. "Papa." She held him with her eyes. "Don't think it would be better if he died." She saw him flinch at her words, but she had to say it. "Save him, Papa, and I will let him go."

"That's not our concern now." He moved swiftly, scrubbing his hands while Vittorio prepared his instruments.

"It's my concern, Papa." Her throat burned with tears wanting release. Her voice shook. "I want him to live. I need him to live."

Her papa stopped scrubbing. "He will live if God is willing." The stern intensity of his face warned her.

She glanced at Vittorio, knowing as she did that he had not been told about Flavio's father. He wouldn't guess Papa could choose to let Quillan die. But would he notice if Papa did? She would be there for that. She looked back at her papa, the doctor. There was sadness in his eyes. Sadness that she doubted him? How could she not?

He said, "I will do all I can. Now prepare or leave us." Papa finished his scrubbing and dosed Quillan with chloric ether. The smell wafted up from the cloth to Carina, standing at his head. She held her breath to avoid the fumes as she turned and washed her hands thoroughly in case Papa would call on her. Then she pulled a full apron over her dress and resumed her post at Quillan's head.

Papa swabbed Quillan's belly with carbolic acid, feeling with his fingers for the worst of the swelling. She had witnessed surgeries before, but when Papa cut Quillan she felt it as her own flesh. Tears forced their way through her closed eyelids. *Signore Dio. Caro Signore.*

Before the disinfectant qualities of carbolic acid, Quillan would surely have died from such a cut alone. She lost track of time, focused only on keeping Quillan's head between her hands, repeating a dose of anesthetic when Papa indicated the need. He worked silently, cutting, suturing, and disinfecting, draining the blood and toxic fluids. Part of the intestine had been crushed, and Papa had to cut away the damaged part before sewing it back together. Then he closed up the incision, poulticed and bandaged it.

Quillan's head shifted in her hands. Carina lifted the bottle of chloric ether and looked to her father. "More?"

He shook his head. "There's enough in him for us to set the bones."

Quillan's whole body shuddered when Papa and Vittorio reseated the hip joint; he jerked when they aligned the femur of his right leg, broken in two places. Papa worked a long time over the leg, removing shards of bone from the gash and shaking his head. At last he sutured the leg, wrapped, and cast it in plaster. By the time they set and cast the ulna of Quillan's right arm and his left collarbone, he did not respond. Pain was its own anesthetic. Last of all they swabbed and bandaged the cuts and gashes, suturing the worst of them.

At last Papa stood back. At no time had Carina suspected he did anything but his best for Quillan. He looked drained as he washed up once again. Carina met his eyes, searching his thoughts. She would know if Papa thought Quillan would die. She always knew. He tried now to shield her, but his face was grave. "I don't know, daughter." Then lower, "I've done what I can." And his eyes pierced. "*All* that I can."

She nodded, believing him. But her heart was breaking anyway. What if Papa's skill was not enough? Was this why God had insisted she surrender Quillan? Did He know so soon He would call him away forever? *Let him live, Signore. Please let him live.*

Carefully Papa and Vittorio lifted Quillan to the litter. So much of him was bandaged and cast in plaster, they did not attempt to dress him. They laid him on the single bed near the wall and covered him with fresh sheets and a wool blanket.

"I'll sit with him." Carina pulled a chair to the bedside.

Papa spooned morphine into the side of Quillan's mouth. "He must be still. If he shows any agitation, call me immediately."

Carina nodded. Papa must know she would watch more closely than even he himself. Did he see her pain? His hand on her shoulder as he left told her that yes, he knew.

Flavio hunched down against the hollow of the old oak's trunk, shaking and horrified. What had he done? What would happen to him now? He pressed his face into his hands. He could have left Quillan Shepard trapped beneath the burning wagon to die. Then no one would know his part in it.

Did anyone suspect, or was Quillan Shepard the only one who could testify against him? Giocco might guess, but he'd been paid too well to tell. And Flavio had never said what he wanted the dynamite for. But those thoughts were simply distracting him from the full horror of what he found inside himself. How could he do such violence?

He kept hearing the screams, the groans, the agony he had caused another man. It didn't matter now that it was Quillan Shepard, the one Carina loved. He saw the man's face contorted with pain, his moan of "Oh, God." And it was that moan that had spurred Flavio to action.

He had gripped the wagon, just starting to burn, and with more than human strength lifted it to free the man he wanted to destroy. His malice had failed and mercy interceded. Why? For the same reason he now quaked at his own violence? Dottore DiGratia was right. His temper was dangerous. Now he knew what he could do, but knowing it, he could never do it again. It sickened him.

"Oh, God." He repeated Quillan's words. "Oh, God." Had God used him to free the man who called on Him in pain? Had God turned Flavio's own heart to help before it was too late? Was it Quillan's begging for the helpless animals? Flavio loved animals, their warm breath and simplicity. The distress of the horses had contributed, yes, but there was more.

Whatever it was, he was fiercely thankful he had acted as he did. As horrified as he felt now, how much worse would it be if he had left the man to burn? But he could still die. Flavio remembered the wagon crashing down on him, the scream of pain, and he had felt the weight of it himself when he tried to raise it up. Quillan Shepard could die, and it would be on Flavio's soul forever.

He shuddered. If Gesù was a myth and God a tool for priests to frighten children, why now did he feel such a trembling for his soul? He wouldn't believe he had a soul if he didn't feel it crying out against him now. He was like Cain, being cursed by the very ground he walked on. Everyone would know. His own soul convicted him.

"Oh, God." The words came without thought. Flavio didn't pray. He never prayed. *"Prayer is for the weak and simple,"* another of his papa's teachings. Flavio had been frightened when his papa said that. Didn't he know it would offend Gesù? But Papa had laughed at his fears. *"Offend a fairy tale? I'll take my chances."*

"God." Flavio dropped his head back against the tree and closed his eyes. Year after year he had gone through the motions with the very religious Lanzas. But he had never entered in, never counted himself among the weak and simple, never earned his papa's disdain. Even when he could no longer picture his father's face, the things Papa had told him stayed with him. But they were wrong.

God was real, and He had acted when Quillan Shepard called, even turning the hand of his enemy to rescue him, giving him supernatural strength. Flavio moaned. He was wicked and despicable. Yet God had used him when Quillan called.

Twenty-three

"I thirst," He cried out from the cross, pained in heart and soul and
bone, an aching need, heartbreaking loss, *"Father, why am I alone?"*

— *Quillan*

AS THE SLANTING RAYS of thin spring sunlight faded to
gray, Carina held Quillan's hand and prayed. "Il Padre Eterno,
hear me, please. I beg you for his life. I surrender all claims to his
love, to any love. If my wickedness, my selfishness has brought
this evil on him, forgive me." What if she had not asked to go
home? Had left her family when she saw their hearts were hard?
What if...? Oh, so many what-ifs.

Mamma brought her minestrone and bread. The steam was
pungent with tomato and turnips and cabbage and beans, savory
with bacon and onions and basil and thyme, hearty and whole-
some. But Carina shook her head. Her body floated in limbo with
Quillan's. How could she eat, how could she sleep when Quillan
balanced between life and death, fever rising and consuming him.

The heat of his hand sent her heart rushing with fear. His eyes
were hollowed pits, his flesh bruised and crusted with scabs, inci-
dental injuries that would have mattered except when compared
to the snapping of bones and crushing of organs. He was a
shadow of his former vitality. Carina had never seen him sick, not
even a sniffle. He had never complained of aches nor weariness.
To see him reduced to this . . .

Was it kinder for him to die? If he were lost to her anyway,
should she plead so desperately for his life? But that was her own
sorrow speaking. Wouldn't Quillan want to live? Dabbing his lips

with a cloth and trickling water onto his furrowed tongue, she felt hollowed by grief until there was nothing left.

Papa checked him every two hours, even all through the night. He changed the poultice, which was all but steaming on the incision. He gave him more morphine to keep him unconscious while his body became an inferno. He removed the blanket, then the sheet, and bathed Quillan's flesh with cool cloths. Unlike the followers of Benjamin Rush, Papa did not believe in a fever victim sweating out the toxins. But Quillan's skin was dry, so no natural perspiration was cooling the heat that built inside. Nor did Papa bleed him as so many would. Besides, Quillan had lost enough blood on his own.

Carina watched and helped, scarcely taking her eyes from Quillan's face, listening for each labored breath. In the morning, Mamma came with a small cup of strong espresso and cream. Carina drank it. She refused, however, the warm crusty bread with honey from Giuseppe's bees.

"Eat it, Carina. What good is it for you to waste away?"

"I couldn't keep it down." And then when Quillan's fingers quivered, she returned to her vigil, bread and Mamma forgotten.

Vittorio and Papa consulted. If the fever raged out of control much longer, they would open him up again and search for infection, cutting, cauterizing, and treating with carbolic acid again. The skin of Quillan's belly was fiery red, but there was little pus or smell, so Papa was hesitant to interfere.

"Every surgery has both the possibility for good and great harm, Vittorio. We must balance the hope with the risk." But he removed the bandage, treated the incision again with carbolic acid, and poulticed it. He did not rebandage it. They kept the sheet folded down from Quillan's waist to leave the wound open to the air.

"That's best for now. Let's see what his body does today."

It did nothing but burn, and though the fever rose no higher, it subsided not at all. Quillan lay as though dead, sapped by fever and lulled by morphine. His breath was shallow now with a slight wheeze. Papa raised Quillan's head with a second pillow, but feared to move him more than that. He held vigil with Carina, reading from one scientific text or another and continuing his ministrations.

Carina's eyes grew heavy with exhaustion. In spite of her fear, she could not hold them open. Her head nodded, then dropped to her breast. Papa's hand restored consciousness, but he only said, "Go to bed. I'll wait with him."

She looked into Papa's careworn face. Could she trust him? They had been at odds from the day she returned, and Quillan was the center of the conflict. But looking at him now, she had to believe Papa was expending himself to the best of his abilities. She nodded and went upstairs. Sleep engulfed her almost before she had undressed and fallen in a heap to her bed.

———————

Burn, burn, he was burning. The fire had caught and filled him. His flesh melted from his bones. His tongue cracked. His throat ached. How long could he burn before he was consumed? Eternal flames. He could burn forever. No!

Quillan heard voices, but there was something wrong with the words. They were different somehow, yet he imagined he knew what they meant. Not all, though. Some were just sounds, interspersed with the others. *Fever—bones—dangerous—cool, not cold— keep him tied—might awaken soon—no, no fire—we must keep the air pure.*

Air pure. He was burning, yet he smelled no smoke. Did he imagine meaning in the strange words, and what was it that was wrong with them? He swam closer to the surface. *Eye motions—not long now—pain—no more morphine.* Morphine? That word had sounded right, different from the others. And then he realized the speech was Italian.

A jolt of panic sent fire through him. He fought to open his eyes. But they were as immobile as the rest of him. He had tried to shift, or thought he had. None of his limbs would move, nor, he was fairly certain, would his head. At least nothing responded to his efforts. Had he really tried, or did he just think he had?

It was too hard to figure out. He was so tired. There was something else, something demanding to be recognized. Pain. Yes, there was pain.

———————

Starting down the stairs the next morning, Carina saw Father Esser leaving the treatment room. Panic nearly took her legs from under her. Had Papa called him to give last rites? Was Quillan dying? Or dead? She flung herself down the stairs as the priest passed through the back door.

She ran down the hall and crashed into the sickroom gasping, "Quillan!"

Papa spun, splashing the bowl of water down his front, and stared at her. *"Santa Maria!"*

With inexpressible relief, Carina heard Quillan breathing, strained and thick but not rattling and, God forbid, not stopped. And then another terrible thought occurred. She stalked inside. "Why was Father here?"

"Shh." Papa frowned, looking behind him. "Do you want to wake him?"

Carina lowered her voice but not the intensity. "Papa, why was Father here?" Though she was willing to live without Quillan if God wished it, she would not stand for their marriage, their love to be called invalid.

"He brought me a letter."

"What letter?" She would not be put off so easily.

"From someone you know." Papa set down the bowl, grabbed a cloth, and wiped his shirt.

From someone she knew? To Father Esser? "From whom?"

"Father Charboneau."

Carina's heart jumped. "Father Antoine! What did he say?"

"Read it for yourself." Papa motioned to the sheet of stationery lying on his instrument table.

She snatched it up with greedy fingers, her eyes passing over the greeting to the body of the letter. "In response to your concern, I can only say that I know this marriage to be not only true but blessed of God." *Oh, blessed Father Antoine!* "Any efforts to sever that which I joined in God's holy presence would be wrongful and dire. I trust to your holy calling to show wisdom in this matter."

She pressed the letter to her breast, closing her eyes on tears of joy. God did not want her separated from Quillan! Her marriage was not wrong; it was blessed of God. She turned and met Papa's eyes. "What do you think now?"

He sighed, glancing at Quillan's still form. One eyebrow twitched. "I think we must do our best for this man, your husband."

Carina rushed to him, caught him in her arms, and buried her face against his chest. Her papa! Her papa understood. At last he understood.

Papa stroked her hair, then caught her head between his hands. "Which doesn't excuse your marrying without my consent."

"I'm sorry, Papa. Truly." Sorry for hurting him, surely, but not for marrying, not for the marriage God blessed.

"Yes. Well." He separated from her and glanced at Quillan. She followed his gaze. "How is he?"

"The same."

She dropped to the chair beside the bed and touched Quillan's chest. It was like a hot loaf from the oven. "How long can he bear it?"

"It could be helping. Not all fever is detrimental. If it goes no higher . . ." Papa spread his hands. "There's no smell of putrefaction." He refilled the bowl and dropped the cloth in. "Bathe him with this, what parts of him are not covered in bandages and plaster." There was a note in Papa's voice, a familiar tone of sympathy she knew so well. He cared about his patient.

Carina squeezed the water from the cloth. Quillan's left arm was bound across his chest to keep his collarbone immobile. A band had been stretched across his chest and upper arms, tying him to the bed, she guessed, in case he tried to move before Papa thought him ready. There was also a band across his forehead, probably to protect the collarbone. His ribs were wrapped, his right arm cast and his leg, as well. Yes, there was little of him that had not been hurt in some way. But strangely, looking at him now, she felt hope.

Flavio could stand it no longer. He had to know. He left his retreat, the small frame building the Lanzas had erected for him to paint and draw in, a place of light and breezes. But today it suffocated him. He had to know if God had charged murder to his soul, and if there would be an earthly punishment as well as eternal flames.

He went to the stable and called for his stallion, ill-used these last days but hopefully forgiving today. He paced while the servant saddled the horse and brought it to him. Then he swung astride and took off for the DiGratias. He was not certain Quillan would have been taken there. If he had died at the quarry ... But no, he couldn't think that way! At any rate, Carina would know where he'd been taken.

Flavio reined in sharply. Carina. She would also know the truth, that he had done that violence to her husband. How could she not when he had struck her with his own hand? The horse sidestepped, tossing at the rein. Flavio looked over the hills to where the DiGratia land joined the Lanzas'.

The horse pulled in an impatient circle, bad tempered about being told to run then made to stop. Frowning, Flavio brought the horse back toward the Lanza farm. He couldn't go, couldn't look Carina or her father in the eyes and inquire whether he had done enough to kill or only enough to maim and torture. He who despised violence in any form. He, the great pacifist.

What must they think of him? Carina would hate him. There would not even be pity in her eyes now. And the dottore? Would he regret that he ever took that six-year-old boy under his wing? Flavio hung his head. "Oh, God." Those two words had been his steady diet ever since they were uttered by Quillan Shepard in the extremity of his pain.

Flavio's chest burned. He should put an end to it. A rope from the studio rafter? He urged the horse forward. Was he such a coward? But the thought of release from this guilt was potent. Like Judas Iscariot? Hadn't Judas betrayed the one he loved as Flavio betrayed Carina? *Oh, God.*

He returned the horse to the stable and secured a length of rope. With its coils on his shoulder, he went back to the studio. It was no longer a haven. No place was. He was like Cain, saying it's too much to bear. It was himself he couldn't bear. He had become an animal, the antiphony of all he despised. As wicked and dark as the rioting crowd who had killed his papa. Flavio was one of them. He sat on the stool before his easel and rested the rope across his knees. He felt its strength, its coarse fibers.

He swallowed, looped one end and began to form a noose. When he had it finished, he looked at it with fascination. How simply the rope slid through the knot, open and closed. The sunbeams crept across the floor, finally lengthening and slanting as he sat hour after hour, looking at the hangman's knot in his lap.

"When you find a man's weakness, use it." He'd found his own weakness, hadn't he? His anger had driven him to violence, in

spite of his beliefs. It was only time until he did it again, wasn't it? What if Quillan Shepard didn't die? What if he recovered and lived happily with Carina? Would Flavio strike again? But somehow the thought didn't bring rage. Nor even choking despair. Why not? The cool gray early evening light replaced the golden shafts.

"Flavio!" It was Mamma Lanza. "*Pranzo*—dinner, come and eat."

He blinked as though coming out of sleep. How had the hours passed without his carrying out his intention? He looked at the rope in his hands, raised it, and studied the knot. Then he coiled it and laid it against the wall. When the despair came, as he knew it would, then . . .

———

At last the awful stillness eased. Like shackles from his mind, Quillan felt the heaviness depart, and he swam up and up into . . . pain. Oh, God, was there any part that didn't hurt? He blinked, taking in a soft gray light, broken by a dim golden glow somewhere to one side. He tried to turn to see, but his head would not obey.

"Wait a moment." A male voice, not unfamiliar, yet he couldn't place it. Someone fumbled with something near his head. "I have permission to unbind your head as long as you understand that any sharp motion will put torsion on the collarbone."

Quillan couldn't see who was speaking. The voice seemed to come from behind him.

"There." A figure stood and pulled a cloth band from his forehead.

Quillan looked up with his eyes only.

"You'll know if you disturb the bone, believe me." It was Carina's brother Vittorio.

Quillan closed his eyes. He must be more confused than he thought. Something wet dabbed his lips, and he sucked before he realized what he was doing. It was an automatic motion, something from the fog he'd climbed out of.

"Are you in pain?"

Quillan didn't want to probe that question. "Where am I?"

"Dr. DiGratia's treatment room. Do you remember anything?"

Quillan frowned. Dr. DiGratia—Carina's father? He didn't understand. But it hurt to think. It hurt to breathe. And he still couldn't move. Wait . . . one leg seemed to respond. His left.

"Don't do that. You need to be very still. You've had a delicate surgery. Well, more than that, but that's most fragile at the moment."

Yes, Quillan felt fragile. His throbbing right leg was completely stiff; he could do nothing with it at all, and the hip pained him sharply. His right arm also seemed stiff, and both were bound against his chest. He tried to lift his head to see down his body. It was more than he could manage. He couldn't remember ever feeling so weak, so helpless. He swallowed, wishing desperately for water.

As though Vittorio had read his mind he brought a glass and a spoon. "Let this run down the side of your tongue so you don't choke."

Quillan took the water like a baby, then closed his eyes again, too exhausted to wonder anymore. After a time, he heard two voices conversing, the same he'd heard before. Again they spoke Italian. *He—awake a moment. Yes—asked where—* so many of the words Quillan hadn't learned yet. The other voice was deeper. Dr. DiGratia's. *We will see.*

Quillan felt hands near his throat. Fingers probed along the collarbone. Quillan remembered. He had felt it break, heard it snap when he fell, before the wagon landed on top of him. He winced when the fingers found the spot, then forced his mind to clear. The hand stopped probing and reached for the edge of the sheet. With a tiny motion, Quillan gripped the wrist and opened his eyes.

Startled, the doctor looked at him. Their gaze locked. Quillan glared, or thought he did. He wasn't sure his face obeyed, but the doctor seemed to get the message.

"You can relax. I'm only going to bathe you."

Quillan maintained his grip. "No, you're not."

"Cleanliness is essential to recovery." With his other hand, Dr. DiGratia folded the sheet down across Quillan's chest.

Feeling exposed and helpless, Quillan tightened the squeeze on the man's wrist, though it sent aching throbs up his arm and across his shoulder to his neck. "I'll wash myself."

"Will you? Which hand will you use?" The doctor's frank stare sent panic through him.

Quillan stared down his chest: the right arm trapped in plaster, the left bound up across his chest to the wrist. He had only movement enough to grab the doctor's hand when it passed from his shoulder to his chest. Sudden claustrophobic panic choked up. He tried to sit but couldn't, feeling the band strapped across his ribs. His legs were immobile, and one felt stiff as a log. An indistinguishable pain grew inside him. He felt like a trapped animal. "What's wrong with me?"

"It would be shorter to name what's not." Dr. DiGratia folded the sheet again, exposing his belly. Quillan tensed. The air of the room was warm, but his flesh quivered. Vittorio came over with a bowl of scented water. Quillan sniffed.

"It's arnica for bruising." Dr. DiGratia said, gently working a bandage loose from the lower right side of Quillan's abdomen.

Quillan recognized the source of burning pain, although it seemed to penetrate all through him. What had happened there? Something worse than anything he'd known before.

"Laudanum, I think, Vittorio."

"No." Quillan shook his head, clenching his teeth, though the thought of dulling the pain was hypnotic.

The doctor raised his brows, but Quillan was not about to have his senses lulled again, no matter how much it hurt. He wasn't sure why he'd been put into the care of Carina's father, but he knew enough not to lose his wits again. It would be a simple thing for Dr. DiGratia to remove him permanently from Carina's life.

"It's not for pain only. We must keep the intestine relaxed, allow the surgery to heal." The doctor nodded to Vittorio, who set the aromatic bowl on the table beside the doctor and prepared the opium tincture.

Surgery on his intestine? And he was alive to protest? Dr. DiGratia must be as skilled as Carina claimed. That brought scant comfort.

The doctor soaked a cloth in the bowl and wrung it out, then began swabbing Quillan's skin. "Your fever broke last night. Do you remember the delirium?"

Delirium. How did one remember delirium? But Quillan did

have a vague sense of thrashing, reliving the explosion, the crushing pain of the wagon upon him as it began to burn. Crying out for his horses. He wondered now where they were. Had someone cared for them?

"Once the perspiration began, I guessed you would come out of your stupor. But now I must wash the perspiration away so it does not putrefy your wounds." The doctor continued to swab him with the warm cloth.

Cringing inside, Quillan resisted the comfort of that warm swabbing. He couldn't remember ever being touched in a healing, nurturing way, except for Carina. Where was she? He wanted to ask, but he feared she had been locked in some corner of the mansion, as far from him as possible.

Vittorio brought the tincture of opium.

Dr. DiGratia unfastened the strap across Quillan's ribs. "Help me get his back first." They raised him only enough to rub his back with the warm cloth, then wipe it dry and lay him back down.

Quillan's ribs shot with pain, but they were nothing to the throbbing wound in his abdomen and the muscles surrounding it. The doctor raised quizzical brows. "Now you will accept your medicine?"

Awareness of the pain grew until it sapped his thought, his will. Quillan closed his eyes and nodded.

"I thought as much. Vittorio."

Again Vittorio spooned the liquid into the side of his mouth. Quillan swallowed, lulled into a false complacency that evaporated the moment Dr. DiGratia lowered the sheet. Humiliated and fiercely resentful, he lay still while the rest of him was cleaned. Had he ever felt so stripped and vulnerable? *God, what are you doing?* Only the image of Christ likewise stripped and humiliated kept him from kicking with his one good leg. That, and the weakness that again overcame his fury.

Twenty-four

No horror terrifies the soul, like rendering the flesh unwhole;
Poor feeble spirit tethered by a mangled man too dense to die.

— *Quillan*

WHEN CARINA WENT INTO the treatment room she breathed the scent of arnica and rosemary. The room was warmer than the rest of the house, and she noted the coal burning steadily in the brazier. Quillan slept, peaceful now after his thrashing—what thrashing he could do last night, tied to the bed, chest and head. But Papa told her he had wakened.

The restraints were removed now. Papa must believe the worst was past. She dropped down beside Quillan. She had left him only when the sweat poured from his skin, cooling the fever and ending his delirious rantings. Papa had promised it was a good thing and that Quillan would be stronger by morning. He looked stronger, and praise be to God, he felt warm, not fiery. It was a miracle.

Five days of burning fever. Papa had grown silent and grim as Quillan's delirium worsened. But when it gave way to drenching sweat, Papa seemed satisfied, though to her eye, Quillan had looked the worst yet. This morning, though, he seemed fresh and restful. What a change had occurred between the time Papa ordered her to bed and now!

She looked at the face of her husband, smelled laudanum on his breath. His sleep was drugged, then, but Papa knew what he was doing. His chin was covered in beard, the mustache grown over his upper lip. His whiskers ranged down his neck in a W

317

shape. She touched his face, smoothed back his hair, and stroked her fingers through it. If he awoke it would be to a loving touch, but he didn't. His hair was damp and clumped. Though they had bathed his skin throughout the fevered days, no one had washed his hair.

She stood, filled a pitcher from the pot of water on the warming surface over the brazier, and took from the cabinet a shallow dish shaped like a large shaving bowl with an indentation in the side. She set them and a small jar of hair soap on the table beside the bed. Gently raising Quillan's head, she put the shallow pan beneath him, resting his neck in the hollow of its side and laying his hair down in the bowl. Then she slowly poured the warmed water over his hair, starting at the front of his scalp.

"I said no!" He jerked, and she nearly dropped the pitcher.

"Easy now or you'll soak yourself." Carina poured half of the pitcher over his hair and set it down.

"Carina?" He opened his eyes, then closed them again, breathing thickly. "If it's not really you . . ."

Heart rushing with love and relief, she bent and kissed his mouth. "Who do you think it is? My papa?"

He scowled, drawing his face into a tight mass, and his eyes opened stormily.

Grazie, Dio! If he could be so angry, he must be getting strong! "What's the matter?" She dipped her fingers into the jar of soap.

"What's the matter? I have to lie like a baby while your father . . ."

She worked the lather into his hair, scrubbing with her fingers. "While Papa what?"

He clamped his mouth shut, seemingly torn between anger and the irresistible comfort of her fingers on his scalp. She balled and lathered his hair, working out the snarls, the sweat, the last of the blood and dirt, then poured the rest of the water from the pitcher to rinse it. He sighed softly as she wrung his hair and wrapped it in a towel. Then she slid the bowl out and set it aside.

She smiled at the begrudged loosening of his face. Suddenly overwhelmed that he was truly awake and speaking to her, she kissed his damp forehead. "Caro mio, I was so afraid."

His face contorted, his mouth working before any words came out. Then he sucked in a breath and said, "Carina, what's wrong with me? Am I paralyzed? Why can't I move anything?"

She stared into his face. "Paralyzed? No. Immobilized."

"Why? Why am I strapped down like an animal?"

She saw the same fear he'd betrayed in the cave. He could not stand to be trapped. Panic shot through his eyes like flashes of heat lightning. "*Pace*, caro. Peace." She stroked his hair back. "You're no longer tied. That was to keep you still while you raved. To protect you from hurting yourself."

"Then why can't I move my leg?"

She looked down. "It's heavy with plaster, and your hip was injured, as well. You haven't the strength, that's all."

"And my arms?"

"Your right is broken, but Papa set and cast it. Your left is whole, though the collarbone—"

"Yes, I feel it. And my ribs?"

"Three are broken on your right side."

He nodded slowly. "Where the wagon fell."

She caught his hand between hers as it lay just beneath his chin. "What happened, Quillan?"

His throat worked against her fingers, and his eyes slipped away from hers. "Nitro is chancy stuff."

"What?" She fought sudden tears. Why wouldn't he look at her? Did he lie? She sensed it, saw it. "Tell me the truth, Quillan."

He looked at her now. "It's unstable, even when neutralized somewhat by the sawdust in dynamite. It's the risk you take." He had made his eyes like plates, shutting her out. Why?

"You did this to yourself?"

He didn't answer. "Do you know where my horses are? Are they all right?"

"In our stable." Why was he evading her? To protect Flavio? She laid her palm against his cheek. "Did Flavio do this?"

He closed his eyes. "Carina . . . I'm tired." He was. Overwhelmingly so.

She reached up and stroked his face. "Sleep, then. Every time you wake you'll be stronger than the last."

He caught her hand, opening his eyes once more. "Will you be here? Will they keep you away?"

"I'll be here. If I leave for a moment I'll be back. Don't worry. Just rest. Get strong."

He closed his eyes.

Signore, he is so weak. He can't be expected to remember. Maybe he doesn't know, didn't see what happened. Maybe it was only an accident. She was the one jumping to conclusions. What proof had she that Flavio caused it? She touched her cheek and remembered his face with his soul torn asunder. She closed her eyes. That was why she suspected him.

Quillan slept through the day, obviously worn out from such small exertion that morning. Papa came in at regular intervals to check his pulse, his incision, his temperature. "Did he speak with you?" he asked Carina softly during one examination.

She nodded. "He asked what was wrong with him."

Papa felt the glands beneath Quillan's jawline. "Some swelling," he said as much to himself as her. "The glands would be enlarged by so much injury."

"Will he be all right, Papa? Will he heal?"

Her papa cocked his head. "Healing is mending, Carina. Is the mended cloth what it was before?"

She felt a sinking in her heart. "Then he won't . . ." She couldn't voice her disappointment.

"Will bones that knit be as bones never broken? I don't know. Will a body cut open have the integrity of one never exposed?" He spread his hands. "I don't know." He looked up, and his sudden keen stare took her by surprise. "Did he say what happened?"

She looked into her papa's face. Did he also suspect? "He said nitro is unstable."

Papa stood and washed his hands at the basin, shook the water from them, then reached for the towel. "That was all?"

She dropped her eyes to Quillan's sleeping face. Should she tell Papa what she suspected? What if she were wrong? Anyway, it was Quillan's choice. "He was very tired. He couldn't speak long."

Papa turned slightly, and she felt his doubt. As Quillan said, the whole world knew what she felt and thought. Did she have any right to blame Flavio without proof? How could she know? Quillan would not or could not say. But Flavio could.

The thought sent fire through her veins. Go to Flavio? Confront him? That would mean leaving Quillan's side. Papa would watch him, though Quillan seemed not too happy about that. Still, the question harried her, now that worrying whether Quillan would live no longer consumed all her thoughts.

"You are wan, Carina." Papa hung the towel and straightened his vest. "Take some air."

She looked up. Had he guessed even these last thoughts? Did he suggest she should go? Impossible. But nonetheless, he had given her the opportunity. She stood. "Yes, Papa. Do you need anything?"

He shook his head and went to his bookshelf. While he searched the spines, she went out the door. She could take a horse, but it wasn't so far. It was two miles and more through the vineyard and the Lanzas' pasture to their house, a little shorter to Flavio's studio. That's where she would find him, painting or brooding.

She took the path from the house to the near vineyard. The vines had been gathered into heaps, ready for burning. The ground looked pocked and lanced. Her heart broke. Ah, the weeping vines. She passed between the rows, cursing the ground that harbored the parasite, which destroyed the roots like sin the soul.

Hill after decimated hill she passed. Her brothers and their workers had been busy while Papa tended Quillan, busy ripping out the grapes and tossing them to be burned. Such desolation, such waste.

Then she came to a field of vines and stopped short at the wonder. A green mist softened the black gnarly branches. She stared all along the rows of grapes. How had they been spared? Rapt, she passed among them. Had this field been overlooked? Was this a weak attempt that would be ignored when the workers came to yank them out?

Deeper into the vineyard she went. She could sense its vitality. These vines were alive, thriving even. Papa had found a viable rootstock. They were small, yes, in their first year of planting, but they were strong. *Oh, Signore!* She felt such hope. She crossed through the pastures of the Lanzas' cattle and saw the small wooden house that was Flavio's retreat.

She stopped walking, wondering for a moment what she was doing. Did she want to know? Could she bear to know? If Flavio had injured Quillan so brutally ... But knowing could be no worse than wondering. She moved forward to the door between two flowering quince. Flavio loved them because they bore vibrant, orange-red blooms.

His stallion, Juno, grazed nearby. Carina passed between the plants and stopped at the door. She knocked, then opened the door herself and walked in.

Flavio sat on a tall stool before an easel with a brush in his hand. But the brush was dry. It had not been dipped in paint. He turned slowly and looked at her, his face showing too much. He lowered his eyes. "He told you, then?"

Carina stood silent, not wanting to understand what he said, but God help her, she did. Her suspicions were right, what she had known in her heart, in spite of Quillan's evasion. How could she ever look at Flavio again with anything but hatred? She shook with it. "He told me the nitro was unstable. That it was a risk he took."

Flavio looked up, searched her face. "He said that? That was all?"

"Perhaps his memory is not as keen as yours, since even now he fights for his life." Her voice broke.

Flavio dropped the brush, caught his face in his hands, and groaned. "He will live, though?"

"You want to know so you can finish the job?"

He slid his fingers into his hair, pressing his palms to his eyes. "I know you despise me. But it's nothing to what I feel for myself. Look there." He pulled one hand free and pointed to the corner of the floor where a rope lay.

She looked closely, saw the hangman's noose atop the coils.

"I don't even have the courage to use it."

She stared at him. "Why would you use it, Flavio?"

His hands dropped to his lap. "Because of what I am."

Yes, she thought. He deserved to die, to hang from a rope by his own hand. His cruelty, infidelity, violence . . . Her throat tightened painfully. She took a step toward him. She could help, kick the stool out if he hadn't the courage to jump. The thought horrified her. She recalled Quillan's terse answers, telling her nothing, protecting this . . . this man she had once loved.

Yes, she could hurt him. But instead, she put a hand to his shoulder. From somewhere deep inside her came the words, "If Quillan doesn't condemn you, who will?"

Flavio started to weep. "My own soul."

"Your soul has been forfeit from birth. What difference is there now?"

"Oh, God . . ." It was more a moan than words.

She didn't want to say it, to offer him the peace she knew he could have. She wanted to walk away, to run, to leave him to his

322

rope. Why should she stop his suffering when Quillan's was so much worse, when Quillan might never be the same? None of them would be the same!

Again she spoke resolutely. "God will forgive you if you let him. We have all gone astray, but He draws us to himself just as you gather the cows before a storm, Flavio. Surrender to Him. Know His peace."

"How can God forgive when you hate me so deeply?"

Yes, he had seen it in her face; how could he not? She showed it to the world. She wanted him to see, to know, to suffer in that knowledge. Her hands tightened at her sides. "What I feel is at war with what I know. God will forgive you, and so will I." She would have to, or this new bitterness would destroy all she had won.

Flavio shook with sobs. "I got him out, Carina. I freed him or he would have burned."

Dio! Was it true? She shuddered, pictured Quillan charred black like his wagon. Had Flavio prevented that?

"He asked only to let his horses free, but I lifted it, his wagon, with more strength than my own. I lifted it and got him out. Then I ran."

She suddenly clutched his head, overcome with gratitude that he had not let Quillan die. "Grazie, Flavio."

He wrenched his head up. "Grazie? After what I did?"

"He would not be alive."

Flavio shook his head. "God help me, Carina, I wish I had died in his place."

She let him go. "You don't have to." But she could go no further. It was up to Flavio now to accept the grace and forgiveness God offered. "I have to go back. Quillan will want me there when he wakes."

Flavio looked into her face, searching for some redeeming thread. She closed her eyes, breathing painfully. "If Quillan won't speak against you, neither will I." She opened her eyes and faced him. "If there are none to condemn you, what right have you to condemn yourself? Ask God's forgiveness."

He swallowed, then followed bleakly with his eyes as she turned away. She stopped at the door, reversed herself to cross the room. Without looking at Flavio, she lifted the rope and carried it out with her.

As she walked home, her heart swelled with love for Quillan. However misplaced his silence was, he kept it honorably. What a different man she joined in one flesh than she might have. God had removed her from a love that was corrupt to a redeeming love, for both herself and Quillan. Maybe even her angry flight had been God's urging. How else could He unite her with the man He had chosen? *Oh, Signore. Your ways are bigger than mine. Grazie, Dio. Grazie.*

Carina came in like a breeze, her cheeks no longer wan but touched with color. Her hair tumbled loose and her limbs moved with grace and ease. Quillan watched silently as she brought a small bowl to the bedside and pulled a stool close. He could turn his head, but it hurt the collarbone, so he followed her with his eyes.

This was the first day he felt clearheaded enough to respond. His other awakenings, day and night—how many days he didn't know—had been foggy and confused, ending in exhaustion. He was so tired of being tired. Gently, she eased his head and shoulders up and pushed a wedge-shaped pillow beneath. One thing hadn't changed. He was too weak to assist or resist, and it galled him.

"There," she said, stroking his head. That galled, too. He couldn't touch her back.

She sat and took a bowl into her lap, stirring with the tiny spoon inside, releasing steam and aroma. Quillan swallowed in anticipation. Had anything but water passed his lips?

She brought the spoon to her own and sipped. "A little hot." She stirred more and the beefy bouquet reached his nose and teased. At last she brought the spoon to his lips.

Quillan frowned. "Unbind my arm and I can feed myself." Trussed up like a chicken with his arms across his chest, he could do nothing!

"Take the broth, Quillan." She touched the spoon to his lips. They parted in spite of him and he swallowed.

Her smile was infuriating, so indulgent. The spoon touched his lips again and liquid seeped through. Broth, food for babies and invalids. He wanted real food and working arms.

"Sei impaziente."

"Impatient? What do you expect?"

She swirled the spoon in the bowl. "You don't have to holler."

He scowled. "I'm not hollering."

"Your face is."

"My—"

She snuck another spoonful in, and he swallowed furiously. "Stop that."

Carina cradled the bowl in her lap. "What should I stop? Feeding you?"

"Stop feeling so smug about it."

She laughed. "You like helping, but you don't like to receive it, do you?"

Receive? Being fed like a baby, an invalid, like Leona Shepard, out of her wits and—

"I see the storm in your eyes."

Quillan glared at his wife. "Are you enjoying this?"

"No more than you, when you ordered me to bed." She bent and kissed his forehead.

He struggled against the tight wrapping, which trapped his left arm to his chest, and the sling that immobilized his right in its cast. Even that much movement brought pain. And exhaustion.

"If you're too difficult, I'll have Papa feed you."

Quillan couldn't make his face more murderous. He wanted to throw the bowl of insipid broth right through the window and stalk out of that house. He wanted no part of Dr. DiGratia or any of them. Trying to win Carina's family had cost him too much. He would take Carina and go.

"You're in pain, aren't you? Why don't you ask when you need medicine?"

"I don't need laudanum, I need peace. And I won't find it here." Again that feeling of entrapment. He had no control!

She set the bowl down and kissed his lips. He couldn't reach his hands into her hair or hold her there when she drew away. Having his arms bound and useless scared him more than he wanted to show. It was horrible to be so trapped, so helpless.

"It's all right. You're welcome here." Carina lifted the bowl again. "Father Antoine validated our marriage, Quillan. They accept—"

"I don't care about any of that. I don't want their acceptance, their pity...."

She drew back, irked. "No, you have enough of your own, it seems."

The rebuke stung. Did she blame him? Wasn't it enough that he protected Flavio, kept silent about his throwing the dynamite, causing all this wreckage? Quillan felt a wave of terror. Would he be crippled and helpless the rest of his life? When the casts came off, the bandages removed, would he hobble around like Alan Tavish, or like Cain with only one leg?

What was wrong with his leg? All he got from Dr. DiGratia was, "We must wait and see." He didn't want to wait! He wanted his arms back, his legs to work, his bowels to digest more than broth!

"Caro mio." Carina kissed him again.

He wanted to grab her, hold her. And he could do nothing! "Don't patronize me. I don't need human acceptance and comfort. I surrendered it all."

Her face changed. "Was that so hard? Haven't you done that all your life? Turned your back on anyone who could hurt you and depended on yourself?"

Why was she scolding him? "Not myself now. On God."

"Bene." She shrugged one shoulder. "Did God set your bones? Mend your intestine? Has God fed you and bathed you and seen to your comfort?"

He flushed hotly but couldn't answer that. He was living and breathing today because of the care he had received. And it wasn't directly God's hand, of course. It was Dottore DiGratia's.

"Maybe you need to surrender your independence."

He did not want to hear that. Did she know something they wouldn't tell him? Would he be helpless, forever dependent on others, unable to reject their succor? Fear seared his innards.

"Now that would be surrender, eh?" She leaned close, kissed one eye and then the other, kissed his cheeks, then his lips again. He groaned.

The door opened and Dr. DiGratia came in. Carina straightened, but her face was flushed and her mouth turned up, her features maddeningly like her father's. Surrender his independence? Never!

Quillan scowled from one to the other. "I want my arm unbound."

"Do you." The doctor spoke dryly, obviously not at all concerned with his wants. He walked over to the bed. "Let me see." He pressed with one finger on the collarbone and Quillan hollered. The doctor straightened. "Maybe not just yet."

If his arm had been loose Quillan would have coldcocked him, even if it broke the collarbone again. Carina looked reproachfully at her father. So now she understood?

Dr. DiGratia shook the thin glass tube he'd been sticking into Quillan's mouth every day, several times a day. He poked it in once more. "Under your tongue."

"It's a clinical thermometer, Quillan." Carina patted his elbow. "It tells us your body temperature."

Us. The dottore and her. Quillan sank back against the stiffly stuffed backrest she had placed behind him. At least with the thermometer in his mouth she couldn't keep spooning soup at him. Simmering, he endured the time that he had to hold the tube under his tongue.

Carina was right. The pain was persistent. His gut felt like fire, the muscles too offended to lift him at all. Carina had to raise him up and prop things behind just to elevate him enough to eat broth without choking. Any motion at all made the ribs throb, and shifting the weight from his rear sent pain into the hip. His leg might as well be blown off at the knee for all he could do with it. Several times a day he was rolled to one side or the other like a piece of meat on a spit. And the greatest horror was the swaddling. Was he no longer a man?

Carina was right again; he had pity aplenty. *But, Lord! What am I supposed to do? You told me you were the vine. If I remained in you, rejecting everything else* . . . Hadn't it said that? Jesus said remain in Him. Didn't that mean forsake the rest?

He opened his mouth so Dr. DiGratia could remove the clinical thermometer. How had Carina known he'd never seen one before? He had almost never been sick, and the two times that he could recall, no one had poked thermometers at him, bathed him, and . . . Well, Augusta Tabor had spoon-fed him, but only the once. Quillan's frown deepened.

The doctor held the tube between his fingertips and studied it. "Hmm." No more explanation than that. Quillan had had enought of "hmm"s and "we'll see"s. Dr. Gratia went to the glass-faced cabinet and opened the door, fingering through the small bottles. He took down two—one that looked like dried leaves and smelled sweetly pungent when he unstoppered it, and another grayish white powder. He pinched a couple grains of the powder into a porcelain cup, then put a few of the leaves into a square of muslin and tied it shut with thread.

Quillan watched in spite of himself as the doctor poured boiling water over both, dissolving the powder and steeping the leaves. He looked up suspiciously when the cup was held out to him. "What is it?"

"Sassafras and monkshood." A tremor at the corners of his mouth clued Quillan to ignore what came next. "Not enough to poison, I hope. Just to control the fever."

"Is it rising?" Carina took the cup and held it to Quillan's lips.

Quillan sipped. *Not enough to poison . . . he hoped.* Very funny. He made a face.

"From his sour temper, no doubt."

Carina glanced at her papa, then back to him. Quillan refused to look ashamed. "Be kind, Papa," was all she said, and she urged a second sip of the steaming concoction between Quillan's lips. Her eyes softened. "I think something for pain, as well."

The doctor turned, and Quillan met his quizzical glance with undisguised resentment.

"Yes," the doctor said.

Quillan flushed at the implication that pain was making him cross. But the thought of the warm, formless effect of laudanum softened his resistance. He'd told Carina he didn't want it, but the thought worked on him now like a seductress.

"Not opium, I think." Again the doctor reached into his cabinet, bringing out a larger bottle half filled with powder, then stirred it into another batch of tea. "Willow bark."

Quillan shook his head. Was Dr. DiGratia some herbalist from the dark ages? He wanted to demand laudanum. Only his pride kept him silent, and the next gulp of sassafras tea. The fewer trips Carina made to his mouth with the cup the better. Every one reminded him of her words, *"Maybe you need to surrender your independence."* She wiped a dribble from his chin, shaved that morning by Vittorio.

Quillan drank the willow bark tea, certain he would need the opium tincture anyway. But in a while it did seem to dull the edge. After the doctor left, he said, "What does your father have against laudanum? He was free enough with it at the start."

"He doesn't want you habituated."

Quillan leaned his head back. Habituated. Was he? He knew smoking the drug made addicts; he'd seen the Chinamen weaving home from the dens, but . . . He swallowed his disappointment. He should be thankful Dr. DiGratia was not the sort to be draining his blood and dosing him into a stupor.

Maybe he was in better hands than he wanted to admit, in spite of the dry, terse comments and tyrannical pokes. Then there were Carina's hands, working the tension from his brow and temples. Healing hands, nurturing hands, human hands. He closed his eyes, letting her fingers ease his pain. He was tired. His annoyance and fear drained him. Carina stroked the weariness from his brow, then leaned close and whispered in his ear, "T'amo." And she kissed the same ear. No opium was necessary to spread that kind of warmth.

Caught between Quillan and her papa, Carina had felt like a fox between two hounds. They were both too stubborn to give the other any ground. So Papa accepted her marriage. Could he not extend some courtesy to Quillan? And Quillan, couldn't he go a little way toward showing gratitude and forgiveness?

She felt him slip into sleep under her gentle massage and slowly removed her hands. Let him sleep now, and perhaps he would wake in better humor. She brushed a kiss across his forehead and left. Mamma was in the kitchen, working garlic pulp into the focaccia. She could have a Chinese cook like Gelsomina did, but Mamma loved the feel of the dough beneath her palms, the steam of the savory sauces on the stove, the heat of the oven as she removed the crisply browned fishes and roasts. Carina understood.

"How is he?" Mamma asked without looking up, making the best of that to which she must resign herself. She had stopped harping when she read Father Antoine's letter. No matter how heartbreaking the match, it was done.

"He is cross. He wants more than broth, and it frets him to be so helpless."

Mamma smiled. She couldn't help it, though she hid it at

once. "How long does Papa say before he can eat?"

Carina shrugged. "Papa is equally cross. He doesn't say."

Now Mamma glanced up. "Like two bears, are they?"

"In springtime."

Again Mamma smiled. "It won't hurt your papa to reach a little."

Carina cocked her head. Could Mamma mean that? Did she see it was mostly Papa's pride that had muddled things?

"Eh, soon enough I'll bake him a lasagne with fresh ricotta and spinach from the garden."

Of course Mamma didn't mean Papa; she was thinking of Quillan. Carina's mouth watered, and she knew Quillan would succumb at the first bite. If anything could make peace between them all, it was Mamma's lasagne, dripping cheese and rich tomato sauce.

"I wish he could have it now."

"Your papa knows best." Mamma turned the dough and dimpled it with her fingers.

Carina reached for the cruet and drizzled olive oil over the garlicky circle her Mamma formed. She had to admit Papa was tending Quillan as carefully as she would herself.

Mamma lifted the dough onto the cornmeal-sprinkled baking stone and slid it into the oven. "I have fresh prawns for supper."

Carina looked at the bowl of large gray prawns, their legs like stunted tentacles gathered in the curl of their bodies. "Shall I devein them?" She reached for the small sharp knife when Mamma nodded. What would Quillan think of prawns? Fried with butter and oregano and lemon until they turned pink and firm, their edges crisp and golden. She closed her eyes and pictured his expression as he filled his mouth with a new flavor.

"What is it?" Mamma touched her hand.

Carina opened her eyes, picked up a thin-shelled prawn. "I was thinking how Quillan would look when he tried it for the first time."

"Has he had no shrimp?" Mamma swabbed the marble counter with a hot cloth.

Carina shrugged. "He never saw a crab until San Francisco."

"What did he think of it?"

"He thought it tasted better than it looked." She dangled the prawn from her fingers. "He has a point."

Mamma laughed. "That's why we don't allow men in the kitchen. It's better they don't know."

Carina sliced the blade down the back side of the prawn, splitting the shell and cutting shallowly into the translucent flesh beneath. With the tip of the knife she lifted out the thin blue vein that was really the animal's intestine. Why was it a woman could deal with that thought, but Tony and others grew pale, contending they would never touch a prawn again—until, of course, a plate of them was set sizzling before them in savory buttery sauce.

"Quillan would try anything I make. He loves to watch me cook."

"You've let him in your kitchen?" Mamma slapped the cloth onto the counter with a soft plop.

Carina pictured Mae's kitchen with the long board table where she had served Quillan that first meal of cannelloni, how he had lingered over each bite. What would Mamma think that she had fed him right there at the table where she prepared it? And then the time he had watched her make the ravioli, mixing the pasta with her fingers, the intensity in his eyes as he watched.

She smiled. "Yes, Mamma. Quillan is welcome in my kitchen."

Mamma stared at her a long moment. "Then where can you be separate?"

Carina considered that. She knew what Mamma was asking. Where was her woman's place, her refuge from a husband's expectations, her place to control, to rule. She picked up a second prawn. "I don't want to be separate. I want to be one." She looked up into Mamma's face. She had no doubt Mamma loved Papa, but she had never fought for that love as Carina had. Could she understand?

Brows raised, Mamma lifted the cloth and squeezed the excess water into the washbowl. "You are naïve, Carina." She smiled. "But maybe . . . not so much, eh?"

Carina laughed. "You should see him, Mamma. He watches me as though I speak the lasagne into being. He says it's magic. He thinks my fingers are magic."

Again Mamma paused. "Is it possible—could it be I've missed something all these years?" She looked around the room where the women had always gathered to prepare meal after meal, their world.

"What are you thinking, Mamma?" Carina held the knife poised over the fragile shell.

"I'm trying to imagine your papa in here watching me." She slowly folded the cloth and laid it on the edge of the counter.

"And?" Carina held her breath.

"I would take a spoon to him."

"Mamma!"

Mamma shook her head, laughing. "It's no use, Carina. Your papa could no more sit in here than I could tell him how to grow his vines or cure his patients. We are what we are."

"But, Mamma . . ."

"No, Carina. Some things don't change. Maybe . . . maybe it's different with your man. He is not . . ."

"Italian?"

Mamma shrugged. "Who can explain the humors that flow in the blood?" She rested her hands on the counter. "If you had chosen Flavio . . ."

Carina met her mother's eyes. Would she be condemned again? Would this time of connecting end here with that name mentioned?

Mamma sighed. "Flavio would not have watched you cook, Carina."

Her heart swelled. It was true. Flavio was her own kind, but she had chosen Quillan, or God had.

"Your home will not be the same as mine." There was a wistful note in Mamma's voice.

"Not so different, Mamma."

Smile lines crinkled at her mamma's eyes. "Not in the bedroom, eh?"

Carina looked up, startled.

"Not when your sons come, nor your daughters."

Carina's heart constricted. "I don't know, Mamma." Her cycle was again irregular. She couldn't remember the last time she'd bled.

Mamma waved her hand. "Your husband is capable still. I asked Papa."

Carina flushed. Her parents had discussed that? She swallowed the pain in her throat. "It's not Quillan I'm worried about. After my miscarriage Dr. Felden was unsure if I could—"

"Don't say it, Carina. Of course you can." Mamma crossed

herself, then sobered. "It must have been awful."

Carina nodded slowly, tears stinging her eyes. And then she was in Mamma's arms, the knife and prawn lying where she dropped them, and the scent of Mamma's lemon water and the soft flesh of her throat against Carina's face. She poured out the story of the terrible men and her own temper and the disastrous price her baby had paid. She sobbed.

"Cara mia." Mamma stroked her hair. "And where was your Quillan?"

Carina sniffed. "Away."

Mamma rocked her. "Ah, tesora . . ." She dropped a tear of her own to Carina's face. "If you can forgive him that, you must truly love him."

"With all my heart, Mamma."

Her mamma pressed her face to Carina's hair. "Then God will provide, eh? You hear, Signore? Give them a child again." She squeezed Carina and released her.

Carina laughed, suddenly seeing that Mamma's scolding was really a deep belief that God could and would answer her prayer. Carina knew God would do as He saw best, but silently her heart added its own plea.

"I'll finish the prawns. You go wash your face."

Carina sniffed, grateful for the release the tears had given, but ready to be through with it. She went to the bathhouse and washed, then toweled her face dry and drew in a deep settling breath. God was good. His perfect will would be done. Surely she and Quillan would both recover. She just had to be patient.

She went outside and drank in the spring scent of waking earth, budding and blooming shrubs and bulbs and nut trees. The Gravenstein apple trees would soon be profuse with blossoms and the scent from the rows of forty orange trees just behind the barn indescribable. Everywhere life quickened, and she had to believe it God's promise that hers and Quillan's too would be restored.

Feeling almost buoyant, she wanted to see Ti'Giuseppe. Quillan had taken so much of her time and concern that—

"Mrs. Shepard!"

Carina turned in surprise.

"I am *so* glad to find you." Mr. Pierce hurried over from the gates outside the courtyard. "I've come every day, but your brothers turned me away. I can only hope it isn't at your bequest?"

She was too surprised to be anything but truthful. "I didn't know you had come. What is it you want?" She only hoped her tears didn't show again.

He looked exasperated. "I heard about the accident, but no one seems to know what happened. The men at the quarry shake their heads and mumble with side glances at each other; but get a straight answer? I'd have to be Socrates."

"Mr. Pierce—"

"Now don't put me off, Mrs. Shepard. Quillan and I have a deal, and I find it my duty—"

"A deal?" She dropped her hands to her sides. "What deal?"

"His story, of course. I told you I had an opportunity."

"Yes, but—" She spread her hands wide. "Quillan agreed?"

"Of course."

She looked at him probingly. How much of this was bluster? "My husband was badly injured."

"How badly?"

She shook her head. "The wagon fell on top of him."

"How? How did it fall?"

"An explosion."

He pulled the ever-present pad from his pocket. "What caused the explosion?"

She looked into Mr. Pierce's face. Was it any of his business? Did he have a right to their misery? "You'll have to ask Quillan."

He nodded sharply. "That's all I want. To speak to him."

Unsnagging the hem of her skirt from a honeysuckle bush, she looked back toward the house. "I don't know. Papa will have to decide."

"Mrs. Shepard . . ."

She recognized the cajoling tone and turned back, annoyed. "Mr. Pierce, my husband was nearly killed. My papa is the finest surgeon around. Maybe no one else could have brought him through. I will let him decide."

Mr. Pierce backed up one step, with his palms raised. "All right, all right. But ask, will you? Ask Quillan when we can meet."

She stared at him. How did one become so insensitive and bullheaded?

He removed his hat and fanned his face. "One more thing. Was it your lover who injured him?"

Her breath came out in a rush of indignation. "My lover?"

"I asked around. Flavio Caldrone..."

"Flavio—was not—my lover." She punctuated each phrase with a step in his direction.

"You were betrothed."

He was not as tall as Quillan, but she was aware of her diminutive size in comparison, mainly because she considered slapping him. Instead, she eyed him as she might a particularly odious reptile. "Mr. Pierce, you overstep yourself."

"It must be painful to be the cause of your husband's tragedy.

The breath left her lungs in a huff. "Painful? This is painful!" She kicked his shin with everything in her.

Hopping backward, he gripped his leg and howled, even dropping his pad into the dirt.

She snatched it up. "Now get off my land." With a flourish of skirts, she stalked toward the tiny cottage beside the barn.

"Mrs. Shepard." He gasped, limping behind. "I meant no disrespect."

No disrespect? Seething, she gained Ti'Giuseppe's door, yanked it open, and turned. "Go away, or I'll have my uncle blow your head off."

Mr. Pierce stopped. "Well, all right, then. Tell Quillan I want to see him." He straightened his pants leg, gathering what dignity he could.

She went in and closed the door in his face. Ti'Giuseppe sat by the fire with a smile as wide as his ears, bare gums and all. She took the stool at his side. "I kicked him, Tio."

"Good, good. Nosy one, that."

"Did he talk to you?"

Giuseppe nodded. "Wandered this way when Tony wouldn't let him in the gate."

"What did you tell him?"

"Eh?"

"I said, what did you tell him?"

"Eh?" Giuseppe burst into a wicked laugh.

Carina's mouth dropped open, and she laughed full chested as she hadn't in a long time. "Oh, Tio." She flung her arms around him and squeezed.

"How is he, your man?"

Carina sighed. "Better, but frustrated he can't do everything for himself. He doesn't like to be helped."

Again Giuseppe laughed. "Then he'll learn more than he might have."

Twenty-five

Life stripped of any consequence,
brings one to aching cognizance.
Strength once commanding reality;
Keen, now, the mind knows futility.

— *Quillan*

QUILLAN WINCED ONLY SLIGHTLY when Dr. DiGratia unbound his arm and probed the collarbone. He imagined the doctor's fingers like insect antennae sending information to the brain as his mouth puckered slightly in concentration, and the tendons in his gray-haired forearms rippled with each movement of the fingers.

"Better, eh?" the doctor said.

"Yes," Quillan grudgingly admitted.

Dr. DiGratia pointed to the other arm still in the cast. "That one was a compound fracture. The bone broke through the flesh. It will take longer. But at least you will have one arm now to use."

"Thank you." These last weeks had reduced him to gratitude for the smallest things. Being allowed to fumble about left-handed would be significant. He moved his arm, dismayed by its weakness.

"Atrophy. The muscle will come back with time."

Time. Had it ever hung so heavily and passed so slowly? Quillan no longer had the benefit of invalid exhaustion to sleep away these helpless days. Even the pain had diminished, and nothing was offered to lull him. He chafed as he had never chafed before.

His own body held him trapped. Sometimes the terror was inexpressible, but during the day he did his best to hide it.

The doctor left, and Carina came in smelling flowery and fresh as the breeze the dottore had let in the window once the morning mists evaporated. "Come stai?" She kissed his lips.

How was he? He caught her neck with his freed hand and kissed her back. *"Sto bene—no, benissimo!"* He kissed her again.

She laughed, catching his hand between hers. "You have your arm free?"

"And good as a wet noodle."

She kissed his fingers. "It will strengthen. How are your ribs?"

"Fit as a fiddle—as long as I don't move or breathe."

"Still sore, eh?" She cupped his face in her palm.

"Not so bad." Even the abdominal surgery seemed to be healing well. He was able to raise himself with help. His hip no longer pained him, but it was the leg no one mentioned. It throbbed in the night, and Quillan noted the sickly yellow toes. If holding his arm inert these weeks could render it limp, what would the leg be like when they took the plaster off? "You don't suppose you could spring me loose, do you?"

"Why would you want to be?" She kissed his forehead, but this time he didn't hold her there.

That was the crux of it. Carina was perfectly content now that her flock had swooped him into their midst. She didn't understand that he belonged there no more than he had at the start. And he had no remaining inclination to belong. He learned the language because it was easy and Carina enjoyed speaking it with him, but not because he wanted to be one of them. Jesus was the vine, Quillan the branch—and Carina, too, God help him. But the rest of them could be pruned away, and good riddance. No matter what she said about independence and surrender.

"You're anxious."

"Yes, I am."

She threaded his hair with her fingers. "Healing takes time."

"Well, I don't have time. I need to work, now that . . ."

"That what?" She tipped his chin up with a look of pure indulgence.

He felt a spiteful surge. "Now that everything I have is destroyed."

"A wagon, Quillan. It was only a wagon."

He shook his head. "No, Carina. Everything I had was in that wagon. Every dollar I'd earned except those washed away by the flood. It was all burned to ashes, every cent."

She stared at him. "You kept your money in your wagon?"

"I had a special box built into the frame just above the axle."

"You didn't have it in a bank?"

He dropped his eyes, then shot them up defiantly. "Carina, I was there when Shane Dennison cleaned out that bank."

"He didn't get away with it."

"He has since."

She shook her head uncomprehending. "So the money from the mine . . ."

"And everything else I earned freighting." Quillan spread his fingers. "Up in smoke."

She sat down on the edge of the bed. "How much was it? No, don't tell me; I don't want to know."

"Fifty-four thousand dollars."

She dropped her face into her hands and started to shake. He thought she was weeping until he realized with annoyance it was laughter he heard. She could laugh—now that everything they had, that would have bought them land and a living was gone?

She looked up, still mirthful. "Oh, Quillan, God is merciful."

He shook his head, dumbfounded.

"I know you. I see the wheels turning in your mind. As soon as you are well it would have been off to Alaska or someplace to make your own way and the devil take the world. Now? Now maybe you will see that there are those willing and able to help."

"What are you talking about?"

"You'll see." She started to stand.

He caught her wrist. "See what, Carina?"

She tugged gently until she freed herself. "Is there anything I can bring you?"

He swallowed his frustration. "Yes. The things from my room at the Union Hotel. My journal and Cain's Bible and the books. Bring it all. There's no sense keeping the room when I can't pay for it." He scowled.

She smiled serenely. "I'll be glad to." And she left as though he had just told her the finest news imaginable. Never, as long as he lived, would he understand the mind of his wife.

Carina's heart sang. Before, she could not imagine how she was going to get Quillan to accept Papa's gift, but now? He had little choice now! Ti'Giuseppe hitched the small buggy, and she rode into the plaza and pulled up at the hotel where Quillan had been staying. She marched in to the counter. "Good day, Mr. Renault. I need to collect my husband's things."

Mr. Renault tucked his watch back into his vest pocket. "Is he finished with the room then? He hadn't given word so I've been compelled to charge it each night to his account."

"How much does he owe you?"

"I'll tally the bill." He penciled the figures and handed her the slip.

"I will bring you payment." She tucked the paper into her wrist purse and held out her hand for the key.

"I'll send a man up to carry it all down."

"Thank you."

He cleared his throat. "How is he, if I may ask? Rumor is rampant."

She smiled. "He is improving, thank you."

"I'll tell your friend."

She turned. "My friend?"

"The young man from Denver. He's been in nearly daily asking after Mr. Shepard. Sent him up the other day to fetch something from the room. Didn't you send him?"

"Do you mean Mr. Pierce?"

"That's the name."

Carina gripped her hands into fists. "What did he fetch?"

"It looked like a book. With Mr. Shepard incapacitated, I thought Mr. Pierce was acting as his agent."

Carina turned and charged the stairs. Mr. Pierce had gone too far, and more than his shin would bear the brunt. She went into Quillan's room, and a moment later a youth came in to help her carry everything. As she suspected, Quillan's journal was neither on the table nor in his pack.

She fumed, thinking of the personal and beautiful poems he had shared with her. That Roderick Pierce would not only see them but turn Quillan's words to his own advantage ... She waited fretfully while the youth loaded Quillan's things into her buggy, then gave him a coin and accepted his assistance up to the seat. She slapped the reins. Quillan would not be happy.

Quillan could do nothing but stew. Day after day he pondered the affront. Roderick Pierce had skipped town with his journal and probably felt justified after the scene Carina described of their last encounter. Quillan pictured it easily. As slippery as Pierce was, he had not avoided Carina's kick, though she wouldn't tell him what precipitated it. But that didn't make the theft of his journal anything less than that. The man was a snake.

Dr. DiGratia broke into Quillan's thoughts as he came into the room. His visits were less frequent now that they had moved Quillan to a small porch off the east side of the house. He had a fainting couch that enabled him to sit more easily, though it was less comfortable for sleeping, a side table, and a shelf for the books Carina had brought from the hotel and any of those in her father's collection Quillan might care to read. In his extreme boredom, he did exactly that.

The doctor carried a small saw. "Are you ready to have that off?" He indicated the cast on Quillan's right arm. His dry humor did nothing to improve Quillan's mood.

Quillan held up the arm, which had been out of the sling for several days. The doctor worked silently, sawing through the plaster, then pulling it off the arm. Quillan eyed the lumpy scar where the bone had pushed through muscle and skin. Then he straightened his elbow and felt the expected weakness. It was worse than the left arm had been, though limited use had begun to restore the first to something better than a noodle. As Dr. DiGratia examined this pale, wasted forearm, Quillan considered what it had been.

"A straight mend, it appears." Dr. DiGratia picked up the scraps of cloth and plaster.

"And my leg? Are you taking that plaster off?"

The doctor glanced down at the leg lying as it had been week after week, a plaster log from hip to calf. "Not yet, I think."

"Why not?"

The doctor took a breath, then released it. "The femur was broken twice, one section more nearly crushed. It needs time yet."

Quillan swallowed. "Time for what?"

"For what healing there will be."

Quillan squelched the panic of those words. He was maimed?

Useless? Like Cain? Cain hadn't been useless, a voice inside argued, but Quillan ignored it. How would he support his wife, children when they came? Would Carina even want a cripple for a husband? *Surrender your independence.* And what? Depend on her? He opened and closed his right hand, clenching the fist harder and harder.

Dr. DiGratia paused, the split cast and fragments balanced in his hands. "We will see when the time comes. There's no use imagining the worst."

"I doubt you've told me the worst."

The doctor's chin cocked slightly. "The worst is the leg will not bear your weight, and you'll use a crutch."

Again Quillan pictured Cain hobbling over the rough ground. *Oh, God!* He forced his voice to steady. "When will I know?"

"Once I determine the bone is fused, we will begin to strengthen the leg."

"How can you tell anything through this?" Scowling, Quillan knocked on the plaster near his hip.

"I can't. Maybe it's ready now. But I will err on the side of caution." He fixed Quillan with his blue stare. "Too soon a try might damage the bone beyond repair."

Quillan closed his eyes. He was peevish and unfair in his impatience. Dr. DiGratia had expended much time and effort with his care. "I'm sorry."

A faint smile pulled the doctor's lips. "You must understand my position. One wrong move with you now, and I'll have Carina's ire forever."

Quillan stared at him. That was the first acknowledgment of permanent status he'd had from the man. Why now, when he could offer so little? He'd lost his fortune and even his strength. Now he truly had nothing to offer but himself, and even that was questionable. The tightness in his throat became an ache. Had he misunderstood something somewhere? But though the doctor left him brooding, he could not see it.

Carina passed her papa coming from Quillan's room, the saw and cast pieces in his hand. "His arm is healed?"

"The break is knitted."

"But his arm . . . it will . . ."

Papa paused his stride. "Your husband is strong and determined."

Her husband. To hear it again from Papa's lips assured her of Quillan's place in her family. No one talked anymore of annulling; no one tried to keep her from the man she loved. If only it had come without Quillan's pain. But even in that she was sure God had a purpose.

Vittorio came and took the pieces of the cast from Papa. "Shall I show him how to strengthen the arm?"

Papa nodded. "Slowly today. Strength only. We will train the reflexes later."

Train the reflexes. She thought of Quillan's speed with a gun when he shot the head from the rattlesnake. Train his reflexes?

But Carina felt a surge of pride. Quillan could be in no better hands than her papa's. What if he had landed in the care of a doctor like Miss Preston's father, who would have determined his care by the bumps on Quillan's head or by his complexion and assumed temperament?

Appearances were nothing to Papa, not in his practice of medicine. He knew the body inside and out, which parts knitted to which, which organs performed what duty. Like Leonardo da Vinci he had studied a dead body once, had performed surgery on its parts. Maybe that was disrespectful to the dead. Many people thought so. But to the living it provided invaluable knowledge.

If anyone could bring Quillan through this, it was Papa. And Vittorio. Carina looked up at her serious-faced brother. Yes, he had been as stubborn as the rest, determined to keep her from the man they all considered a usurper. But he had worked tirelessly beside Papa when Quillan arrived injured. He would be a fine doctor in his own right.

Vittorio discarded the cast remains and went into Quillan's room. Carina lingered in the doorway out of Quillan's line of sight and watched her brother greet him with soft-spoken courtesy. Ah, how things had changed. Vittorio lifted Quillan's arm, and Carina saw with dismay the shrunk muscle and limp tissue. She could well imagine training the nerves and muscles to respond again.

Vittorio ran his hand down the arm, nodding. "The bone is sound. But the muscle is not, eh?"

"Not exactly." Quillan looked uncomfortable, annoyed. Why did he persist in his grudge? Couldn't he see they were trying to welcome him as best they could?

"Make a fist." Vittorio watched the hand come together. "Tighter."

Quillan strained.

"Let it go." Vittorio held Quillan's forearm. "Try again. Harder. Try harder."

Quillan's forehead took on a sheen as Vittorio ordered the same motion repeatedly, then switched to the other arm and did the same. If so little cost so much, how would it be to restore strength to the rest of him? She again realized the extent of the trauma to her husband's body, worse by far than her injuries had been, yet she had felt weak as a kitten and helpless. How Quillan must fear that weakness.

She started to pray for strength, then thought of Saint Paul. Maybe it was in Quillan's weakness that God's power would be perfected. That thought was so different from her old demands and cajoling that she paused. She must desire God's will even if it seemed contrary to her own wants and Quillan's. *Padre Eterno, heal my husband as you will. Let this misfortune be turned to good for all and especially the man I love. Grazie, Signore.*

Her heart felt peaceful even as she watched Quillan's frustration grow. He flung his arm down to his side. "Enough! Can't you see it's wasted?"

Vittorio merely nodded, so like Papa in demeanor she was sure that irked Quillan, as well. "Yes, I see." This time Vittorio lifted the arm and studied the tendons as he closed the fingers himself. "That's all for today." He restored Quillan's arm to his side and pointed to the left. "That one is better, eh?"

Quillan shrugged. "I've had some use of it."

"Its injury was not so severe." He touched the collarbone, and Quillan scarcely winced. "Good."

Quillan might not have winced, but Carina saw him squirm. Was it Vittorio's touch he disliked? An affront to his privacy? It was as natural to Vittorio as breath. Italian men touched, kissed, danced, and hugged. She tried to picture Quillan thus and failed. Oh, he touched her with fierce connection. But had she ever seen him reach out to anyone else?

Cain. He had regularly supported, even carried Cain in his

infirmity. And Alan; Quillan gave his strength as Alan needed. That was it. He could touch to help others, especially the old ones, but he did not receive such touch himself. Nor, she supposed, would he take easily to affectionate touch from any but her. She bit her lower lip, smiling slightly at the learning he had yet to do.

Vittorio raised Quillan's chin. "A shave, I think."

"Just bring me a bowl and straight razor."

"And watch you slice your throat?" Vittorio took down a shaving bowl and mixed a lather. He dipped a towel into the water held warm on the brazier, then laid it over Quillan's face.

Carina leaned on the doorway. She'd never seen her husband get shaved. He had as much beard as any man in her family, and it reached down his neck, as well. Vittorio removed the towel and brushed on the lather, then took up the blade.

"I'll do it myself if you'll fetch me a mirror."

Carina stepped into the room. "Behave yourself, Quillan, and let Vittorio shave you. Soon enough you'll do everything yourself."

He turned, gave her a fiery glance, then succumbed to the first scratchy glide of the blade. Carina watched the stripe of bare flesh widen with each stroke of the blade. Quillan's hands lay at his sides, but she saw them clench slightly. Yes, he suffered the care, no more. Then Vittorio took out a small scissors to trim his mustache.

Quillan said, "Leave it."

"Here, let me." Carina took the scissors and sat at Quillan's side. Carefully she clipped the overgrowth of his full, jaunty mustache. What if she took it all the way off? Would his mouth look vulnerable? What if his hair were cut? Would he look gentle and meek? She doubted it.

With her fingertips, she flicked the sides of his mustache free of loose clippings, then leaned in and kissed his lips. Quillan's eyes flicked up to Vittorio, who stood grinning. Carina smiled, too, as Vittorio toweled the flecks of lather from Quillan's throat and jaw.

"There. You are presentable to kiss my sister."

Quillan looked from one to the other, exasperated. Poor man, he didn't know how to take them.

"Go away." Carina shooed her brother with her hand. Then

she turned from Vittorio's departing back to her husband's expectant face.

"Do you intend to make a regular spectacle of me?" He raised a hand into her hair.

She shrugged. "Things are less private here. Our love is part of their lives. My brothers, my parents, cousins, friends—they're all included." She spread her hands. "We are family."

Quillan frowned. "Feels mighty crowded."

She kissed his forehead. "You'll get used to it."

His stormy glance argued back, but both arms came around her in a loose embrace.

She settled into his chest. "You just have to try a little."

"You sound like Vittorio."

She laughed. "How hard was it?"

"Hard." He raised one shaky arm, then dropped it. "I'm weak as a baby."

"But you'll try again."

He met her gaze. "You know I will. The sooner—"

She kissed his mouth, full and feverishly. She didn't want to hear what he thought he would do when his strength returned. She was suddenly glad God might keep him weak some while. Maybe in that time he could learn to keep still.

Twenty-six

One lesson learned through loss of health is time can be a friend.
The plague it places on your mind cannot itself contend,
with what great strides it grants your flesh while bone and sinew knit.
But how a friend can wear a welcome thin if overlong does sit.

— Quillan

CARINA LEFT HER WEARY HUSBAND and went out to the courtyard. Lingering near the fountain, Divina and Nicolo looked up as she stepped out. Nicolo's hand was on Divina's belly, caressing the child—that wasn't his? Carina stared. Did he treasure that baby because it gave him Divina? Or for its own sake? She looked at her cousin in a new light.

Unattractive in comparison to her brothers and especially to Flavio, Nicolo had never occupied much of her thoughts. And none of Divina's, she was sure. Yet standing there together, they seemed content, Nicolo having grown in stature and comeliness by it. She joined them, but Nicolo's hand remained on the swelling gathers of Divina's skirt.

Divina smiled. "Nicolo thinks he can feel a kick."

With a pang, Carina remembered her own baby's soft flutterings. "Can he?"

"Try it." Nicolo lifted his hand and motioned hers into its place.

Carina put her hand on Divina's belly. "Do you feel it inside?" Carina looked into her sister's face, trying not to envy her condition.

347

"Of course." Divina waved her hand. "I've felt it some while now."

A tiny thump touched Carina's palm, and her eyes widened. "I felt it."

"I told you." Nicolo pulled Divina close to his side again. "He's a strong one."

"He might be a girl." Divina nudged his ribs. "With a kick like Carina's."

Carina huffed. "She'll have to work hard to aspire to that." They laughed, Divina's barb scarcely bringing a sting to Carina's old pride. Having so recently kicked Mr. Pierce, she could hardly deny the tendency still existed, but she felt no need to defend herself. Maybe her oversensitivity had made more of Divina's remarks than there ever was.

Anyway, it was Ti'Giuseppe she wanted to see, so she left them to each other and headed for his cottage. She tapped the door, then walked in.

Ti'Giuseppe was not in bed; he sat dozing by his stove, shoulders wrapped in a woolen blanket Flavio's mother had woven for him. Carina crept close and kissed his cheeks, smiling when his gray filmed eyes opened and his lips parted. She held his face between her hands. "How are you, Tio?"

"Bene, cara. Dreaming of heaven."

Her heart lurched in her chest. "Not yet, Tio. I need you still."

He shook his head, smiling. "You have all you need in that young man and the little ones to come. Life is for the young."

"And for the old. What would we do without you?" Tears stung her eyes again at the thought of Nonna's absence. To consider Ti'Giuseppe passing away was too painful. But she knew he was frail, more so, perhaps, than he seemed. If he dreamed of heaven, was God preparing him to go? She caught his hand between hers and kissed his fingers.

"Life has been good to me, Carina." His eyes warmed with the glow from his stove. "When it is time to leave this place, I will leave it content."

"When the time comes. But not yet." She squeezed his hand.

"I think I will see the little one."

"Tio?"

He rested his head against the pressed wooden back of his chair. "The baby."

Carina glanced back to where she had left Divina. "Nicolo has felt it kick."

"Not Divina's baby." Ti'Giuseppe tugged one edge of the blanket higher. "Yours."

She looked into his face. What was he saying? That he would live to see her children? She could only hope so. But the old man did not know that her injuries might keep her from ever bearing a child. "Of course, Tio. You will bless my children."

He closed his eyes. "This one, at least, I will bless."

This one. A ripple ran through her. What do you mean? she wanted to ask, but his breathing had deepened, fluttering his lips over his gums. She slipped her hand out of his and stood. He was still dreaming, her dear Giuseppe. She let him sleep.

Back outside the day's warmth soothed the ache he had brought to her heart. So much loss. Her baby, Nonna, and now fears for Giuseppe. But Quillan grew stronger every day. She must see the good, bask in the blessings.

She went to the stable and saddled a mare. A ride to town would help, and she had errands there. She mounted side saddle and brought the horse around, then rode at a brisk clip. When she reached the plaza, she stopped first at the post office. In some of her hours attending Quillan, she had written her friends in Crystal. Too much time had passed, but with all the strain of the journey, then the trials of their arrival, she had not corresponded with Mae or Èmie as she had expected to. One feverishly thankful letter she had sent to Father Antoine, but she had not heard back from anyone yet.

She waited behind Mrs. Gardener, thinking of the line of miners at the post office in Crystal and the kindness she had found in them as they moved her ahead and gave up their places. Mrs. Gardener collected her mail and moved aside. Carina stepped up to the window. Before she could ask, Mr. Halliford handed her a string-wrapped stack of letters, too thick to hold with one hand.

Her heart jumped as she read the top name. Joe Turner! She clasped the packet to her breast, not looking at the other ones. She would let them surprise her. Letters from people she hadn't even written. Had Mae shared her letter with Joe? Had others heard and sent their regards . . . at three cents an ounce? She laughed. What was three cents to Joe Turner? It was she and Quillan who were penniless. She laughed again and went outside.

What fun she would have reading each letter to Quillan. Would he pretend he didn't care? Or would he listen with his pirate's smile and tease? That depended on his mood these days, which reminded her of her other errand. She tucked the letters into her saddle pouch and led her horse across the plaza, past the train turntable to the goldsmith and jeweler's. She tethered the horse, then went inside. "Good afternoon, Mr. Grady. How is the locket coming?"

"Not finished yet, I'm afraid. Soon."

"But you can repair it?"

The goldsmith looked up with deep-set triangular eyes. "Not as it was. I've had to replace the front. I'm tooling it now."

"But the photograph?"

He smiled and nodded. "Some things are more valuable than gold, aren't they?"

She agreed fervently. "Thank you for your work. Please let me know when you have it finished."

Back out on the street, she prepared to mount when someone called her name—a voice she did not relish hearing. All her good humor vanished, and she stopped with one foot in the stirrup, indignation rising like a tide. He would show his face again? She turned, biting words on her tongue, but he was not daunted at all. What was he made of, this Mr. Pierce?

At the knock on his door, Quillan woke, a warm lethargy permeating his system. But Carina came in looking like thunder.

He jolted up, wincing. "What's the matter?"

She put one hand on her hip. "Someone's here to see you."

"Who?"

She motioned as though that someone might slither through the door, when in fact he came in behind her looking dapper as ever in a black Prince Albert coat and gaiters. The man had gall, Quillan gave him that.

"Quillan." He came forward, hand extended. "Good to see you looking so hale."

Quillan didn't take the extended hand, even though he could finally have done so if he wished. He sent a chilling glare instead.

Pierce waved a hand. "Now I know . . . theft and all that. But see?" He held up the journal. "Once again, no intention to retain said stolen property."

"You have a warped sense of ethics."

Pierce grinned. "Wonder what else I've brought, do you?"

"No."

Pierce laughed. "Well, I know you do, though you'd suck lemons before you'd admit it. I have a contract for a poetry anthology based on the excerpts from the biographical sketches in *Harper's Monthly*."

Quillan tensed. "Excerpts of what?"

"Your poems, of course."

Quillan opened and closed his mouth. He had specifically and repeatedly refused Pierce's requests. The poems in his journal were the words of his heart, not intended for public scrutiny.

"We had a handshake agreement. I had to give them something, and you were . . . unavailable." Pierce spread his hands reasonably, as though Quillan should understand his necessary infamy. "The folks at Harper and Brothers are agog. They're naming you with Emerson and Holmes. They're crazy for American poets to compete with the Brits."

Baffled by the man's obtuseness, Quillan shook his head. What did he care about competing with the British or anyone else? Those poems were his inner turmoil, his . . . He looked at Carina, saw her own indignation. The corner of his mouth flickered. With very little provocation, she would kick Pierce again. He noticed Mr. Pierce stayed out of range.

Quillan fixed Pierce in his stare. "Mr. Pierce . . ."

"Rod."

"I specifically told you those poems were not for publication. I haven't changed my mind."

"Maybe this will." Pierce held out a bank draft. "In advance of your submission. Royalties, of course, would follow."

Quillan neither took nor looked at the check. "What's in it for you?"

"A small percentage from future projects." At least Pierce didn't hedge. "And of course the acknowledgment that I discovered you. That goes a long way in my field."

Quillan laughed. Pierce's audacity was no small thing. Nor what he offered. Another man might have jumped at the chance for fame and recognition. Quillan just wanted to be able to walk again with two sound legs and Carina at his side. His laugh died.

He sank back and crossed his arms, a motion he hadn't managed in weeks. He hoped their paltry condition was not evident. At any rate Pierce didn't look at him like an invalid. Quillan swallowed. "My poetry's not for sale."

Pierce gave a dramatic sigh. "Quillan, what can I say to convince you? America needs a voice that so poignantly describes her soul."

Did he mean that? Did he really think the words that came to him in turmoil, grief, and joy described America's soul?

Mr. Pierce set the check on the bed stand. "I'll leave this. Discuss it with your wife. If she's forgiven my boorish behavior . . ." He glanced at Carina hopefully. "Maybe she can get through to you."

Not likely, Quillan thought, by the expression on her face.

"Mrs. Shepard, I do apologize. I had scanty information and jumped to a conclusion I should never have drawn. I was desperate and thought to provoke you to reveal something—anything— I could use."

Quillan wasn't sure what conclusion Pierce had drawn, but he had certainly provoked Carina, though she had yet to tell him what specifically precipitated her kick. It was obviously scurrilous. Carina crossed her arms, jaw tight and eyes like molten jet.

"Well, then." Pierce turned back to Quillan. "I'll leave you to decide." He started for the door.

"Pierce." Quillan's tone was sharp.

Mr. Pierce turned.

"The journal."

Roderick Pierce drew a breath and released it, then laid the journal atop the check. "Truly, Quillan, you have words that should be heard. It's wrong to hoard them."

Quillan met his frank stare, unsure how to take those last words. Wrong, to keep his private thoughts to himself? Mr. Pierce gave a short nod and walked out.

"Oh!" Carina shook her fists. "He makes me want to—"

"Kick?"

She spun on him. "And you can sit there and smirk?"

Quillan squelched a smile. "What exactly did Mr. Pierce say to you?"

"He wanted to know if my 'lover' had caused your accident."

As soon as the words were out, she seemed to want them back.

Quillan flinched even though he'd done everything he could to keep the truth from her.

She rushed to the couch and dropped down beside him. "Why didn't you tell me?"

"There's nothing to tell."

She caught his hands in hers. "I know Flavio did this. He admitted it."

Quillan raised his brows in surprise. He couldn't believe the man would actually brag on it. Not after—

"Why did you protect him?" Though he looked away, she persisted. "Did you think I wanted that?"

"No." He unfolded his arms, dropped them to his sides.

"Then why?"

Quillan turned back to her. How could he make her see? The harm Flavio had done him mattered less than it might. He was used to the worst in people. But in those moments, knowing he was hopelessly trapped, that fire would consume him as it had his parents, as the worst of his nightmares of melting flesh and charred bones . . . From the extremity of his pain and terror, Flavio had freed him. "Because he could have let me die . . . and didn't."

"Oh, Quillan." Carina pressed in close to his chest, nestling her head beneath his chin.

He wrapped an arm around her, then the other. She understood. She knew his demons. She had brought them out of his own personal darkness and suffered them with him. Rose's diary had brought her tears; Wolf's pictures had broken her heart. But it was to the burned-out cabin she had returned again and again, imagining their final agony. She must know what Flavio had saved him from.

She drew a jagged breath. "He hates himself. I found him with a rope tied into a hangman's noose."

Quillan turned her face up to see the truth. It was there in her eyes. "Why?"

"Because of what he did. What he is."

Quillan looked down at his leg, the leg that might never hold him again. He felt the residual pain in his weakened body. The weeks of helplessness and humiliation, being fed and shaved and bathed while his own hands were bound to his chest. All Flavio's doing. He closed his eyes, fighting the satisfaction of the man's torment.

But it was wrong. He'd spent enough years believing himself a flawed man. He would not wish it even on Flavio. And only he could change it.

"Would he come here if you asked?"

Her face came up as he'd known it would, in wonder and confusion. "I don't know."

He forced his voice to obey his will. "Ask."

She started to straighten.

"Not"—he pulled her close again—"just now." He sank his fingers into her hair. It was a little thing to have his hands back, but it felt immense.

———

Past the amazed stares of Tony, Joseph, and Mamma, Carina led Flavio through the house to the shuttered porch where Quillan waited. She was uncertain even now what her husband intended, though Flavio had asked at once, "Does he mean to accuse me?"

And she had met his gaze. "What if he does?"

Flavio had fought an inner battle that flashed across his face, but he had come. He asked no more questions as they rode together to Papa's house, though his expression had darkened and ebbed by turns as he no doubt pondered the outcome of it all. Now he looked both desperate and resentful. But his inner fiber, the worthy core Carina hoped was still part of him, had brought him to face the man he had wronged.

She pushed open the door. "Quillan, Flavio is here."

Quillan looked up from the couch. He set down Henry Gray's *Anatomy of the Human Body.* She could tell by the sweat on his brow he had not been reading, but rather using it to strengthen his arms; Papa would be irked. Quillan nodded. "Let him in."

She motioned Flavio into the room, then positioned herself beside the bookshelf. The moment Flavio entered she could feel their tension. Flavio might be ashamed of his deed, but he was still Flavio, mercurial and proud. They squared off, both defensive. Though Quillan had asked and Flavio come, had either anticipated the difficulty of coming face to face after such an act?

"I'm sorry I don't have a chair." Quillan indicated the sparse appointments.

Flavio said nothing, but he glanced at Quillan's leg in the cast and lost some of his defiance. "What do you want?"

Quillan seemed to be fighting for his next words. Carina wanted to rush in to his defense, to make Flavio see what he had done, the suffering he had caused. She wanted him to know her husband, who had once been so strong, but now strained to lift a book, to make a fist, to sit up by himself.

Quillan's gaze was steady. "I want to thank you for getting me out."

Carina's whole attention went to Quillan. What had she expected? Accusation, threats, demands. But gratitude?

Flavio glared. "What do you mean?"

Quillan dampened his lips. The tendon in his cheek pulled taut beneath the skin. Could Flavio see the effort Quillan made? He said, "My parents burned to death. It's been my terror all my life."

Carina stared at her husband as though she had never seen him. In truth she *had* never seen him so real. She knew the truth, his inner anguish, his parents' suffering and the fear it had caused Quillan. But to admit such a thing to Flavio? Who tried to kill him? Who might have succeeded.

"I . . ." Flavio turned away.

"I don't know how you got that wagon up. But I'm grateful."

The wagon that had burned up all their wealth, all Quillan's work, that had burned because of Flavio. Yes, she had been thankful for the loss, if it kept Quillan from wandering, but Flavio's hatred and jealousy had almost cost her husband his life. She fought to restrain her anger in the face of Quillan's resolve. Whatever he was doing, she must not interfere.

Flavio's hands tightened into fists, the veins rising blue, knuckles white. Carina held her breath. How would he respond? He could not have guessed this was what Quillan brought him here to say. Did he realize what it cost Quillan to reveal a weakness, a fear? To admit his helplessness to the man who had caused it?

She saw Flavio's confusion. Quillan's word could bring an end to his world. It would not hang him, but he would surely go to jail, and for a man of Flavio's temperament, that was worse than a rope. Yet here was Quillan, expressing gratitude. What could Flavio say? "Prego, my friend—I'm glad I could help"?

Quillan didn't give him a chance. His face hardened, not angry or fierce, but so compelling she felt the force. He held Flavio's eyes just as he so frequently held hers, unable to retreat. His voice stayed low, but still commanded. "I want this over now. I have no grudge with you." They were words of peace, yet they offered no compromise.

Flavio looked at Carina with eyes she had known as long as she could remember. She saw hurt and confusion, but also, faintly, relief. She longed for him to let his anger go, to be done with hating. And then it seemed he was. There was a freshness to his face, the softened lines of hope. Her own anger evaporated as he turned back to Quillan, nodding. "It's over."

It was as though a barrier broke inside Flavio, and Carina imagined peace pouring in. Her heart jumped with gratitude for Quillan's integrity and courage. Quillan held up his hand, shaking slightly with the weakness in the muscle. Slowly, Flavio grasped it, hand to wrist like a brother. One moment they clung, then he left without another look.

Flavio left the house confused, yet less confused than he'd been since Carina's return to Sonoma. Riding over, his stomach had knotted, not just in pondering Quillan Shepard's motives, but in seeing him at all after the last broken and bloody sight. Damage there was, but also strength of a sort Flavio did not understand.

The grip of his hand, shaking as it was, had transmitted a terrible peace, and Flavio imagined it as Moses' hand or some other chosen tool of Il Padre Eterno. Or Cristo himself. *"I have no grudge with you."* How could he say that after what he'd suffered? To call him there and thank him ...

Flavio swallowed. Was it any wonder Carina's heart was lost? There was pain in that thought, but he couldn't fault her. The fault was his, but even that didn't bring him to the black place. It seemed sealed off, and other parts of his mind beckoned, parts he hadn't probed in too long. What power had Quillan's grasp unleashed?

He sighed, passing through the gate to the barn where he had left his horse, but Angelo DiGratia stood outside it. Flavio stopped before him. He hadn't known what he would feel looking into that face again, but he looked now. "You know what I did?"

Angelo dropped his chin, but not his gaze. "Both of us know the worst."

It was true. There were no secrets between them, only guilt. Ti'Angelo had let his papa die; Flavio had tried to kill a man. Yet the one who could have brought Flavio to justice had released him. His papa could not release the doctor. But he could.

At the same moment, they gripped each other's upper arms and held on. Though they did know the worst of each other, there was no animosity left in Flavio for this man he loved, nor the man's daughter, he realized, though there was the pain of loss. The grip of her husband's hand had sealed her from his heart, yet there was no animosity left for Quillan Shepard, either. The terrible strain that had been tearing him apart was gone.

"You've made your peace?" Angelo DiGratia spoke softly as the night descended around them.

Flavio nodded. "I've made my peace." The night felt fresh and new, the air rich with moisture and the scent of the barn.

Ti'Angelo's grip tightened. *"Dio vi benedica."* God bless you. He kissed Flavio on both cheeks. It was both welcome and farewell. Though nothing would be the same, they were healed.

"And you, Ti'Angelo." He kissed the doctor willingly, then took his horse and rode home, not to the house where his parents slept, but to his studio. A canvas stood on the easel, but no paint had touched it. His hand and mind had been paralyzed, though he had sat hour by hour trying to put his skill to it.

Now he mixed his paints and took up his brush. Through the night he worked, forming arches and pools, olive trees and strips of cloud. But in the foreground it was Gesù Cristo, untouched yet by whip and thorns, reaching down to a man on a litter and forgiving his sins.

Twenty-seven

Forgiven, forgotten, the sins once held tight.
Surrender may render one stripped of one's right.
But the chalice of malice one drinks quid pro quo,
is purged of its scourge when we mercy may show.

— *Quillan*

QUILLAN CLENCHED HIS JAW in frustration. For two weeks Carina had read him a letter a day. First Joe Turner, opining his fear that the mineshaft named for Carina would stop producing simply because they had run into some bad rock. Her absence, he was certain, would bring the end to his good luck, and couldn't she consider returning to Crystal? Carina had written back her assurance that the mine was safe and would produce as long as God willed, but no, she was home now and would stay.

Then there was Mae's, filled with the happenings of a town Quillan no longer had time for, men finding fortunes where his had been washed away, earned again, then carried across the country to be burned. He had smugly believed the money had no hold on him since he refused to depend on it. Now he knew that without it he was trapped. And how was he supposed to restore it as an invalid?

Èmie's letter had brought Carina to tears. Stories of the miners she served at Carina's restaurant and of the girls who served with her, and news of the baby she would bear in the fall. Quillan had held Carina close, let her tears soak his shirt, and kissed away her protests that she didn't know why she cried. He knew.

There were other letters from names he hardly knew. One man admitted Joe Turner had offered to pay postage for anyone who wanted to send Carina a letter. She laughed when she read those, describing the men who had come to her Sunday dinners. This one had lost an eye in a drilling accident, that one had seventeen children. How had she come to know so many and care enough to glow when she read their awkward scrawls?

She answered each letter after sharing it with him, but refused to read more than one a day. He suspected it was to help him pass the time that now dragged like overloaded wagons with square wheels. It was her little ritual, and some days it did help.

But today's letter put him in a particularly difficult mood. Carina had paused when she pulled Alex Makepeace's letter at random from the stack. Did she debate sharing it before she knew what it held? But she slit the envelope and spread the sheets across her lap where she sat at the end of the couch beside his useless leg.

"It's from Alex, Quillan. To us."

But he had already seen the address, and his name was not on it.

" 'Dear Carina,' " she faltered, then went on. " 'The cave we found has proved a great venture. Many people come long ways to tour the limestone cavern. I have attached torch holders to the walls in some places to enable the tours better safety and allow its grandeur to be seen. The stalactites and stalagmites are magnificent in the light. The flowstone on the walls glimmers with greens and browns and streaks of white. I have identified all the minerals, but people don't seem interested in all that. They do listen to how the cave was formed and seem inclined to remember that much at least. Not many aspire to geological greatness, I fear.' "

Carina smiled. "Poor Alex. He was always more interested in the makeup of the cave than I." She glanced up, and Quillan forced an even countenance.

She read on, " 'I do include some of the side tunnels in the tours and take people into the crystal chamber. Do you remember you thought it was like the center of a geode?' " Carina paused, no doubt recalling her time with Alex in some fairyland cavern.

Quillan caught his hostile thoughts and forced them to submit. Had he learned nothing? Where was the benevolence he had shown to Flavio, the peace it had brought his own heart?

" 'Tell your husband the painted chamber is sealed off and safe from discovery. It was hard going, but we made it look like a natural slide, and no one so far has suspected. Probably because they do not know enough about the formation of caves to detect the anomaly of weathered outside rock in a limestone cavern.' " There Carina smiled.

Quillan relaxed. Alex had kept his word, and he had to appreciate that much. But he tensed again when she read the next part.

" Èmie's cooking is reminiscent of your own, and I dine thankfully every night, though things are not the same without you. Give your husband my regards. I am indebted to him for my continued position and partial possession of a very successful mine. My regards to you, as well, Carina. Sincerely, Alex Makepeace.' "

Quillan smiled grimly at the irony. Alex Makepeace was growing rich on the mine Quillan had provided him, while he sat disabled and penniless. But when he looked into Carina's face, he knew which of them had come out the richer. "What are you going to answer back?"

She waved the pages. "I'll send my condolences that no one appreciates the mineral content of the flowstone."

Quillan reached for her hand and held it a long moment. "Thank him for sealing off Wolf's chamber."

"I will." She kissed his fingers and stood. "Shall I say anything else?"

He fought a quick battle and won. "Whatever you want, Carina."

Still, he felt stark when she left. He looked down at the casted leg. Would the cast ever come off? And what would remain when it did? He had expected some acknowledgment of improvement. But Dr. DiGratia remained grave and resisted questioning. The leg must be as bad as he imagined.

Quillan picked up Cain's Bible and considered the verse he had made his own, the verse that assured him of God's provision if he remained in him. But how could he remain in God alone when he was so helpless he had to depend on others, as well? He laid aside the Bible and shifted his position on the couch. His backside had never complained so much on the hard box of his wagon as it did now on this couch.

He swung his left leg over the side, easing the casted mate to the edge. Should he try to stand? Even his good leg would atrophy if it sat there much longer. He put his weight on it and raised himself slightly. It suddenly felt like he'd stepped on an anthill. He jerked it up and waited while the blood infused his left foot, but his arms lacked the strength yet to get him up with one leg totally useless and the other half asleep.

He settled back onto the couch. *God, what do you want from me?* He had gone over the words of that verse so many times. He had felt so sure that God wanted him to relinquish every desire for human acceptance, to find his worth in Jesus alone. And he had done so, even if it meant he would lose Carina, as well. On his knees he had surrendered all hope of human attachment. Then God—reversing Himself?—had rendered him completely dependent.

"Maybe you must surrender your independence." Carina's words nagged him as badly as the Lord's had. He would have died without Dr. DiGratia's skills, without the constant care of Carina and her brother, even the broth prepared by her mother. What could Quillan have done for himself? For a time he couldn't even raise a spoon to his mouth, couldn't wash himself.

Now he had use of his arms. He could raise himself, albeit painfully; he could stamp the blood back into his left foot, but he couldn't stand. Not without help. And he couldn't work. His independence was lost. Quillan squirmed. *Anything but that, Lord!* It was asking too much. God's knife had slipped, cut away too much. This branch was too tender to bear it.

Quillan looked at Cain's Bible, as much at odds with it as he'd sometimes been with Cain himself. The words were fixed in his memory, but he didn't understand. Why would God make him surrender his hope of family and acceptance, then make him helpless? The frustration grew until he scowled.

He shook his head, unwilling to think anymore. He needed a distraction, something to chase Carina's words and God's from his mind. In times like this he rued the gift of memory. He picked up the treatise Carina had brought him to practice his Italian. Giuseppe Mazzini's *The Duties of Man.*

Just the thing. He would understand more of that than God's word. Quillan reached for the book and flipped it open to the place he'd marked earlier with a slip of paper. He stared at the foreign words, ciphering them piece by piece and trying to fit them back into a form he recognized.

La famiglia è un paese d'il cuore. The family is a country?—of . . . something. Quillan frowned. His mind was obviously not operating at its best.

Dr. DiGratia came into the room with his usual flicking glance before he used his hands. Had he ever been touched so much in his life? Quillan suffered the back of the man's hand briefly against his forehead, his fingers probing the soft tissue beneath his jaw, the quick grip of that jaw as his face was raised and the sharp momentary scrutiny of his eyes. As usual, Dr. DiGratia said nothing about what he looked for or saw, but Quillan had learned to read his expression. He wasn't dying today, he assumed.

"Open your shirt."

Quillan tucked the paper slip into the page, set the book beside him, and unbuttoned his shirt.

Dr. DiGratia probed his abdomen, which hurt most when encouraged by the doctor's fingers. Then he worked the same magic on Quillan's ribs. Though he winced, Quillan could tell they were healing.

"Very good." A surprising accolade. "Vittorio."

His son came in carrying a pail of river rocks. He set it by the wall and joined his father at the couch.

"Planning to stone me?" Quillan's wry humor earned him the older man's glance.

"I brought you something to use instead of my books." He removed several rocks from the pail, placing them on the floor, then lifted the pail to the bed, holding the handle up.

Quillan caught his meaning and gripped the handle. The weight of the rocks was as much as he could lift left-handed, and it sent an ache through the collarbone. He crossed his right arm over his body and tried it with that one. Again a pain in the bone that had broken, and he could hardly raise it.

"You can adjust the number of rocks."

Quillan realized the benefit to that; much better than trying to raise an ungainly stack of books. "Thank you."

Dr. DiGratia pointed to the book at his side. "That will do you no more good. It's in Italiano."

"I know."

"I'll return it to the shelf." He held out his hand.

Quillan rested his palm atop the book. "If you don't mind, I'll muddle through it still."

The doctor raised his brows. "You are reading Italian?"

"Somewhat." Quillan felt defensive. Would the doctor tell him he had no right to their language, to understand their culture and beliefs?

"Giuseppe Mazzini"—he pronounced it *Matzini*—"was a visionary for the unification of Italy. But he was a republican. Unlike Garibaldi, he did not want the nation unified under a king." The doctor shrugged. "His writings are very powerful. May I?" Dr. DiGratia lifted the book.

He opened to the page Quillan had marked and translated: " 'The family is a country of the heart. There is an angel in the family who, by the mysterious influence of grace, of sweetness, and of love, renders the fulfillment of duties less wearisome, sorrows less bitter.' "

Quillan pictured Carina, and in her all of that: grace, sweetness, love. It did render life less bitter. But he suspected the writing didn't refer to one individual, but an entity created by the whole, the family.

The doctor read on. " 'The only pure joys unmixed with sadness which it is given to man to taste upon earth are, thanks to this angel, the joys of the family.' "

As the doctor read, Quillan felt his spirit shrink. That was what Carina knew, what she valued, what she tried to give to him. But was it what God intended? He felt the doctor's eyes on him, but couldn't meet them, to see there the exclusion he thought didn't matter. But it did. Hearing those words made him realize it did. Was God torturing him?

Dr. DiGratia set the book on the table. "Vittorio, the saw."

Quillan looked up sharply. A saw could mean only one thing. Vittorio brought it, and Dr. DiGratia began cutting the cast from Quillan's leg. Quillan watched with trepidation. What would he see when the plaster came off? A mangled piece of meat, no longer useful? A weight to be dragged along with a crutch?

The plaster peeled off like the bark of a log. The flesh inside was like hairy chicken skin. A jagged scar rose red and angry along the thigh, which was thinner by half what it had been. Quillan moved his toes and felt the awful flexing of what muscle remained. Dr. DiGratia felt the thigh deeply, and Quillan shrank as much from the unaccustomed sensation of touch there as from pain.

"Why do you want to know Italian when in America Italians learn English?"

Quillan tore his eyes from his leg. Was the doctor trying to distract him? "Carina speaks Italian."

"Carina speaks five languages." The doctor raised Quillan's leg at the knee, feeling the break just above it.

That was the worse of the two, Quillan could tell. It hurt as the doctor rotated the leg between his palms, studying his work. He flinched at the hands on his skin, the motion of a leg unused to motion, the bending joint, stiff and sore, and most of all, the flaccid muscle. He forced himself to respond to the doctor's last remark. "Italian is the language of her heart." He met the doctor's glance.

"Take his arm, Vittorio." Dr. DiGratia swung Quillan's right leg to the floor.

His waxy yellow foot turned red, and Quillan hissed his breath sharply between his teeth at the shooting pain and maddening tingle. Vittorio caught him by one arm, the doctor by the other. Quillan resisted. He didn't want to try the leg and fail. *The worst is the leg will not bear your weight.* Fear seized him.

The doctor spread his hand between Quillan's shoulder blades with a soothing warmth. Quillan tried unsuccessfully to release the knotted muscles, to hide the binding tension of that fear. He felt ashamed and at the same time protected. If he never stood, he'd never know, never face life as a one-legged man.

Again he thought of Cain, saw the useless stump of a leg. *"Sometimes in the night when the ghost pains come, I wish it had blown the rest of me up, too. Never thought I'd clobber about on a wood peg. But God knows best."* Quillan had doubted it then, and for all his efforts at faith, he doubted it now.

The doctor said, "I think we should work the muscles first."

Quillan's tension eased. Any reprieve was welcome, even though he knew the muscle would be sore and weak. The doctor reached for the pail and set it on the floor beside Quillan's foot. Quillan stared at the rocks inside the galvanized pail while the doctor wrapped the handle with a cloth.

Vittorio let go Quillan's left arm, probably confused by the abrupt change of plans. He hadn't sensed what Carina's father had sensed, the fear and resistance. The doctor had not missed it, though, and responded as a . . . a father might, with compassion and understanding. Quillan looked down at the graying head of the man lifting the handle of the pail over the foot and ankle of his right leg.

But Dr. DiGratia did not look up. "Try to lift," he said.

Quillan hesitated. Would the bone snap with the effort? Jaw tight, he focused on his leg and tried to lift the pail. It came briefly off the floor, then clamored back down. The doctor removed several stones. "Again."

Quillan tensed the thigh and raised the pail a short distance, then dropped it noisily to the floor. Dr. DiGratia reached up and felt the bone above the knee. Quillan's muscle shook under the doctor's fingers. "Again." The fingers bore deeply into the thigh as Quillan raised the pail, sweat beading on his forehead at such a small effort. "Leave us, Vittorio."

Quillan's breath seized as he dropped the pail. Why did he send his son out? To tell Quillan he was a cripple? The doctor eased Quillan's foot out of the handle and set it on the floor. He looked up into Quillan's face. "Your fear will hold you back."

Quillan swallowed. "I don't want to be less than whole."

"I believe," the doctor said, "the bone has knit well. Shall we try again, we two?"

Something in the way he said the word *two*, linking them together, made Quillan want to try. He sensed the doctor's vested concern. It was important to him. He had worked hard for this moment. Quillan gathered the ragged edges of his will and nodded.

The doctor stood slowly, taking Quillan's arm over his shoulders. Quillan forced his muscles to respond and came up standing, though most of his weight was on the doctor.

"Shift to your right."

Carefully, gingerly, Quillan allowed his right leg to take some of the burden. Pain, but not unbearable. Little strength, but no snapping or splintering of bone. The thigh looked slightly crooked as Quillan looked at it. But that could be the wasted muscle and the scar.

The doctor eased out from under his arm, keeping hold of the small of Quillan's back. "It bears your weight."

Quillan nodded, though the leg had started to shake uncontrollably.

"Sit now." Dr. DiGratia eased him down.

Quillan was amazed by the gentleness of his aid. What brought it now, after their constant brusque sparring? Again the doctor's fingers were on his thigh probing deeply to the bone. Quillan grimaced.

The doctor flicked him a glance. "Painful?"

Quillan glared. What did the man think?

Angelo DiGratia laughed softly. "You and I do not have an easy time between us, eh?"

"It might be easier without the poking and prying."

"Ah." The doctor smiled, deep lines forming between the sides of his nose and his chin. Quillan couldn't recall seeing the man's smile before.

"Then I would not do my duty."

His duty. Was that it? Had he imagined the unity of purpose, of concern? Quillan looked away.

"To my son."

The words jolted through him like lightning. Had he heard right? He looked back at Carina's father, found a look of begrudged affection.

"I don't excuse what you did. But—" he stood—"maybe . . ." He spread his hands like Carina. "Because I have worked so hard to mend you, it makes a bond . . . like family."

Quillan's chest tightened painfully. Had he misunderstood, used God's words to support his own resistance? Was it harder to bear their acceptance than their rejection? "Dr. DiGratia—"

"I think . . . it must be Papa DiGratia."

Papa. Quillan gripped the edge of the couch. *Lord?* Was it allowed him? *If ye abide in me, and my words abide in you, ye shall ask what ye will, and it shall be done unto you.* Ask now, and it would be done. Which did he want? His fierce independence or that sweetness of which the author Mazzini spoke?

The doctor held out his hand. "We will make our peace as you did with Flavio?"

Throat taut, Quillan took his hand.

The doctor, his . . . papa . . . leaned down and kissed both his cheeks. The oddness of it was washed away by the sheer wonder. "You said to judge you by yourself."

Quillan remembered. It had been brash and defiant of him.

Papa DiGratia gripped his forearms. "I have done so."

Their eyes met in mutual esteem. For the first time since Carina, Quillan felt that someone had seen him as he was—not perfect, but neither more nor less flawed than the next man—and accepted him as such. "Thank you."

Papa DiGratia released his arms. He began gathering up his books, Gray's *Anatomy* and other heavy tomes Quillan had no better use for than to work his muscles. He started for the door, then stopped, looked over his shoulder. "You don't need to learn Italian. You already speak the language of Carina's heart."

Twenty-eight

What jaunts the path of life does make, what least the heart foresees,
Beware oh careless traveler of life's tempestuous seas,
Lest path should turn and waves rise up,
and you be blown upon life's breeze.

— *Quillan*

AT THE SOUND of raucous male voices, Carina headed for Quillan's porch. He had to be there, but she could not see him with all her brothers crowded in. Joseph was nearest her, and she tapped his arm. "What is it? What's going on?"

"Nothing to worry you." He held his position.

"*Uno . . . due . . .*"

She tried to press past him and see what they were counting, but Tony's back prevented her. She nudged his shoulder. "What are you doing?"

Tony half turned. "Don't push. There's no room."

Angelo's voice rose up. "You can't do better than that? Carina could swing as well." Laughter from them all.

She could not hear Quillan's answer over her brothers' laughter. What were they up to? She pushed Tony again. "Let me in. What's going on?"

Tony spoke over his shoulder. "We're just helping."

Helping? She rose to tiptoes and caught a glimpse of Vittorio waving Angelo back.

"Give him a moment." He held an arm up toward Lorenzo, as well.

369

"Tired, eh?" Angelo swung playfully, and Quillan, sitting on a stool in the middle of the room, blocked it. Her brother swung again with his left arm and caught Quillan in the shoulder. Quillan grabbed his wrist and jerked his arm down, but Angelo twisted free, grinning. "*Tre* for you."

Carina frowned. There was a time Quillan could have taken Angelo to the floor with no effort at all. Lorenzo feinted toward him, and again Quillan blocked the blow. Two on one, it wasn't fair.

"Stop it." Carina pushed between Tony and Joseph and into the space around Quillan, where Angelo and Lorenzo both danced in and out aiming slaps and pokes. "What do you think you're doing?" She glared at Vittorio, who certainly should have known better after all the time he'd spent nursing Quillan.

He gave her a level glance. "Don't get your hackles up. We're training his reflexes. Building his nerves back."

Angelo swung his palm and smacked Quillan's right arm. Quillan's eyes stormed, but he warned Carina off with a glance. She put her hands to her hips and glared at Vittorio. "How is this helping?"

"He needs to use his arms." Vittorio crossed his own over his chest.

"He does use them. He lifts the pail."

"This is different. Instant motion forces the mind to talk to the arm, and the arm to respond."

Lorenzo moved swiftly and poked Quillan's chest. He darted again, but Quillan smacked him away. At the same time, he blocked Angelo's swing.

Tony caught her arm. "Stop interfering. They're not hurting him."

Angelo flicked the back of Quillan's head, grunting when Quillan elbowed his chest hard. "*Quattro.* That was four." But even as he spoke, he swung again. "Against my twenty."

Quillan caught Angelo's shirt and pulled him close. "You keep score now; I'll settle it later."

"Is that a threat?"

Quillan cocked his head. "A reminder. Once my arms are back . . ."

Lorenzo slapped from the left and caught Quillan above the elbow. Quillan twisted and landed a jab in Lorenzo's belly. Lorenzo staggered into the bookcase and caught his breath with a gasp. Tony and Joseph cheered. "*Cinque!* Five hits."

"You see?" Angelo turned on her. "He doesn't need you. Go stitch some lace."

Carina raised her chin. "I will not." She pressed in toward Quillan's side. "Go aw—" But before she could finish, Angelo bent and caught her up over his shoulder. She pounded his back, but her brothers parted for his exit far more easily than they had for her entrance.

He deposited her in the hall, caught her jaw with his palm, and grinned. "Stay out of it, Carina." Then he kissed her cheek and went back into the porch room.

Fists at her sides, she started to force her way back in, though she knew they'd be more difficult yet.

"Carina." Tia Marta spoke from the end of the hall. "Come dye this thread with me."

Carina turned. "Do you know what they're doing?"

Her aunt nodded. "They're welcoming your husband to the family."

"Welcoming!" Carina planted her hands on her hips.

"You know how it is, Carina. Have you been away so long?" Marta clicked her tongue. "It is a passage. They would not bother if he didn't matter. And it will help him heal."

"Not if he's bruised all over again."

Tia Marta took her arm and led her away from the porch where a fresh wave of cheering rose up, no telling for whom. "They won't hurt him. Your papa told them not to."

"Papa knows what they're doing?"

Tia Marta wrapped her in one plump arm. "Shall we make it red to embroider roses or blue for grapes?" Tia always dyed her own threads from quercitron bark, madder root, indigo, or a dozen other plant parts she had collected from different parts of the world.

But Carina did not care at the moment. She stomped her foot and stalled. "What are they trying to prove? That they can overpower an injured man?"

Marta caught her shoulders and stared into her face. "They're not proving anything. They're letting your Quillan prove himself."

Carina shook her head. "He doesn't need to prove himself. He—"

Tia Marta put fingers to Carina's mouth. "You show your youth, Carina. Every man needs to prove himself. And you were not helping."

"Beh." Carina flicked her fingers beneath her chin. "Quillan's not like them."

Tia Marta laughed. "You'll see. He'll sleep peacefully tonight, and tomorrow things will be different."

"How?"

"He will have the fight inside." Tia Marta tapped her temple.

"The fight?"

"To get strong again and show your brothers."

Carina let her breath out in a huff, then realized it wasn't far from what she'd heard Quillan say himself, warning Angelo not to push him too far. Was it possible they did him a service? He'd been discouraged since the cast came off his leg. He had yet to walk on it, and the weakened condition of his arms worried him, she knew.

She glanced back in the direction of the porch. She could hardly hear them now, and she had to admit that their behavior hadn't been malicious. Taunting and jeering wouldn't hurt Quillan; he was stronger than that. And they were slapping and poking only. But how would Quillan take their affronts to his person? The storm had been there in his eyes, but it was frequently there. Maybe, as Tia Marta said, he would sleep tonight, knowing he had to get strong.

She shook her head. She did not understand her brothers, nor even Quillan sometimes. Men were different, and maybe she should listen to a wiser woman than herself. But as soon as they were finished dying the woolen thread a deep indigo blue, she left Tia Marta and hurried back to Quillan. Hearing voices still, she stopped outside the door. She could only see Tony, seated on an overturned pail.

"Did the horse get up again?"

Quillan's voice held emotion. "Died on the spot. Had to be cut loose and rolled over the side. I told that driver if he ever strained a beast on that pass again he'd be the one rolled over the side."

"Did you ever lose a horse yourself?"

A pause. "A few. Two in a flood, and one to avalanche."

"Avalanche." Tony spread his hands. "Snow?"

Would Quillan talk about Jack? Carina leaned into the wall beside the door.

"Avalanche."

Tony shook his head. "That would be something to see."

"I don't think Jack felt that way. He died beneath his twin. I was trapped and couldn't get to them."

Carina turned her back to the wall, fingers resting on her lips. Tony was not just being civil. He and Quillan were really talking. She didn't know where the others were, but for now they had finished their sport.

"You were trapped by the avalanche?"

"Buried in a mine. I would have burrowed out if it were only me, searched for my horses at once. But I had Carina and another to think of."

Carina sagged. Would he have burrowed into twenty feet of chunks and powder to save his team? He could not have made it but would have died trying. Thankfully he had her and Father Antoine to think of.

"How did you get out?"

"Built a tower. Father Charboneau down on all fours, I stood on his back, and Carina stood on my shoulders."

Tony laughed. "She has always been a tiger. *Piccola* tigre. She is small but tenacious." Then he paused. "Wasn't she afraid of the height?"

Carina peeked around to see Tony leaning forward earnestly. "She has been afraid of heights ever since she fell from the roof."

"Doesn't stop her," Quillan said. "She crawled down a deadly slope to retrieve her things, even though the sight over the edge would send a grown man shaking."

"What things?" Tony spread his hands.

"Things I'd toppled over the side with her wagon."

Tony sat silent, not comprehending. "You sent her wagon over the side of the pass? Like the horse?"

"Biggest mistake of my life." Carina could hear Quillan's rogue smile. And that was enough eavesdropping.

She stalked into the room. "He wanted the road cleared for his own mighty wagon, and my little broken one was in the way."

"Talk about hell to pay." Quillan reached out and circled Carina's waist, pulling her close.

Tony laughed. "You don't have to tell me. I grew up with her." He rubbed his shin.

Quillan laughed. "More than one man's experienced that, but not I. Yet."

Carina sent him a blazing glare. "I wouldn't dream of kicking my husband. Only my brothers." She swung a playful kick Tony's way.

"And irksome reporters." Quillan's grin broadened.

Now she wished she hadn't walked in. But Quillan tugged her down to sit beside him on the couch, arm still around her waist. His strength seemed improved already. Even if the others had bullied, their intentions had been good. And Tony had stayed to talk with Quillan. Carina's heart warmed. Surely he would see their efforts and want to stay.

Tony crossed his wrists over one knee. "So how in the world did you break her?"

Quillan's arm tightened. "Oh, no trouble there. She prefers rogue pirates to natty scoundrels."

"He saved me from an unsavory cad."

"Tell me."

Sitting beside him, Carina learned more about Quillan's dealings with Mr. Beck than she had known. She interjected some details Quillan had not heard, as well. Together, their story amazed Tony, whose admiration for Quillan was evident.

"I knew you hadn't married him to spite Flavio."

Carina thought back to those tumultuous days in Crystal, Berkley Beck's advances, and Quillan's insults. She could hardly believe herself that things had happened as they had. Quillan must have sensed her thoughts, for his hand on her side spread protectively.

She settled against him, smiling at Tony. "So you see why all of you and Papa could not keep us apart."

"I saw that from the start." Tony spread his hands. "But there was Flavio."

"That's settled now." Quillan's voice was even.

"A man of war and a man of peace." Tony turned to her. "You've chosen well, baby sister."

That, she knew already.

Quillan's leg shook as he lowered the pail to the floor, this time controlling its descent. He grunted his relief of the burning in his thigh.

Vittorio nodded. "Buono." He slipped the pail handle off Quillan's ankle. "Now stand."

With one hand on Vittorio's shoulder, Quillan pulled himself up. The leg was holding better each time he tried, though not without support. So much damage took time. But he was determined. Just as his arms were gaining muscle and dexterity—he'd walloped the breath from Angelo that afternoon—so the leg would get strong again, as well.

"And step."

Such a little thing, to lift and place the foot. Yet he had to focus like a baby toddling its first awkward steps. Carina came in, arms crossed over a packet held to her chest. Her eyes shone with encouragement. Quillan stepped.

"All right." Vittorio eased him back down on the couch. "More tomorrow."

"Naturally."

"Missing even one day would set you back."

Quillan had grown accustomed to Vittorio's dry manner. Where Angelo was fiery and blusterous, Lorenzo smoldered, and Joseph jeered, Vittorio was quiet and reserved. Of them all, he preferred Tony's quick laugh and earnest bearing. But in some ways he seemed to have earned their respect, even Vittorio, who like Papa DiGratia, showed little emotion beyond a warming of the eyes and occasional smile.

Vittorio put on his vest and turned to his sister. "He's all yours."

She turned with a warm smile. "I know."

Quillan's heart jumped. As soon as Vittorio was past the threshold, Quillan held out his arms.

She came to him, bent, and kissed his neck. "You stand so well now!"

"You don't do so bad yourself." He pulled her down beside him. "What's this?"

She held out the thick envelope. "It came for you."

He took it and read: " 'Quillan Shepard, care of Angelo DiGratia.' " No return address, but it had been stamped in

Denver. Did all the world know he was in the doctor's care? He frowned.

"Well, open it, Quillan! I'm dying of curiosity."

Quillan turned it over and studied it, musing. "I'd like to see it in private, if you don't mind."

Her mouth dropped open in just the pout he'd expected. "In private? We have no secrets. I read you every one of my letters, even—"

"Alex's?" He chucked her chin, and she thumped him in the chest.

"Yes, even Alex's."

He clicked his tongue. "Well, I'm not sure your emotional nature can withstand this, my dear."

"Oh!" She swiped for the letter, but he jerked it out of her reach. She threw her hands into her lap. "You are a rogue to tease when you know I—"

His mouth crooked up. "You what, Carina?"

"Open the letter, or I'll bring you no supper."

He raised his brows. "And what is Mamma making tonight?"

"Whatever it is, you'll wish you had it." She jerked her chin pointedly. "Now open the letter."

Quillan looked down at it. He'd been joking when he suggested reading it privately. But it did unsettle him. Why no return address? Tucking Carina's head to the side of his jaw, he tore the envelope open and pulled out the papers.

The first was a copy of the train robbery article Pierce had written about him. Maybe it was another attempt by the unwavering rogue to get hold of his poems. But the second was another page from a Wyoming newspaper. That was something different. Quillan looked at the lead article.

Robber cut down by clerk's foresight. Quillan read on. *Notorious bank and train robber Shane Dennison was shot dead Wednesday at the Fort Laramie bank.* Quillan stared at the page. The Fort Laramie bank. He recalled the way his hands had trembled when Dennison had thrown him the bags and told him to run. Was the man insane to try that bank again? He pictured Shane's cocky face. *"No one gets the better of me, Quillan. You stick around long enough, you'll see."* Had that one failure niggled inside until he had to tempt fate once more?

Bank clerk Simon Blessing claims he saw the notorious outlaw in a poker game at the saloon. "I recognized the mole under his lip from the new posters." Certain there could be trouble, he alerted bank owner Thaddeus Marsh. Law officers were ready when Dennison made his move on the bank. Dennison was shot trying to exit the window. Two partners were captured and await trial.

Still leaving his men to take the fall. But this time, Shane hadn't made his escape. He'd found a bullet instead. Quillan read on. "He looked just like his face on the posters," Blessing said. "There was no doubt in my mind it was Dennison."

And it was Quillan's sketch they'd used for the new posters. He'd drawn the mole that clerk recognized. Quillan stared at the page. Carina leaned close. "They got Shane Dennison?"

"Shot him." Quillan swallowed. It was a strange feeling to know he'd helped to bring the man down. Though he'd been willing to shoot during the robbery to protect those aboard the train, he felt only numb now. Dennison deserved the retribution of the law. But he had been the first friend Quillan had, even if he had been a false one.

He looked back at the other papers in his lap. The next was a cashier's check for two hundred dollars. He pushed it aside to read the letter beneath.

My esteemed sir. Quillan had to grin. It would appear my earlier judgments were in error. Earlier judgments? Whose letter was this? He glanced to the bottom of the sheet and froze. William Wallace DeMornay III.

Quillan's breath escaped in a rush. William DeMornay?

"What is it?" Carina took the letter and read, " 'My esteemed sir. It would appear my earlier judgments were in error. You must forgive my skepticism. Men of my position are often targets of unscrupulousness. As an officer of the Union Pacific Railroad, I am honored to present you this portion of the reward for the capture of the notorious Mr. Shane Dennison, the amount being one third divided between yourself, Mr. Simon Blessing, and Mr. Thaddeus Marsh.' " She glanced up, still obviously unaware of who it was that addressed him.

" 'As to your previous claims, my wife has informed me that she believes your story and has legitimate reason for doing so.' " Now her eyes shot to the bottom of the page, and she gasped. "Quillan, it's from your grandfather. He's an officer of the railroad?"

Tabor had mentioned that, but Quillan had forgotten. He might not have been so eager to save the train if he'd remembered. "So it appears."

"But this is remarkable. What fortunate serendipity. He says, 'At some time in the near future, I would like to discuss the matter further with you. Yours very sincerely, William Wallace DeMornay III.'" Carina looked up. "Quillan, he knows. He acknowledges you."

"He knew before."

"You know the railroad barons are criticized and envied. He had to be cautious. It wasn't because of you that he acted as he did. How did he say it?" She perused up the letter. "Men of his position are 'targets of unscrupulousness.' That explains his behavior."

"Does it?" Quillan was not so sure.

Carina flicked her fingers across the page. "He wants to discuss your relationship."

Quillan jerked his chin toward the wall, resisting her words. Here she was again, explaining matters of the heart. But it still stung that William DeMornay had accused him of wanting money instead of listening to his intentions.

She turned his face back, caught it between her palms. "Quillan, your grandfather made a mistake. He admits as much. But that doesn't change the relationship any more than his denial changed the truth."

Quillan sighed and looked down at the last paper in the packet. Another letter in a genteel if spidery hand. *My dear Quillan.* It was from his grandmother. *You must know how deeply we regret our error. Perhaps it will not be easy for you to forgive, but I pray you will not find it impossible. You have your mother's nature.*

Quillan glanced up at Carina. He suddenly missed his mother's locket with a piercing ache. He wanted to see, once again, that sweet face.

I can only beg you understand my hesitance. After so many years of wondering, longing, weeping, and finding at last some thin peace, to resurrect the pain was not easy. For William it was harder yet. He blamed himself for his daughter's ruin. Because he knew the man's reputation, he refused to countenance their courtship request, but Rose was snared by the scoundrel's iniquity. William would have forgiven her, I believe, if given the chance. It broke his heart when she disappeared.

Quillan wrinkled his brow. William DeMornay seemed too cold and stiff for broken hearts. But maybe, like himself, his grandfather built walls to protect against the pain.

Think kindly on him, Quillan. As you have loved your mother, so William loved her first. Never were two so inseparable. Joy died in him the day she left.

A sharp pang lodged in his chest at those words. He'd spent most of his life hating his mother because he misunderstood. How could he blame William for coping as poorly?

Carina cupped his chin and turned his face up. "Are you all right?"

How did she see inside him? His throat tightened painfully. "What am I supposed to do?"

"What does she say?"

He looked back down. " 'Would you permit us to visit? William also extends this request. I pray you will consider it. Yours humbly and sincerely, Annelise DeMornay.' "

"Annelise! Rose was named for her mamma."

Quillan folded the letter.

"And she wants to come visit. Write her back, Quillan. Tell them to come, of course to come."

Quillan sagged. How could he see them now, with his pathetic arms, his crippled leg? He had gone to them strong and independent, and they had called him a thief. How would they look at him now? With pity?

"Quillan." Carina reached into her pocket, then caught his hand and placed her closed fist inside it. When she opened her fingers, something heavy and round rested there. She drew her hand away.

His mother's locket, the front different and the catch, but he knew the weight and shape of it. He looked up, questioning.

"It was damaged in the accident. I had it repaired."

He pushed the release that opened the new front and saw his mother's face. The photo bore one scratch, but the rest was unmarred. He stared into his mother's eyes, remembering their aqua brilliance. The same color as Annelise DeMornay's.

Carina folded both hands behind his neck. "They're Rose's parents, Quillan. And they need you."

He looked from the locket to his wife's face. Did she always have to be right? "So I should let them come."

"You should welcome them."

His mouth pulled sideways. "With something more than grim acceptance."

"Exuberant joy."

He laughed. "Being not overly endowed with exuberance, I'll leave that to you." But he felt suddenly light. Not only had God given him Carina's family, but it seemed he meant to extend it once again. Grandparents. He took a moment to savor the thought. The Lord's abundance amazed him. He had gone from being totally alone to winning Carina, being accepted by her family—though that was still a mixed blessing with her brothers—to having the DeMornays acknowledge him.

He lowered his forehead to Carina's. "Do you suppose he'd foot me a loan for a new wagon?"

Carina punched his chest.

"Ow. I've had my reflex training, thank you." He caught her face and kissed her, then hung the locket around her neck.

"What are you doing?" She pressed the locket to her breast.

"I want you to have it." He stroked back her curtain of hair. "I have nothing else to give you these days."

She caught his face between her hands. "You have yourself." She kissed him back. He had thought she might.

———

Still warm inside from the meal they had all shared around the table, Carina helped Quillan down from the small grape wagon. Ah, what a wonderful time it had been, all gathered together at the long table for Quillan's first meal with the family. They had all been there, her brothers and their wives, Divina and Nicolo, Tia Marta and Gelsomina and Ti'Giuseppe, beaming his bare gums in delight. Quillan had swallowed Mamma's lasagne like a ravening wolf, then held up his goblet when Papa and the others raised theirs.

Papa's voice was strong and sincere. "This wine was made from grapes grown and ripened before phylloxera weakened a single vine on our land. With God's help, we will all grow this strong, mellow this deeply, and warm this well." He had raised the goblet an inch higher to Quillan, sitting alongside her at the table. "Welcome to the family."

Though his arms were stronger now, almost what they'd been,

Carina had noticed the shake of Quillan's goblet as he drank. Now, as she helped him, his muscles tightened and bunched as he eased his weight onto the cane and stepped down. The foot of the cane sank into the soft ground at the edge of the vineyard, the one she had discovered in bud, now burgeoning with green leaves and trailing tendrils. Quillan breathed deeply as he looked out at the scene.

"Do you like it?"

He nodded silently, his larynx working up and down.

"From the edge of this young vineyard, across that field and citrus orchard, up to the top of the hill there." She pointed to the oak-capped hill. "This is the land Papa gives us."

He stood in silence a long time, his eyes absorbing what his mind struggled to take in.

"It's a gift, Quillan. He wants us to have it."

"But I haven't earned it."

"You don't have to." She slipped her hand inside his free one. "It's Papa's gift, Quillan. Only accept it."

He started slowly down between the vines, using the cane to balance.

"Can you manage on the soft ground?"

He nodded. "I can manage. I may never lose the limp, though."

"Eh." She waved her fingers. "What's a pirate without a limp?"

He turned and smiled. "Or a poet?"

Surprised, she stepped up close. "Is that an announcement?"

He shrugged, shifting his weight on the cane. "It's something I could do if . . . until this leg heals."

She knew his concern, but she believed the Lord would and was healing Quillan's leg. Only Papa could have put the bone together as well as he did. Now Quillan's constitution and God's mercy must do the rest.

"But it's more than that." Quillan shook his head. "Carina, since I was first able to connect letters into words, I've read the stories and poems other people have written. Sometimes it kept me sane. Always it gave me something. What if they had all kept their words to themselves? Hoarded them."

She remembered Mr. Pierce's admonition, that it was wrong for Quillan to keep his words to himself. Carina looked into her husband's face. Had he so healed he could share his soul at last?

If that were so, who was she to stop him? She rested her hand atop his on the cane head. "Mr. Pierce will burst like grapes shattering on the vine."

"I think he'll recover." Quillan's mouth torqued to one side.

It would be a strange alliance—fiercely private Quillan and unscrupulous Roderick Pierce. But she sensed a purpose in him, and a peace. "In the meantime, we must decide where to build our villa."

Quillan looked back over the land. "Near the vineyard. I want to see it from every window."

Carina laughed. "We'll have to put it in the middle, then."

He nodded. "Jesus said He's the vine and I'm the branch. I thought it meant I could only have Him, that all else must be cut away. But look, Carina." He pointed out over the field. "How every branch reaches across to another, so tangled I can't say where one ends and the next begins."

She wove her fingers between his. "The blooms of one vine bring fruit to another." She touched her belly, almost tempted to increase his wonder. But she would wait, savoring the knowledge that like this field resisting the pestilence, the night they'd spent together in the midst of all the trouble would bear fruit. How had Ti'Giuseppe known? But she would save it for another moment, when there was room in Quillan for more. *Ah, Signore, you work all things for our good, because we love you!*

Acknowledgments

Thanks to members of the Historical Society of Sonoma
who helped me research their town.
Special thanks to Robert Parmalee and Michelle Kazeminejad
for their time and information.
My thanks also to Sarah Long and Bethany House Publishers.

*Not to us, O Lord, Not to us but to your name give
glory because of your kindness, because of your truth.*

PSALM 115:1 NASB

CAPTIVATING TALES FROM AN UNFORGETTABLE ERA

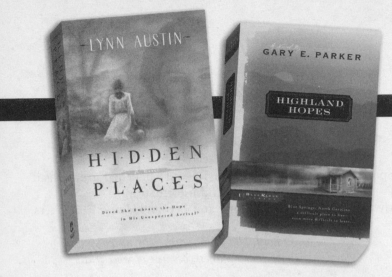

CAN GOD TURN HER TEARS INTO LAUGHTER?

Hidden Places is a spellbinding story of how one woman's prayers are answered in the most unlikely of ways. Eliza Wyatt, a widowed mother of three, asked God for an angel to help keep her family alive. She is desperately struggling to run the family orchard as the country around her plunges into economic ruin. But when a stranger in need and a crazy widow are the only answers she receives, Eliza thinks God may not be listening. Are these strangers really the answer to her prayers?

Hidden Places by Lynn Austin

A STORY OF TRIALS, TRIUMPHS, AND FAMILY TIES SURPASSING THEM ALL

"Blue Ridge folks keep their tales in their minds...folded up like a stack of quilts—just waiting for the time when they can pull them out and spread them open." This is exactly what Abigail Porter—an unpretentious, 100-year-old matriarch—does for her great-granddaughter, painting a tale of tragedy, humor, and triumphant faith. Abigail's life has never been easy—not since her momma died giving birth. Discover how this young girl without a mother grows to be a loving woman of God.

Highland Hopes by Gary Parker

⬧ BETHANYHOUSE 11400 Hampshire Ave.S., Bloomington, MN 55438
1-800-328-6109 www.bethanyhouse.com